D1152504

MORDECAI RICHLER

Barney's Version

WITH FOOTNOTES AND AN AFTERWORD BY
Michael Panofsky

VINTAGE BOOKS
London

Laois County Library
Leabharlann Chontae Laoise
Acc. No. ......13892......
Class No. ....
Inv. No. ....

WITHDRAWN FROM STOCK

Published by Vintage 1998

2 4 6 8 10 9 7 5 3 1

Copyright © 1997 Mordecai Richler Productions Ltd

Mordecai Richler has asserted his right under the Copyright, Designs
and Patents Act 1988 to be identified as the author of this work

This book is sold subject to the condition that it shall not,
by way of trade or otherwise, be lent, resold, hired out,
or otherwise circulated without the publisher's prior
consent in any form of binding or cover other than that
in which it is published and without a similar condition,
including this condition, being imposed on the
subsequent purchaser

This copyright page should be read in conjunction
with the Acknowledgements on p.409

First published in Great Britain by Chatto & Windus in 1997

Vintage
Random House, 20 Vauxhall Bridge Road,
London SW1V 2SA

www.vintage-books.co.uk

Addresses for companies within The Random House Group Limited
can be found at: www.randomhouse.co.uk/offices.htm

The Random House Group Limited Reg. No. 954009

A CIP catalogue record for this book
is available from the British Library

ISBN 9780099554462

The Random House Group Limited supports The Forest
Stewardship Council (FSC), the leading international forest
certification organisation. All our titles that are printed on
Greenpeace approved FSC certified paper carry the FSC logo.
Our paper procurement policy can be found at:
www.rbooks.co.uk/environment

Mixed Sources
Product group from well-managed
forests and other controlled sources
www.fsc.org Cert no. TT-COC-2139
© 1996 Forest Stewardship Council
FSC

Printed and bound in Great Britain by
CPI Bookmarque, Croydon, CR0 4TD

For Florence,
and in memory of four absent friends:
Jack Clayton, Ted Allan, Tony Godwin
and Ian Mayer

I

CLARA
1950–1952

ONE

TERRY'S the spur. The splinter under my fingernail. To come clean, I'm starting on this shambles that is the true story of my wasted life (violating a solemn pledge, scribbling a first book at my advanced age), as a riposte to the scurrilous charges Terry McIver has made in his forthcoming autobiography: about me, my three wives a.k.a. Barney Panofsky's troika, the nature of my friendship with Boogie, and, of course, the scandal I will carry to my grave like a humpback. Terry's sound of two hands clapping, *Of Time and Fevers*, will shortly be launched by The Group (sorry, the group), a government-subsidized small press rooted in Toronto, that also publishes a monthly journal, *the good earth*, printed on recycled paper, you bet your life.

Terry McIver and I, both Montrealers born and bred, were in Paris together in the early fifties. Poor Terry was no more than tolerated by my bunch, a pride of impecunious, horny young writers awash in rejection slips, yet ostensibly confident that everything was possible – fame, adoring bimbos, and fortune lying in wait around the corner, just like that legendary Wrigley's shill of my boyhood. The shill, according to report, would surprise you on the street to reward you with a crisp new dollar bill, provided you had a Wrigley's chewing-gum wrapper in your pocket. Mr. Wrigley's big giver never caught up with me. But fame did find several of my bunch: the driven Leo Bishinsky; Cedric Richardson, albeit under another name; and of course Clara. Clara, who now enjoys posthumous fame as a feminist icon, beaten on the anvil of male chauvinist insentience. My anvil, so they say.

I was an anomaly. No, an anomie. A natural-born entrepreneur. I hadn't won awards at McGill, like Terry, or been to Harvard or Columbia, like some of the others. I had barely squeezed through high school, having invested more time at the tables of the Mount

Royal Billiards Academy than in classes, playing snooker with Duddy Kravitz. Couldn't write. Didn't paint. Had no artistic pretensions whatsoever, unless you count my fantasy of becoming a music hall song-and-dance man, tipping my straw boater to the good folks in the balcony as I fluttered off stage in my taps, yielding to Peaches, Ann Corio,[1] Lili St. Cyr, or some other exotic dancer, who would bring her act to a drum-throbbing climax with a thrilling flash of bare tit, in days long before lap-dancers had become the norm in Montreal.

I was a voracious reader, but you would be mistaken if you took that as evidence of my quality. Or sensibility. At bottom, I am obliged to acknowledge, with a nod to Clara, the baseness of my soul. My ugly competitive nature. What got me started was not Tolstoy's *The Death of Ivan Ilyich*, or Conrad's *Secret Agent*, but the old *Liberty* magazine, which prefaced each of its articles with a headnote saying how long it would take to read it: say, five minutes and thirty-five seconds. Setting my Mickey Mouse wristwatch on our kitchen table with the checkered linoleum cloth, I would zip through the piece in question in, say, four minutes and three seconds, and consider myself an intellectual. From *Liberty*, I graduated to a paperback John Marquand *Mr. Moto* novel, selling for twenty-five cents at the time in Jack and Moe's Barbershop, corner of Park Avenue and Laurier in the heart of Montreal's old working-class Jewish quarter, where I was raised. A neighbourhood that had elected the only Communist (Fred Rose) ever to serve as a member of parliament, produced a couple of decent club fighters (Louis Alter, Maxie Berger), the obligatory number of doctors and dentists, a celebrated gambler-cum-casino owner, more cut-throat lawyers than needed, sundry school teachers and *shmata* millionaires, a few rabbis, and at least one suspected murderer.

Me.

I remember snowbanks five feet high, winding outside staircases that had to be shovelled in the sub-zero cold, and, in days long before snow tires, the rattle of passing cars and trucks, their wheels encased in chains. Sheets frozen rock hard on backyard clotheslines. In my bedroom where the radiator sizzled and knocked through the night, I eventually stumbled on Hemingway, Fitzgerald, Joyce,

---

[1] The correct spelling is Coreo.

Gertie and Alice, as well as our own Morley Callaghan. I came of age envying their expatriate adventures and, as a consequence, made a serious decision in 1950.

Ah, 1950. That was the last year Bill Durnan, five times winner of the Vezina trophy, best goalie in the National Hockey League, would mind the nets for my beloved Montreal Canadiens. In 1950, *nos glorieux* could already deploy a formidable defence corps, its mainstay young Doug Harvey. The Punch Line was then only two-thirds intact: in the absence of Hector "Toe" Blake, who retired in 1948, Maurice "The Rocket" Richard and Elmer Lach were skating on a line with Floyd "Busher" Curry. They finished second to bloody Detroit in the regular season and, to their everlasting shame, went down four games to one to the New York Rangers in the Stanley Cup semi-finals. At least The Rocket enjoyed a decent year, finishing the regular season second in the individual scoring race with forty-three goals and twenty-two assists.[2]

Anyway, in 1950, at the age of twenty-two, I left the chorus girl I was living with in a basement flat on Tupper Street. I withdrew my modest stash from the City and District Savings Bank, money I had earned as a waiter in the old Normandy Roof (a job arranged by my father, Detective-Inspector Izzy Panofsky), and booked passage to Europe on the *Queen Elizabeth*,[3] sailing out of New York. In my innocence, I was determined to seek out and be enriched by the friendship of what I then thought of as the pure of heart, artists, "the unacknowledged legislators of the world." And those, those were the days when you could smooch with college girls with impunity. One, Two, Cha-Cha-Cha. "If I Knew You Were Coming, I'd've Baked a Cake." Moonlit nights on deck nice girls wore crinolines, cinch belts, ankle bracelets, and two-tone saddle shoes, and you could count on them not to sue you for sexual harassment forty years later, their suppressed memories of date-rape retrieved by lady psychoanalysts who shaved.

Not fame, but fortune eventually found me. That fortune, such

---

[2]Actually, Richard finished fourth in the scoring race. Ted Lindsay, of the Detroit Red Wings, won the title with twenty-three goals and fifty-five assists. Sid Abel came second, Gordie Howe third, and then Richard.

[3]It was the *Queen Mary*, which made its last voyage in 1967, encountering the *Queen Elizabeth* at sea at 12:10 a.m., on September 25, 1967.

as it is, had humble roots. To begin with, I was sponsored by a survivor of Auschwitz, Yossel Pinsky, who changed dollars for us at black-market rates in a curtained booth in a photography shop on the rue des Rosiers. One evening Yossel sat down at my table in The Old Navy, ordered a *café filtre*, dropped seven sugar cubes into his cup, and said, "I need somebody with a valid Canadian passport."

"To do what?"

"Make money. What else is left?" he asked, taking out a Swiss Army knife and beginning to clean his remaining fingernails. "But we should get to know each other a little better first. Have you eaten yet?"

"No."

"So let's go for dinner. Hey, I won't bite. Come, boychick."

And that's how, only a year later, Yossel serving as my guide, I became an exporter of French cheeses to an increasingly flush, postwar Canada. Back home Yossel arranged for me to run an agency for Vespas, those Italian motorized scooters that were once such a hot item. Over the years I also dealt profitably, with Yossel as my partner, in olive oil, just like the young Meyer Lansky; bolts of cloth spun in the islands of Lewis and Harris; scrap metal, bought and sold without my ever having seen any of it; antiquated DC-3s, some of them still being flown North of Sixty; and, after Yossel had moved to Israel, one step ahead of the gendarmes, ancient Egyptian artifacts, stolen from minor tombs in the Valley of the Kings. But I have my principles. I have never handled arms, drugs, or health foods.

Finally I became a sinner. In the late sixties, I began to produce Canadian-financed films that were never exhibited anywhere for more than an embarrassing week, but which eventually earned me, and on occasion my backers, hundreds of thousands of dollars through a tax loop-hole since closed. Then I started to churn out Canadian-content TV series sufficiently shlocky to be syndicated in the U.S. and, in the case of our boffo "McIver of the RCMP" series, which is big on bonking scenes in canoes and igloos, in the U.K., and other countries as well.

When it was required of me, I could rhumba as a latter-day patriot, the Great Cham's last refuge of the scoundrel. Whenever a government minister, a free-marketeer responding to American pressure, threatened to dump the law that insisted (and bankrolled to a yummy degree) so much Canadian-manufactured pollution on our airwaves, I did a quick change in the hypocrite's phonebooth, slipping into my Captain Canada mode, and appeared before the committee. "We are defining Canada to Canadians," I told them. "We are this country's memory, its soul, its hypostasis, the last defence against our being overwhelmed by the egregious cultural imperialists to the south of us."

I digress.

Back in our expatriate days, we roistering provincials, slap-happy to be in Paris, drunk on the beauty of our surroundings, were fearful of retiring to our Left Bank hotel rooms lest we wake up back home, retrieved by parents who would remind us of how much they had invested in our educations, and how it was time for us to put our shoulders to the wheel. In my case, no airmail letter from my father was complete without its built-in stinger: "Yankel Schneider, remember him, he had a stammer? So what? He's become a chartered accountant and drives a Buick now."

Our loosy-goosy band included a couple of painters, so to speak, both of them New Yorkers. There was the loopy Clara and the scheming Leo Bishinsky, who managed his artistic rise better than Wellington did, you know, that battle in a town in Belgium.[4] He left a ball to go to it. Or interrupted a game of bowls. No, that was Drake.

A garage in Montparnasse served as Leo's atelier, and there he laboured on his huge triptychs, mixing his paints in buckets and applying them with a kitchen mop. On occasion he would swish his mop around, stand back ten feet, and let fly. Once, when I was there, the two of us sharing a toke, he thrust his mop at me. "Have a go," he said.

"Really?"

"Why not?"

Soon enough, I figured, Leo would get a shave and a haircut and join an advertising agency in New York.

I was dead wrong.

Go know that forty years later Leo's atrocities would be hanging in the Tate, the Guggenheim, MOMA, and The National

---

[4]Waterloo, where the Duke of Wellington, and the Prussian Field Marshal Gebhard Leberecht von Blücher defeated Napoleon on June 18, 1815.

Gallery in Washington, and that others would be sold for millions to junk-bond mavins and arbitrage gurus who were often outbid by Japanese collectors. Go anticipate that Leo's battered Renault[5] deux-chevaux would one day be succeeded, in a ten-car garage in Amagansett, by a Rolls-Royce Silver Cloud, a vintage Morgan, a Ferrari 250 berlinetta, and an Alfa Romeo, among other toys. Or that to mention his name today, in passing, I could be accused of name-dropping. Leo has appeared on the cover of *Vanity Fair* in Mephistophelean guise, replete with horns, magenta cape and tails, painting magic symbols on the nude body of a flavour-of-the-month starlet.

In the old days you could always tell who Leo was screwing, because, *tout court*, a white-bread-and-cashmere-twin-set young woman out of Nebraska, working for the Marshall Plan, would turn up at La Coupole and think nothing of picking her nose at the table. But today renowned fashion models flock to Leo's Long Island mansion, vying with one another to proffer pubic hairs that can be worked into his paintings along with bits of beach glass, bluefish skeletons, salami butts, and toenail clippings.

Back in 1951 my gang of neophyte artists flaunted their liberation from what they, *de haut en bas*, denigrated as the rat race, but the sour truth is, with the shining exception of Bernard "Boogie" Moscovitch, they were all contenders. Each one as fiercely competitive as any *Organization Man* or *Man in the Grey Flannel Suit*, if any of you out there are old enough to remember those long-forgotten best-sellers, modish for a season. Like Colin Wilson. Or the hula hoop. And they were driven by the need to succeed as much as any St. Urbain Street urchin back home who had bet his bundle on a new autumn line of *après-ski* wear. Fiction is what most of them were peddling. Making it new, as Ezra Pound had ordained before he was certified insane. Mind you, they didn't have to cart samples round to department store buyers, floating on "a smile and a shoe-shine," as Clifford Odets[6] once put it. Instead, they shipped their

---

[5]Actually, the 2CV was a Citroën. It was introduced at the Paris Motor Show in 1948, and taken out of production in 1990.

[6]Not Odets, but Arthur Miller in *Death of a Salesman*, p. 138. Viking Press Inc., New York, 1949.

merchandise off to magazine and book editors, enclosing a stamped, self-addressed envelope. Except for Boogie, my anointed one.

Alfred Kazin once wrote of Saul Bellow that, even when he was still young and unknown, he already had the aura about him of a man destined for greatness. I felt the same about Boogie, who was uncommonly generous, at the time, to other young writers, it being understood that he was superior to any of them.

In one of his manic moods Boogie would throw up lots of smoke, deflecting questions about his work by clowning. "Look at me," he once said, "I've got all the faults of Tolstoy, Dostoievsky, and Hemingway rolled into one. I will fuck just about any peasant girl who will have me. I'm an obsessive gambler. A drunk. Hey, just like Freddy D., I'm even an anti-Semite, but maybe that doesn't count in my case as I'm Jewish myself. So far, all that's lacking in the equation is my very own Yasnaya Polyana, a recognition of my prodigious talent, and money for tonight's dinner, unless you're inviting me? God bless you, Barney."

Five years older than I was, Boogie had scrambled up Omaha Beach on D-Day, and survived the Battle of the Bulge. He was in Paris on the GI Bill, which provided him with one hundred dollars monthly, a stipend supplemented by an allowance from home, which he usually invested, with sporadic luck, on the *chemin de fer* tables in the Aviation Club.

Well now, never mind the malicious gossip, most recently revived by the lying McIver, that will pursue me to the end of my days. The truth is, Boogie was the most cherished friend I ever had. I adored him. And over many a shared toke, or bottle of *vin ordinaire*, I was able to piece together something of his background. Boogie's grandfather, Moishe Lev Moscovitch, born in Bialystok, sailed steerage to America from Hamburg, and rose by dint of hard work and parsimony from pushcart chicken peddler to sole proprietor of a kosher butcher shop on Rivington Street in New York's lower East Side. His first-born son, Mendel, parlayed that butcher shop into Peerless Gourmet Packers, suppliers of K-rations to the U.S. army during the Second World War. Peerless emerged afterward as purveyors of Virginia Plantation packaged ham, Olde English sausages, Mandarin spare ribs, and Granny's Gobblers (frozen, oven-ready turkeys) to supermarkets in New York state and New England. En route, Mendel, his name laundered to Matthew

Morrow, acquired a fourteen-room apartment on Park Avenue, serviced by a maid, a cook, a butler-cum-chauffeur, and an English governess off the Old Kent Road for his first-born son, Boogie, who later had to take elocution lessons to rid him of his Cockney accent. In lieu of a violin teacher and a Hebrew *malamud*, Boogie, who was counted on to infiltrate the family deep into the WASP hive, was sent to a military summer camp in Maine. "I was expected to learn how to ride, shoot, sail, play tennis, and turn the other cheek," he said. Registering for camp, Boogie, as instructed by his mother, filled out "atheist" under "Religious Denomination." The camp commander winked, crossed it out, and wrote "Jewish." Boogie endured the camp, and Andover, but dropped out of Harvard in his sophomore year, in 1941, and joined the army as a rifleman, reverting to the name Moscovitch.

Once, responding to persistent inquiries from an earnest Terry McIver, Boogie allowed that in the opening chapter of his discombobulating novel-in-progress, set in 1912, his protagonist disembarks from the *Titanic*, which has just completed its maiden voyage, docking safely in New York, only to be accosted by a reporter. "What was the trip like?" she asks.

"Boring."

Improvising, I'm sure, Boogie went on to say that two years later, his protagonist, riding in a carriage with the Archduke Francis Ferdinand of Austria-Hungary and his missus, drops his opera glasses as they bounce over a bump in the road. The archduke, big on *noblesse oblige*, stoops to retrieve them, thereby avoiding an assassination attempt by a Serb nutter. A couple of months later, however, the Germans invade Belgium all the same. Then, in 1917, Boogie's protagonist, shooting the breeze with Lenin in a Zurich café, asks for an explanation of surplus value, and Lenin, warming to the subject, lingers too long over his *millefeuille* and *café au lait*, and misses his train, the sealed car arriving in the Finland Station without him.

"Isn't that just like that fucking Ilyich?" says the leader of the delegation come to greet him on the platform. "Now what is to be done?"

"Maybe Leon would get up and say a few words?"

"A few words? Leon? We'll be standing here for hours."

Boogie told Terry he was fulfilling the artist's primary function – making order out of chaos.

"I should have known better than to ask you a serious question," said Terry, retreating from our café table.

In the ensuing silence, Boogie, by way of apology, turned to me and explained that he had inherited, from Heinrich Heine, *le droit de moribondage*.

Boogie could yank that sort of conversation-stopper out of the back pocket of his mind, propelling me to a library, educating me.

I loved Boogie and miss him something awful. I would give up my fortune (say half) to have that enigma, that six-foot-two scarecrow, lope through my door again, pulling on a Romeo y Julieta, his smile charged with ambiguity, demanding, "Have you read Thomas Bernhard yet?" or "What do you make of Chomsky?"

God knows he had his dark side, disappearing for weeks on end – some said to a *yeshiva* in Mea Shearim and others swore to a monastery in Tuscany – but nobody really knew where. Then one day he would appear – no, materialize – without explanation at one of the cafés we favoured, accompanied by a gorgeous Spanish duchess or an Italian contessa.

On his bad days Boogie wouldn't answer my knock on his hotel-room door or, if he did, would say no more than "Go away. Let me be," and I knew that he was lying on his bed, high on horse, or that he was seated at his table, compiling lists of the names of those young men who had fought alongside him and were already dead.

It was Boogie who introduced me to Goncharov, Huysmans, Céline, and Nathaniel West. He was taking language lessons from a White Russian watchmaker whom he had befriended. "How can anybody go through life," he asked, "not being able to read Dostoievsky, Tolstoy, and Chekhov in the original?" Fluent in German and Hebrew, Boogie studied the Zohar, the holy book of the Kabbalah, once a week with a rabbi in a synagogue on rue Notre-Dame-de-Lorette, an address that delighted him.

Then years ago, I collected all eight of Boogie's cryptic short stories that had been published in *Merlin*, *Zero*, and the *Paris Review*, with the intention of bringing them out in a limited edition, each volume numbered, elegantly printed, no expense spared. The story of his that I've read again and again, for obvious reasons, is a variation on a far from original theme, but brilliantly realized, like everything he wrote. "Margolis" is about a man who walks out to buy a package of cigarettes and never returns to his wife and child, assuming a new identity elsewhere.

I wrote to Boogie's son in Santa Fe offering him an advance of ten thousand dollars, as well as a hundred free copies and all profits that might accrue from the enterprise. His response came in the form of a registered letter that expressed amazement that I, of all people, could even contemplate such a venture, and warning me that he would not hesitate to take legal action if I dared to do such a thing. So that was that.

Hold the phone. I'm stuck. I'm trying to remember the name of the author of *The Man in the Grey Flannel Suit*. Or was it *The Man in the Brooks Brothers Shirt*? No, that was written by the fibber. Lillian what's-her-name? Come on. I know it. Like the mayonnaise. Lillian Kraft? No. *Hellman. Lillian Hellman*. The name of the author of *The Man in the Grey Flannel Suit* doesn't matter. It's of no importance. But now that it's started I won't sleep tonight. These increasingly frequent bouts of memory loss are driving me crazy.

Last night, sailing off to sleep at last, I couldn't remember the name of the thing you use to strain spaghetti. Imagine that. I've used it thousands of times. I could visualize it. But I couldn't remember what the bloody thing was called. And I didn't want to get out of bed to search through cookbooks Miriam had left behind, because it would only remind me that it was my fault she was gone, and I would have to get out of bed at three o'clock anyway to piss. Not the swift bubbly torrent of my Left Bank days, no sirree. Now it was dribble, dribble, dribble, and no matter how hard I shook it, a belated trickle down my pyjama leg.

Lying in the dark, fulminating, I recited aloud the number I was to call if I had a heart attack.

"You have reached the Montreal General Hospital. If you have a touch-tone phone, and you know the extension you want, please press that number now. If not, press number 17 for service in the language of *les maudits anglais*, or number 12 for service *en français*, the glorious language of our oppressed collectivity."

Twenty-one for emergency ambulance service.

"You have reached emergency ambulance service. Please hold

and an operator will come to your assistance as soon as our strip-poker game is over. Have a nice day."

While I waited, the automatic tape would play Mozart's *Requiem*.

I groped to make sure my digitalis pills, reading glasses, and dentures were within easy reach on the bedside table. I switched on a lamp briefly and scooped up my boxer shorts to check them out for skid marks, because if I died during the night I didn't want strangers to think I was dirty. Then I tried the usual gambit. Think of something else, something soothing, and the name of the spaghetti thingumabob will come to you unsummoned. So I imagined Terry McIver bleeding profusely in a shark-infested sea, feeling another tug at what was left of his legs just as a rescuing helicopter is attempting to winch him out of the water. Finally what remains of the lying, self-regarding author of *Of Time and Fevers*, a dripping torso, is raised above the surface, bobbing like bait in the churning waters, sharks lunging at it.

Next I made myself a scruffy fourteen-year-old again, and unhooked, for that first whoopie time, the filagreed bra of the teacher I shall call Mrs. Ogilvy, even as one of those nonsense songs was playing on the radio in her living room:

> Mairzy doats,
> and dozy doats,
> andlittlelambseativy,
> akid'lleativytoo,
> wouldn'tyou?

To my astonishment, she didn't resist. Instead, terrifying me, she kicked off her shoes and began to wriggle out of her tartan skirt. "I don't know what's got into me," said the teacher who had awarded me an A+ for my essay on *A Tale of Two Cities*, which I had cribbed, paraphrasing here and there, from a book by Granville Hicks. "I'm robbing the cradle." Then, in my mind's eye, she spoiled everything, adding, with a certain classroom asperity, "But shouldn't we strain the spaghetti first?"

"Yeah. Sure. But using what thingumajig?"

"I fancy it *al dente*," she said.

And now, giving Mrs. Ogilvy a second chance, hoping for a

better return this time, I travelled back through memory lane again and tumbled onto the sofa with her, incidentally hoping for at least a semi-demi-erection in my decrepit here and now.

"Oh, you're so impatient," she said. "Wait. Not yet. *En français, s'il vous plaît?*"

"What?"

"Oh, dear. Such manners. We mean 'I beg your pardon,' don't we? Now then, let's have 'not yet' in French, please."

"*Pas encore.*"

"Jolly good," she said, sliding open a side-table drawer. "Now I don't want you to think me a bossy boots, but please be a considerate lad and roll this on to your pretty little willy first."

"Yes, Mrs. Ogilvy."

"Give me your hand. Oh, have you ever seen such filthy fingernails? There. Like that! Gently does it. Oh yes, please. *Wait!*"

"What have I done wrong now?"

"I just thought you'd like to know it wasn't Lillian Hellman who wrote *The Man in the Brooks Brothers Shirt*. It was Mary McCarthy."

Damn damn damn. I got out of bed, slipped into the threadbare dressing-gown which I couldn't part with, because it was a gift from Miriam, and padded into the kitchen. Rummaging through drawers, I yanked out utensils and named them one-two-three: soup ladle, egg timer, tongs, pie splicer, vegetable peeler, tea strainer, measuring cups, can opener, spatula . . . and hanging on a wall hook, there it was, the thingumabob used to strain spaghetti, *but what was it called?*

I've survived scarlet fever, mumps, two muggings, crabs, the extraction of all my teeth, a hip-socket replacement, a murder charge, and three wives. The first one is dead and The Second Mrs. Panofsky, hearing my voice, would holler, even after all these years, "Murderer, what have you done with his body?" before slamming down the receiver. But Miriam would talk to me. She might even laugh at my dilemma. Oh, to have this apartment resonate with her laughter. Her scent. Her love. The trouble is, Blair would probably be the one to answer the phone, and I had already blotted my copybook with that pretentious bastard the last time I called. "I would like to speak to my wife," I said.

"She is no longer your wife, Barney, and you are obviously inebriated."

He would say "inebriated." "Of course I'm drunk. It's four o'clock in the morning."

"And Miriam's asleep."

"But it's you I wanted to talk to. I was cleaning out my desk drawers here and I found some stunning nude photographs of her when she was with me, and I was wondering if you would like to have them, if only to know what she looked like in her prime."

"You're disgusting," he said, hanging up.

True enough. But, all the same, I danced round the living room, doing my take on the great Ralph Brown's Shim Sham Shimmy, a tumbler of Cardhu in hand.

There are some people out there who take Blair to be a fine fellow. A scholar of distinction. Even my sons defend him. We appreciate how you feel, they say, but he is an intelligent and caring man, devoted to Miriam. Bullshit. A drudge on tenure, Blair came to Canada from Boston in the sixties, a draft-dodger, like Dan Quayle and Bill Clinton, and, consequently, a hero to his students. As for me, I'm dumbfounded that anybody would prefer Toronto to Saigon. Anyway I've got his faculty group fax number and, thinking of how Boogie would have taken advantage of that, I sit down and wing one to Blair occasionally.

Fax to Herr Doktor Blair Hopper né Hauptman
From Sexorama Novelties

ACHTUNG
PRIVATE AND CONFIDENTIAL

Dear Herr Doktor Hopper,

Pursuant to your inquiry of January 26, we welcome your idea of introducing to Victoria College the old Ivy League practice of requiring selected coeds to pose naked for posture photographs, front, profile, and back. Your notion of introducing garter belts and other accessories is inspired. The project has, as you put it, great commercial potential. However, we will have to assess the actual photographs before we can take up your suggestion to market a new set of playing cards.

Sincerely,
Dwayne Connors
Sexorama Novelties.

P.S. We acknowledge your return of our 1995 TOY BOYS calendar, but cannot send you a refund due to the fact that the August and September pages are stuck together.

12:45 a.m. Now I held the spaghetti thingumajig in my liver-spotted hand, wrinkled as a lizard's back, but I still couldn't put a name to it. Flinging it aside, I poured myself a couple of inches of Macallan, picked up the phone, and dialled my eldest son in London. "Hiya, Mike. This is your six a.m. wake-up call. Time for your morning jog."

"As a matter of fact, it's 5:46 here."

For breakfast my punctilious son would munch crunchy granola and yoghurt, washed down with a glass of lemon water. People today.

"Are you okay?" he asked, and his concern just about brought tears to my eyes.

"In the pink. But I've got a problem. What do you call the thingee you strain spaghetti with?"

"Are you drunk?"

"*Certainly not.*"

"Didn't Dr. Herscovitch warn you that if you started up again it would kill you?"

"I swear on the heads of my grandchildren, I haven't had a drop in weeks. I no longer even order *coq au vin* in restaurants. Now will you answer my question, please?"

"I'm going to take the phone in the living room, hang up here, and then we can talk."

Mustn't wake Lady Health Fascist.

"Hi, I'm back. Do you mean a colander?"

"Of course I mean a colander. It was on the tip of my tongue. I was just going to say it."

"Are you taking your pills?"

"Sure I am. Have you heard from your mother lately?" I blurted out compulsively, having sworn I'd never ask about her again.

"She and Blair stopped over here for three days on

October 4th,[7] on their way to a conference in Glasgow."

"I don't give a damn about her any more. You don't know what a pleasure it is not to be reprimanded because I forgot to lift the seat again. But, speaking as a disinterested observer, she deserved better."

"You mean you?"

"Tell Caroline," I said, lashing out, "that I read somewhere that lettuce bleeds when you chop it up and carrots suffer traumas when you pluck them out of the ground."

"Dad, I hate to think of you all alone in that big empty apartment."

"As it happens, I have what I think they now call 'a resource person,' or is it 'a sex worker,' staying with me tonight. What boors like me used to call a skirt. Tell your mother. I don't mind."

"Why don't you fly over and haunt our house for a while?"

"Because in the London I remember best the obligatory first course in even the most stylish restaurant was grey-brown Windsor soup, or a grapefruit with a maraschino cherry sitting in the middle like a nipple, and most of the people I used to hang out with there are dead now, and about time too. Harrods has become a Eurotrash temple. Everywhere you turn in Knightsbridge there are rich Japs shooting movies of each other. The White Elephant is kaput, so is Isow's, and L'Etoile ain't what it used to be. I have no interest in who's banging Di or whether Charles is reincarnated as a tampon. The pubs are intolerable, what with those noisy slot machines and pounding jungle music. And too many of our people there are something else. If they've been to Oxford or Cambridge, or earn more than a hundred thousand pounds a year, they are no longer Jewish, but 'of Jewish descent,' which is not quite the same thing."

I've never really been rooted in London, but I was once there in the fifties for three months, and another time in 1961 for a stay of two, missing the Stanley Cup playoffs. Mind you, that was the year the heavily favoured Canadiens were eliminated in six games, in the semi-finals, by the Chicago Black Hawks. I still wish I had caught the second game, in Chicago, which the Hawks won 2–1, after

---

[7]According to my diary, Blair and my mother stopped over on October 7th, and the conference was in Edinburgh.

fifty-two minutes of overtime. That was the night referee Dalton McArthur, that officious bastard, penalized Dickie Moore, *in overtime*, for tripping, enabling Murray Balfour to pot the winning goal. An outraged Toe Blake, then our coach, charged onto the ice to bop McArthur one, and was fined $2,000. I had flown over to London in '61 to work on that co-production with Hymie Mintzbaum that led to such a nasty fight, resulting in our being estranged for years. Hymie, born and bred in the Bronx, is an anglophile, but not me.

You simply can't trust the British. With Americans (or Canadians, for that matter) what you see is what you get. But settle into your seat on a 747 flying out of Heathrow next to an ostensibly boring old Englishman with wobbly chins, the acquired stammer, obviously something in the City, intent on his *Times* crossword puzzle, and don't you dare patronize him. Mr. Milquetoast, actually a judo black belt, was probably parachuted into the Dordogne in 1943, blew up a train or two, and survived the Gestapo cells by concentrating on what would become the definitive translation of Gilgamesh from the Sin-Leqi-Inninni; and now – his garment bag stuffed with his wife's most alluring cocktail dresses and lingerie – he is no doubt bound for the annual convention of cross-dressers in Saskatoon.

Once again Mike told me that I could have their garden flat. Private. With my own entrance. And how wonderfully dreadful it would be for his children, who had adored *Friday the 13th*, to get to know their grandfather. But I hate being a grandfather. It's indecent. In my mind's eye, I'm still twenty-five. Thirty-three max. Certainly not sixty-seven, reeking of decay and dashed hopes. My breath sour. My limbs in dire need of an oil-lube job. And now that I've been blessed with a plastic hip-socket replacement, I'm no longer even bio-degradable. Environmentalists will protest my burial.

On one of my recent annual visits to Mike and Caroline, I arrived laden with gifts for my grandchildren and her ladyship (as Saul, my second-born son, has dubbed her), my *pièce de résistance* reserved for Mike: a box of Cohibas, acquired for me in Cuba. It pained me to part with those cigars, but I hoped it would please Mike, with whom I had a difficult relationship, and it did delight him. Or so I thought. But a month later one of Mike's associates, Tony Haines, who also happened to be a cousin of Caroline's, was in Montreal on a business trip. He phoned to say he had a gift from

Mike, a side of smoked salmon from Fortnum's. I invited him to meet me for drinks at Dink's. Pulling out his cigar case, Tony offered me a Cohiba. "Oh, wonderful," I said. "Thank you."

"Don't thank me. They were a birthday gift from Mike and Caroline."

"Oh, really," I said, lumbered with another family grievance to nurse. Or cherish, according to Miriam. "Some people collect stamps, or bookmatch covers," she once said, "but with you, my darling, it's grievances."

On that visit Mike and Caroline settled me into an upstairs bedroom, everything mod, from Conran or The General Trading Company. A bouquet of freesias and a bottle of Perrier on my bedside table but no ashtray. Opening the bedside-table drawer, searching for something I could use, I blundered on a pair of torn pantyhose. Sniffing them, I recognized the scent at once. Miriam's. She and Blair had shared this bed, contaminating it. Yanking back the sheets, I searched the mattress for tell-tale stains. Nothing. Har, har, har. Professor Limp Prick couldn't cut the mustard. Herr Doktor Hopper né Hauptman probably read aloud to her in bed instead. His deconstructionist pensées on Mark Twain's racism. Or Hemingway's homophobia. All the same, I retrieved a canister of pine spray from the bathroom and fumigated the mattress, and then remade the bed after a fashion before climbing back into it. Now the sheets were riding up on me, a maddening tangle. The room stank of pine scent. I opened a window wide. Freezing cold it was. An abandoned husband, I was obviously destined to perish of pneumonia in a bed once graced by Miriam's warmth. Her beauty. *Her treachery.* Well now, women of her age, suffering hot flushes and confusions, sometimes unaccountably begin to shoplift. If she were arrested, I would refuse to be a character witness. No, I would testify that she had always been light-fingered. Let her rot in the slammer. Miriam, Miriam, my heart's desire.

MIKE, BLESS him, is filthy rich, which he atones for by still wearing his hair in a ponytail and favouring blue jeans (Polo Ralph Lauren's, mind you), but, happily, no earrings. Or Nehru jackets any longer. Or Mao caps. He's a property baron. Owner of some choice houses in Highgate, Hampstead, Swiss Cottage, Islington, and Chelsea, which he accumulated before inflation hit, and converted into flats.. He's also into some things off-shore, which I'd rather not know about, and deals in commodity futures. He and Caroline live in modish Fulham, which I remember before the DIY-trained yuppies invaded. They also own a dacha high in the hills of the Alpes-Maritimes, not far from Vence, a vineyard running down its slopes. In three generations, from the *shtetl* to the makers of Château Panofsky. What can I say?

Mike is a partner in a restaurant for the smart set. It's in Pimlico, called The Table, the chef ruder than he is talented which is *de rigueur* these days, isn't it? Too young to remember Pearl Harbor, or what happened to the Canadians taken prisoner at – at – you know, that impregnable outpost in the Far East. Not the one where the dawn comes up like thunder, no, but the place where the Sassoons struck it rich. Singapore? No. The place like the name of the gorilla in that film with Fay Wray. *Kong*. Hong Kong. And, look, I know that Wellington defeated Napoleon at Waterloo, and I remember who wrote *The Man in the Grey Flannel Suit*. Come to me unbidden. *The Man in the Grey.Flannel Suit* was written by Frederic Wakeman[8] and the movie starred Clark Gable and Sydney Greenstreet.

Anyway, too young to remember Pearl Harbor, Mike invested heavily in the Japanese market in the early days and dumped everything at the propitious moment. He rode gold through the OPEC scare, whipping his stake past the finishing line, doubling it, and made another killing speculating in sterling in 1992. He had bet on Bill Gates before anybody had heard of E-mail.

Yes, my first-born son is a multi-millionaire with both a social and a cultural conscience. He's a member of a trendy theatre board, a promoter of in-your-face plays wherein top people's leggy daughters feel free to pretend to shit on stage and RADA guys simulate bum-fucking with abandon. *Ars longa, vita brevis*. He's one of the more than two hundred backers of the monthly *Red Pepper* magazine ("feminist, anti-racist, environmentalist and internationalist");

---

[8] *The Man in the Grey Flannel Suit* was written by Sloan Wilson (1955); and it was *The Hucksters*, by Frederic Wakeman, that was made into a movie starring Clark Gable, Deborah Kerr, and Sydney Greenstreet: MGM, 1947. Now also shown in computer-coloured version.

and, not without a redeeming sense of humour, he has added my name to the subscription list. The most recent issue of *Red Pepper* includes a full-page ad, an appeal for donations by London Lighthouse, which features a photograph of a sickly young woman, her staring eyes rimmed with dark circles, looking into a hand-held mirror.

"SHE TOLD HER HUSBAND THAT SHE WAS HIV+. HE TOOK IT BADLY."

What was the poor bastard supposed to do? Take her to dinner at The Ivy to celebrate?

In any event, as Mr. Bellow has already noted, more die of heartbreak. Or lung cancer, speaking as a prime candidate.

True, Mike shops for shiitake mushrooms, Japanese seaweed, Nishiki rice, and shiromiso soup at Harvey Nichols food hall, but, emerging on Sloane Street, he always remembers to buy a copy of the *Big Issue* from the bum lurking there. He owns an art gallery in Fulham that has proven itself, as it were, having twice been charged with obscenity. He and Caroline make a point of buying works by as-yet-unknown painters and sculptors who are, in Mike's parlance, "on the cutting edge." My up-to-the-minute, state-of-the-art son is into gangsta rap, information highways (as distinct from libraries), "dissing," quality time, Internets, all things cool, and every other speech cliché peculiar to his generation. Mike has never read the *Iliad*, Gibbon, Stendhal, Swift, Dr. Johnson, George Eliot, or any other now discredited Eurocentric bigot, but there isn't an over-praised "visible minority" new novelist or poet whose book he hasn't ordered from Hatchards. I'll wager he never stood for an hour contemplating Velásquez's portrait of that royal family,[9] you know the one I mean, in the Prado, but invite him to a vernissage that promises a crucifix floating in piss or a harpoon sticking out of a woman's bleeding arsehole, and he's there with his chequebook. "Oh," I said, determined to keep our trans-Atlantic phonecall going, "I don't mean to pry, but I do hope you've spoken to your sister recently."

"Watch it. You're beginning to sound just like Mom."

"That's no answer."

---

[9] *Las Meninas.*

"There's no point in phoning Kate. She's either just rushing out, or is in the middle of a dinner party, and can't talk now."

"That doesn't sound like Kate."

"Come on, Dad. As far as you're concerned, she can do no wrong. She was always your favourite."

"That's not true," I lied.

"But Saul phoned yesterday to ask what I thought of his latest diatribe in that neo-fascist rag he writes for. Hell, it had only arrived in that morning's mail. He's incredible, really. It took him fifteen minutes to bring me up to date on his imaginary health problems and work difficulties, and then to denounce me as a champagne socialist and Caroline as a penny-pincher. Who's he living with these days, may I ask?"

"Hey, I see the British are up in arms, because calves are being shipped to France, where they're confined to crates, instead of being booked into the Crillon. Has Caroline joined the demos?"

"You can do better than that, Dad. But do come and see us soon," said Mike, his voice stiffening, and I guessed that Caroline had just floated into the room, glancing pointedly at her wristwatch, unaware that I was paying for the phonecall.

"Sure," I said, hanging up, disgusted with myself.

Why couldn't I have told him how much I love him, and what pleasure he has given me over the years?

What if this were to be our last conversation?

"But death, you know," wrote Samuel Johnson to the Reverend Mr. Thomas Wharton, "hears not supplications, nor pays any regard to the convenience of mortals."

And what if Miriam and I were never to be reconciled?

TWO

WE have all read too much in literary journals about the unjustly neglected novelist, but seldom a word about the justly neglected, the scratch players, brandishing their little distinctions, *à la* Terry McIver. A translation into Icelandic, or an appearance at a Commonwealth arts festival in

Auckland (featuring a few "writers of pallor," as the new nomenclature has it, as well as an affirmative action mélange of Maori, Inuit, and Amerindian good spellers). But, after all these years as a flunk, my old friend and latter-day nemesis has acquired a small but vociferous following, CanLit. apparatchiks to the fore. That scumbag is ubiquitous in Canada these days, pontificating on TV and radio, giving public readings everywhere.

It was through that self-promoting bastard's father, who is also traduced in *Of Time and Fevers*, that I met Terry in the first place. Mr. McIver, sole prop. of The Spartacus Bookshop on St. Catherine Street West, was the most admirable, if innocent, of men. A scrawny Scot, bred in the Gorbals, he was the illegitimate son of a laundry woman, and a Clydeside welder who fell on the Somme. Mr. McIver would urge books on me by Howard Fast, Jack London, Emile Zola, Upton Sinclair, John Reed, Edgar Snow, and the Russian, you know, Lenin's laureate, what's-his-name? Anathema to Solzhenitsyn. *Come on, Barney. You know it.* There was a splendid movie made in Russia about his memoirs of childhood. Hell, it's on the tip of my tongue. First name Max – no, Maxim – surname like a goyishe pickle. Maxim Cornichon? Don't be ridiculous. Maxim Gherkin? Forget it. Gorki. Maxim Gorki.

Anyway, the bookshop had to be negotiated like a maze, towering stacks of second-hand books here, there, and everywhere, that could be sent tumbling if you didn't mind your elbows, as you followed Mr. McIver's slapping slippers into the back room. His sanctuary. Where he sat at his roll-top desk, elbows peeking out of his ancient, unravelling cardigan, conducting seminars on the evils of capitalism, serving students toast and strawberry jam and milky tea. If they couldn't afford the latest Algren or Graham Greene, or that first novel by that young American, Norman Mailer, he would lend them a brand new copy, providing they promised to return it unsoiled. Students demonstrated their gratitude by pilfering books on their way out and selling them back to him the following week. One or two even dipped into his cash register, or stiffed him with a bad cheque for ten or twenty dollars, never turning up at the bookshop again. "So you're going to Paris," he said to me.

"Yes."

This, inevitably, led to a lecture on the Paris Commune.

Doomed, like the Spartacus League in Berlin. "Would you mind taking a parcel to my son?" he asked.

"Of course not."

I went to pick it up at the McIvers' airless, overheated apartment that evening.

"A couple of shirts," said Mr. McIver. "A sweater Mrs. McIver knitted for him. Six tins of sockeye salmon. A carton of Player's Mild. Things like that. Terry wants to be a novelist, but . . ."

"But?"

"But who doesn't?"

When he retreated to the kitchen to put up the tea kettle, Mrs. McIver handed me an envelope. "For Terence," she whispered.

I found McIver in a small hotel on the rue Jacob and, amazingly, we actually got off to a promising start. He flipped the parcel onto his unmade bed, but slit open the envelope immediately. "You know how she earned this money?" he asked, seething. "These forty-eight dollars."

"I have no idea."

"Babysitting. Coaching backward kids in algebra or French grammar. Do you know anybody here, Barney?"

"I've been here for three days and you're the first person I've talked to."

"Meet me at the Mabillon at six and I'll introduce you to some people."

"I don't know where it is."

"Meet me downstairs, then. Hold on a minute. Does my father still run those ad hoc symposiums for students who laugh behind his back?"

"Some are fond of him."

"He's a fool. Eager for me to be a failure. Like him. See you later."

NATURALLY I was sent an advance copy of *Of Time and Fevers*, compliments of the author. I've struggled through it twice now, marking the blatant lies and most offensive passages, and this morning I phoned my lawyer, maître John Hughes-McNoughton. "Can I sue somebody for libel who has accused me, in print, of being a wife-abuser, an intellectual fraud, a purveyor of pap, a drunk with a penchant for violence, and probably a murderer as well?"

"Sounds like he got things just about right, I'd say."

No sooner did I hang up than Irv Nussbaum, United Jewish Appeal *capo de capos*, phoned. "Seen this morning's *Gazette*? Terrific news. Big-time drug lawyer was shot dead in his Jaguar, outside his mansion on Sunnyside last night, and it's splashed all over the front page. He's Jewish, thank God. Name's Larry Bercovitch. Today's going to be a hummer. I'm sitting here going through my pledge cards."

Next, Mike rang with one of his hot stock-market tips. I don't know where my son gets his inside market information, but, back in 1989, he tracked me down at the Beverly Wilshire Hotel. I was in Hollywood at the time for one of those television festivals, where they even have an award, rather than an electric chair in place, for the director of the "most brilliant" commercial. I had not come in quest of prizes but in search of markets for my rubbish. Mike said, "Buy *Time* shares."

"No 'hello.' No 'How are you, Daddy dear?' "

"Phone your broker as soon as I hang up."

"I can't even read that magazine any more. Why should I invest in it?"

"Will you please do as I say?"

I did, and bastard that I am, I was already anticipating the satisfaction I would squeeze out of dropping my bundle and blaming him for it. But a month later both Warners and Paramount pounced, the shares more than doubling in value.

I'm running ahead of myself. Filling my peddler's office that evening in Beverly Hills, I was obliged to take two functionally illiterate NBC-TV executives to dinner at La Scala; and mindful of Miriam's parting admonition, I was resolved to be civil. "You should send somebody else to L.A.," she had said, "because you're bound to end up having too much to drink and insulting everybody." And now, into my third Laphroaig, I espied Hymie Mintzbaum at another table with a bimbo young enough to be his granddaughter. Following that brawl in London, whenever Hymie and I ran into each other here or there over the years, at the international stations of the show-business Cross (Ma Maison, Elaine's, The Ivy, L'ami Louis, et cetera, et cetera), we acknowledged each other's presence with no more than a nod. I would occasionally see him, accompanied by a fawning starlet wannabe, and pick up his gravelly voice drifting over tables in one restaurant or another. "As Hemingway once said to me . . ." or "Marilyn was far more intelligent than most people realized, but Arthur wasn't right for her."

Once, in 1964, Hymie and I actually got to exchange words.

"So Miriam didn't take my advice," he said. "She finally married you."

"We happen to be very happy together."

"Does it ever start unhappily?"

And that night, more than twenty years later, there he was again. He nodded. I nodded. Hymie had obviously endured a face-lift since I had last seen him. He now dyed his hair black and wore a bomber jacket, designer jeans, and Adidas. As luck would have it, we all but collided in the men's room. "You damn fool," he said, "when we're dead it will be for a long time and it won't matter that the film we did in London was from Boogie's original story."

"It mattered to me."

"Because you were consumed with guilt?"

"After all these years, the way I look at it is Boogie was the one who betrayed me."

"That's not the way most people see it."

"He should have turned up at my trial."

"Rising from the grave?"

"Flying in from wherever."

"You're incorrigible."

"Am I?"

"Prick. You know what I'm doing now? A film-of-the-week for ABC-TV. But it's a very exciting script and could lead to big things. I'm with a Freudian analyst these days. We're working on a sensational script together and I'm fucking her, which is more than I ever got from any of the others."

Back at my table, one of the young executives, his smile reeking of condescension, said, "You know old Mintzbaum, do you?"

The other one, shaking his head, said, "For Christ's sake, don't encourage him to come to our table, or he'll start to pitch."

"Old Mintzbaum," I said, "was risking his life in the Eighth Army Air Force before you were born, you smug, insufferably boring, little cretin. As for you, you cliché-mongering little shit," I added, turning to the other one. "I'll bet you pay a personal trainer to time your laps in your goddamn swimming pool every morning. Neither of you are fit to shine old Mintzbaum's shoes. Fuck off, both of you."

1989 THAT was. I'm jumping all over the place. I know, I know. But seated at my desk these endgame days, my bladder plugged by an enlarged prostate, my sciatica a frequent curse, wondering when I will be due for another hip-socket, anticipating emphysema, pulling on a Montecristo Number Two, a bottle of Macallan by my side, I try to retrieve some sense out of my life, unscrambling it. Recalling those blissful days in Paris, in the early fifties, when we were young and crazy, I raise my glass to absent friends: Mason Hoffenberg, David Burnett, Alfred Chester, and Terry Southern, all dead now. I wonder whatever became of the girl who was never seen on the boulevard Saint-Germain without that chirping chimpanzee riding her shoulder. Did she go home to Houston and marry a dentist? Is she a grandmother now and an admirer of Newt? Or did she die of an overdose like the exquisite Marie-Claire, who could trace her lineage back to Roland?

I dunno. I just dunno. The past is a foreign country, they do things differently there, as E.M. Forster[1] once wrote. Anyway, those, those were the days. We had not so much arrived in the City of Light as escaped the constraints of our dim, provincial origins, in my case the only country that declared Queen Victoria's birthday a national holiday. Our lives were unstructured. Totally. We ate when we were hungry and slept when we were tired, and screwed whoever was available whenever it was possible, surviving on three dollars a day. Except for the always elegantly dressed Cedric, a black American who was the beneficiary of a secret source of funds about which the rest of us speculated endlessly. Certainly it wasn't family money. Or the pathetic sums he earned for stories published in the *London Magazine* or *Kenyon Review*. And I dismissed as a canard the rumour rife among some other Left Bank black Americans that, in those days of crazed anti-Communism, Cedric received a

---

[1]Actually, it was L.P. Hartley in *The Go-Between*, page 1. Hamish Hamilton, London, 1953.

monthly stipend from the FBI, or CIA, to inform on their activities. Whatever, Cedric wasn't hunkered down in a cheap hotel room but was ensconced in a comfortable apartment on the rue Bonaparte. His Yiddish, which he had acquired in Brighton Beach, where his father worked as an apartment-building janitor, was good enough for him to banter with Boogie, who addressed him as the *shayner reb* Cedric, the *shvartzer goan* of Brooklyn. Ostensibly without racial hang-ups, and fun to be with, he went along with Boogie's jest that he was actually a pushy Yemenite trying to pass as black because it made him irresistible to young white women who had come to Paris to be liberated, albeit on a monthly allowance from their up-tight parents. He also responded with an admixture of warmth and deference whenever Boogie, our acknowledged master, praised his latest short story. But I suspected his pleasure was simulated. With hindsight, I fear that he and Boogie, constantly jousting, actually disliked each other.

Make no mistake. Cedric was truly talented, and so, inevitably, one day a New York publisher sent him a contract for his first novel, offering him a $2,500 advance against royalties. Cedric invited Leo, Boogie, Clara, and me to dinner at La Coupole to celebrate. And we did whoop it up, happy to be together, going through one bottle of wine after another. The publisher and his wife, said Cedric, would be in Paris the following week. "From his letter," said Cedric, "I gather he thinks I'm one dirt-poor spade, living in a garret, who will jump at his invitation to dinner."

This led us into jokes about whether Cedric could order chitlins at Lapérouse, or turn up barefoot for drinks at the Deux Magots. And then I made my gaffe. Hoping to impress Boogie, who could usually be counted on for the invention of our most outlandish pranks, I suggested that Cedric invite his publisher and his wife to dinner at his apartment, where the four of us would pretend to be his hired help. Clara and I would cook, and Boogie and Leo, wearing white shirts and black bow-ties, would serve the table. "I love it," said Clara, clapping hands, but Boogie wouldn't have it.

"Why?" I asked.

"Because I fear our friend Cedric here would enjoy it too much."

An ill-wind passed over our table. Cedric, feigning fatigue, called for the bill, and we dispersed separately into the night, each

one troubled by his own dark thoughts. But, within days, the
episode was forgotten. Once again we took to gathering in Cedric's
apartment late at night, after the jazz clubs had closed, digging into
his stash of hashish.

Those days not only Sidney Bechet, but also Charlie Parker
and Miles Davis were playing in small *boîtes de nuit* which we frequented. Lazy spring afternoons we would pick up our mail and
some gossip at Gaït Frogé's English Bookshop on the rue de Seine,
or saunter over to the Père Lachaise cemetery to gawk at the graves
of Oscar Wilde and Heinrich Heine, among other immortals. But
dying, a blight common to earlier generations, did not enter into
our scheme of things. It wasn't on our dance cards.

Each age gets the arts patrons it deserves. My bunch's bene-
factor was Maurice Girodias, né Kahane, sole prop. of Olympia
Press, publishers of the hot stuff in the Traveller's Library. I can
remember waiting for Boogie more than once on the corner of the
rue Dauphine as he ventured into Girodias's office on the rue de
Nesle, lugging last night's twenty-odd pages of porn, and, if he were
lucky, coming away with maybe five thousand sustaining francs, an
advance against a stroke-book to be delivered as soon as possible.
Once, to his amusement, he collided with the vice squad, the men in
trenchcoats from *La Brigade Mondaine* (The Worldly Brigade), who
had barged in to seize copies of *Who Pushed Paulo*, *The Whip Angels*,
Helen and Desire, and Count Palmiro Vicarion's *Book of Limericks*:

> When Titian was mixing rose madder,
> His model was poised on a ladder.
> "Your position," said Titian,
> "Inspires coition."
> So he nipped up the ladder and 'ad 'er.

On a whim, or just because a motorcycle ride was suddenly
available, we would take off for a few days in Venice, or bum a ride
to the *feria* in Valencia, where we could catch Litri and Aparicio
and the young Dominguin in the Plaza des Toros. One summer
afternoon, in 1952, Boogie announced that we were going to
Cannes to work as film extras, and that's how I first met Hymie
Mintzbaum.

Hymie, built like a line-backer, big-featured, with black hair,

curly as a terrier's, brown eyes charged with appetite, big floppy
ears, prominent nose misshapen, twice-broken, had served with the
American Army Air Force 281st Bomb Group, based in Ridgewell,
not far from Cambridge, in 1943; a twenty-nine-year-old major,
pilot of a B-17. His gravelly voice mesmerizing, he told Boogie and
me – the three of us seated on the terrace of the Colombe d'Or in
St.-Paul-de-Vence, that summer of '52, into our second bottle of
Dom Pérignon, every flute laced with Courvoisier XO, Hymie's
treat – that his squadron's brief had been daylight precision
bombing. He had been in on the second raid on the Schweinfort
ball-bearings factory in which the Eighth Air Force had lost 60 out
of the 320 bombers that had set out from East Anglia. "Flying at
25,000 feet, the temperature 50 below zero, even with heated flying
suits," he said, "we had to worry about frostbite, never mind Goer-
ing's personal squadron of ME-109s and FW-190s, circling, waiting
to pick off stragglers. Do either of you young geniuses," he asked,
the designation "geniuses" delivered in italics, "happen to know the
young woman seated in the shade there, second table to our left?"

   Young geniuses. Boogie, that most perspicacious of men, couldn't
handle liquor, it made him sloppy, so he didn't grasp that we were
being patronized. Obviously Hymie, who was pushing forty at the
time, felt threatened by the young. Clearly my manhood, if not
Boogie's, was in question as I had never been blooded in combat.
Neither was I old enough to have suffered sufficiently through the
Great Depression. I hadn't cavorted in Paris in the good old days,
immediately after its liberation, knocking back martinis with Papa
Hemingway at the Ritz. I hadn't seen Joe Louis floor Max Schme-
ling in the first round and couldn't understand what that meant to a
yid coming of age in the Bronx. Or caught Gypsy Rose Lee strip-
ping at the World's Fair. Hymie suffered from that sour old man's
delusion that anybody who had come after him was born too late.
He was, in our parlance, a bit of a drag. "No," I said. "I have no idea
who she is."

   "Too bad," said Hymie.

   Hymie, blacklisted at the time, was shooting a French *film noir*
under a pseudonym in Monte Carlo, an Eddie Constantine flick,
Boogie and I working as extras. He called for another Dom Pérignon, instructed the waiter to leave the Courvoisier XO bottle on
the table, and asked for olives, almonds, fresh figs, a plate of crev-

ettes, some pâté with truffles, bread, butter, smoked salmon, and anything else you've got for nibbles there.

The sun, which had been warming us, began to sink behind the olive-green hills, seemingly setting them alight. A donkey-drawn wagon, led by a grizzly old geezer wearing a blue smock, passed clippity-clop below the terrace's stone retaining wall, and we caught the scent of its cargo of roses on the evening breeze. The roses were bound for the perfumeries in Grasse. Then a fat baker's boy puffed by our table, one of those huge wicker baskets of freshly baked baguettes strapped to his back, and we could smell that too. "If she's waiting for somebody," said Hymie, "he's shamefully late."

The woman with the gleaming hair seated alone two tables to our left appeared to be in her late twenties. Somebody's gift package. Her fine arms bare, her linen shift elegant, long bare legs crossed. She was sipping white wine and smoking a Gitane, and when she caught us sneaking glances at her, she lowered her eyes, pouted, and reached for the book in her straw shoulder bag, *Bonjour tristesse*,[2] by Françoise Sagan, and began to read.

"Do you want me to invite her over to join us?" asked Boogie.

Hymie scratched his purply jaw. He made a face, wrinkling his forehead. "Naw. I think not. If she joined us, it could spoil everything. Gotta make a phonecall. Back in a couple of minutes."

"He's beginning to bug me," I said to Boogie. "As soon as he get's back, I think we ought to split, man."

"No."

Hymie, back soon enough, began to drop names, a failing I cannot tolerate. Hollywood manna. John Huston, his buddy. Dorothy Parker, big trouble. The time he had worked on a screenplay with that stool-pigeon Clifford Odets. His two-day drunk with Bogie. Then he told us that his commanding officer had summoned all the air crews to a briefing in a Nissen hut before they took off on their first mission. "I don't want any of you girls faking mechanical trouble three hundred miles short of the target area, dropping your bombs on the nearest cow patch, and dashing for home. Gosh darn it. Holy smoke. You would be failing Rosie the Riveter, not to mention all those 4-F hymies raking it in on the black market

---

[2] It had to be some other book, as *Bonjour tristesse* wasn't published until 1954.

stateside and fucking the girls you left behind. Better shit yourselves than try that story on me." Then he added, "Three months from now two-thirds of you will be dead. Any stupid questions?"

But Hymie survived, demobilized with some fifteen thousand dollars in the bank, most of it won at the poker table. He made straight for Paris, moving into the Ritz, he said, and not drawing a sober breath for six months. Then, down to his last three thousand dollars, he booked passage on the *Ile de France*, and lit out for California. Starting as a third-assistant director, he bullied his way up the ladder, intimidating studio executives, who had served with honour on the War Bond drives on the home front, by wearing his flight jacket to dinner parties. Hymie churned out a *Blondie*, a couple of Tim Holt westerns, and one of Tom Conway's *The Falcon* series, before he was allowed to direct a comedy featuring Eddie Bracken and Betty what's-her-name? You know, like the stock-market brokers. Betty Merrill Lynch? No. Betty Lehman Brothers? Come off it. Betty like in those ads. When la-de-da speaks, everybody listens. *Hutton*. Betty Hutton. He was once nominated for an Academy Award, was three times divorced, and then the House Un-American Activities Committee caught up with him. "This sleaze-bag Anderson, my comrade," he said, "a five-hundred-dollar-a-week screenwriter, was sworn in by the committee and told them he used to come to my house in Benedict Canyon to collect weekly Party dues. How was I to know he was an FBI agent?"

Surveying our table, Hymie said, "There's something missing. *Garçon, apportez-nous des cigares, s'il vous plaît.*"

Then a Frenchman, obviously past it, well into his fifties, pranced onto the terrace. He was sporting a yachting cap, his navy blue blazer with the brass buttons tossed over his shoulder like a cape: he had come to claim the young woman who sat two tables to our left. She rose to greet him, a butterfly disturbed, with a flutter of delight.

"*Comme tu es belle*," he cooed.

"*Merci, chéri.*"

"*Je t'adore*," he said, stroking her cheek with his hand. Then he called peremptorily for the waiter, *le roi le veut*, flashed a roll of francs bound with a gold clasp, and settled the bill. The two of them drifted toward our table, where she obliged him to stop, indicating the remnants of our feast with a dismissive wave of her hand, saying, "*Les Américains. Dégueulasses. Comme d'habitude.*"

"We don't like Ike," said the Frenchman, tittering.

"*Fiche-moi la paix,*" said Hymie.

"*Toi et ta fille,*" I said.

Stung, they moved on, arms around each other's waist, and strolled toward his Aston-Martin, the old man's hand caressing her bottom. He opened the car door for her, settled in behind the wheel, slipped on his racing driver's gloves, made an obscene gesture at us, and drove off.

"Let's get out of here," said Hymie.

Piling into Hymie's Citroën, we sped to Hauts-de-Cagnes, Hymie and Boogie belting out synagogue songs they remembered as we charged up the all but perpendicular hill to Jimmy's Bar on the crest, and that's when my mood began to curdle. Wintry is my soul's season. And that evening, perfect but for my fulminating presence, my heart was laden with envy. For Hymie's war experiences. His charm. His bankroll. For the effortless manner in which Boogie had been able to establish a rapport with him, their joshing now often excluding me.

Years later, shortly after the murder charges against me had been dismissed, and Hymie was home again, now that the blacklist was a nightmare past, he insisted that I recuperate at the beach house he had rented for the summer in the Hamptons. "I know you don't want to see anyone in your mood. But this is just what the doctor ordered. Peace and quiet. Sea. Sand. Pastrami. Divorcées on the make. Wait till you taste my kasha. And nobody will know anything about your troubles."

Peace and quiet. Hymie. I should have known better. The most generous of hosts, he furnished his beach house with wall-to-wall guests almost every night, most of them young and all of whom he set out to seduce. He would regale them with stories of the great and near-great he claimed to have known. Dashiell Hammett, a prince. Bette Davis, misunderstood. Peter Lorre, his kind of guy. Ditto Spence. Passing from guest to guest, he would illuminate them, like a lamp-lighter. He would whisper into the ear of each young woman that she was the most gorgeous and intelligent on Long Island, and confide in each of the men that he was uniquely gifted. He wouldn't allow me to brood in a corner, but literally thrust me on one woman after another. "She's wildly attracted to you." Going on to introduce me, saying, "This is my old friend Barney Panofsky and he's dying to meet you. He doesn't look it, I know, but he just got away with the perfect crime. Tell her about it, kid."

I took Hymie aside. "I know you mean well, Hymie, but the truth is I'm committed to a woman in Toronto."

"Of course you are. You think I don't hear you coming on like a pimply teenager on the phone after I've gone to bed?"

"Are you listening in on the extension in your bedroom?"

"Look, kid, Miriam's there, and you're here. Enjoy."

"You don't understand."

"No, it's you who doesn't understand. When you get to be my age, what you regret is not the times you cheated a little, but the times you didn't."

"It's not going to be like that with us."

"I'll bet when you were a kid you clapped hands for Tinkerbell."

Early every morning, rain or shine, Hymie, who was then being treated by a Reichian analyst, would trot on to the dunes and let out primal screams sufficiently loud to drive any sharks lingering in the shallows back to sea. Then he would start on his morning jog, accumulating a gaggle of everybody else's children en route, proposing marriage to eleven-year-old girls and suggesting to nine-year-old boys that they stop somewhere for a beer, eventually leading them to the local candy store for treats. Back at the beach house, he would make both of us salami omelettes garnished with mounds of home fries. Then, immediately after breakfast, still hoarse from his dune therapy, Hymie, who was connected to the world outside by his phone, would put in a call to his agent: "What are you going to do for me today, you *cacker*?" Or he would get a producer on the line, cajoling, pleading, threatening, honking phlegm into his handkerchief, lighting one cigarette off another. "I've got it in me to direct the best American film since *Citizen Kane*, but I never hear from you. How come?"

I was often wakened in the early morning hours by Hymie hollering into the phone at one or another of his former wives, apologizing for being late with an alimony payment, commiserating over an affair that had ended badly, or shouting at one of his sons, or his daughter in San Francisco. "What does she do?" I once asked him.

"Shop. Get pregnant. Marry, divorce. You've heard of serial killers? She's a serial bride."

Hymie's children were a constant heartache and an endless financial drain. The son in Boston, a Wiccan, and proprietor of an occult bookshop, was writing the definitive book on astrology. When not contemplating the heavens, he was given to writing bad cheques on earth, which Hymie had to make good. His other son, a wandering rock musician, was in and out of expensive detox clinics, and had a weakness for hitting the road in stolen sports cars which he inevitably smashed up. He could phone from a lock-up in Tulsa, or a hospital in Kansas City, or a lawyer's office in Denver, to say there had been a misunderstanding. "But you mustn't worry, Dad. I wasn't hurt."

Not yet a father myself, I deigned to lecture him. "If I ever have children," I said, "once they reach the age of twenty-one they're on their own. There has to be a cut-off point."

"The grave," he said.

Hymie supported a shlemiel of a brother, who was a Talmudic scholar, and his parents in Florida. Once, I found him weeping at the kitchen table at two a.m., surrounded by cheque books, and scraps of paper on which he had made hurried calculations. "Anything I can do?" I asked.

"Yeah. Mind your own business. No, sit down. Do you realize that if I had a heart attack tomorrow, there would be twelve people out on the street, without a pot to piss in? Here. Read this." It was a letter from his brother. He had finally caught up with one of Hymie's movies on late-night television: prurient, obscene, meretricious, and an embarrassment to the family's good name. If he must make such trash, couldn't he use a pseudonym? "Do you know how much money he's in to me for, that *momzer*? I even pay his daughter's college fees."

I was not good company. Far from it. Waking in a sweat at three a.m., convinced I was still wasting away in that slammer in St. Jérôme, denied bail, a life sentence my most likely prospect. Or dreaming that I was being weighed again by that somnolent jury of pig farmers, snow-plough men, and garage mechanics. Or, unable to sleep, grieving for Boogie, wondering if the divers had messed up, and if, against all odds, he was still tangled in the weeds. Or if his bloated body had surfaced in my absence. But an hour later my concern would yield to rage. He was alive, that bastard. I knew it in my bones. Then why hadn't he shown up at my trial? Because he hadn't heard about it. He was on one of his retreats in an ashram in India. Or he was in a heroin-induced stupor in a hotel in San Francisco. Or he was in that Trappist monastery on Big Sur, trying to kick, studying his list of the names of the dead. Any day now I would get one of his cryptic postcards. Like the one that once came from Acre:

> In those days there was no king in Israel, but every man did that which was right in his own eyes.
>
> Judges, 17:6.

The day after my release from prison, I had driven out to my cottage on the lake, jumped into my outboard, and covered every inch of the shoreline as well as the adjoining brooks. Detective-Sergeant O'Hearne had been waiting for me on my dock. "What are you doing here?" I'd demanded.

"Walking in the woods. You were born with a horseshoe up your ass, Mr. P."

Late one night Hymie and I sat on the deck, the two of us sipping cognac. "You were such a bundle of nerves when we first met," he said. "Sweating anger and resentment and aggression under that assumed hipster's carapace. But who would have guessed that one day you would get away with murder?"

"I didn't do it, Hymie."

"In France you would have got off with a slap on the wrist. *Crime passionnel* is what they call it. I swear I never thought you'd have the guts."

"You don't understand. He's still alive. Out there somewhere. Mexico. New Zealand. Macao. Who knows?"

"According to what I've read, afterwards there was never any money withdrawn from his bank account."

"Miriam found out that there were three break-ins into summer cottages on the lake in the days following his disappearance. That's how he probably found some clothes."

"Are you broke now?"

"My lawyer. Alimony. Neglected business affairs. Sure I'm broke now."

"We're going to write a screenplay together."

"Don't be ridiculous. I'm not a writer, Hymie."

"There's a hundred and fifty big ones in it for us, split two ways. Hey, wait a minute. I mean one-third for you, two-thirds for me. What do you say?"

Once we settled into work on the script, Hymie would rip scenes out of my typewriter and read them over the phone to a former mistress in Paris, a cousin in Brooklyn, his daughter, or his agent. "Now you listen to this, it's fabulous." If the reaction wasn't what he expected, he would counter, "It's only a first draft and I did tell Barney it wouldn't work. He's a novice, you know." His cleaning lady's opinion was solicited, he consulted his analyst, handed out pages to waitresses, and made revisions based on their criticisms. He could charge into my bedroom at four a.m. and shake me awake. "I just had a brilliant idea. Come." Slurping ice cream out of a bucket retrieved from the fridge, he would stride up and down in his boxer shorts, scratching his groin, and begin to dictate. "This is Academy Award stuff. Bullet-proof." But the next morning, rereading what he had dictated, he would say, "Barney, this is a piece of shit. Now let's get serious today."

On bad days, dry days, he might suddenly sink to the sofa and say, "You know what I could do with now? A blow-job. Technically, you know, that's not being unfaithful. What am I worrying about? I'm not even married now." Then he would leap up, pluck his copy of *The Memoirs of Fanny Hill* or *The Story of O* from a bookshelf, and disappear into the toilet. "We should do this at least once a day. It keeps the prostate in check. A doctor told me that."

Back at Jimmy's Bar, in 1952, we hit the road in Hymie's Peugeot[3] again, and the next thing I remember is one of those crowded, tiny, smoke-filled bar-tabacs with a zinc-topped counter in an alley off the market in Nice, and the three of us knocking back cognacs with the porters and truck drivers. We drank toasts to Maurice Thorez, Mao, Harry Bridges, and then to La Pasionaria and El Campesino, in honour of the two Catalan refugees in the company. And then, laden with gifts of tomatoes that still reeked of

---

[3]Described as a Citroën on page 33.

the vine, spring onions, and figs, we moved on to Juan les Pins, where we found a nightclub open. " 'Tailgunner Joe,' " said Hymie, "my intrepid comrade-in-arms Senator Joseph McCarthy, that cockroach, actually never flew into battle...."

Which was when a seemingly comatose Boogie suddenly shifted gears, going into overdrive. "When the witch hunt is over," he said, "and everybody is embarrassed, as they were after the Palmer Raids, McCarthy may yet be appreciated with hindsight as the most effective film critic ever. Never mind Agee. The senator certainly cleaned out the stables."

Hymie would never have taken that from me, but, coming from Boogie, he decided to let it fly. It was amazing. Here was Hymie, an accomplished and reasonably affluent man, a successful film director, and there was Boogie, poor, unknown, a struggling writer, his publications limited to a couple of little magazines. But it was an intimidated Hymie who was determined to win Boogie's approval. Boogie had that effect on people. I wasn't the only one who needed his blessing.

"My problem," Boogie continued, "is that I have some respect for the Hollywood Ten as people, but not as writers of even the second rank. *Je m'excuse*. The third rank. Much as I abhor Evelyn Waugh's politics, I would rather read one of his novels any day than sit through any of their mawkish films again."

"You're such a kidder, Boogie," said a subdued Hymie.

" 'The best lack all conviction,' " said Boogie. " 'while the worst/ Are full of passionate intensity.' So said Mr. Yeats."

"I'm willing to admit," said Hymie, "that our bunch, and I include myself in that lot, possibly invested so much integrity in our guilt-ridden politics we had little left for our work. I suppose you could argue that Franz Kafka didn't require a swimming pool. Or that George Orwell never attended a script conference, but..." And then, unwilling to tangle with Boogie, he unleashed his anger on me. "And I hope I will always be able to say the same for you, Barney, you condescending little prick."

"Hey, I'm not a writer. I'm merely hanging out. Come on, Boogie. Let's split."

"Leave my friend Boogie out of this. At least he speaks his mind. But I have my doubts about you."

"Me too," said Boogie.

"Go to hell, both of you," I said, leaping up from the table and quitting the nightclub.

Boogie caught up with me outside. "I expect you won't be satisfied until he punches you out."

"I can take him."

"How does Clara put up with your tantrums?"

"Who else would put up with Clara?"

That made him laugh. Me too. "Okay," he said, "let's get back in there, and you make nice, understand?"

"He bugs me."

"Everybody bugs you. You're one mean, crazy son of a bitch. Now if you can't be a mensch, you can at least pretend. Come on. Let's go."

Back at the table, Hymie rose to rock me in a bear hug. "I apologize. Humbly I do. And now we can all do with some fresh air."

Settling into the sand, on the beach in Cannes, we watched the sun rise over the wine-dark sea, eating our tomatoes, spring onions, and figs. Then we shed our shoes, rolled up our trouser bottoms, and waded in up to our knees. Boogie splashed me, I splashed him back, and within seconds the three of us were into a water fight, and in those days you didn't have to worry about turds or used condoms drifting in on the tide. Finally we repaired to a café on the Croisette for *oeufs sur le plat*, brioches, and *café au lait*. Boogie bit the end off a Romeo y Julieta, lit up, and said, "*Après tout, c'est un monde passable,*" quoting only God knows who.[4]

Hymie stretched, yawned, and said, "Got to go to work now. We begin shooting at the casino in an hour. Let's meet for drinks at the Carlton at seven tonight and then I know of a place in Gulf-Juan where they make an excellent bouillabaisse." He tossed us his hotel keys. "In case you guys want to wash up or snooze or read my mail. See you later."

Boogie and I strolled as far as the harbour to look at the yachts, and there was that French sugar-daddy, sunning himself on his teak deck, out on the Mediterranean endlessly rocking, his squeeze nowhere in sight. He looked absolutely pathetic, wearing reading glasses, his sunken belly spilling over his bikini, as he perused *Le*

[4]Voltaire.

Figaro. The stock-market pages, no doubt. Obligatory reading for those without an inner life. "*Salut, grandpère,*" I called out. "*Comment va ta concubine aujourd'hui?*"

"*Maricons,*" he hollered, shaking his fist at me.

"Are you going to let him get away with that?" asked Boogie. "Knock his teeth out. Beat the shit out of him. Anything to make you feel better."

"Okay," I said. "Okay."

"You're a fucking menace," he said, leading me away.

THREE

THE script Hymie and I wrote on Long Island was never produced, but less than a year later, in 1961, he phoned me from London. "Come on over. We're going to write another picture together. I'm so excited about this project I've already written my Academy Award acceptance speech."

"Hymie, I've got a full plate over here. I spend every weekend in Toronto with Miriam, or she flies here and we go to a hockey game together. Why don't you get yourself a real writer this time?"

"I don't want a real writer. I want you, darling. It's from an original story I bought years ago."

"I can't leave here just like that."

"I've already booked you on a first-class flight leaving Toronto tomorrow."

"I'm in Montreal."

"What's the difference. It's all Canada, isn't it?"

Outside, it was 15 degrees below zero, and another cleaning lady had quit on me. There were mouldy things sprouting in my fridge. My apartment stank of stale tobacco and sweaty old shirts and socks. In those days I usually started my morning with a pot of black coffee fortified with cognac and a stale bagel I had to soak in water and heat up in an oven encrusted with grease. I was then already divorced from The Second Mrs. Panofsky. I was also a social pariah. Adjudged innocent by the court but condemned as a murderer, incredibly lucky to walk, by just about everybody else. I had taken to playing childish games. If the Canadiens won ten in a row, or if Beliveau scored a hat trick on Saturday night, there would be a postcard from Boogie on Monday morning, forgiving me my red-hot outburst, those harsh words I swear I didn't mean. I tracked down and wrote or phoned mutual friends in Paris and Chicago and Dublin and, you know, that artsy desert pueblo-cum-Hollywood-*shtetl* in Arizona, favoured by short producers in cowboy boots, with those health-food restaurants where you can't smoke and everybody pops garlic and vitamin pills with their daily fibre. It's not far from where they made the atom bomb, or from where D.H. Lawrence lived with what's-her-name. Santa something.[1] But nobody had seen or heard from Boogie, and some resented my inquiries. "What are you trying to prove, you bastard?" I visited Boogie's old haunts in New York: The San Remo, The Lion's Head. "Moscovitch," said the bartender in the San Remo, "he was murdered somewhere in Canada, I thought."

"The hell he was."

At the time, I was also having my problems with Miriam, who would change everything for me: then, now, and forever. She was still vacillating. Moving to Montreal to marry me would mean giving up her job with CBC Radio. Furthermore, to her mind, I was a difficult man. I phoned her. "Go ahead," she said, "London will be good for you and I need some time alone."

"No, you don't."

"I can't think with you here."

"Why not?"

"You're devouring me."

"I want you to promise that if I'm in London for more than a month you'll fly over for a few days. It won't be a hardship."

She promised. So why not, I thought. The work wouldn't be rigorous. I needed the money desperately and all Hymie required was sympathetic company. Somebody to sit at the typewriter and guffaw at his one-liners, while he worked the phone, striding up and down, honking, chatting up bimbos, agents, producers, or his analyst: "I just remembered something significant."

Hymie's film turned out to be one of his iffy patchwork-quilt projects, the financing stitched together by pre-selling distribution

[1] Santá Fe in New Mexico.

to individual territories: the U.K., France, Germany, and Italy. His once curly black hair had faded grey as ash, and he was now given to cracking his knuckles and picking at the fat of his palms with his thumbnails, rendering the flesh painfully raw. He had shed his Reichian analyst for a Jungian, whom he visited every morning. "She's incredible. A magus. You ought to see her yourself. Great tits."

Hymie now suffered from insomnia, he chewed tranquillizers, and did the occasional line. He had been through an LSD session with the then modish R.D. Laing. His problem was that nobody in Hollywood was in need of his services any more. His phonecalls to most agents and studio executives in Beverly Hills went unanswered or were returned some days later by an underling, one of whom actually asked Hymie to spell his name. "Call me back, sonny," said Hymie, "when your voice has changed." But, as promised, we did whoop it up together in that suite Hymie had taken in the Dorchester, where he was encouraging the chambermaid to write poetry, and a waiter in the dining room to organize a staff union. We smoked Montecristos and sipped brandies and sodas while we worked, and called room service to send up smoked salmon and caviar and champagne for lunch. "You know something, Barney, we may never be able to check out of here, because I don't know if my backers can handle the bill." My long phonecalls to Toronto, often twice daily, included. "Hey," Hymie would say, breaking off in the middle of acting out a scene, "you haven't spoken to your sweetiepoo in six hours. Maybe she's changed?"

Early one afternoon, maybe ten days into our collaboration, I phoned again and again. No answer. "She told me she'd be home tonight. I don't understand."

"We're supposed to be working here."

"She's a terrible driver. And they had freezing rain there this morning. What if she's been in an accident?"

"She's gone to a movie. Or dinner with friends. Now let's get some work done here."

It was five a.m., London time, before somebody picked up her phone. I recognized the voice at once. "McIver, you bastard, what in the hell are you doing there?"

"Who is this?"

"Barney Panofsky is who, and I want to speak to Miriam at once."

Laughter in the background. The clinking of glasses. Finally, she came to the phone. "My God, Barney, why are you still up at this hour?"

"You have no idea how worried I've been. You told me you'd be in tonight."

"It's Larry Keefer's birthday. We all went out to dinner and I invited everybody back here for a nightcap."

"Why didn't you call me when you got in?"

"Because I assumed you'd be asleep."

"How come McIver's there?"

"He's an old friend of Larry's."

"You're not to believe a word he says about me. He's a pathological liar."

"Barney, I've got a room full of guests here, and this is getting to be very embarrassing. Go to sleep. We'll talk tomorrow."

"But I – "

"Sorry," she said, her voice hardening. "I forgot. How could I? Chicago beat Detroit 3–2 tonight. Bobby Hull scored twice. So the series is tied now."

"That's not why I called. I don't care about that. It's you I – "

"Good night," she said, hanging up.

I considered waiting a couple of hours and then calling back, ostensibly to apologize but actually to make sure she was alone now. Fortunately, on reflection, I dismissed this as a bad idea. But I was in a rage, all the same. How that prick McIver must have enjoyed himself! "You mean he calls you from London for the hockey scores? Amazing."

FLUSH OR BROKE, Hymie lived like royalty. So just about every night we dined at either the Caprice, the Mirabelle, or The White Elephant. Providing it was only the two of us, Hymie was the most engaging of companions, a born raconteur, charming beyond compare. But if there was a visiting Hollywood biggie at the next table, he was instantly transmogrified into a supplicant, who would tell one obviously irritated oaf how exciting it would be to work with him, and another that his last, unappreciated film was actually a production of genius. "And I'm not saying that just because you're here."

A couple of days before Miriam was due to fly into London at last, I made the mistake of trying to have a serious conversation with Hymie. "She's very sensitive, so I want you to make an effort not to be vulgar."

"Yes, Daddy."

"And your latest 'discovery,' that idiot Diana, is certainly not joining us for dinner while Miriam's here."

"Say we're in a restaurant, and I have to go and make weewee, do I put up my hand to ask permission?"

"And none of your prurient Hollywood gossip, please. It would bore the hell out of her."

I needn't have been apprehensive about Miriam meeting Hymie. She adored him at first sight, dinner at The White Elephant. He made her giggle harder than I ever had, that bastard. He got her to blush. And, to my amazement, she couldn't get enough of his salacious stories about Bette Davis, Bogie, or Orson. There I was, mooning over my loved one, my smile goofy in her presence, but definitely *de trop*.

"He told me you were intelligent," said Hymie, "but he never once mentioned that you were so beautiful."

"He probably hasn't noticed yet. It's not like I ever scored a hat trick or the winning goal in overtime."

"Why marry him when I'm still available?"

"Did he say I had agreed to marry him?"

"I didn't. I swear. I said I *hoped* that you would – "

"Why don't the two of us meet for lunch tomorrow, while I give him some typing to do?"

Lunch? They were gone for four hours, and when Miriam finally tottered into our hotel room, she was flushed and slurring her words, and had to lie down. I had booked us into the Caprice for dinner, but couldn't get her out of bed. "Take Hymie," she said, turning over and starting to snore again.

"What did you talk about for so long?" I asked Hymie later.

"This and that."

"You got her drunk."

"Eat up, boychick."

Once Miriam had flown back to Toronto, Hymie and I

resumed our carousing. Hell for Hymie wasn't other people, as Camus had it,[2] but being without them. When I would quit our table at The White Elephant or the Mirabelle, pleading fatigue, he would move on to another table, uninvited but making himself welcome by dazzling the company with anecdotes about bankable names. Or he would slide over to the bar, chatting up whatever woman was seated alone there. "Do you know who I am?"

One night it still chills me to remember, Ben Shahn turned up at The White Elephant with a group of admirers. Hymie, who owned one of Shahn's drawings, took this as a licence to intrude at his table. Pointing a finger at Shahn, he said, "Next time you see Cliff, I want you to tell him for me that he's a dirty rat."

Cliff, of course, was Odets, who had babbled to the Un-American Activities Committee, naming names.

Silence settled like a shroud over the table. Shahn, unperturbed, raised his glasses to his forehead, peering quizzically at Hymie, and asked, "And who shall I say was the messenger?"

"Never mind," said Hymie, shrinking before my eyes. "Forget it." And retreating, he seemed momentarily befuddled, old, unsure of his bearings.

Finally, several months later, the day came when I sat with Hymie in a Beverly Hills screening room and watched the titles and credits of our film roll past. Startled, I read:

FROM AN ORIGINAL STORY BY BERNARD
MOSCOVITCH

"You bastard," I hollered, yanking Hymie out of his seat, shaking him, "why didn't you tell me it was from a story by Boogie?"

"Touchy touchy," he said, pinching my cheek.

"Now, as if I didn't have enough to handle, people will say I'm exploiting his work."

"Something bothers me. If he was such a good friend, and he's still alive, why didn't he show at your trial?"

In response, I reached back and managed to crunch Hymie's twice-broken nose for a third time, something I had longed to do ever since he had taken Miriam out for that four-hour lunch. He

---

[2]Actually, it was Jean-Paul Sartre.

countered by pumping his knee into my groin. We carried on
pounding each other, rolling over on the floor, and it took three
men from the unit to untangle us, even as we went on cursing each
other.

FOUR

POETRY comes naturally to the Panofskys. Take my father,
for instance. Detective-Inspector Izzy Panofsky departed this
vale of tears in a state of grace. Thirty-six years ago today he
died of a heart attack on the table of a massage parlor in Montreal's
North End, immediately after ejaculating. Summoned to claim my
father's remains, I was taken aside by the visibly shaken young
Haitian girl. She had no last words to impart to me, but did point
out that Izzy had expired without signing his credit-card slip. A
dutiful son, I paid for my father's final squirt of passion, adding a
generous tip and apologizing for the inconvenience to the establishment. And this afternoon, on the anniversary of my father's death, I
made my annual pilgrimage to the Chevra Kadisha cemetery and, as
I do every year, emptied a bottle of Crown Royal rye whisky over
his grave and, in lieu of a pebble, left a medium-fat smoked meat on
rye and a sour pickle on his gravestone.

Were ours a just God, which he isn't, my father would now
dwell in heaven's most opulent bordello, which would also include a
deli counter, a bar with a brass rail and spitoon, a cache of White
Owl coronas, and a 24-hour TV sports channel. But the God we
Jews are stuck with is both cruel and vengeful. To my way of
looking, Jehovah was also the first Jewish stand-up comic, Abraham
his straight man. "Take thy son," the Lord said unto Abraham,
"thine only son Isaac, whom thou lovest, and get thee into the land
of Moriah; and offer him there for a burnt offering upon one of the
mountains which I will tell thee of." And Abe, the first of too many
Jewish grovellers, saddled his ass and did as he was told. He built an
altar, and laid the wood in order, and bound Isaac his son, and laid
him on the altar upon the wood. "Hey, Daddy-o," said a distressed
Isaac, "behold the fire and the wood, but where is the lamb for the

burnt offering?" In response, Abe stretched forth his hand, and took the knife to slay his son. At which point Jehovah, quaking with laughter, sent down an angel who said, "Hold it, Abe. Lay not thy hand upon thy son." And Abraham lifted up his eyes, and looked, and beheld behind him a ram caught in a thicket by the horns; and Abraham went and took the ram, and offered him up for a burnt offering in the stead of his son. But I doubt that things were ever the same again between Abe and Izzy.

I'm digressing. I know, I know. But this is my one and only story, and I'm going to tell it exactly how I please. And you are now into a short detour into that territory that Holden Caufield once deprecated as that Nicholas Nickleby[1] sort of crap. Or was it Oliver Twist? No, Nickleby. I'm sure of it.

Once Clara asked me, "How come your family immigrated to Canada, of all places? I thought the Jews went to New York."

I was born Canadian, I explained, because my grandfather, a ritual slaughterer, was short two sawbucks and a fin. It was 1902 when Moishe and Malka Panofsky, newly wed, went to be interviewed by Simcha Debrofsky of the Jewish Immigrant Aid Society in Budapest. "We want the papers for New York," said my grandfather.

"Siam isn't good enough for you? India you don't need? Sure, I understand. So here's the phone and now I'll ring Washington to tell the president, 'You short of greenhorns there on Canal Street, Teddy? You need more who can't speak a word of English? Well, good news. I've got a couple of shleppers here who are willing to settle in New York.' If it's the *goldene medina* you want, Panofsky, it costs fifty dollars American cash on the table."

"Fifty dollars we haven't got, Mr. Debrofsky."

"No kidding? Well, I'll tell you what. I'm running a special here today. For twenty-five dollars I can get you both into Canada."

Mine was not the legendary Jewish mother, a striver, fawning on her only son, no sacrifice too great if it meant he would enjoy a better life. Back from school, whacking open the front door, I'd holler, "Maw, I'm home."

"Sh," she'd say, a finger held to her lips, as she sat by the radio

---

[1] In fact, it was *David Copperfield*. See *Catcher in the Rye*, by J.D. Salinger, page 1. Little, Brown, Boston, 1951.

listening to "Pepper Young," "Ma Perkins," or "One Man's Family." Only when there was a commercial break would she allow, "There's peanut butter in the ice-box. Help yourself."

The other kids on the street envied me, because my mother didn't care how I did at school, or what time I came home at night. She read *Photoplay*, *Silver Screen*, and other fanzines, worrying about what would become of Shirley Temple, now that she was a teenager; whether Clark Gable and Jimmy Stewart would come home safely from the war; and if Tyrone Power would ever find an enduring love. Other mothers on Jeanne Mance Street force-fed their sons Paul de Kruif's *Microbe Hunters*, hoping it would inspire them to study medicine. Or cheated on the grocery money, saving up to buy *The Books of Knowledge*, ideal for a headstart in life. Dunkirk, The Battle of Britain, Pearl Harbor, the siege of Stalingrad passed like distant clouds, but not Jack Benny's feud with Fred Allen, which deeply troubled her. What we used to call the funnies were more real to her than I ever was. She wrote to Chester Gould, demanding that Dick Tracy marry Tess Trueheart. When Raven Sherman died in the arms of her sweetheart, Dude Hennick, in *Terry and the Pirates*, she was one of the thousands who sent a telegram of condolence. She longed for Daisy Mae to catch up with Li'l Abner on Sadie Hawkins Day, before he was seduced by Wolf Gal or Moonbeam McSwine.

My five-foot-ten father, who had been to see *Naughty Marietta* with Nelson Eddy and Jeanette MacDonald maybe five times, and whose favourite tune was "Indian Love Call," wished to join the RCMP, but he was pronounced too short. And so, having decided to settle for the Montreal police force, he went to see The Boy Wonder on Schnorrers' Day.

Jerry Dingleman, a.k.a. The Boy Wonder, usually conducted business from the penthouse suite of his plush gambling establishment on the far shore of the St. Lawrence River, but on Wednesdays he was available to local losers in a poky little office off the dance floor of the Tico-Tico, one of several nightclubs he owned. Wednesdays were known to The Boy Wonder's inner circle as Schnorrers' Day, and from ten to four the supplicants came and went.

"Why do you want to become a cop, of all things?" Dingleman asked my father, amused.

"I would be grateful to you for life, Mr. Dingleman, if, you know, like you would help me with my chosen endeavour."

The Boy Wonder put in a phonecall to Tony Frank, and then told my father he had to report to Dr. Eustache St. Clair for a medical. "And what do you remember to do first, Izzy?"

"Take a bath?"

"Why, a man with your acumen will make a detective in no time."

But a month later The Boy Wonder, stopping for two medium-fat on rye at Levitt's on the Main, was surprised to see that my father was still cutting meat behind the counter. "Why aren't you in uniform?" he asked.

"Dr. St. Clair said I wasn't acceptable because of the holes I got left in my face from acne."

Dingleman sighed. He shook his head. "Didn't he tell you that it could be cured?"

So Izzy Panofsky made another appointment with Dr. St. Clair, and this time, as instructed, he clipped a hundred-dollar bill to his application form, and passed the medical. "In them days," my father once told me, chewing on a mushy White Owl, "if you was a goy and had flat feet and a big belly, well, they used to bring them in from the Gaspé, all over the place, big fat guys, and you had to pay to get on the force." From the beginning, he said, pinching one nostril and shooting a payload out of the other, there was trouble. "The judge who swored me in, a lush with popping eyes, looked startled sort of. 'Aren't you a Jew?' he asked. And at the police school, where I was taught jujitsu and wrassling, the goys were always testing me. Irish *shikers* and French-Canadian *chazerim*. Dummies. Ignorantuses. I mean like I had at least finished seventh grade and was never plucked, not once."

On his first beat, Notre-Dame-de-Grâce, my over-eager father made too many arrests, so he was shifted downtown. Strolling on St. Catherine Street, watchful, he promptly apprehended a pick-pocket outside the Capitol Theatre where Helen Kane, the one and only Boop-Boop-a-Doop Girl, was starring. My upright dad anticipated a citation for his diligence, but, instead, he was pulled into a back room in the station and threatened by two detectives. " 'If you want to stay here,' they said, 'Christ, don't you ever bring in one of these guys again.' They was licensed, if you get my meaning."

Other cops fattened on vigorish from crooks and their lawyers, but my pappy couldn't be bought. "Like I had to be straight, Barney," he said. "I mean my name was Panofsky and I couldn't afford to have them say 'the goddamn Jew.' That's all I needed, Christ, they used to say *if I slipped on a hair*, you know what I mean, they would have me hung."

Over the years my straight-shooting father soured as he witnessed Irish *shikers* and French-Canadian *chazerim*, guys he broke into the force himself, being promoted over him. Izzy remained a detective-sergeant for nine years. "When I was finally promoted to inspector you know what they done, it made me sick, they went to the union and made up a story that I hadn't passed my exams in shooting. I used to check out my men, you know. I was sincere. They hated me like hell. So they went to the union and complained about me."

Izzy Panofsky's problems on the force were endless.

"Hey, when I went to pass an exam on promotions, Gilbert was on the board then, he says to me how come the Jews are smarter? I got two answers, I says. You're wrong. There's no such thing as a super-human. But the only thing I got to tell you, if you take a dog and kick him around he's got to be alert, he's got to be more sharper than you. Well, we've been kicked around for two thousand years. We're not more smarter, we're more alert. My other answer is the story about the Irishman and the Jew. How come you're smarter, the Irishman asks the Jew. Well, we eat a certain kind of fish, the Jew says. In fact, I've got one right here, and he shows it to the Irishman. Christ, the Irishman says, I'd like to have that fish. Sure, the Jew says, give me ten bucks. So he gives it to him. Then the Irishman looks at it good and says, hey, that's no fish, that's a herring. So the Jew says, you see, you're getting smarter already."

FIVE

LAST night I dreamt that McIver had been nicked on the ankle by a deer tick, and had stupidly dismissed it as a mosquito bite. Lying in his bed on the twentieth floor of The Four Seasons Hotel in Toronto a month later, the dreaded Lyme's Disease pulsing through his blood stream, flooding it, McIver was wakened by a horn honking in his room and then a panicky voice coming over the p.a. system: "We have a serious fire here. The elevators aren't working. Black smoke has made the stairways temporarily impassable. Guests should remain in their rooms and spread wet towels under the door. Good luck and thank you for choosing The Four Seasons Hotel." Choking smoke began to seep into McIver's room, but, overcome by paralysis, he couldn't even raise his arms, never mind move his legs. Flames consumed his door and began to dance round him, licking at a stack of *Of Time and Fevers* on the floor, every copy as yet unsigned, therefore still qualifying as collectors' items . . . and that's when I leaped out of my own bed with a song in my heart. I retrieved my morning papers from outside my apartment door, made coffee, and soft-shoed into my kitchen, singing: "Take your coat and grab your hat . . ."

Turned to the Montreal *Gazette* sport pages first, a lifelong habit. No joy. The fumblebum Canadiens, no longer *nos glorieux*, had disgraced themselves again, losing 5–1 to – wait for it – The Mighty Ducks of California. Toe Blake must be spinning in his grave. In his day only one of his inept bunch of millionaires could have played in the N.H.L., never mind suiting up for the once legendary *Club de hockey canadien*. They don't have one guy willing to stand in front of the net, lest he take a hit. Oh for the days when Larry Robinson would feed a long lead pass to Guy Lafleur, lifting us out of our seats, chanting, "Guy! Guy! Guy!" as he went flying in all alone on the nets. *He shoots, he scores*.

The phone rang and of course it was Kate. "I tried your line maybe five times last night. The last call must have been at one o'clock. Where were you?"

"Darling, I appreciate your concern. Honestly I do. But I'm not your child. I'm your father. I was out."

"You have no idea how I worry about you all alone there. What if, God forbid, you had a stroke and couldn't come to the phone?"

"I'm not planning on it."

"I was on the verge of calling Solange to ask her to see if you answered your door."

"Maybe I should phone you every night after I come in."

"Don't worry about waking me. You could leave a message on our answering machine, if we're asleep."

"Bless you, Kate, but I haven't even had breakfast yet. We'll talk tomorrow."

"Tonight. Are you having fried eggs and bacon in spite of your promise?"

"Stewed prunes. Muesli."

"Yeah. I'll bet."

I'm rambling again. Wandering off the point. But this is the true story of my wasted life and, to come clean, there are only insults to avenge and injuries to nurse. Furthermore, at my age, with more to remember and sort out than there is to look forward to, beyond the infirmaries waiting in the tall grass, I'm entitled to ramble. This sorry attempt at – at – you know, my story. Like Waugh wrote about his early years. Or Jean Jacques Rousseau. Or Mark Twain in that Life on the what's-it-called river book. Christ Almighty, I soon won't even be able to remember my own name.

You strain spaghetti with a colander. Mary McCarthy wrote *The Man in the Brooks Brothers Suit* or *Shirt*. Whichever. Walter "Turk" Broda was the goalie for the Toronto Maple Leaf team that won the Stanley Cup in 1951. Stephen Sondheim it was who wrote the lyrics for *West Side Story*. *I've got it. I didn't have to look it up. The Mississippi, Life on.*

To recap. This sorry attempt at *autobiography*, triggered by Terry McIver's calumnies, is being written in the dim hope that Miriam, reading these pages, will be overwhelmed by guilt.

"What's that book you're so absorbed in?" asks Blair.

"Why, this critically acclaimed best-seller is the autobiography of my one true love, you inadequate little shmuck on tenure."

Where was I? Paris 1951 is where. Terry McIver. Boogie. Leo. Clara, of blessed memory. Nowadays when I open a newspaper I turn to the Dow Jones first and then to the obits, checking the latter page for enemies I have outlasted and icons no longer among the quick. 1995 got off to a bad start for boozers. Peter Cook and a raging Colonel John Osborne both gone.

1951. Quemoy and Matsu,[1] if anybody can find those pimples on the China Sea now, were being shelled by the Commies, a prelude, according to some, to an invasion of what was then still called Formosa. Back in America everybody was still scared by The Bomb. Something of a jackdaw, I still own the Bantam paperback of *How to Survive an Atomic Bomb*:

> Written in question-and-answer form by a leading expert, this book will tell you how to protect yourself and your family in case of atomic attack. There is no "scare talk" in this book. Reading it will actually make you *feel better*.

Rotarians were digging A-bomb fall-out shelters in their back yards, laying in supplies of bottled water, dehydrated soups, sacks of rice, and their collection of *Reader's Digest* condensed books and Pat Boone[2] records to help while away the contaminated weeks. Senator Joe McCarthy and his two stooges, Cohn and Schein, were on a rampage. Julius and Ethel Rosenberg were for it, and just about everybody liked Ike for '52. In not yet querulous Canada Inc., instead of a prime minister we were being managed by an avuncular CEO, Louis St. Laurent. In Quebec, my cherished Quebec, the thuggish Maurice Duplessis was still premier, riding herd over a gang of thieves.

Mornings, waking late, our bunch could usually be found at the Café Sélect or the Mabillon, gathered at the table where Boogie Moscovitch presided, reading the *International Herald-Tribune*, starting with Pogo and the sports pages, monitoring how Duke Snider and Willie Mays had performed the night before. But Terry

---

[1]Quemoy and Matsu are in the Taiwan Straits, and the mainland Communists did not begin shelling until August 1958. Threatened by the American Secretary of State, John Foster Dulles, they suddenly confined the bombardments to only odd days of the month. Then, in March 1959, the bombardments ceased altogether, without explanation.

[2]Pat Boone did not have his first hit single until 1955: "Two Hearts, Two Kisses".

never joined us. If Terry was to be seen at a café table, he would be seated alone, annotating his Everyman's Library edition of Walter Savage Landor's *Imaginary Conversations*. Or scribbling a rebuttal to Jean-Paul Sartre's lead essay in the latest issue of *Les Temps Modernes*. Even in those days Terry appeared not to be worried that, to quote MacNeice,[3] "not all the candidates pass." No sir. Terry McIver was already sitting for his portrait of the handsome young artist fulfilling his manifest destiny. He was intolerant of frivolity. A rebuke to the rest of us time-wasters.

One evening, strolling down the boulevard Saint-Germain des Prés, bound for a bottle party Terry hadn't been invited to, I caught a glimpse of him maybe half a block ahead, slowing his pace, hoping I'd ask him to join us. So I stopped to look at the books in the window of La Hune, until he faded into the distance. Late another night, a far from sober Boogie and I, ambling down the boulevard Montparnasse, searching café terraces for friends from whom we might cadge a drink or a roach, came upon Terry at the Café Sélect, writing in one of his notebooks. "I'll bet you ten to one," I said, "that the covers of his notebooks are numbered and dated out of consideration for future scholars."

Terry, a man of daunting integrity, naturally took a dim view of Boogie. For a much-needed five hundred dollars, Boogie had churned out a steamy novel, for Maurice Girodias's Traveller's Companion series. *Vanessa's Pussy* was dedicated to the unquestionably constant wife of the Columbia professor who had failed Boogie in a course on Elizabethan poetry. The dedication read:

To the lubricious Vanessa Holt,
in fond memory of priapic nights past

Boogie had thoughtfully sent copies of *Vanessa's Pussy* to his professor and Columbia's arts faculty dean, as well as to the editors of the *New York Times Book Review* and the book pages of the *New York Herald-Tribune*. But it is difficult to know what any of them made of it because Boogie had written *Vanessa's Pussy* under a pseudonym: Baron Claus von Manheim. A disdainful Terry

---

[3]Auden, actually. *Selected Poems*, Faber & Faber, London, 1979.

returned his complimentary copy unread. "Writing," he said, "is not a job, it's a calling."

Be that as it may, such was the success of *Vanessa's Pussy* that Boogie was promptly commissioned to deliver more. The rest of us, eager to help out, gathered at the Café Royal St.-Germain, long since displaced by Le Drugstore, to improvise sexual epiphanies that could be savoured in a gym, under water, or taking advantage of all the artifacts available in an equestrian's tack room or a rabbi's study. Terry, naturally, eschewed these late-night seminars, appalled by our salacious laughter.

Boogie's second Traveller's Companion opus, by the Marquis Louis de Bonséjour, proved him to be a man ahead of his time, a literary innovator, who intuited karaoke, inter-active TV, computer porn, CD-Roms, Internet, and other contemporary plagues. The virile hero of *Scarlet Lace*, blessed with monstrous equipage, went unnamed, which is not to say he was anonymous. Instead, wherever his name should have appeared, there was a blank space, enabling the reader to fill in his own name, even as one of his gorgeous, sex-inflamed conquests, enjoying multiple orgasms, called out, "———, you wonderful man," in gratitude.

It was Clara, a compulsive dirty talker, who contributed the most imaginative but outlandish pornographic ideas to Boogie, which was surprising, considering what I then took to be her problems. We had, by this juncture, begun to live together, not as a consequence of a deliberate choice we had made but having casually slipped into it, which is the way things were in those days.

Put plainly, what happened is that late one night Clara – suffering from *le cafard*, she said – announced that she simply couldn't face her hotel room again, because it was haunted by a poltergeist. "You know that hotel was a Wehrmacht brothel during the war," she said. "It must be the spirit of the girl who died there, fucked God knows how many times through every possible orifice." Then, only after she had harvested sympathetic looks from the rest of us at the table, did she giggle and add, "Lucky thing."

"Where will you sleep, then?" I asked.

"Bite your tongue," said Boogie.

"On a bench at the Gare Montparnasse. Or under the Pont Neuf. The only *clochard* in town who graduated *magna cum laude* from Vassar."

So I took her back to my room, where we passed a celibate night, Clara sleeping fitfully in my arms. In the morning she asked me to be a sweetheart and fetch her canvases and drawings and notebooks and suitcases from Le Grand-Hôtel Excelsior on the rue Cujas, assuring me that I would only have to tolerate her for a couple of nights, until she found a more agreeable hotel. "I'd come along to help you," she said, "but Madame Defarge," which is what she called the concierge, "hates me."

Boogie grudgingly agreed to accompany me to the hotel. "I hope you know what you're getting into," he said.

"It's only for a couple of nights."

"She's crazy."

"And you?"

"Don't worry. I can handle it."

Drugs is what we were talking about. Boogie had graduated from hashish to horse. "We should try everything," he said. "Kvetchy Jewish princesses before they go home to marry doctors. Arab boys in Marrakesh. Black chicks. Opium. Absinthe. The mandrake root. Magic mushrooms. Stuffed derma. Halva. Everything on the table and under. We only get to go around the block once. Except for Clara, of course."

"What's that supposed to mean?"

"Miss Chambers of Gramercy Park and Newport is into reincarnation. It comes with her trust fund. Didn't you know that much about her?"

Clara's things included, among other items, a two-volume edition of *The Secret Doctrine* by H.P. Blavatsky, a water-pipe, a dictionary of Satanism, a stuffed owl, several volumes on astrology, palmistry charts, a deck of tarot cards, and a framed portrait of Aleister Crowley, The Great Beast 666, wearing the head-dress of Horus. But the concierge wouldn't let us remove anything until I had paid her 4,200 francs in overdue rent. "Money disgusts me," said Clara. "Yours. Mine. It doesn't matter. It's not worth talking about."

It would be inaccurate to describe Clara as tall. Long is what she was. Skinny enough for a rib count. Her hands constantly in movement, adjusting her shawls, smoothing her skirts, brushing back her hair, peeling the labels off wine bottles. Her fingers were nicotine- and ink-stained, her nails broken or bitten to the quick.

Ears the shape of teacup handles protruded from her hair – "It's the colour of shit," she said. "I hate it" – that cascaded to her narrow waist. She had only the faintest of eyebrows, her huge black eyes lit with intelligence. And scorn. And panic. She was sickly pale, which she emphasized by applying full moons of rouge to her cheeks and by wearing orange, green, or purple lipstick, depending on her mood. Her breasts, she felt, were too full for her figure. "With jugs like these," she said, "I could nurse triplets." She complained that her legs were too long and scrawny and her feet too large. But for all her disparaging remarks about her appearance, she could never pass a café mirror without pausing to admire herself. Oh, her rings. I forgot to mention her rings. A topaz. A blue sapphire. And, her favourite, an ankh.

Years before it became modish, Clara wore loose, beaded, ankle-length Victorian dresses and high button shoes, retrieved from the flea market. She also draped herself in shawls, the colours often conflicting, which struck me as odd, considering she was a painter. Boogie dubbed her "The Conversation Piece," as in "*Sauve qui peut*. Here comes Barney and The Conversation Piece." And, to come clean, I enjoyed that. Couldn't write. Didn't paint. And even then I was not a likeable man. Already a sour, judgmental presence. But suddenly I had acquired a distinction of sorts. I had become an intriguing fellow. I was nutty Clara's keeper.

Clara was a compulsive toucher, which annoyed me once we had begun to live together. She was given to collapsing into laughter against other men's chests at café tables, stroking their knees. "If Grouchy wasn't here with me, we could go somewhere and fuck now."

Memory test. Quick, Barney. Names of the Seven Dwarfs. Grouchy, Sneezy, Sleepy, Doc. I know the names of the other three. Got them right just last night. They'll come to me. I'm not going to look them up.

Clara especially enjoyed teasing Terry McIver, which I approved of heartily. Ditto Cedric Richardson, long before he won celebrity as Ismail ben Yussef, scourge of Jewish slave-traders past and slumlords present, and nemesis of ice-people everywhere.

Keeping track of what became of everybody is what sustains me in my dotage. It's amazing. Mind-boggling. The scheming Leo Bishinsky coining millions with his japes on canvas. Clara, who despised other women, enjoying posthumous fame as a feminist

martyr. Me, stricken with limited notoriety as the chauvinist pig
who betrayed her, a possible murderer to boot. The unspeakably
boring novels of Terry McIver, that pathological liar, now on university courses throughout Canada. And my once beloved Boogie
out there somewhere, bruised beyond belief, unforgiving, fulminating. He had picked up my copy of *Rabbit, Run*, and, startling me,
said, "I can't believe you read such shit."

Grouchy, Sneezy, Soc . . . Snoopy? *No, you idiot. That's the dog in
Pogo. I mean Peanuts.*

Onwards. These days I come across an account of Ismail ben
Yussef's latest pronouncement to be quoted in *Time* but instead of
being outraged I find myself chuckling at the photograph of Cedric
sporting a fez, dreadlocks, and a kaftan coloured like a rainbow.
Once, I actually wrote him a letter.

Salaam, Ismail:

I am writing to you on behalf of The Elders of Zion Foundation. We are raising money to establish mugging fellowships
for black brothers and sisters in everlasting memory of three
young bloodsucker kikes (Chaney,[3] Goodman and Schwerner),
who ventured into Mississippi in 1964 to register black voters
and, as a consequence, were murdered by a gang of ice-people.
I trust we can count on your contribution.

Possibly you could also help me with a philosophical con-
undrum. I happen to agree with Louis Farrakhan's *aperçu* that
the ancient Egyptians were black. As further evidence, let me
cite *Flaubert in Egypt: A Sensibility on Tour*. Anticipating Sheik
Anta Diop's claim that civilization's cradle was black, he wrote
of the Sphinx: " . . . its head is grey, ears very large and protruding like a negro's . . . (and) the fact that the nose is missing
increases the flat, negroid effect . . . the lips are thick . . ."

But, holy cow, if the ancient Egyptians were black, then so
was Moses, a prince in Pharaoh's court. And then it follows that
the slaves whom Moses liberated were also black, or he would
have stuck out like the proverbial "n— in the woodpile," and
the notoriously contrary Israelites would have complained,

---

[4]Actually, James E. Chaney, 21, was black.

"Listen here, have we sunk so low that we're going to wander through a desert for forty years led in circles by a *schvartzer*?"

So, assuming that Moses and his tribe were black, what perplexes me is that when the undeniably eloquent Farrakhan denounces my people, is it possible that, unbeknownst to him, he is in fact just another self-hating Jew, like Philip Roth?

I look forward to your reply, bro, not to mention your cheque and enclose a stamped, self-addressed envelope.

Allah Akbar!

Your old friend and admirer
Barney Panofsky

I'm still waiting for a reply.

Rereading this old letter of mine recently, I suffered one of my frequent attacks of spiritual voice-mail: Miriam, my conscience, tripping me up again.

If I could turn the clock back it would be to those days when Miriam and I couldn't keep our hands off each other. We made love in the woods and on a kitchen chair, after quitting a tedious dinner party early, and on hotel-room floors and trains, and once we were nearly caught at it in a bathroom at the Shaar Hashomiyim synagogue at one of Irv Nussbaum's fund-raising dinners. "You could have been excommunicated," she said. "Just like Spinoza."

One memorable afternoon, we did it on my office carpet. Miriam had arrived unexpectedly, coming straight from her obstetrician, pronounced fit, six weeks after she had given birth to Saul. She locked the door, shed her blouse, and stepped out of her skirt. "I was told that this is where you audition actresses."

"Oh, my God," I said, simulating shock, "what if my wife happens to drop by?"

"I am not only your wife," she said, tugging at my belt, "and the mother of your children. I'm also your whore."

Bliss it was to be alive when we would be wakened by children in their pyjamas tumbling helter-skelter into our bedroom and leaping onto the bed.

"Mommy's got nothing on."

"Neither has Daddy."

How could I have failed to pick up the early distress signals, rare as they were? Once, on her return from what I had hoped would be a fun dinner with her former CBC Radio producer, Kip Horgan, that meddling bastard, she seemed distracted. She began to straighten picture frames on the walls and plump up sofa cushions, always a bad sign. "Kip's disappointed in me," she said. "He thought I'd never settle for being a housewife."

"That's not what you are."

"Of course I am."

"Shit."

"Don't you get upset now."

"Let's go to New York for the weekend."

"Saul is still running a fever – "

"Ninety-nine and a sixteenth?"

" – and you promised to take Mike to the hockey game on Saturday night." Then, out of nowhere, she added, "If you're going to leave me, I'd rather you did it now, before I'm old."

"Can I have ten minutes to pack?"

Later, we worked out that Kate was probably conceived that night. Damn damn damn. If Miriam's gone, it is surely due to my insensitivity. *Mea culpa*. All the same, it strikes me as unfair that I still have to defend myself against her moral judgments. My continuing need for her approbation is pathetic. Twice now I have stopped myself on the street to remonstrate with her, a crazy old coot talking to himself. And now, my letter to Cedric in hand, I could hear her say, "Sometimes what you find funny is actually nasty, calculated to wound."

Oh, yeah? Well, just maybe I'm the one who has the right to feel wounded. How could Cedric, once one of our band of brothers, take to the college pulpits, chastising me and my kind for our religion and skin colour? Why did such a talented young man eschew literature for the vulgar political stage? Hell, given his gifts, I'd be scribbling day and night.

I'd like Farrakhan, Jesse Jackson, Cedric *et al.* to get off my back. Yes, Miriam. I know, Miriam. I'm sorry, Miriam. Had I endured what they and their kind had in America, I, too, would be prepared to believe that Adam and Eve were black, but Cain turned white with shock when God condemned him for murdering Abel. All the same, it ain't right.

Anyway, back in our Left Bank days, Cedric was seldom seen

without a white girl on his arm. Clara, simulating jealousy, usually greeted him with, "How long before I get my ticket punched?"

She took a different tack with Terry. "For you, honey-child, I'd be willing to dress as a boy."

"But I much prefer you as you are, Clara. Always tricked out like a harlequin."

Or, an avid Virginia Woolf reader, Clara would pretend to espy a tell-tale stain on his trousers. "You could go blind, Terry. Or haven't they heard about that in Canada yet?"

Clara not only did troubled non-figurative paintings, but also frightening ink drawings, crowded with menacing gargoyles, prancing little devils, and slavering satyrs, attacking nubile women from all sides. She committed poetry as well, inscrutable to me, but published in both *Merlin* and *Zero*, earning her a request from James Laughlin of New Directions Press to see more. Clara shoplifted. Sliding things under her voluminous shawls. Tins of sardines, bottles of shampoo, books, corkscrews, postcards, spools of ribbon. Fauchon was a favourite haunt, until she was denied entry. Inevitably, she was once caught snatching a pair of nylon stockings at the MonoPrix, but got off, she said, by allowing the fat, greasy flic to drive her to the Bois de Boulogne, and come between her breasts. "Just like my dear Uncle Horace did when I was only twelve years old. Only he didn't boot me out of a moving car, laughing as I tumbled head over heel, calling me filthy names, but presented me with a twenty-dollar bill each time to keep our secret."

Our room, in the Hôtel de la Cité, on the Ile de la Cité, was perpetually dark, its one small window looking out on an interior courtyard narrow as an elevator shaft. There was a tiny wash-basin in the room, but the communal toilet was down a long hallway. It was a squatter, no more than a hole in the floor, with elevated grips for your shoes, and a clasp fixed to the wall offering paper squares scissored out of the politically relevant *L'Humanité* or *Libération*. I bought a Bunsen burner and a small pot, so that we could hard boil eggs to eat in baguette sandwiches for lunch. But the crumbs attracted mice, and she wakened screaming when one skittered over her face during the night. Another time she opened a dresser drawer to retrieve a shawl and stumbled on three newly born mice nesting there, and began to shriek. So we gave up eating in our room.

We languished in bed a good deal of the time, not making love but in search of warmth, dozing, reading (me into Jacques Prévert's *Paroles*, which she scorned), comparing difficult childhoods and congratulating each other on our amazing survivals. In the privacy of our refuge, far from the café tables where she felt compelled to shock or, anticipating criticism, to pick at the scabs of other people's weaknesses, she was a wonderful storyteller, my very own Scheherazade. I, in turn, entertained her with tales of the exploits of Detective-Inspector Izzy Panofsky.

Clara abhorred her mother. In a previous life, she said, Mrs. Chambers must have been an ayah. Or, in another spin of the reincarnation wheel, Chinese, her feet bound in childhood, taking little mincing steps in The Forbidden City during the days of the Ming Dynasty. She was the ultimate wifey. "*Très mignonne*. Hardly a virago," said Clara. Her husband's philandering she took to be a blessing, as it meant she no longer had to suffer him between the sheets. "It is astonishing to what lengths a man will go," she once said to Clara, "to achieve thirty seconds of friction." Having provided Mr. Chambers with a son, Clara's younger brother, she felt that her duty was done, and was delighted to move into her own bedroom. But she continued to thrive as an exemplary chatelaine, managing their Gramercy Park brownstone and Newport mansion with panache. Mrs. Chambers was a member of the Metropolitan Opera Company board. Giuseppe di Stefano had sung at one of her soirées. Elisabeth Schwarzkopf was a frequent dinner guest. Mrs. Chambers had made a point of taking Kirsten Flagstad to lunch at Le Pavillon after the Jews had taken against her. "My mother would suffer a stroke if she knew I was living with a Jew," said Clara, tickling my nose with one of her ostrich boas. "She thinks you're the poison contaminating America's bloodstream. What have you got to say to that?"

Her father, she once told me, was a senior partner in John Foster Dulles's old law firm. He kept Arabian horses and once a year flew over to Scotland to fly-fish for salmon on the Spey. But another time I heard her say that he was a Wall Street broker and a cultivator of rare orchids, and when I asked her about that, once we were alone together, she countered, "Oh, you're so fucking literal. What does it matter?" and she ran off, disappearing round a corner of the rue de Seine, and didn't return to our room that night. "As a matter of interest," I asked, when she showed up at the Pergola the next evening, "where did you stay last night?"

"You don't own me, you know. My pussy's my own."

"That's no answer."

"It just so happens my Aunt Honor is staying at the Crillon. She put me up. We ate at Lapérouse."

"I don't believe you."

"Look," she said, and digging into her skirts, she produced a wad of one-thousand-franc notes, and threw them at me. "Take whatever I owe you for room and board. I'm sure you've been keeping track."

"Is it all right if I charge interest?"

"I'm taking the train to Venice with my aunt tonight. We're staying with Peggy Guggenheim."

Shortly after one o'clock in the morning a week later, Clara returned to our room, undressed, and slid into bed with me. "We drank endless Bellinis at Harry's Bar with Tennessee Williams. Peggy took us to Torcello for lunch one day. For your sake, I visited the Campo del Ghetto Nuovo. Had you lived there back then you wouldn't have been allowed out after ten o'clock at night. I was going to send you a postcard from the Rialto," she said, "to say there's no news to report, but I forgot."

In the morning, I couldn't help noticing the angry scratches running down her back. A veritable trail. "Peggy keeps Russian greyhounds," said Clara. "They got over-excited when I wrestled with them on the rug."

"Nude?"

"We should try everything. Isn't that what your mentor said?"

"Boogie's not my mentor."

"Look at you. Raging inside. You want to kick me out, but you won't. Because you enjoy showing me off, your crazy, upper-middle-class *shiksa*."

"It would help if you bathed occasionally."

"You're not an artist, like the rest of us here. You're a voyeur. And when you go home to make money, which is inevitable, given your character, and you've married a nice Jewish girl, somebody who shops, you'll be able to entertain the guys at the United Jewish Appeal dinner with stories about the days you lived with the outrageous Clara Chambers."

"Before she became famous."

"If you don't enjoy me now, you will in retrospect. Because what you're doing here is loading up your memory bank. Terry McIver has got you down pat."

"Oh yeah? What does that creep have to say about me?"

"If you want to know what Boogie was thinking yesterday, listen to Barney today. He calls you Barney like the player piano. Always playing somebody else's music because you have none of your own."

Stung, I belted her one, hard enough to bang her head against the wall. And when she came at me with her fists, I knocked her to the bed. "Were you with a guy called Carnofsky?" I asked.

"I don't know what you're talking about."

"I'm told somebody by that name has been showing a photograph of you here and there, making inquiries."

"I know no such person. I swear to God, Barney."

"Have you been shoplifting again?"

"No."

"Passing bad cheques? Anything I should know about?"

"Oh, wait. Now I've got it," she said, her eyes filled with guile. "I had an art teacher in New York called *Ch*arnofsky. A real sicko. He used to follow me to my loft in the Village and stand outside and watch the window. There were obscene phonecalls. Once he exposed himself to me in Union Square."

"I thought you didn't know anybody called Carnofsky."

"I just remembered, but it was *Ch*arnofsky. It has to be him, that pervert. He mustn't find me, Barney."

A week passed before she would leave our hotel room again, and even then she was furtive, her face obscured by shawls, and avoiding our usual haunts. I knew she was lying about Carnofsky, or Charnofsky, but I didn't twig to what was going on. Had I understood, I might have been able to save her. *Mea culpa* yet again. Shit. Shit. Shit.

SIX

"SAUL, it's me."

"Who else would phone me this early in the morning?"

"It's ten-thirty, for Christ's sake."

"I was up reading until four. I can feel the flu coming on. I had a very soft bowel movement yesterday."

Once, when he was only eighteen, a raging Saul opened the front door of our house, dropping his books, and exclaiming, in that disgusting manner of his, "Shit. Shit. Shit," before barging into the living room, where I sat with Miriam. "This has been a godawful day," he said. "I got into an argument with that cretin on tenure, who is my philosophy professor. I stupidly ate lunch at Ben's and my stomach's been upset ever since. I've probably got food poisoning. I just about punched out a damn fool librarian and I don't know what I've done with my English 240 notes, not that it's worth writing down anything that babbling idiot says. I had to wait forty minutes for my bus. I quarrelled with Linda. I've got another fierce headache. I hope we're not eating pasta for dinner again." Only then did he notice that Miriam's leg, propped up on a hassock, was in a cast. "Oh," he said, "what happened?"

"Your mother fractured her ankle this morning, but you mustn't let that worry you."

Now I said, "Remember I once took you and the others to see *Snow White and the Seven Dwarfs*? There was Sneezy, Sleepy, Doc, Grouchy and – "

"Grouchy? You mean Grumpy, don't you?"

"That's what I said. The other three, please."

"Happy."

"I know that. And?"

"I can't remember the other two offhand."

"Think."

"Damn it, Daddy. I haven't even brushed my teeth yet."

"I hope I didn't waken Sally."

"Sally's toast. You mean Dorothy. Naw, she's already left for work. Shit. Shit. Shit."

"What's wrong now?"

"She didn't leave the *Times* on my bed and I can see she forgot to take my laundry with her. Look, I'm going to try to get back to sleep now, if you don't mind?"

He's brilliant, my Saul, far more intelligent than I am, but charged with discontent. Sour. Abrasive. Cursed with a ferocious temper, which I take to be a most unattractive quality. But he is also blessed with something of Miriam's beauty. Her grace. Her originality. I adore him. Before graduating *magna cum laude* from McGill, he condescended to sit for a Rhodes scholarship competition, and, having won one, declined it in his own incomparable style. "Cecil Rhodes," he told the committee, "was a vicious imperialist and his scholarship fund would be more honourably used making restitution to the blacks he exploited. I don't want anything to do with his blood money." Eschewing Oxford, Saul went on to do his post-graduate work at Harvard. But, naturally, my boy did not accept his degree, which in those days he considered a bourgeois stigma.

My sons short-circuited somewhere. Crossed wires. Mike, a militant socialist, is sinfully rich and married to an aristo. But Saul, born again a neo-conservative, is dirt poor and lives in squalor in New York, in an East Village loft, where the infatuated girls come and go, cooking and sewing and boiling his underwear. Saul ekes out a living of sorts writing polemics for the right-wing trades: the *American Spectator*, the *Washington Times*, *Commentary*, and the *National Review*. A volume of his essays has been published by The Free Press, and I never pass an out-of-town bookshop without slapping three expensive art books down on the counter, and asking, "Would you happen to have a copy of Saul Panofsky's brilliant *Minority Report*?" If they answer no, I say, "Well, in that case, I won't be needing any of these."

Saul's a raver. His right-wing diatribes, inarguably well written, are offensive, homophobic, totally without compassion for the poor, but they also amuse me no end, because back in 1980, when he was a mere seventeen-year-old, Saul was a Marxist firebrand. He was a passionate supporter of Quebec's independence, which he pronounced a rite of passage, necessarily brief, that would yield to North America's first workers' state, after his bunch had marched on Quebec City's Winter Palace, but not before eleven a.m. He also spoke at thinly attended meetings denouncing Israel as a racist state and demanding justice for the Palestinians. "If God bequeathed Canaan to the descendants of Abraham then that also included Esau's progeny."

In those days Saul was no longer living at home, in the house I had acquired in Westmount after Michael was born, but was rooted in a commune, largely composed of middle-class Jewish kids, in a cold-water flat on St. Urbain Street, right in my old neighbour-hood. I wander down there occasionally in unavailing quest of familiar faces and old landmarks. But, like me, the boys I grew up with moved on long ago: those who prospered to Westmount, or Hampstead, and the ones who are still struggling to the nondescript suburbs of Côte St. Luc, Snowdon, or Ville St. Laurent. These streets now teem with Italian, Greek, or Portuguese kids, their parents as out of breath as ours once were, juggling overdue house-hold bills. Signs of the times. The shoeshine parlour where I used to take my father's fedoras to be blocked has been displaced by a unisex hair stylist. The Regent Theatre, where I could once catch a double feature for thirty-five cents, and enjoy three hours of uninterrupted necking with the notorious Goldie Hirschorn, is boarded up. The lending library where I took out books (*Forever Amber*; *Farewell, My Lovely*; *King's Row*; *The Razor's Edge*) for three cents a day no longer exists. Mr. Katz's Supreme Kosher Meat Mart has yielded to a video rental outlet: ADULT MOVIES OUR SPECIALTY. My old neighbourhood now also boasts a New Age bookstore, a vegetarian restaurant, a shop that deals in holistic medicines, and a Buddhist temple of sorts which cater to the needs of Saul and his bunch and others like them.

Some bunch that was that Saul was involved with. Posters of the usual suspects hung on the walls. Lenin. Fidel. Che. Rosa Lux-emburg. Louis Riel. Dr. Norman Bethune. FUCK PIERRE TRUDEAU was spray-painted on one wall and VIVE LE QUEBEC LIBRE on another. The flat reeked of dirty socks and stale farts and pot. Half-eaten pizzas were abandoned here and there. I used to visit occasionally. Once Saul emerged grudgingly from a bedroom to greet me, his long brown hair tumbling to his shoulders, a Cree headband hugging his forehead like a slipped halo, a book about the Chinese revolution in hand. He promptly began to lecture me, in the admiring presence of his comrades, about the rigours of the Long March.

"Long March, baloney," I said, lighting a Montecristo. "That was a hike, kid. A Sunday picnic. I'll tell you a long march. Forty years, trudging through the desert, without egg rolls or Peking Duck, your ancestors and mine – "

"You think everything's a joke. The pigs are filming all our rallies."

"Saul, my boy, *abi gezunt.*"

The lanky black girl in bra and panties curled up on a mattress on the floor began to stir. "What does that mean?" she asked.

"It's a saying of our forefathers. You know, the slumlords of Canaan. It means 'so long as you're groovy.' "

"Oh, why don't you just fuck off," she said, rising, and slouching out of the room.

"What an enchanting young lady. Why don't you bring her home to dinner one night?"

Another girl – dumpy, sleepy-eyed, nude – blundered in from a room and drifted into the kitchen, wiggling her ass at me. "May I ask, which one of these delectable creatures is your girlfriend?"

"We don't go in for property rights here."

Another young revolutionary, his greasy hair caught in a pony-tail, sailed in from the kitchen, sipping coffee out of a jam jar. "Who's the old prick?" he asked.

"Don't talk to my father like that," said Saul. Then, pulling me aside, he whispered, "I don't want you or Mum to worry, but they might come for me."

"The health department?"

"The RCMP. My activities are not unknown."

He had a point. A year earlier Saul, putting in a catch-up term at Wellington College, had discovered that it had investments in American branch-plants, one of which manufactured spark plugs used in Israeli tanks. Outraged, Saul's bunch had risen as one and barricaded themselves into the faculty club. They immediately alienated certain professors who, although disposed to be of the new left, suddenly found themselves cut off from booze on credit. The manifesto of The 18th of November Fifteen was dropped out of a faculty club window and broadcast between helicopter traffic reports on Pepper Logan's CYAD morning call-in talk show. It set out the following demands:

That Wellington divest itself of investments in companies that served fascist or racist states.

That in recognition of the past exploitation of the Québécois collectivity, the White Niggers of North America, fifty per cent of Wellington courses should now be taught in French.

That if studies of the disposable past were to continue they should no longer go by the appellation "history" but, instead, "his and herstory."

Police barricades went up outside Wellington, but no siege guns were put in place. Bed sheets with slogans daubed on them were draped from windows. DEATH TO THE PIGS. VIVE LE QUEBEC LIBRE. REPATRIATE THE FLQ FREEDOM FIGHTERS. The electricity was cut off on the third day, which meant that The 18th of November Fifteen could no longer watch themselves on TV. When furniture was broken up and burned in various fireplaces, it aggravated Judy Frishman's asthma. Then, once they ran out of usable wood, Marty Holtzman caught cold. He could see his mother camped on the far side of the barricades, armed with his cashmere sweater and sheepskin-lined coat, but at that tantalizing distance this only fed his sneezing fits. A chocolate-bar diet was adequate for some, but it made Martha Ryan's skin break out, so she refused to pose bare-chested at the window any more for cameramen, putting vanity before the cause. Not surprisingly, she was denounced as a bourgeois cunt at that night's cell meeting.

Inevitably, the close quarters, the dark, and the freezing temperatures made for dissension in the ranks. Greta Pincus ran out of allergy pills and asked to be released for health reasons. It was discovered that Donald Potter, Jr. was surreptitiously squirting contact lens fluid into his eyes in the bathroom, not sharing with the two comrades who had run out of theirs. Potter was denounced. He countered by accusing the others of being prejudiced against gays. Molly Zucker pleaded to be let out on Thursday for her appointment with her analyst, but the vote went against her. The toilets, which hadn't been flushed for days, became unendurable. So, on the ninth day of the siege, the frustrated 18th of November Fifteen decided to walk out in time for the CBC-TV National News deadline. They marched out in a disciplined file, heads held high, saluting with clenched fists even as they were loaded into the waiting paddy wagon. I stood watching, a distraught Miriam at my side, digging her nails into the palm of my hand hard enough to make me wince.

Beneath Miriam's seemingly serene nature, there was a woman warrior waiting to leap out. Put another way, anybody going for a stroll in the woods in our country knows enough not to wittingly pass between a bear and her cubs, but I would rather risk a mauling by a grizzly any day than threaten Miriam's children.

"Will they beat up Saul once they get him into the station?" she demanded.

"They won't mess with this bunch. Some of their parents are too well connected. Besides, there are lawyers waiting with bail, John Hughes-McNoughton among them. Saul will be home tomorrow morning."

"We're going to follow the paddy wagon to the station and warn those bastards if they so much as lay a finger on Saul – "

"Miriam, that's not the way to handle it."

Her hot tears notwithstanding, I insisted on driving her home. "You think I'm not worried? Of course I am," I said. "But you're such an innocent. You have no idea how things work. You don't get anywhere threatening the cops. Or signing petitions. Or writing letters to the editor. What you do here is sweet-talk the right people, spreading a little vigorish where it counts. And that's what Hughes-McNoughton and I will be up to starting tomorrow."

"We could at least go down to the station and sit there until he gets out on bail in the morning."

"Miriam, no."

"I'm going."

"The hell you are."

We began to struggle, and finally she collapsed in my arms, heaving with sobs, which did not subside until I led her to bed. Five a.m. I found her pacing up and down in the living room, where she greeted me with her most chilling look. "God help you, Barney Panofsky, but you'd better be right about how to handle this."

"Don't worry," I said, but the truth was that my confidence was more than somewhat forced.

Saul was released on bail later that morning. Undeniably the ringleader, he was accused, among other things, of disturbing the peace and of the wilful destruction of private property. Nobody knew precisely what charges would be laid by Wellington, but as I hastily explained to Miriam, Calvin Potter, Sr. was on the board of governors and Marty Holtzman's father sat in Trudeau's cabinet.

After breakfast I compiled a list of helpful names and then I called Saul into the library, Miriam and Kate trailing after to protect him. "I don't want you to worry, comrade," I said. "Maître Hughes-McNoughton is going to see some people here, and I'm going to meet with others in Ottawa."

"Yeah, sure. That figures. This society is rotten to the core."

"Lucky for you it is, because you're facing two years in the slammer is how John sees it, and I've been there, you won't like it. So you are not to say a word to reporters or any other running dogs of imperialism until this is over. No manifestos. No pensées of Chairman Saul. Understand?"

"Will you please not threaten him," said Miriam.

"I'm willing to listen to you, Mom, because you don't find it necessary to shout in order to make your feeble points, and you don't contribute funds to the upkeep of the Israeli army of occupation in the homeland of the Palestinians."

"Saul, prison isn't what you think it is. If they lock you up for only six months they will be gang-raping you every night."

"I don't have to sit here and listen to your homophobic prejudices."

"Shit. Shit. Shit."

"I will not do anything to compromise my comrades."

"Spartacus has spoken."

"Darling, listen to your father. You won't be asked to compromise anybody."

The judge, I found out, would be Mr. Justice Bartolomé Savard of Saint-Eustache, who was reputed to be something of a womanizer and bon vivant. John had once introduced me to him at Les Halles. "I am a great admirer of your people," he said. "For sure mine could learn a lesson from yours on how to stick together, come water or high hell."

I hurried home to comfort Miriam with the news. "We've struck gold, my love. The judge just happens to be the brother of my one-time saviour, the good Bishop Sylvain Gaston Savard."

But she did not respond as I had hoped. "I would like you to tell me why," she said, "you have never admitted to anybody the real reason why you were responsible for the English translation of that idiotic book about his appalling aunt. Don't think I'm never asked about it."

I had not only paid for the privately printed English edition of that little monograph in praise of Sister Octavia, but I had also been obliged, at the time, to contribute a goodly chunk of the cost of raising a statue to the bitch in Saint-Eustache. Bishop Savard hoped his aunt would be beatified one day, if not for her noble work among the poor, then at least for her 1937 campaign to get her people not to buy from Jew shopkeepers "who had cheating in their blood."

"Because," I said, "if the truth were known it would only make matters worse."

"You're not being honest," she said, clearly irritated with me. "It's because after all these years you're still trying to please Boogie. He would be delighted to know you had created a scandal. 'You see, Boogie, appearances notwithstanding, I can still *épater les bourgeois*, just like you taught me.'"

"You're taking a sleeping pill tonight."

"No, I'm not."

I drove to Ottawa, where I just happened to run into Graham Fielding, the lanky deputy minister of justice, in the lobby of the Château Laurier, and the two of us repaired to the National Arts Centre restaurant across the street. Fielding was the scion of an immensely rich Montreal stockbroker family. His wife, who cut his hair and darned his socks, was not allowed to shop for clothes on her own: instead, he accompanied her once a year to the Oxfam Nearly New store. We had first met and knocked back a couple of beers together one night many years ago in Paris, when he was studying at the Sorbonne. Nudging fifty now, constantly prodding the bridge of his horn-rimmed glasses with his forefinger, Fielding still had the appearance of a precocious schoolboy, the class snitch. We were well into our second round when he summoned the waiter to bring him his very own box of Montecristos. Isn't that nice of him, I thought? Then I watched him select a cigar for himself, allowing the waiter to snip and light it for him before waving him off. Amused, I told him how deeply I admired his wife's geometric paintings, all of them done in different shades of yellow, and how it was a damn shame that she had not yet exhibited in New York, where her work *was bound to fetch big bucks*. If she would be good enough to send me some slides, I would pass them on to the great Leo Bishinsky, an old pal of mine. Then I told him about Saul, burnishing the tale to make it as entertaining as possible.

"You do realize," said Fielding, withdrawing his long legs from under the table, "that prosecutions by provincial authorities are a world unto themselves."

"Graham, I would never have mentioned the case to you if I thought you could influence the proceedings in any fashion. That would be most improper," I said, calling for the bill. I left him my card. "And please don't forget to send me those slides."

Next I imposed on an old friend to take me to lunch at the Mount Royal Club on a day I knew Calvin Potter, Sr. would be there. Stopping at his table, I congratulated him on his daughter's engagement to Senator Gordon McHale's son, who had such a bright political future. "Unfortunately, Calvinism dies hard," I said. "Old Gordon, for instance, simply cannot tolerate homosexuality. He thinks it's a disease."

Changing the subject, Potter inveighed against wanton destruction and wildfire radicalism, and insisted that Wellington's young vandals, his son included, be taught a lesson.

"You're right, but my concern is for innocent family bystanders. Should there be a prolonged trial the private peccadilloes of some of the offenders, a few of them obviously sexually confused – albeit temporarily, it goes without saying – would be magnified by the press, given their insatiable appetite for scandal among their social superiors."

Calling in a marker here, and a marker there, I wangled an invitation to Club Saint-Denis, where I cornered the provincial minister of justice and argued passionately that Canada had no culture to speak of that wasn't French-Canadian. And that weekend I went on a retreat to the Benedictine abbey of Saint-Benoît-du-Lac, where I was able to renew the acquaintance of the good Bishop Sylvain Gaston Savard, the devoted nephew of the odious Sister Octavia. We embraced, as old friends should, and sat down to chat. The bishop told me about the sad state of repair of his cathedral in Saint-Eustache, and the dire need of funds to restore it to its former glory. "Now that's very interesting," I said, "because I am so grateful to this province – no, this nation struggling to be born – for the sustenance it has given me and my family, and I'd like to put some-

thing back into Quebec. But of course it would be improper of me
to be of any help while your brother is to sit in judgment on my
errant son."

So even Miriam had to agree that I had done everything possible, and the trial itself started unnervingly well. As a matter of fact,
to begin with, it was something of an anti-climax. Wellington's
lawyers did not go for the jugular, perhaps mollified because parents
of the accused had promised to endow a chair of visible minority
social studies at the college. A subdued, appropriately pale Saul
wore a suit and answered questions in such a timorous voice that
Judge Savard had to ask him more than once to speak up.

On the morning that Saul and his comrades were to be sentenced, sympathizers gathered in front of the court-house. They
wielded placards that read FREE THE 18TH OF NOVEMBER FIFTEEN.
REMEMBER LES PATRIÓTES. Fortunately the judge, who had never
enjoyed such attention before, was in an expansive mood. Summing
up, he recalled his own struggles as a rebellious youth in Saint-
Eustache. Coming of age, he added, at a time when you couldn't be
served in French in an Eaton's department store and the recipes on
macaroni boxes were in English only. He remembered the Great
Depression. The Second World War, which he had watched in
newsreels. He allowed that the times were calculated to try the
souls of young men and women. There was the Cold War. Drugs.
Pollution. Promiscuity. Pornographic magazines and movies.
Unfortunate tensions between the English and French in Quebec.
A lamentable decline in church – and, he added, eyes a-twinkle –
synagogue attendance. So the young, he ventured, were obviously
troubled, especially the more sensitive among them. But this, he
pointed out, did not entitle them to run amok, destroying private
property. Nobody was above the law. And yet – and yet – he
wondered aloud, would it serve any point to incarcerate the sons
and daughters of respectable, law-abiding families with common
criminals? Yes, certainly, if they held to their radical beliefs. No, just
possibly, if they had come to repent sincerely. Then, having given
Saul his cue, he asked if – before he was sentenced – he had anything to say for himself.

Alas, Saul was now aware of the reporters, as well as his many
admirers in the courtroom. Hushed, expectant. "Well, young man,"
said Mr. Justice Savard, prodding him, his smile benign.

"I don't give a flying fuck what you sentence me to, you old fart, because I do not recognize the authority of this court. You are just another running dog of imperialism." Then, saluting with a clenched fist, he hollered, "Power to the people. *Vive le Québec libre.*"

Miriam, convinced that Saul had blown it, was horrified. And maître Hughes-McNoughton and I, fearful that all our efforts had been in vain, exchanged despairing glances. While Mr. Justice Savard tried to restore order there was nothing for it but for me to flee the court for a much-needed smoke.

Within minutes a smiling Miriam emerged, followed by a disappointed Saul, who was promptly embraced by Mike and Kate. "He's got a suspended sentence," said Miriam, "provided that he is responsible for no further outrages, and lives at home. There is also a fine to be paid."

Only then did I catch a glimpse of the good Bishop Sylvain Gaston Savard approaching, bearing a portfolio filled with architects' plans, and builders' estimates, his smile large.

SEVEN

STORY in this morning's *Gazette* about the former cafeteria manager at the Smithsonian Museum in Washington, who was awarded $400,000 after the jury heard that his boss had called him an "old fart." The cafeteria manager, who was a stripling at the time, a mere fifty-four-year-old, claimed that his boss regularly made age-related remarks to him, including, "Check out Jim's grey hair"; "How are you doing, old man?" and "Here comes the old man, get out the wheelchair."

Alas, just like Jim, I'm running out of road. Yesterday, released into a downpour from the torture chamber of the man who manipulates my back once my sciatica becomes intolerable, I couldn't find a taxi. So I boarded a Sherbrooke Street bus. Jam-packed. No seats available. But sitting right before me there was a fetching young woman, mini-skirted, legs crossed. I immediately began to undress her in my mind's eye, undoing zippers and snaps tantalizingly slowly. She must have been psychic, for, lo and behold, unless she was suffering from a nervous tic, she was giving *me* the eye. Actually smiling at old Barney Panofsky, making my aging heart skip a beat. I smiled right back at her. Leaping up, she said, "Now why don't you sit down, sir?"

"I am perfectly capable of standing," I said, poking her back into her seat.

"Well," she said, "serves me right for being considerate in this day and age."

Onwards. At the risk of offending my neighbours, maybe even inviting a law suit, like Jim's boss, that age-ist boor, the truth is that the building I call home in downtown Montreal is actually a rich old fart's castle. There's no moat or drawbridge, but, all the same, it could easily qualify as a fortress for besieged anglophone septuagenarians who tiptoe about in terror of our separatist provincial premier, whose school nickname was "The Weasel." Most of my neighbours have unloaded their Westmount family mansions and shifted their stock portfolios to Toronto for safe keeping, as they wait for the *québécois pure laine* (that is to say, racially pure francophones) to vote in a second referendum on independence of a sort, yes or no, for this provincial backwater called Quebec.

Our building was recently disposed of by the Teitelbaums, sold retail to a new bunch out of Hong Kong, their suitcases laden with cash. It's called the Lord Byng Manor, after Viscount Byng, the British general who led thousands of Canadians to the slaughter in the battle of Vimy Ridge in 1917, and later went on to become one of our governors general. The Hong Kong bunch, fingers to the wind, want to rename our stately pile of granite Le château Dollard des Ormeaux, in honour of an early hero of New France. Dollard des Ormeaux is said by some to have sacrificed himself and his sixteen young companions to save Ville-Marie, as Montreal was known in 1660, in a battle with a band of three hundred Iroquois at the Long Sault. Or, conversely, he was a fur trader with his eye on the main chance, who came to a deserved bad end when his raiding party was ambushed. In any event, my neighbours are outraged by this insult to their anglophone heritage, and a petition is circulating to protest the proposed name-change.

One of my neighbours, once a feared federal cabinet minister but now in his eighties, has gone gaga. He is still a natty dresser, never without his tweed hat, regimental tie, hacking jacket, and cavalry twill trousers. But his eyes have emptied out. Weather permitting, his keeper, a cheerful young nurse, airs him out once a day, taking him for a turn round the courtyard. Then they subside onto a bench in the sun, the nurse dipping into a Harlequin paperback and the former cabinet minister sucking jellybeans, watching the cars come and go in the parking lot, and writing down their licence numbers on a pad. Whenever I pass, he smiles and says, "Congratulations."

The senator who recently moved into our penthouse is none other than Harvey Schwartz, liquor tycoon Bernard Gursky's former *consigliere*. Harvey is worth kazillions. He and Becky own a Hockney, which I wish were mine, a Warhol, a painting by what's-his-name, who used to ride a bicycle over his canvases,[1] and a Leo Bishinsky, constantly rising in value. I stopped the Schwartzes in the lobby recently, the two of them obviously bound for a charity costume ball, tricked out like a twenties mobster and his moll. "Well, I'll be gol-darned," I said, "if it ain't Bonnie and Clyde Schwartz. Don't shoot."

"Ignore him," said Harvey. "He's drunk again."

"One minute," I said. "You know that Bishinsky you own?"

"You've never been invited to our apartment," said Harvey, "and you never will be. Forget it."

"I thought you'd be delighted to know that I worked on it too. Let fly with a wet mop Leo handed me one day."

"That's the most ridiculous thing I ever heard," said Becky.

"Ten to one you've never even met Bishinsky," said Harvey, brushing past me.

We also boast a gaggle of divorcees of a certain age in the Lord Byng Manor. My favourite, an anorexic with a helmet of lacquered hair dyed blonde, breasts once as flat as yesterday's flapjacks, and legs as thin as pipe cleaners, hasn't spoken to me since we ran into each other after she had returned from a second-chance clinic in Toronto, where she had gone for a face-lift and a boob refill. I had greeted her in the lobby with a kiss on the cheek.

"What are you staring at?" she demanded.

"I'm waiting to see if the dent remains in place."

---

[1] Jackson Pollock (1912–1956).

"Bastard."

I no longer really have to go into my production office, where I am considered a spent force. I could live anywhere. In London with Mike and Caroline. In New York with Saul, and whoever is his latest squeeze. Or in Toronto with Kate. Kate's my darling. But in Toronto I'd be bound to run into Miriam and Blair Hopper né Hauptman, Herr Doktor Professor of Nostrums.

CBC Radio, overjoyed to have Miriam back in Toronto, immediately found a niche for her. Reverting to her maiden name, Greenberg, which first brought her to national attention as an arts reporter, she now presides over a morning classical-music program called "By Special Request." It enables listeners to ask for any recording they fancy, treating us to the insufferably cute stories behind their selection. I tape these shows, tracking the tunes most popular with Mr. and Mrs. Front Porch. They are, in no special order, "The William Tell Overture," "The Moonlight Sonata," "The Warsaw Concerto," "The Four Seasons," "The 1812 Overture." I play these tapes back at night, seated in the dark, a Macallan in hand, savouring the voice of my one true love, pretending she is not on the radio but in our bathroom, going about her nightly ablutions, preparing for bed, where she will curl into me, warming my old bones, and I will cup her breasts until I fall asleep. Riding sufficient Macallan, my pretence will go so far as even to allow me to call out to her, "I know you're worried about my smoking, darling, so I'm putting out my cigar right now and coming straight to bed."

Poor Miriam. Her program's a clunker. Between playing records, she is obliged to read her listeners' letters aloud; once – to my everlasting glee – a letter that purported to come from a Mrs. Doreen Willis of Vancouver Island:

Dear Miriam,

I hope you don't mind my being so familiar, but out here on Vancouver Island we tend to think of you as family. So here goes. Blush blush blush. Forty years ago today I was on the "yellow brick road" to Banff with Donald on our honeymoon. We drove a Plymouth Compact. It was blue, my favourite colour. I also like ochre, silver, and lilac. I don't mind canary yellow *on some people*, if you know what I mean? But I simply can't stand maroon. It was raining cats and coyotes. And then, what? A flat tire. I was fit to be tied. Donald, then in the early stages of multiple sclerosis, although we hardly suspected it at the time (I thought he was just too clumsy), wasn't able to fix it. And little me? Well I wasn't going to risk getting axle grease on my brand new two-piece polka-dot suit with semi-fitted top ending just below the waist. It was turquoise. Then along came a Good Samaritan in the nick of time to save our bacon. Whoops. I'm sure you don't eat it with your name, but no offence, eh? We were exhausted by the time we arrived at the Banff Springs Hotel. All the same, Donald insisted that we celebrate our safe arrival with a couple of Singapore Slings. The bartender had his radio on and Jan Peerce was singing "The Bluebird of Happiness." I tell you it gave me goose-pimples. It fit our mood to a T. Today is our fortieth wedding anniversary and Donald, who has been confined to a wheel-chair for years, is feeling blue (my favourite colour, natch). But I want you to know he still retains his sense of humour. I call him Shaky, which makes him giggle so hard, I then have to wipe his chin and blow his nose. Oh well, for better or for worse, isn't that what we pledged, *although some wives I could name don't honour it.*

Please play Jan Peerce's recording of "The Bluebird of Happiness" for Donald, as I know it will lift his spirits. Many thanks from a faithful listener.

Yours,
Doreen Willis

Gotcha, I thought, pouring myself a big one, slipping into a soft-shoe shuffle. Then I sat down and began to scribble notes for another letter.

In my declining years, I continue to linger in Montreal, risking icy streets in winter in spite of my increasingly brittle bones. It suits me to be rooted in a city that, like me, is diminishing day by day. Only yesterday, it seems, the separatists officially launched their referendum campaign with a show performed before a thousand true believers in Quebec City's Grand Théâtre. Their prolix, if

decidedly premature, Declaration of Sovereignty, recited by a
spotlit duo, owed more to Hallmark cards than to Thomas
Jefferson.

> We, the people of Quebec, declare we are free to choose
> our future.
> We know the winter in our souls. We know its blustery
> days, its solitude, its false eternity and its apparent deaths.
> We know what it is to be bitten by the winter cold.

We are dealing with a two-headed beast: our provincial
premier, a.k.a. The Weasel, and his minions in Quebec City, and
Dollard Redux, the fulminating leader of the Bloc Québécois in
Ottawa. Dollard Redux has lit a fire here. Soon the only English-
speaking people left in Montreal will be the old, the infirm, and
the poor. All that's flourishing now are FOR SALE/ A VENDRE signs,
sprouting up every day like out-of-season daffodils on front lawns,
and there are stores with TO LET/ A LOUER signs everywhere on
once fashionable streets. In the watering-hole I favour, on Crescent
Street, there is a wake at least once a month for the latest regular
who has had his fill of tribalism and is moving to Toronto or Vancouver. Or, God help them, Saskatoon, "a good place to bring up
children."

Dink's is the name of the bar I repair to for lunch just about
every day and again at five in the afternoon, an hour when the place
is thick with sour old farts. That adorable gamin who is my personal
assistant at Totally Unnecessary Productions, the indispensable
Chantal Renault, is familiar with my routine. Ignoring the men,
who are always stirred by her presence, she tends to come and go
with cheques that have to be signed and more exasperating problems. Happily Arnie Rosenbaum is no longer with us. Arnie, who
was in my class at Fletcher's Field High, is the nebbish I once
foolishly hired to run the Montreal office of my cheese-importing
business. Prompted by guilt, I kept him on when I prematurely
went into TV production back in 1959, finding a place for him in
accounts. Those days. Christ Almighty. One step ahead of creditors,
I used to delay settling lab, film-stock, and camera-rental bills until
the last possible moment. Then there was Arnie to cope with.
Teeth-grinding Arnie, who was suffering from halitosis, asthma,

ulcers, and flatulence, his maladies exacerbated by the torments he was subjected to by his boss, Hugh Ryan, our resident chartered accountant. One day Arnie would come in to find an entry that wasn't his own in one of his ledgers, obliging him to waste hours in futile calculations. Another day, popping what he took to be one of his pills, he would, before the morning was out, be struck with a sudden attack of diarrhoea. Then there was the afternoon Arnie caught up with me at Dink's and thrust his raincoat onto the bar. "I'm just coming from the cleaners," he said. "Look what they found in my pockets." Condoms. A vibrator. A torn pair of tiny black panties. "What if it had been Abigail who had emptied my pockets?"

I also loathed Hugh, but didn't dare fire him. He was the nephew of our federal minister of finance and a frequent dinner guest in the homes of the presidents of the Bank of Montreal and the Royal. Without his assurances, my line of desperately needed credit would be severed. "Arnie, if you only learned to ignore him, he would stop bugging you. But I'll speak to him."

"One day, so help me, I'll pick up a knife and ram it between his shoulder blades. Fire him, Barney, I could do his job."

"I'll think about it."

"That's exactly what I expected. Thanks for nothing," he said.

AMONG THE regulars at Dink's these days there are a few divorcees, a number of journalists, including Zack Keeler, the *Gazette* columnist, a couple of bores to be avoided, some lawyers, a marooned New Zealander, and a likeable gay hairdresser. Our star turn and my best friend there is a lawyer, who usually claims his bar stool at noon and doesn't surrender it until seven, when we yield Dink's to ear-splitting rock music and the young, there to make out.

John Hughes-McNoughton, born into Westmount affluence, misplaced his moral compass years ago. His thin hair dyed brown, he is a tall, scrawny, stoop-shouldered man, his blue eyes radiating scorn. John was a brilliant criminal lawyer until he was undone by two costly alimony settlements and a deadly mixture of booze and irreverence. Defending a notorious swindler-cum-lounge lizard some years back, a man charged with the sexual assault of a woman he had picked up in the Esquire Show Bar, John made the mistake of going out to a long liquid lunch at Delmo's before returning to the courtroom to deliver his summing up. Floating into the well of the court, slurring his words, he said, "Ladies and gentlemen of the jury, it is now my duty to make an impassioned speech in defence of my client. Then you will benefit from the judge's unbiased summary of the evidence you have heard here. And following that, ladies and gentlemen of the jury, you, in your wisdom, will pronounce on whether you find my client innocent or guilty. But, honouring Juvenal, who once wrote *probitas laudatur et alget*, which I won't insult you by translating, let me admit that I am far too drunk to make a speech. In all my years in court, I have yet to come across an unbiased judge. And you, ladies and gentlemen of the jury, are incapable of deciding whether my client is innocent or not." Then he sat down.

In 1989, John addressed public meetings in support of a quirky new anglophone protest party that would elect four members to our so-called National Assembly in Quebec City. He also published corrosive op-ed pieces here and there ridiculing the province's loopy language laws, which ordained, among other foolish things, that henceforth English, or even bilingual, commercial signs would be *verboten*, an affront to the *visage linguistique* of *la belle province*. In those contentious days even Dink's suffered a visit from an inspector (or tongue trooper, as we called them) from the *Commission de protection de la langue française*. This latter-day, pot-bellied *patriote* in a Hawaiian shirt and Bermuda shorts was saddened to discover a banner suspended from the bar that read:

ALLONS-Y EXPOS
GO FOR IT, EXPOS

His manner beyond reproach, the inspector allowed that the sentiment was admirable but, unfortunately, the sign was illegal, because the English lettering was the same size as the French, whereas the law clearly stated that the French must be twice the size of the English. It was past three p.m. when the inspector pronounced and a well-oiled John was already into his shouting mode. "When you can send in an inspector who is twice the size of us anglophones," he hollered, "we'll take down the sign. Until then, it remains in place."

"Are you *le patron?*"

"*Fiche le camp. Espèce d'imbécile.*"

Six months later John was in the news. He had failed to pay his provincial income tax for the past six years. An oversight. So he summoned reporters to Dink's. "I am being persecuted," he said, "because I am an anglophone, a spokesman for my people who have been denied their constitutional rights. Rest assured I will not be intimidated or silenced. And I will survive. For, as Terence put it, *fortes fortuna juvat.* That's spelt T,E,R,E,N,C,E, gentlemen."

"But have you paid your taxes or not?" asked a reporter from *Le Devoir.*

"I refuse to countenance hostile questions put to me by politically motivated reporters from the francophone press."

Riding a surfeit of vodka and cranberry juice, his preferred tipple, John could be truly obnoxious, his favourite foil the harmless gay hairdresser he shouts at, denouncing him as a bowel-troweller or worse, infuriating Betty, our incomparable barmaid, as well as everybody else in the bar. Betty, born to her job, sees to it that nobody who is not a certified member of our group is ever seated at our end of the horseshoe-shaped bar. She fields unwanted phone-calls with panache. If, for instance, Nate Gold's wife calls, she will look directly at Nate for a sign, even as she calls out, "Is Nate Gold here?" She cashes cheques for Zack Keeler, among others, and hides them until she is assured they will not be returned NSF. When drink has rendered John too much to bear, she will take him gently by the arm, and say, "Your taxi is here."

"But I didn't order a . . ."

"Yes, you did. Didn't he, Zack?"

John is certainly a scoundrel, but he is also an intelligent man and an original, a species this city is short of. Furthermore, I am permanently in his debt. Even though I'm sure he suspected I was guilty, he defended me with wizardry in court. He was there for me when only Miriam's visits to the prison in St. Jérôme stood between me and a breakdown.

"Of course I believe you," she had said then, "but I think you haven't told me everything."

To this day when the officer who was in charge of the investigation, Detective-Sergeant Sean O'Hearne, puts in an appearance at Dink's, John does his utmost to humiliate him. "If you must impose yourself on the quality here, O'Hearne, you're going to have to pay for your own drinks, now that you've retired."

"If I were you, maître Hughes hyphen McNoughton, I would mind my own business."

"*Ite, missa est,* you viper. So do not trouble my client here. You can still be charged with harassment, you know."

Raskolnikov has nothing on me. Or, put another way, to each suspect his own Inspector of Police Porfiry. O'Hearne continues to keep tabs on me, hoping for a deathbed confession.

Poor O'Hearne.

All of us who frequent Dink's in the afternoon have suffered time's depredations, but the years have been especially unkind to O'Hearne, now in his early seventies. Once he had been built square as a boxer, a stranger to flab, Warner Brothers tough, with a weakness for Borsalinos, kipper ties, and bespoke tailoring acquired on the arm. In days gone by his mere presence in Dink's, or any other Crescent Street watering-hole, was sufficient to empty the place of dealers in drugs, stolen goods, or call-girls, none of whom wanted O'Hearne to see them spending lavishly. But nowadays O'Hearne, his residue of snowy white hair still parted down the middle or spine, stray strands slicked down either side like bleached salmon ribs, was not so much corpulent as beer-bloated, his blubber seemingly without substance. Prick him with a fork, I thought, and he would spurt fat like sausage in a pan. Jowly he was, sweaty, his double-chin wobbly, his belly immense. He no longer chain-smoked Player's Mild, but he was left with, and often overcome by, such a wet, bronchial cough as to make the rest of us resolve to reread our wills when we got home. The last time he stopped by to check me out, heaving himself into the bar stool beside me, wheezing, he said, "You know what worries *me* most? Cancer of the rectum. Having to shit into a Glad bag attached to my hip. Like poor old Armand Lemieux. Remember him?"

Lemieux was the one who put the cuffs on me.

"I sit in the crapper every morning now," he said, "and an hour passes before I'm done. It comes out in angry little bits."

"That's very interesting, your excreta. Why don't you go in for a check-up?"

"You eat Japanese?"

"Not if I can help it."

"I tried that new place on Bishop, The Lotus Blossom, or whatever the hell they call it, and they brought me raw cold fish and hot wine. Listen here, I said to the waitress, I like *hot* food and *cold* wine. Take it away and try again, eh? Hey, I get a lot of reading done these days."

"Sitting on the crapper?"

"Lemieux remembers you like yesterday. The way you handled it, he says, you had to be a genius."

"I'm touched."

"Lemieux's got himself a nice bit of stuff for an old cop. An Italian widow, with boobs out to here, who runs a dépanneur in the North End. But what can it be like for her, eh? I mean he's in the sack with her, woosh woosh woosh, and she takes a peek and that fucken Glad bag is filling up. Am I boring you?"

"Yes."

"You know, after all these years The Second Mrs. Panofsky, as you insist on calling her, still has me around for the occasional dinner."

"You're lucky. Of all my wives so far, she was the best cook. I don't mind you telling her that," I said, hoping my calumny would be reported to Miriam.

"I don't think she'd appreciate the compliment coming from you."

"She still accepts my monthly cheques."

"Let's be serious for a moment. It's like her life stopped right there and then. She's got the trial transcripts bound in morocco, and she goes over it again and again, making notes, looking for loopholes. Hey, tell me the difference between Christopher Reeve and O.J."

"I wouldn't know."

"O.J. will walk," he said, guffawing.

"You're such an oaf, Sean."

"Don't you get it? Reeve is that actor, he played Superman, who had this riding accident and is paralyzed for life. O.J. is guilty as hell, you know. Just like you. Ah, come on. Lighten up. That's all water over the dam. In your position, I might have done the same thing. Nobody blames you."

"Why do you keep coming in here, Sean?"

"I enjoy your company. Really I do. Would you do something for me? Leave me a letter, saying what you did with it." ·

"The body?"

He nodded.

"But you're bound to go first, Sean. With the weight you're carrying around these days you're just begging for a heart attack."

"I'll see you out, Panofsky. Guaranteed. You leave me that letter. I promise to read it and destroy it. I'm curious is all."

EIGHT

IRV NUSSBAUM was on the phone again this morning before I even had my coffee. "Terrific news," he said. "Turn on CJAD. Quick. Kids painted a swastika on the walls of a Talmud Torah school last night. Broke windows. Bye now."

And a compelling item out of Orange County, California, in today's *Globe and Mail*. A seventy-year-old woman, taking care of her cancer-ridden husband – changing his diapers, feeding him, sleeping only a few hours a night because of his incessant TV watching – just about snapped. She splashed her significant other of thirty-five years with rubbing alcohol and set him on fire when she discovered that he had eaten her chocolate bar. "I'd gone out for a minute to the mailbox and when I came back, it was gone. I knew there was nobody else there, so it must have been him," she said. "He gets candy, too, every day. But he took mine. So I fetched a teaspoonful of rubbing alcohol and threw it at him. I had matches in my pocket. It just went up. I really didn't mean to do it. I was just scaring him."

I had a one o'clock appointment, and set out in a foul mood, but in good time. Unlike Miriam, I took pride in being punctual. Then, suddenly, I stopped. All at once I couldn't remember what I was doing on . . . the sign on the corner said Sherbrooke Street. I had no idea where I was going. Or why. Overcome by dizziness, sliding in sweat in spite of the cold, I shuffled over to the nearest bus stop and collapsed on a bench. A young man waiting for the bus, his baseball cap worn back to front, leaned over me and said, "Are you okay, pops?"

"Shettup," I said. Then I began to mutter what is becoming my mantra. Spaghetti is strained with the device I have hanging on my kitchen wall. Mary McCarthy wrote *The Man in the Brooks Brothers Suit*. Or *Shirt*. Whichever. I am once a widower and twice divorced. I have three children – Michael, Kate, and the other boy. My favourite dish is braised brisket with horseradish and latkes. Miriam is my heart's desire. I live on Sherbrooke Street West in Montreal. The street number doesn't matter, I'd know the building anywhere.

My heart thudding, threatening to fly free of my chest, I groped for a Montecristo, and managed to light and then pull on it. Smiling weakly at the concerned young man who still hovered over me, I said, "I'm sorry. I didn't mean to be rude to you."

"I could call an ambulance."

"I don't know what came over me. But I'm fine now. Honestly." He seemed dubious.

"I'm going to meet Stu Henderson at Dink's. It's a bar on Crescent Street. I turn left at the next block and there it is."

Stu Henderson, a struggling freelance TV producer, who used to be with the National Film Board, was waiting for me at the bar. John, already rooted on his customary stool, sat beside him, seemingly lost in a reverie. Back in 1960, Stu had already made a prize-winning but boring documentary about the Canadair CL-215, a water bomber, then still being tested on various Laurentian lakes, that could scoop up 1200 gallons of water without coming to a full stop, and drop it on the nearest forest fire. And now he had come to pitch a project to me. He was looking for seed money for an independently produced documentary about Stephen Leacock. "That's very intriguing," I said, "but I'm afraid I'm not into cultural projects."

"Considering all the money you've made producing shlock, I –"

A glassy-eyed John intruded, "*Non semper erit aestas*, Henderson. Or, in the vernacular, no soap."

I suffer from a wonky system of values, acquired in my Paris salad days and still with me. Boogie's standard, whereby anybody who wrote an article for the *Reader's Digest*, or committed a best-seller, or acquired a Ph.D., was beyond the pale. But churning out a pornographic novel for Girodias was ring-a-ding. Similarly, writing for the movies was contemptible, unless it was a Tarzan flick, which would be a real hoot. So coining it in with the idiotic "McIver of the RCMP" was strictly kosher, but financing a serious documentary about Leacock would be *infra dignitatem*, as John would be the first to point out.

Terry McIver, of course, did not subscribe to Boogie's value system. As far as he was concerned, we were an unforgivably flippant bunch. Louche. Our shared political stance, nourished by the *New Statesman*, resolutely left-wing, struck him as pathetically naïve. And Paris was a political circus in those days, animal acts to the fore. One night the rabidly anti-Communist goons of *Paix et Liberté* pasted up posters everywhere that showed the Hammer and Sickle flying from the top of the Eiffel Tower, the caption underneath reading, HOW WOULD YOU LIKE TO SEE THIS? Early the next morning Communist toughs went from poster to poster, gluing the Stars and Stripes over the Soviet flag.

Clara, Boogie, Cedric, Leo, and I sat on the terrace of the Mabillon, drunkenly accumulating beer coasters on the day General Ridgway, fresh out of the Korean War, drove into Paris, replacing Eisenhower at SHAPE. Only a thin, bored crowd of the curious had turned out to look over the general, yet the gendarmes were everywhere, and the boulevard Saint-Germain was black with Gardes Mobiles, their polished helmets catching the sun. All at once, the Place de l'Odéon was clotted with Communist demonstrators, men, women, and boys squirting out of the side streets, whipping out broomsticks from inside their shapeless jackets and hoisting anti-American posters on them. Clara began to moan. Her hands trembled.

"RIDGWAY," the men hollered.

"*À la porte*," the women responded in a piercing shriek.

Instantly the gendarmes penetrated the demonstration, fanning out, swinging those charming blue capes featured in just about every French tourist poster I've ever seen, capes that were actually weighed down with lead pipe in the lining. Smashing noses. Cracking heads. The once disciplined cry of *Ridgway à la porte* faltered, then broke. Demonstrators retreated, scattered, clutching their bleeding heads. And I ran off in pursuit of a fleeing Clara.

Another day a German general came to Paris, summoned by
NATO, and French Jews and socialists paraded in sombre silence
down the Champs-Elysées, wearing concentration camp uniforms.
Among them was Yossel Pinsky, the rue des Rosiers money-changer
who would soon become my partner. "*Misht zikh nisht arayn*," he
said. Don't mix in here. The Algerian troubles had begun. Gendarmes began to raid Left Bank hotels one by one, looking for Arabs
without papers. Five o'clock one morning they pounded on our
door and demanded to see passports. I produced mine, even as
Clara, hitching the blankets to her chin, cowered in bed, whimpering. Her feet protruded, each toenail painted a different colour.
A veritable rainbow. "Show them your passport, for Christ's sake."

"I can't. I'm naked."

"Tell me where it is."

"No. You mustn't."

"Goddamn it, Clara."

"Shit. Fuck." Gathering her blanket round her as best she
could, still whimpering, even as the gendarmes grinned at each
other, she fished her passport out of the bottom of a suitcase,
showed it to them, and locked the suitcase again.

"They saw my coozy, those filthy bastards. They were staring
at it."

I ran into Terry that afternoon at the Café Bonaparte, where I
had gone to play the pinball machine. My initial bond with Terry
stemmed from the fact that we were both Montrealers. Me, off
Jeanne Mance Street in the city's old working-class Jewish quarter,
and Terry out of the marginally better-off, Waspy Notre-Dame-de-
Grâce neighbourhood, where his father had scraped together a
mean living out of his second-hand bookshop that specialized in
Marxist texts. His mother had taught in an elementary school until
parents protested they didn't want their children watching documentaries about life on a communal farm in the Ukraine, rather
than Bugs Bunny cartoons.

If most of us were broke, Terry was destitute. Or so it seemed.
There were days when his diet was limited to a baguette and a *café
au lait*. He wore drip-dry shirts, which he rinsed in his hand basin
and hung out to dry overnight. A girl he knew, who was lodged at
the *cité universitaire*, used to cut his hair for him. Terry survived by
writing six-hundred-word articles for UNESCO that were distri-

buted free to newspapers round the world. For thirty-five dollars he would churn out an erudite piece commemorating the centennial of a famous writer's birth, or the fiftieth anniversary of the first performance of Marconi's first wireless message or Major Walter Reed's discovery that yellow fever was carried by mosquitoes. He was barely tolerated by our bunch, as I may have mentioned earlier, so if there was a party anywhere the word that bounced from café to café was, "For God's sake, don't tell Terry." Terry, the pariah. But I grew perversely fond of him and took him out to dinner once a week in a restaurant I favoured on the rue du Dragon. Clara never joined us. "He's the most *dégoûtant* person I have ever laid eyes on," she said, "totally *déraciné*, a *frondeur*. And, furthermore, he has a bad aura and is constantly directing elementals at me." But then she didn't care for Yossel either. "He gives me the chills. He stinks of all the world's evil."

Terry intrigued me. The rest of us, blithely unselfconscious, didn't brood over whatever our ages were at the time: twenty-three, or twenty-seven, or whatever. We didn't think in terms of life spans. Or, put another way, shells had not yet begun to land close to the trench. Terry, however, was aware that he was young and experiencing his "Paris period." His life was not his to enjoy and spend recklessly, like Onan's seed. It was a responsibility. A trust. Like a black-and-white drawing in a child's colouring book that was his to crayon, filling it in with the utmost autobiographical care, mindful of future criticism. So he appeared to relish rather than endure penury, a rite of his literary passage. Dr. Johnson had known worse. So had Mozart. Everything he did and heard was fodder for his journals, the entries twisted as I discovered too late.

Terry, who mocked his parents' politics, nevertheless inherited some of their prejudices, inveighing against all things American. He despaired of Coca-Cola culture. The New Rome. "Remember the night," he said, "Cedric took us out to celebrate his signing a contract for his novel, being so damned ostentatious about his new affluence. I didn't want to rain on his fanfaronade, the clash of those Nubian cymbals, so I was mute at the time, which you, no doubt, ascribed to envy. But the truth is Scribner's had just sent back the first three chapters of my novel-in-progress with a flattering letter and a caveat. Alas, there was negligible interest in matters Canadian. Would you consider resetting your novel in Chicago? Hugh

MacLennan, whom I hold in no high regard, was right in this instance, 'Boy meets girl in Winnipeg. Who cares?' And how are things going with the unpredictable Clara these days?"

"She would have joined us for dinner, but she wasn't feeling well."

"You needn't prevaricate with me. I don't suffer from your compulsion to be approved of, surely an appurtenance of your Jeanne Mance Street heritage. But what I don't fathom is why you persist in trailing after Boogie like a poodle."

"You're such a prick, Terry."

"Come now. You worship that mountebank. You have even acquired some of his gestures." Terry – having scored, he felt – leaned back and regarded me with a condescending smile.

Terry's initial publication was in *Merlin*, one of the little magazines current in Paris at the time. "Paradiso" was insufferably poetic, Joycean, *written*, and sent us chortling to our dictionaries to look up words: didynamia, mataeology, *chaude-mellé*, sforzato.

I am now a collector of sorts of Canadiana, my special interest the journals of early travellers to Lower Canada, and dealers regularly send me catalogues. I recently espied the following entry in one of them:

Exceedingly Rare and in Fine Condition

McIver, Terry. The author's first publication, "Paradiso," a short story. An early but seminal pointer to the future obsessions of one of our master novelists. *Merlin*, Paris. 1952.
See Lande, 78; Sabin, 1052.
C$300.

One night an exuberant Terry caught up with me at the Café Royal Saint-Germain. "George Whitman read my story," he said, "and has asked me to read at his bookshop."

"Why, that's terrific," I said, feigning enthusiasm. But I was in a foul mood for the rest of the day.

Boogie insisted on accompanying Clara and me to the bookshop opposite Notre-Dame Cathedral. "Unmissable," said Boogie, obviously stoned. "Why, in years to come people will ask, where were you the night Terry McIver read from his *chef-d'oeuvre*? Less fortunate men will be bound to say, I was cashing in my winning Irish Sweepstakes ticket, or I was screwing Ava Gardner. Or Barney will be able to boast he was there the night his beloved Canadiens won yet another Stanley Cup. But I will be able to claim I was present on the night literary history was being made."

"You're not coming with us. Forget it."

"I shall be humble. I will gasp at his metaphors and applaud each use of *le mot juste*."

"Boogie, I want your word that you're not going to heckle him."

"Oh, stop being such a kvetch," said Clara. "You're not Terry's mother."

Folding chairs had been provided for forty, but there were only nine people there when Terry began to read, a half-hour late.

"I believe Edith Piaf is opening somewhere on the Right Bank tonight," said Boogie, *sotto voce*, "otherwise, there would surely have been a better turnout."

Terry was in mid-flight when a bunch of Letterists barged into the bookshop. They were supporters of *Ur, Cahiers pour un dictat culturel*, which was edited by Jean-Isador Isou. The redoubtable Isou was also the author of *A Reply to Karl Marx*, a slender riposte that was peddled to tourists by pretty girls on the rue de Rivoli and outside the American Express – tourists under the tantalizing illusion that they were buying the hot stuff. The Letterists believed that all the arts were dead and could only be resurrected through a synthesis of their collective absurdities. Their own poems, which they usually recited in a café on the Place Saint-Michel, consisted of grunts and cries, incoherent arrangements of letters, set to an anti-musical background and, for a time, I was one of their fans. And now, as Terry continued to read in a monotone, they played harmonicas, blew whistles, pumped the rubber bulb of a klaxon and, hands cupped under armpits, made farting noises.

Deep down, I'm a homer. I root for the Montreal Canadiens and, when they were still playing ball in Delormier Downs, our Triple-A Royals. So I instinctively sprang to Terry's defence. "*Va te faire foutre! Tapettes! Salauds! Petits merdeurs! Putes!*" But this only served to spur on the rowdies.

A flushed Terry read on. And on. And on. Seemingly in a

trance, his fixed smile chilling to behold. I felt sick. *Hold the phone.*
Yes, I was truly concerned for him, but, bastard that I am, I was
equally relieved that he hadn't drawn a crowd. Or won acclaim.
Afterwards, I told Boogie and Clara I would catch up with them at
The Old Navy, but first I was taking Terry out for a drink. Before
we parted, Boogie startled me, saying, "I've heard worse, you
know."

Terry and I met at a café on the boulevard Saint-Michel, and sat
on the terrace, the only people there, a couple of Canucks who
didn't mind the cold. "Terry," I said, "those clowns were out for
blood and wouldn't have behaved any differently had Faulkner been
reading there tonight."

"Faulkner is over-estimated. He won't endure."

"All the same, I'm sorry for what happened. It was brutal."

"Brutal? It was absolutely wonderful," said Terry. "Don't you
know that the first performance of Mozart's *Marriage of Figaro* was
booed in Vienna and that when the Impressionists first showed their
work they were laughed at?"

"Yeah, sure. But – "

" ' . . . you ought to know,' " he said, obviously quoting somebody, " 'that What is Grand is necessarily Obscure to Weak men.
That which can be made Explicit to the Idiot is not worth my
care.' "

"And just who said that, may I ask?"

"William Blake wrote that in a letter to the Reverend Dr. John
Trusler, who had commissioned some watercolours from him and
then criticized the results. But what did you think, not that it
matters?"

"Who could hear in all that racket?"

"Don't be evasive with me, please."

Sufficiently irritated by now to want to crack his carapace of
arrogance, I knocked back my cognac and said, "All right, then.
Many are called, but few are chosen."

"You're pathetic, Barney."

"Right. And you?"

"I'm surrounded by a confederacy of dunces."

That prompted a laugh from me.

"Now why don't you just settle the bill, because after all it was you who invited me, and move on to wherever you're meeting your oafish Trilby and foul-mouthed Paphian?"

"My foul-mouthed what?"

"Harlot."

The Second Mrs. Panofsky once observed that in the absence of heart there was a knot of anger swirling inside me. And now, my blood surging, I leapt up, lifted Terry out of his chair and smashed him hard in the face, his chair toppling over. Then I stood over him, crazed, fists ready to fly. Murder in my heart. But Terry wouldn't fight back. Instead he sat on the pavement, smirking, nursing his bleeding nose with a handkerchief. "Good night," I said.

"The bill. I haven't got enough money on me. Settle the bill, damn you."

I threw some franc notes at him, and was just about to flee when he began to tremble and sob brokenly. "Help me," he said.

"What?"

" . . . my hotel . . ."

I managed to get him to his feet and we started to walk, his teeth chattering, his legs rubbery. We had only gone a block when he began to shake. No, vibrate. He sank to his knees and I held his head, as he vomited again and again. Somehow or other, we made it back to his room on the rue Saint-André-des-Arts. I got him into bed, and when he started to tremble again, I piled whatever clothes I could find on top of his blankets. "It's the flu," he said. "I'm not upset. This has nothing to do with my reading. You're not saying anything."

"What should I say?"

"There's no doubting my talent. My work will last. I know that."

"Yes."

Then his teeth began to chatter at such a rate I feared for his tongue. "Please don't go yet."

I lit a Gauloise and passed it to him, but he couldn't handle it.

"My father can hardly wait for me to fail and to join him in misery."

He began to weep again. I grabbed the wastepaper basket and held his head, but for all his heaving he could bring up nothing but a string of green slime. As soon as the retching stopped, I brought him a glass of water. "It's the flu," he said.

"Yes."

"I'm not upset."

"No."

"If you tell any of the others you saw me like this I'll never forgive you."

"I won't say a word to anybody."

"Swear it."

I swore it, and sat with him until his body stopped jerking, and he fell into a troubled sleep. But I had been a witness to his cracking and that, dear reader, is how you make enemies.

NINE

I'M determined to be fair. A reliable witness. The truth is, Terry McIver's novels, including *The Money Man*, in which I fill the large role of the acquisitive Benjy Perlman, are untainted by imagination. His novels are uniformly pedestrian, earnest, as appetizing as health food and, it goes without saying, devoid of humour. The characters in these novels are so wooden they could be used for kindling. It is only in Terry's journals that fantasy comes into play. Certainly the Paris pages are full of invention. A sicko's inventions. Mary McCarthy once observed that everything Lillian Hellman wrote was a lie, including "and" and "but." The same can be said of Terry's journals.

Following, a sampler. Some pages from the journals of Terry McIver (Officer of the Order of Canada, Governor General's Award winner), as they will soon appear in his autobiography, *Of Time and Fevers*, published by the group, Toronto, which gratefully acknowledges the assistance of mediocrity's holy trinity: the Canada Council, the Ontario Arts Council, and the City of Toronto Arts Council.

Paris. Sept. 22, 1951. Couldn't get anywhere with Céline's Mort à Crédit this morning. It was recommended to me by the touchingly insecure P——, which is not surprising, considering that he is burdened with his own inchoate rage against the world. I have the most tenuous of relationships with P——, imposed on me as we are both Montrealers, which hardly amounts to propinquity.

P—— turned up in Paris one day last spring, furnished with my address by my father. He knew nobody here, and, consequently, sought me out daily. He would interrupt me at work, inviting me out to lunch and demanding, in return, that I provide him with the names of the cafés he should frequent, and pleading for introductions. Within a week, he had mastered the fashionable Negro idiom, swallowing it whole. Once, memorably, he came upon me on the terrace of the Mabillon, where I was reading Evelyn Waugh's *Vile Bodies*.

"Is it a drag, or is it any good, man?"

"I beg your pardon?"

"Would I dig it?"

Eventually I succeeded in unloading him onto a clatch of frivolous Americans, whose company I did my utmost to avoid. To begin with they were far from grateful, but soon they discovered that P——, determined to ingratiate himself, could be hit easily for money. Leo Bishinsky borrowed from him to buy canvases and paints, and the others sponged off him, each according to his need. In passing, I once said to Boogie, "I see you've got yourself a new friend."

"Everybody is entitled to his own Man Friday, don't you think?"

Boogie, enduring a long losing streak at the gaming tables, and threatened with eviction from his hotel, got P—— to settle his rent.

In common with other autodidacts, P—— feels compelled to brandish whatever he is reading, his conversation burnished with quotes from their work. Sprung from the ghetto's mean streets, vulgarity comes naturally to him, but he is also inclined to both drunkenness and fisticuffs, which is surprising, considering his Jewish origins. A denial? Possibly.

Born in Montreal, raised in an English-speaking home, P—— still tends to invert many of his sentences, as if they were translated from the Yiddish, as in, "He was a hateful bastard, Clara's doctor," or, after the fact, "Had I known it would have been different, my behaviour." I must remember to use this peculiar syntax when writing a Jew's dialogue.

P——'s countenance is not unpleasant. Black curly hair hard as steel wool. Shrewd tradesman's eyes. Satyr's mouth. Tall, shambly, and given to strutting. He still seems adrift here, out of his league, but now an acolyte of one of the quartier's most obnoxious poseurs whom he trails after as if he were his catamite, his Ganymede, which is not the case. Neither of them is queer.

Wrote 600 words today and then tore them up. Inadequate. Mediocre. Like me?

Paris. Oct. 3, 1951. S——'s husband is in Frankfurt on business, and so she sent me a *pneumatique* this morning, inviting me to dinner in our *oubliette*, a bistro on the rue Scribe, where neither of us was likely to encounter anybody we knew. A prudent bourgeoise, fearful of wagging tongues ("*Elle entretient un gigolo. Tiens donc*"), S—— reached for my hand under the table and slipped me sufficient francs to settle the bill.

I have served as S——'s dutiful lover for three months now. She picked me up one summer night on the terrace of the Café de Flore. Seated alone at the table next to mine, she smiled, indicated the book I was reading, and said, "Not many Americans are capable of reading Robbe-Grillet in French. I must confess even I find him difficult."

She admits to being forty, but I suspect she's somewhat older, as witness her stretch marks. S——, now my self-appointed houri, is in no immediate danger of being confused with Aphrodite, but she is pleasingly pretty, slim. She begins to imbibe in the morning ("Gin and eet, *comme la reine anglaise*"), and she consumed most of the wine at dinner tonight, prodding me to indicate that her legs are spread apart under the table, an invitation for me to remove a shoe and sock and then massage her with my toes.

Later we repair to my disgusting little hotel room which she affects to adore, because it gratifies her *nostalgie de la boue*, as well as her concept of what's appropriate to a struggling young artist. We copulate twice, once fore, and once aft, and then I refuse her cunnilingus. This makes her sulk. She does brighten, however, when, on her insistence, I read to her from my work-in-progress. She pronounces it *merveilleux, vraiment incroyable*.

S—— dreams of being celebrated in my pages, and has picked the name of Héloise for herself. In spite of the driving rain and my fatigue I walk her back to her Austin-Healey, parked at a discreet distance, assuring her of my high esteem for her beauty, wit, intelligence. Back in my room, I immediately sit down to write 500 words, describing, while it is still fresh in my mind, how orgasm makes her shudder.

Wakened with a sneezing fit at 2 a.m. Reached for my thermometer and discovered I had a temperature of 99.2. My pulse was fast. Joints ached. I knew I shouldn't have gone out in the rain.

Paris. Oct. 9, 1951. A letter from my father has been lying on my table for ten days and this morning I finally risk opening the depressingly thick envelope.

I can visualize my father writing this letter in his cramped handwriting, seated at his oak roll-top desk in the rear of the bookshop. He would be smoking an Export A, a toothpick piercing the butt to keep it going until it threatened to scorch his lips. The desk's surface would include a spike thick with unpaid bills, and a cigar box for the collection of paper-clips, elastics, and postage stamps from foreign countries for the French-Canadian postman he is proselytizing. There would also be the remnants of his lunch. The remains of his dry hard-boiled egg, which he never finishes, or a leaky sardine sandwich. An apple core. Sucking his yellow teeth, he writes with an old-fashioned cork-handled pen, even as he still shaves with a straight razor and shines his cracked wingtip shoes every morning.

His letter, as usual, begins with a litany of political bile. Julius and Ethel Rosenberg have naturally been found guilty and sentenced to death. The H-Bomb has been tested in the Pacific, a provocation to the Soviet Union and other People's Democracies. Twenty-one Communist leaders have been arrested in the U.S., charged with conspiracy to teach and advocate the overthrow of the government. Then he gets down to the nitty-gritty. Mother is no better. She cannot be left alone at home, so he wheels her to the bookshop every morning, and soon there will be ice and snow, and how will he manage, his arthritis is so bad? She snoozes or reads in the rear of the bookshop until he is ready to lower the shutters and wheel her home. Home, where he will bathe her, soothing her with rubbing alcohol, and then heat her a bowl of Campbell's tomato soup followed by diced carrots and corn niblets, everything out of cans. Or fry her a couple of eggs in stale bacon grease, the edges burnt lacy brown. He will read to her at night in his smoker's voice, overcome by coughing fits, bringing up phlegm into a filthy handkerchief: Howard Fast, Gorky, Ilya Ehrenburg, Aragon, Brecht. In the absence of a crucifix, a framed copy of Mao's tribute to Comrade Norman Bethune hangs over their bed, which now requires a rubber undersheet for her sake. Some nights he will brush out her knotted grey hair, even as he sings her to sleep:

> Join the Union fellow workers
> Men and women side by side
> We will crush the greedy shirkers
> Like a sweeping surging tide
> For united we are standing
> But divided we will fall
> Let this be our understanding
> All for One and One for All.

My father writes that he now finds it all but impossible to cope. If I come home, he will forgive me my sins of omission and commission. I could have the back bedroom, with the radiator that sizzles and knocks through the night. With

the window that offers the inspiring view of other people's
Penman's long underwear flapping on the backyard clotheslines, and sheets frozen rock-hard in winter. I could write in the
mornings, looking in on Mother from time to time, emptying
the slop basin in her wheelchair, a spur to my appetite for
lunch. Then I could relieve him in the afternoons, tending to
the bookshop, peddling Marxist nostrums to comrades.
Dealing with the occasional innocent who wanders in to
inquire, "Would you have a copy of Norman Vincent Peale's
The Power of Positive Thinking?" Or, perhaps, Gayelord
Hauser's *Look Younger, Live Longer*? He would pay me twenty-
five dollars a week.

"I am not getting any younger, and neither is your devoted
mother, and we require your help, as our lives draw to a close."

And what about my life, I wonder? Why should I sacrifice it
for their sake? I would rather slit my wrists, as poor Clara[1]
did (Clara, whose prodigious talent I was one of the first to
recognize), than return to that bleak house. That so-called
"home" to which I could never bring my friends after school
lest they be lectured on the history of the Winnipeg general
strike, and be laden with pamphlets to take to their parents.

Rereading my father's missive, I take up a pencil and correct
his grammar and punctuation. I also note, typically, that in all
of its seven pages there is no inquiry as to my state of mind.
Not an iota of interest in my work-in-progress.

Inevitably, this filial summons brings on a migraine.
Working proves impossible. I stroll through the Jardin du Lux-
embourg, emerging on the rue Vavin, then on to
Montparnasse. This was foolish of me, for all that exercise
whets my appetite, and I have no money for lunch. Passing the
Dôme, I espy P——, conspiring with the hustler now said to be
one of his intimates. He is a rue des Rosiers money-changer.

A wasted day, fallow, not a word written.

Paris, Oct. 20, 1951. UNESCO cheque, long overdue, has still not

---

[1]The entry for Clara, in McIver's handwritten journals, lodged in the
University of Calgary, reads: "I would rather slit my wrists, as C—— did
(unsuccessfully, *faute de mieux*, like everything else she has undertaken)."
Notebook 31, Sept.–Nov. 1951, page 83.

arrived. Story returned from the *New Yorker* with a printed rejection slip. Irwin Shaw's effusions are more to their taste. I should have known better.

S— is always beautifully dressed by Dior or Chanel. I could survive for months on the cost of just one of those outfits. That pearl necklace with the diamond clasp. Those rings. The Patek Philippe wristwatch. Her husband is a Crédit Lyonnais executive. He hasn't made love to her for more than a year. She has decided he is a *tante*, but that he can go "*à voile et à vapeur*," as she once said.

S— has been shopping on the rue Faubourg St.-Honoré again. On my return from the market on the rue de Seine, the concierge presents me with a small package, tied with a ribbon, that has been delivered by hand. It is from Roger et Gallet. A bottle of scent for men. Three bars of perfumed soap. Oh, the arrogance of the rich.

Then, just as I have settled in at my table, she arrives out of breath, unaccustomed as she is to climbing five flights of stairs. "I only have an hour," she says, her kiss reeking of her garlicky lunch.

"But I'm in the middle of work."

She has brought a chilled bottle of Roederer Crystal, and is already undressing. "Hurry," she says.

300 words today. That's all.

Paris. Oct. 22, 1951. The patronizing P— invited me to lunch today in that cheap restaurant on the rue du Dragon, and of course he expects gratitude in return. He has come into some money, he says, as a consequence of a dubious deal with his money-changer accomplice. Oozing concern, he offers to lend me some. My need is exigent, but I turn him down as he is not the sort I wish to be indebted to. P— is only ostensibly caring. He is blatantly insecure and tenders favours in the hope of binding his betters to him.

Later we stroll as far as the Jeu de Paume together, where he is much taken by the Seurats.

"Seurat is credited with invention, a new style," I say, "but he, as well as some of the Impressionists, were probably short-sighted and painted things as they actually saw them."

"That's ridiculous," he says.

Paris. Oct. 29, 1951. The clatch gathered at a table in the Mabillon. Leo Bishinsky, Cedric Richardson, a couple whose names I can't remember, a girl new to me with glistening hairy armpits, and of course P——, accompanied by both his Svengali and his Clara. Responding to their faux-friendly greetings, I stop briefly at their table, refusing to be provoked by Boogie's taunts. They are all high on hashish, which renders them even more boring than usual.

For my own jollification, I have tried to come up with a cognomination that would be appropriate for that bunch. The Yahoos? The Sluggards? I finally settle on The Motley Crew.

They have come over not to absorb French culture but to meet each other. Not one of them has bothered to read Butor, Sarraute, or Simon. On an evening when I can afford to take in the latest Ionesco, or a Louis Jouvet performance, they can be found cheering Sidney Bechet at the Vieux Colombier. Gathered at their table at one café or another, they will argue endlessly about the merits of Ted Williams vs. Joe DiMaggio or, if P—— is in one of his tiresome hockey moods, Gordie Howe vs. Maurice Richard. Or they will challenge each other to recall the lyrics to an Andrews Sisters song. Or lines spoken in the film of *Casablanca*. They will congratulate each other and troop off together if they discover a cinema showing an old Bud Abbott and Lou Costello comedy, or an Esther Williams musical, and afterwards they will repair to The Old Navy or the Mabillon, to guffaw for hours on end.

Paris. Nov. 8, 1951. George Whitman has insisted that I read at his bookshop. I suppose James Baldwin wasn't available.

Forty-five people are there when I begin, including P—— and his chums, who have obviously come to mock me. Then a bunch of Letterists, sent for by Boogie no doubt, turn up to demonstrate. But they are sadly mistaken if they think they can intimidate me. I carry on in spite of their braying, for the sake of those who have come to listen.

P——, clearly delighted to have seen me attacked, invites me out afterwards for drinks and an opportunity to gloat. Solicitous beyond belief, he offers to lend me money again. Possibly, he suggests, I should return to Montreal and take a teaching job. "You, with your McGill scholarship and Arts Medal," he says with ill-concealed envy.

"Those who can't preach," I tell him.

Insulted, he attempts to sneak off without settling the bill. I insist that I had only come to the café at his invitation. Caught out, seething, he hoists me out of my chair, and punches me in the nose, bloodying it. Then he flees into the night, leaving me to pay the bill.

It is not the first time P— has tried to settle a contretemps with his fists. Nor, I suspect, will it be the last. He is a violent man. Capable of murder one day, I fear.[2]

TEN

HELLO, hello. Reb Leo Bishinsky is in the news again. MOMA is mounting a retrospective, which will next travel to Toronto's AGO, world-class at last. Leo's photograph in the *Globe and Mail* reveals that he now wears a rug – made out of his collection of the pubic-hairs-of-celebrated-models from the look of it. He is bare-chested, beaming, embraced by his twenty-two-year-old mistress, a veritable Barbie doll, her arms entwined round his huge, hairy, pastrami-barrel belly. I miss Leo. I really do. "Before I start work in the morning," Leo confided to the *Globe's* reporter, "I venture out into the surrounding woods and listen to the trees."

The *Globe's* page three yields even richer ore.

Forget Abelard and Héloïse. Never mind Romeo and Juliet. Or Chuck and Di. Or Michael Jackson and the Beverly Hills' orthodontist's number-one son. This morning's *Globe* offers an all-Ontario twisteroo on such poignant tales of romance. A guy named Walton Sue got married yesterday, thereby, according to the *Globe's* reporter, "adding another act to the almost Shakespearean tale of

---

[2] The entry in McIver's handwritten Notebook 31, Sept.–Nov. 1951, page 89, does not include the last sentence. "Capable of murder one day, I fear," had to be added later, after the fact.

love, money, and family feuding in which he and his wife have been cast as unlikely protagonists." Walton Sue, who has been physically and mentally disabled since he was hit by a car fifteen years ago, has now married wheelchair-bound Ms. Maria DeSousa, who suffers from cerebral palsy. They were wed in a "secret" ceremony in Toronto's Old City Hall courthouse attended by more media than family, wrote the *Globe* reporter.

Sue's problem was that his father, who strongly objected to the marriage, controlled his $245,000 settlement from the accident. But the day before yesterday a lawyer had Sue declared incapable of managing his property, thus shifting control of the money to the Public Guardian and Trustees of Ontario, which enabled Sue and Ms. DeSousa to move into an apartment for the disabled.

I'm not poking fun at this couple, to whom I wish a hearty *mazel tov*. My point is that I think being mentally disabled gives Sue a better shot at a happy marriage than I ever had, and I speak as a veteran who has struck out three times. The last time wed to a woman "whom age cannot wither, nor custom stale,"[1] but who ultimately adjudged me unworthy of her, which was an understatement. Miriam, Miriam, my heart's desire.

Were my first wife still alive, I would invite her, The Second Mrs. Panofsky, and Miriam to a bang-up lunch at Le Mas des Oliviers – a symposium on the conjugal failings of Barney Panofsky, Esquire. Cynic, philanderer, boozer, player piano. And murderer as well, perhaps.

Le Mas des Oliviers, my favourite restaurant here, provides proof that this troubled, divided city still has its redeeming values. Its salvation, the continuing devotion to pleasure by our movers and shakers. In Montreal they do not jog or nibble a quick salad after their noonday squash game, a disease money-driven Toronto suffers from. Instead, they congregate at Le Mas for three-hour lunches, digging into generous portions of *côtes d'agneau* or *boudin*, washed down with bottles of St. Julien, followed by calls for cognac and cigars. This is where contending lawyers, and judges as well, meet to settle their disputes amicably, but only after they have regaled each other with the day's most salacious gossip. There are more

---

[1] "Age cannot wither her, nor custom stale / Her infinite variety . . ." *Antony and Cleopatra*, Act 2, Scene 2.

mistresses than wives to be seen. The Tory party's Québécois godfather accepts tributes at his usual table, his manner munificent.
Provincial cabinet ministers who can render fat highway contracts
to the deserving hear out supplicants at other tables. I sometimes
frequent the Jewish sinners' round table, Irv Nussbaum presiding,
my transgressions forgiven, or mentioned only in the hope of pro-
voking laughter.

I brought Boogie here the day before I wed The Second Mrs.
Panofsky.

Boogie, had he survived until now, would be seventy-one years
old, possibly still wrestling with that first novel that was going to
astonish the world. That's rotten of me. Vengeful. But years have
passed since I expected he would ring my doorbell, if not tomorrow
then the day after. "Have you read Lovecraft?"

Long gone are the nights when I would waken with a start at
four a.m. to drive out to my cottage on the lake on a crazed hunch.
Banging open the front door, shouting Boogie's name, unavailingly,
and then retreating to the dock, staring into the waters where I had
last seen him.

"I met him only that one time at your wedding," Miriam once
said, "and I'm sorry to say I thought he was pathetic. Don't look at
me like that, please."

"I'm not."

"I know we've been through what happened that last day on the
lake a hundred times. But I still feel you're holding something back.
Did the two of you quarrel?"

"No. Certainly not."

The pleasures of my cherished cottage in the mountains, some
seventy miles north of Montreal, have diminished somewhat over
the years. True, after they put in the six-lane Laurentian Autoroute
in the sixties, it took me an hour, rather than the best of two, to
reach it. But unfortunately the autoroute has also made the lake
accessible to commuters as well as the computer literate who maintain offices in their cottages. Peeling off the autoroute, my retreat is
no longer approached on a treacherous loggers' road, gearing down
for protruding rocks and avoiding the deepest holes, my scraped
muffler system in need of annual renewal. I don't regret the fallen
trees that sometimes blocked my path, but I do miss the risky one-
lane wooden bridge over the Chokecherry River, its rushing waters

menacingly high during the spring run-off. It was displaced long ago by a proper steel-and-concrete bridge. And the loggers' road, widened in the late fifties, is now paved and ploughed in winter. We have also benefited from political progress. This jewel of a lake, which I still think of as Lake Amherst, was renamed Lac Marquette in the seventies by the *Commission de toponymie*, which is in charge of cleansing *la belle province* of the conqueror's place-names. And where once only canoes and sailboats could be seen on a twenty-three-mile lake, our summers are now polluted by flotillas of power-boats and water-skiers. Fighter planes from the NATO base in Plattsburg sometimes pass overhead, rattling windows. We also suffer the occasional trans-Atlantic jumbo jet on a flight path for Mirabelle airport and there are three tycoons who fly in for week-ends in their own little seaplanes. But back in the old days I recall our then pristine waters disturbed only once by an airplane. It was one of those damn water-bombers that were being tested in 1959, I think it was, and it roared in on the lake, gulping up God knows how many tons of water, and lifted off to drop its load on some distant mountain. Why, when I first came out here there were only five cottages on the lake, including mine, but they now number more than seventy. To my amusement, I have come to fill the quaintsy office of the old codger of the lake, invited to neighbours' cottages to regale their children with tales about the days when the speckled trout were plentiful and we were without electricity or telephones, never mind cable-TV or satellite dishes.

I stumbled on my Yasnaya Polyana by accident. Invited out to a friend's cottage on another lake one weekend, back in 1955, I took a wrong turn and found myself on a loggers' road that came to an abrupt stop at what appeared to be an abandoned lodge high on a hill overlooking the lake. There was a FOR SALE sign with an agent's name banged into a post on the sinking porch. The front door was locked and the windows were boarded up, but I managed to pry one open and climb inside, scattering squirrels and field mice. The lodge, I discovered, had been built as a fishing retreat by a Bostonian in 1935, and had been on the market for ten years, which didn't surprise me considering the appalling shape it was in. But I was smitten on first sight, and acquired it, and the surrounding ten acres of meadow and woods, for an astonishingly cheap ten thou-sand dollars. For the next four years, I camped out there in a sleeping-bag just about every weekend in summer, making do with paraffin lamps and delicatessen, mouse traps laid down everywhere, quarrelling with the slo-mo local contractors who were making it habitable. I installed a gas generator in my third year, but didn't get round to having the cottage winterized, or putting up the out-buildings and boat-house until Miriam and I were married. I maintain the elaborate tree house, where the kids used to play, to this day. For my grandchildren, perhaps.

Agitated, I now began to stride up and down my living-room floor. Somebody was coming to interview me at eleven, but I could no longer remember who. Or why. I had left myself a Post-It note, but now I couldn't find it. Yesterday, seated in my Volvo, preparing to turn into Decarie, I was suddenly at a loss as to how to gear down to third. Pulling over to the curb, I rested, then rammed the clutch home, and practised shifting gears.

Wait. I've got it. The young woman coming to see me is the hostess of "Dykes on Mikes," on McGill University's student radio, and is working on a Ph.D. thesis about Clara. This will not mark the first time I have been interrogated about her. There have been visits, or letters of inquiry, from feminists as far afield as Tel Aviv, Melbourne, Cape Town, and that city in Germany where Hitler led the march on parliament. You know, the British prime minister with the umbrella was there. Peace in our time is what he promised. Damn damn damn. It's the city where they have the famous beer festival. Pilsner? Molson's? No. It sounds like the name of the little people in *The Wizard of Oz*. Or like that painting of "The Shout"[2] by . . . by Munch. *Munich*. Anyway my point is, the martyred Saint Clara's admirers are legion, and have two things in common: they take me for an abomination and fail to understand that Clara intensely disliked other women, whom she considered rivals for the male attention she thrived on.

Hanging over my mantelpiece to this day is one of Clara's overcrowded, tortured pen-and-ink drawings. It depicts a gang-rape of virgins. An orgy. Gargoyles and goblins at play. The chortling satyr drawn in my image clutches a nude Clara by the hair. She is on her knees and I am forcing myself into her open mouth, taking advantage of her scream. I have been offered as much as $250,000

---

[2] "The Scream".

for this charming tableau, but nothing could make me part with it. Appearances to the contrary, I'm really a sentimental old coot.

And now I prepared myself for a visit from what Rush Limbaugh has dubbed a feminazi. Probably wearing a nose-stud and nipple-rings and knuckle-dusters. A German army helmet. Shitkicker boots. Instead, I opened my door to an awfully demure young thing, a mere wisp of a girl, chestnut hair not crew-cut but flowing; smiling sweetly she was, wearing granny glasses, a Laura Ashley dress, and dainty pumps. She immediately endeared herself to me by admiring the photographs of tap-dance immortals which line my walls: Willy "Pickaninny" Coven, creator of the Rhythm Waltz; Peg Leg Bates, caught in mid-flight; The Nicholas Brothers, of Cotton Club fame; Ralph Brown; the young James, Gene, and Fred Kelly in their bellhop uniforms, photographed at the Nixon Theatre in Pittsburgh in 1920; and, of course, the great Bill "Bojangles" Robinson, shown wearing his top hat, white tie, and tails, *circa* 1932. Ms. Morgan set up her tape recorder and produced a sheaf of questions, softening me up with the usual – "How did you meet Clara?" "What attracted you to her?" et cetera et cetera – before she fired her first missile. "In all the accounts I have read, it seems that you were indifferent to Clara's great gifts as a poet and a painter, and did nothing to encourage her."

Amused, I tried to get a rise out of Ms. Morgan. "Let me remind you of what Marike de Klerk, wife of South Africa's former prime minister, once said in church. 'Women are unimportant. We're here to serve, to heal the wounds, to give love –' "

"Oh, you're such a card," she said.

" 'If a woman inspires a man to be good,' said Madame de Klerk, 'he is good.' Let's say, if only for argument's sake, that Clara failed to fill that office."

"And you failed Clara?"

"What happened was inevitable."

Clara was terrified of fire. "We live on the fifth floor," she said. "We wouldn't have a chance." Unexpected knocks on our hotel-room door made her freeze, so friends learned to announce themselves first. "It's Leo," or "It's the Boogie man. Put all your valuables into a bag and pass them through the door." Rich food made her vomit. She suffered from insomnia. But, given sufficient wine, she would sleep, a mixed blessing because that prompted nightmares from which she would waken trembling. She didn't trust strangers and was even more suspicious of friends. She was allergic to shellfish, eggs, animal fur, dust, and anybody indifferent to her presence. Her periods brought on headaches, cramps, nausea, and vile temper. She endured lengthy attacks of eczema. She kept a plugged earthenware jug under our window, a Bellarmino, filled with her own urine and fingernail clippings, to throw back evil spells. She feared cats. Heights scared her. Thunder petrified her. She was frightened of water, snakes, spiders, and other people.

Reader, I married her.

Given that I was a horny twenty-three-year-old at the time, it wasn't because Clara was such a sexual wildcat. Our romance, such as it was, was not enriched by abandon between the sheets. Clara, the compulsive flirt and dirty talker, turned out to be as prudish with me, in any event, as the mother she professed to abhor, denying me what she denigrated as my "thirty seconds of friction" time and again. Or enduring them. Or did her utmost to stifle any joy we might have salvaged out of our increasingly rare and frustrating couplings. After all these years, it's her admonitions that I remember.

"I want you to scrub it with soap and hot water first and then don't you dare come inside me."

She condescended to fellate me once, and was immediately sick to her stomach in the sink. Humiliated, I dressed in silence, quit the room, and tramped along the *quais* as far as the Place de la Bastille and back again. On my return, I discovered that she had packed a suitcase and was sitting on the bed, hunched over, shivering, in spite of wearing layers of her shawls. "I would have been gone before you got back," she said, "but I'm going to need money for another room somewhere."

Why didn't I let her go, while I could still have managed it with impunity? Why did I take her in my arms, rocking her even as she sobbed, undressing her, easing her into bed, stroking her until she slipped her thumb into her mouth and began to breathe evenly?

I sat by her bedside for the remainder of the night, chain-smoking, reading that novel about the Golem of Prague, by what's-his-name, Kafka's friend, and early in the morning I went to the market to fetch her an orange, a croissant, and a yoghurt for breakfast.

"You're the only man who ever peeled an orange for me," she said, already working on the first line of the poem that is now in so many anthologies. "You're not going to throw me out, are you?" she asked in her little girl's Mother-may-I-take-a-step voice.

"No."

"You still love your crazy Clara, don't you?"

"I honestly don't know."

Exhausted as I was, why didn't I give her money right then, and help her move into another hotel?

My problem is, I am unable to get to the bottom of things. I don't mind not understanding other people's motives, not any more, but why don't I understand why *I* do things?

In the days that followed, Clara couldn't have been more contrite, docile, ostensibly loving, encouraging me in bed, her simulated ardour betrayed by her tense, unyielding body. "That was good. So wonderful," she'd say. "I needed you inside me."

Like fuck she did. But, arguably, I needed her. Don't underestimate the nursing sister longing to leap out of somebody even as cantankerous as I am. Looking after Clara made me feel noble. Mother Teresa Panofsky. Dr. Barney Schweitzer.

Scribbling away here and now at my roll-top desk at two in the morning in twenty below zero Montreal, pulling on a Montecristo, trying to impose sense on my incomprehensible past, unable to pardon my sins by claiming youth and innocence, I can still summon up in my mind's eye those moments with Clara that I cherish to this day. She was an inspired tease, and could make me laugh at myself, a gift not to be underestimated. I loved our moments of shared tranquillity. Me, lying on our bed in that box of a hotel room, pretending to read, but actually watching Clara at her work table. Fidgety, neurotic Clara totally at ease. Concentrating. Rapt. Her face cleansed of its often disfiguring turbulence. I was inordinately proud of the high esteem others, more knowledgeable than I, had for her drawings and published poems. I anticipated a future as her guardian. I would provide her with the wherewithal to get on with her work, liberated from mundane concerns. I would take her back to America and build her a studio in the countryside with northern light and a fire escape. I would protect her from thunder, snakes, animal fur, and evil spells. Eventually, I would bask in her fame, playing a dutiful Leonard to her inspired Virginia.

But, in our case, I would be ever watchful, safeguarding her against a mad walk into the water, her pockets weighed down with rocks. Yossel Pinsky, the Holocaust survivor who would become my partner, had met Clara a couple of times, and was skeptical. "You're not a nice man any more than I am," he said, "so why try? She's a *meshugena*. Ditch her before it's too late."

But it was already too late.

"I SUPPOSE YOU want me to have an abortion," she said.

"Hold on a minute," I said. "Let me think." I'm twenty-three years old is what I thought. Christ Almighty. "I'm going out for a walk. I won't be long."

She was sick again in the sink while I was out and, on my return, she was dozing. Three o'clock in the afternoon and Clara, the insomniac, was in a deep sleep. I cleaned up as best I could and an hour passed before she got out of bed. "So there you are," she said. "My hero."

"I could speak to Yossel. He would find us somebody."

"Or he could manage it himself with a coat hanger. Only I've already decided I'm going to have the baby. With you or without you."

"If you're going to have the baby I suppose I should marry you."

"Some proposal."

"I'm only mentioning it as a possibility."

Clara curtsied. "Why, thank you, Prince Charmingbaum," she said, and then she hurried out of our room and down the stairs.

Boogie was adamant. "What do you mean, it's your responsibility?"

"Well, it is, isn't it?"

"You're crazier than she is. Make her have an abortion."

That evening I searched for Clara everywhere, and finally found her seated alone at La Coupole. I leaned over and kissed her on the forehead. "I've decided to marry you," I said.

"Gee whiz. Wow. Don't I even get to say yes or no?"

"We could consult your I Ching, if you like?"

"My parents won't come. They would be mortified. *Mrs.* Panofsky. Sounds like a furrier's wife. Or maybe the owner of a clothing store. Everything wholesale."

I found us a fifth-floor apartment on the rue Notre-Dame-des-Champs, converted from four *chambres de bonne*, and we were married at the *mairie* in the *sixième*. The bride wore a cloche hat, a ridiculous veil, an ankle-length black wool dress, and a white ostrich feather boa. Asked if she would take me as her lawfully wedded husband, a stoned Clara winked at the official, and said, "I've got a bun in the oven. What would you do?" Boogie and Yossel were both in attendance and there were gifts. A bottle of Dom Pérignon, four ounces of hashish implanted in knitted blue booties from Boogie; a set of six Hôtel George V sheets and bath towels from Yossel; a signed sketch and a dozen diapers from Leo; and an autographed copy of *Merlin*, featuring his first published story, from Terry McIver.

Making the arrangements for the wedding, I finally got a peek at Clara's passport, and was startled to discover the name on it was Charnofsky. "Don't worry," she said. "You caught yourself a blue-blood *shiksa*. But when I was nineteen I ran off with him and we were married in Mexico. My art teacher. Charnofsky. It only lasted three months, but it cost me my trust fund. My father disinherited me."

Once we moved into our apartment, Clara began to stay up into the early morning hours, scribbling in her notebooks or concentrating on her nightmarish ink drawings. Then she slept in until two or three in the afternoon, slipped out of our apartment, and was not seen again until evening when she would join our table at the Mabillon or Café Sélect, her manner delinquent.

"As a matter of interest, Mrs. Panofsky, where were you all afternoon?"

"I don't remember. Walking, I suppose." And then, digging into her voluminous skirts, she would say, "I brought you a gift," and would hand me a tin of pâté de foie gras, a pair of socks and, on one occasion, a sterling silver cigarette lighter. "If it's a boy," she said, "I'm going to call him Ariel."

"Now that comes trippingly off the tongue," said Boogie. "Ariel Panofsky."

"I vote for Othello," said Leo, his smile sly.

"Fuck you, Leo," said Clara, her eyes hot, suffering one of her unaccountable but increasingly frequent mood changes. Then she turned on me. "Maybe Shylock would be most appropriate, all things considered?"

Surprisingly, once Clara was over her morning sickness, playing house together turned out to be fun. We shopped for kitchenware and bought a crib. Clara made a mobile to hang over it and painted rabbits and chipmunks and owls on the walls of our nursery. I did the cooking, of course. Spaghetti bolognese, *the pasta strained with a colander*. Chopped chicken liver salad. And, my *pièce de résistance*, breaded veal chops garnished with potato latkes and apple sauce. Boogie, Leo with one or another of his girls, and Yossel often came to dinner, and once even Terry McIver, but Clara refused to tolerate Cedric, who had failed to appear at our wedding. "Why not?" I asked.

"Never mind. I just don't want him here."

She also objected to Yossel.

"He has a bad aura. He doesn't like me. And I want to know what you two are up to."

So I settled her on the sofa and brought her a glass of wine. "I've got to go to Canada," I said.

"*What?*"

"I'll only be gone for three weeks. A month at most. Yossel will bring you money every week."

"You're not coming back."

"Clara, don't start."

"Why Canada?"

"Yossel and I are going into the cheese-export business together."

"You're joking. The cheese business. It's too embarrassing. Clara, you were married in Paris, weren't you? Yes. To a writer or a painter? No, a cheese fucking salesman."

"It's money."

"You would think of that. I'll go crazy all alone here. I want you to get me a padlock for the door. What if there's a fire?"

"Or an earthquake?"

"Maybe you'll do so well with the cheese that you'll send for me in Canada and we could join a golf club, if they have them there yet, and invite people in to play bridge. Or mah-jong. I'm not becoming a member of any synagogue ladies fucking auxiliary and Ariel's not going to be circumcised. I won't allow it."

I managed to register a company in Montreal, open an office, and hire an old schoolfriend, Arnie Rosenbaum, to run it, all within three febrile weeks. And Clara grew accustomed, even seemed to look forward to, my flying to Montreal every six weeks, providing I returned laden with jars of peanut butter, some Oreos, and at least two dozen packs of Lowney's Glosette Raisins. It was during my absences that she wrote, and illustrated with ink drawings, most of *The Virago's Verse Book*, now in its twenty-eighth printing. It includes the poem dedicated to "Barnabus P." That touching tribute which begins,

> he peeled my orange and more often me,
> > > Calibanovitch,
> my keeper.

I was in Montreal, hustling, and Clara was into her seventh month, when Boogie tracked me down in my room at the Mount Royal Hotel early one morning.

"I think you had better answer it," said Abigail, the wife of my old schoolfriend who managed our Montreal office.

Boogie said, "You better grab the first flight back."

I landed at oh whatever in the hell that airport was called before it became de Gaulle[3] at seven a.m. the following morning, and made right for The American Hospital. "I'm here to see Mrs. Panofsky."

"Are you a relative?"

"Her husband."

A young intern, contemplating his clipboard, looked up and regarded me with sudden interest.

"Dr. Mallory would like to have a word with you first," said the receptionist.

I took an instant dislike to Dr. Mallory, a portly man with a fringe of grey hair who radiated self-regard and had obviously never treated a patient worthy of his skills. He invited me to sit down and

_____

[3] Charles de Gaulle airport never existed under any other name. The airport referred to is doubtless Le Bourget.

told me that the baby had been stillborn, but Mrs. Panofsky, a healthy young woman, would certainly be able to bear other children. His smile facetious, he added, "Of course I'm telling you this, because I take it you are the father."

He seemed to wait on my response.

"Yes."

"In that case," said Dr. Mallory, flipping his colourful braces, his riposte obviously rehearsed, "you must be an albino."

Taking in the news, my heart thudding, I delivered Dr. Mallory what I hoped was my most menacing look. "I'll catch up with you later."

I found Clara in a maternity ward with seven other women, several of whom were nursing newly born babes. She must have lost a good deal of blood. Pale as chalk she was. "Every four hours," she said, "they attach clamps to my nipples and squeeze out the milk like I was a cow. Have you seen Dr. Mallory?"

"Yes."

" 'You people,' he said to me. 'You people.' Brandishing that poor, wizened dead thing at me as if it had slid out of a sewer."

"He told me I could take you home tomorrow morning," I said, surprised at how steady my voice was. "I'll come by early."

"I didn't trick you. I swear, Barney. I was sure the baby was yours."

"How in the hell could you be so sure?"

"It was just once and we were both stoned."

"Clara, we seem to have an attentive audience here. I'll come for you tomorrow morning."

"I won't be here."

Dr. Mallory was not in his office. But two first-class airplane tickets to Venice and a confirmation slip for reservations at the Gritti Palace sat on his desk. I copied the number of the hotel reservation slip, hurried over to the nearest Bureau de Poste, and booked a call to the Gritti Palace. "This is Dr. Vincent Mallory speaking. I wish to cancel tomorrow night's reservations."

There was a pause while the desk clerk flipped through his file. "For the entire five days?" he asked.

"Yes."

"In that case, I'm afraid you will lose your deposit, sir."

"Why, you cheap little mafioso, that doesn't surprise me," I said, and hung up.

Boogie, my inspiration, would be proud of me. That master prankster had played far worse tricks on people, I thought, beginning to wander aimlessly. Raging. Murder in my heart. I ended up, God knows how, in a café on the rue Scribe, where I ordered a double "Johnnie Walkair." Lighting one Gauloise off another, I was surprised to discover Terry McIver ensconced at a table in the rear of the café with an over-dressed older woman who was wearing too much make-up. Take it from me, his "pleasingly pretty" Héloise was squat, a dumpling, puffy-faced, with more than a hint of moustache. Catching my eye, equally startled, Terry withdrew her multi-ringed hand from his knee, whispered something to her, and ambled over to my table. "She's Marie-Claire's boring aunt," he said, sighing.

"Marie-Claire's affectionate aunt, I'd say."

"Oh, she's in such a state," he whispered. "Her Pekinese was run over this morning. Imagine. You look awful. Anything wrong?"

"Everything's wrong, but I'd rather not go into it. You're not fucking that old bag?"

"Damn you," he hissed. "She understands English. She's Marie-Claire's aunt."

"Okay. Right. Now beat it, McIver."

But he did not leave without a parting shot. "And in future," he said, "I'd take it as a kindness if you didn't follow me."

McIver and "Marie-Claire's aunt" quit the café without finishing their drinks and drove off *not* in an Austin-Healey but in a less than new Ford Escort.[4] Liar, liar, liar that McIver.

I ordered another double Johnny Walkair and then went in search of Cedric. I found him in his favourite café, the one frequented by the *Paris Review* crowd as well as Richard Wright, the Café le Tournon, high on the rue Tournon. "Cedric, old buddy of mine, we've got to talk," I said, taking his arm, and starting to propel him out of the café.

"We can talk right here," he said, yanking his arm free, and directing me to a table in the corner.

"Let me buy you a drink," I said.

---

[4] The Ford Escort did not go into production until 1968.

He ordered a *vin rouge* and I asked for a Scotch. "You know," I said, "years ago my Daddy once told me that the worst thing that could happen to a man is to lose a child. What do you think, man?"

"You've got something to say to me, spit it out, *man*."

"Yes. Quite right. But I'm afraid it's bad news, Cedric. You lost a son yesterday. My wife's. And I am here to offer condolences."

"Shit."

"Yeah."

"I had no idea."

"That makes two of us."

"What if it wasn't mine either?"

"Now there's an intriguing thought."

"I'm sorry, Barney."

"Me too."

"Now do you mind if I ask you a question?"

"Shoot."

"Why in the hell did you marry Clara in the first place?"

"Because she was pregnant and I thought it was my duty to my unborn child. My turn now."

"Go ahead."

"Were you screwing her after as well as before? We were married, I mean."

"What did she say?"

"I'm asking you."

"Shit."

"I thought we were friends."

"What's that got to do with it?"

Then I heard myself saying, "That's where I draw the line. Fooling around with the wife of a friend. I could never do that."

He ordered another round and this time I insisted that we click glasses. "After all," I said, "this is an occasion, don't you think?"

"What are you going to do about Clara now?"

"How about I turn her over to you, Daddy-o?"

"Nancy wouldn't dig that. Three in a bed. Not my scene. But I do thank you for the offer."

"It was sincerely meant."

"I appreciate that."

"Actually, I think it was awfully white of me to make such an offer."

"Hey, Barney, baby, you don't want to mess with a bad nigger like me. I might pull a shiv on you."

"Hadn't thought of that. Let's have another drink instead."

When the *patronne* brought over our glasses, I stood up unsteadily and raised mine. "To Mrs. Panofsky," I said, "with gratitude for the pleasure she has given both of us."

"Sit down before you fall down."

"Good idea." Then I began to shake. Swallowing the boulder rising in my gorge, I said, "I honestly don't know what to do now, Cedric. Maybe I should hit you."

"Goddamn it, Barney, I hate to tell you this, but I wasn't the only one."

"Oh."

"Didn't you know that much?"

"No."

"She's insatiable."

"Not with me she wasn't."

"Maybe we ought to order a couple of coffees, then you can hit me if it will make you feel better."

"I need another Scotch."

"Okay. Now listen to your Uncle Remus. You're only twenty-three years old and she's a nut-case. Shake her loose. Divorce her."

"You ought to see her. She's lost lots of blood. She looks awful."

"So do you."

"I'm afraid of what she might do to herself."

"Clara's a lot tougher than you think."

"Was it you who made those scratches on her back?"

"What?"

"Somebody else then."

"It's over. Finito. Give her a week to get her shit together and then tell her."

"Cedric," I said, breaking into a sweat, "everything's spinning. I'm going to be sick. Get me into the john. Quick."

ELEVEN

THE intense, hennaed Solange Renault, who had once played Catherine in *Henry V* at our Stratford, was obliged to settle long ago for the continuing role of the French-Canadian settlement nurse in my "McIver of the RCMP" series.

(Private joke. I often request the weekly script that's to be sent to Solange, and rewrite some of her lines for her amusement.

NURSE SIMARD: By Gar, de wind she blow lak 'ell out dere tonight. Be careful de h'ice, everybody.

Or NURSE SIMARD: Look dere, h'it's Fadder St.-Pierre 'oo comes 'ere. Better lock up de alcool and mind it your h'arses, guys.)

Actually, I have made it my business to find work for Solange in just about everything done by Totally Unnecessary Productions Ltd., going back to the seventies. Sixty something years old now, still nervously thin, she persists in dressing like an ingenue but otherwise is the most admirable of women. Her husband, a gifted set designer, was taken out by a massive heart attack in his early thirties, and Solange has brought up, and seen to the education of her daughter, the indomitable Chantal, my personal assistant. Saturday nights, providing the new, improved, no-talent, chicken-shit Canadiens are in town, each one a multi-millionaire, Solange and I eat an early dinner at Pauzé's, and then repair to the Forum, where once *nos glorieux* were just about invincible. My God, I remember when all they had to do was to leap over the boards in those red-and-white sweaters and the visiting team was a goner. Those, those were the days. Fire-wagon hockey. Soft but accurate passes. Fast as lightning wrist shots. Defencemen who could hit. And no ear-piercing rock music played at 10,000 decibels, while a face-off was held up for a TV commercial.

Anyway it now seems that my traditional if increasingly exasperating Saturday night out with Solange is threatened. I'm told I behaved like a hooligan again last Saturday night, embarrassing her. My alleged offence happened during the third period. The effete Canadiens, already down 4–1 to the Ottawa Senators, for Christ's sake, were on their so-called power play, scrambly, a minute gone and yet to manage a shot on the nets. Savage, that idiot, passed to an open wing, enabling a slo-mo Ottawa defenceman, a journeyman who would have been lucky to make the QSHL in the old days, to ice the puck. Turgeon collected it, glided to centre ice, and golfed it into the corner, Damphousse, and Savage scrambling after, throwing up snow just short of the mêlée. "Goddamn that Turgeon," I hollered, "with his contract, he's earning something like $100,000 a goal, Beliveau was never paid more than $50,000[1] for the whole season and he wasn't afraid to carry the puck over the blue line."

"Yes, I know," said Solange, rolling her eyes. "And Doug Harvey never made more than $15,000 a year here."

"I told you that. You didn't know it."

"I'm not denying you told me that, I don't know how many times. Now will you please be quiet and stop making an exhibition of yourself."

"Look at that! Nobody parked in front of the net, because he might have to take an elbow. We'll be lucky if Ottawa doesn't score another short-handed goal. Shit! Fuck!"

"Barney, please."

"They ought to trade Koivu for another Finnish midget," I said, joining in the chorus of boos.

A no-name Senator hopped out of the penalty box, gathered in the puck, skated in all alone on our petrified goalie, who naturally went down too soon, and lifted one over his blocker arm. 5–1 Ottawa. Disgusted fans began to cheer the visitors. Programs were thrown on the ice. I yanked off my rubbers and aimed them at Turgeon.

"Barney, control yourself."

"Shettup."

"I beg your pardon?"

"How am I supposed to concentrate on the game with your non-stop chattering?"

The game was almost over before I noticed that a touchy Solange had quit her seat. Ottawa won 7–3. I retreated to Dink's, grieving over a couple of Macallans before I called Solange. But it was Chantal who answered the phone. "I want to speak to your mother," I said.

---

[1] In 1970–71, his last season with the Canadiens, Beliveau was actually paid $100,000.

"She doesn't want to speak to you."

"She behaved childishly tonight. Walking out on me. I lost my rubbers, and tripped on the ice outside and almost broke a leg before I found a taxi. Did you watch the game on TV?"

"Yes."

"That prick Savard never should have traded Chelios. If your mother won't come to the phone, I'm getting into a taxi and I'll be at your place in five minutes. She owes me an apology."

"We won't answer the door."

"You make me sick, both of you."

Guilt-ridden, and late as it was, there was nothing for it but for me to phone Kate to tell her how badly I had behaved. "What do I do now?" I asked.

"Send flowers first thing tomorrow morning."

But flowers were for Miriam, and to send them to anybody else, Solange included, would amount to a betrayal. "I think not," I said.

"Chocolates?"

"Kate, are you busy tomorrow?"

"Not especially. Why?"

"What if I flew in for the day and the two of us went out for a bang-up lunch."

"In The Prince Arthur Room?"

Even after all these years, I choked up.

"Daddy, are you there?"

"Book us a table at Prego's."

"May I bring Gavin?"

Damn damn damn. "Sure," I said, but early Sunday morning I cancelled out. "I'm not up to it today, darling. Maybe next week."

Monday morning, if only to demonstrate to my employees that I'm not yet totally dispensable, and can still do more than sign cheques, I went into the office, where Chantal immediately greeted me with bad news. Our latest, godawful expensive pilot was rich in meaningful, life-enhancing action: gay smooching, visible minority nice guys, car chases ending in mayhem, rape, murder, a soupçon of S & M, and a dab of New Age idiocies. I had hoped it would fill CBC-TV's nine p.m. Thursday slot but we had lost out to an even more appalling series to be produced by The Amigos Three bunch in Toronto. It was the second time this year that *goniff* Bobby Tarlis, who ran Amigos Three, had done us in. Worse news. Suddenly the once puissant "McIver of the RCMP" series was slipping in the ratings, and CBS was threatening to drop it. This prompted a visit to my office by my Trinity of Twits: Gabe Orlansky, story editor, accompanied by executive producer Marty Klein, and director Serge Lacroix. An apprehensive Chantal trailed after them, notebook in hand. The Trinity agreed we had to goose up the cast for openers. Case in point. Solange Renault, who had played the settlement nurse since the series began eight years earlier, was now far too old. "She could be killed off," said Gabe.

"Then what?" I asked, coming to the boil.

"Do you ever take in 'Baywatch'?"

"You mean we're going to have bimbos in handkerchief-size bikinis frolicking in the snow North of Sixty?"

"I think we've got a consensus here, among your creative people, that we need a new nurse," said Gabe. "So I want you to look at these."

"I hope you're not screwing her, Gabe. Three months after a triple bypass. Shame on you."

"We've got to shake things up, Barney. Get rid of the deadwood. I had a focus group look at two new episodes and the character they found least simpatico was played by Solange."

"Speaking of deadwood, before Solange goes, all of you get the chop. Furthermore, I'm going to ask Solange to direct at least two episodes this season."

"What are her qualifications?" asked Serge.

"She's literate. And, unlike any of you here, suffers from good taste. So, arguably, she's overqualified, but my mind's made up. Now look here, our problem is not Solange, but hackneyed storylines. How about something unpredictable for a change? Say, an ignoble Eskimo. Or an ostensibly sage Indian medicine man who makes his predictions based on *The Farmer's Almanack*? Hey, I've got it. Now that Sikh RCMP recruits are allowed to wear turbans, how about a new RCMP corporal, a Jew who wears a yarmulke, accepts bribes, and bargains at the Hudson's Bay store? Now scoot, all of you, and I want to see some fresh scripts soon. Like yesterday."

Chantal lingered behind. "I'm afraid they're right about Solange."

"Of course they're right, but she's your mother, for Christ's sake, and she'll drive us both crazy if she isn't acting. That's all she lives for. You know that."

"Are you really going to ask her to direct?"

"Don't try to anticipate me. Oh, and Chantal, I really can't bring myself to read any of those scripts. You're the one who's going to have to do it for me. And would you please ask Gabe for those photographs," I said, avoiding her gaze. "I think I'd better have another look."

Next I started on the in-tray of unsolicited mail that Chantal had left me.

Dhaka, Sept. 21, 1995

Sir,

With great respect I beg to state I shall remain ever grateful if you yourself kindly read and respond to my following humble appeal. I am Khandakar Shahryer Sultan, a Bangladeshi student. I lost my mother in her childhood and since then I had to strugle much. Despite much problem I have got graduation degree in English studies from Dhaka University.

I have been desirous and trying much for many years to go to Canada or such any country to study the art of television, which in you excel. But I am undone. I have none here to help me to go abroad.

So I have been writing to many great persons like you in different countries for some help. I'd like to study in your country if you can convince a University or some quarter for a scholarship and it would be best for me. If you like I shall stay with your family and serve you as possible.

If you are not able to do so, yet kindly send me some donation ($50 or $100 or as is possible) for the collection of necessary money in order to go to Canada for education. Many have sent me some and thus I have collected much. I hope I will be able to collect necessary money soon and my dream will come true. So don't forget to send some.

If you send bank-note or draft cheque, make the envelope untransparent send it with *guaranteed* mail. Account No. 20784, Sonali Bank, Dilusha Branch, Dhaka. Or INTERNATIONAL MONEY ORDER is the best way.

I am awaiting your kind response. I beg your pardon for any wrong.

Sincerely,
Khandakar Shahtyer Sultan

Totally Unnecessary Productions Ltd.
1300 Sherbrooke St. West
Montreal, QUE H3G 1J4 Canada
Oct. 5, 1995

From the Desk of Barney Panofsky
Dear Mr. Sultan,

I have, as requested, sent an international money order for $200 in an untransparent envelope, to Account No. 20784, Sonali Bank, Dilusha Branch, Dhaka.

I have also discussed your case with the incomparably rich Professor Blair Hopper, Victoria College, University of Toronto, Toronto, Ont., Canada, and he is eager to hear from you. However, it would be best if you did not mention my name in your correspondence with the esteemed professor.

Sincerely,
Barney Panofsky

P.S. The professor's home phone number is 416 819 2427 and he won't mind if you call collect at any hour of the day or night.

There was also a letter from The Great Antonio.

LIVING LEGEND GREATEST OF THE GREAT HUMAN STRENGTH AT 510 LBS., 225 KILOS, STRONGEST MAN IN THE WORLD. PREHISTORIC MAN STRONG LIKE 10 HORSES. PULLING 4 BUSES TIED TOGETHER WITH A CHAIN, WEIGHT 70 TONS FOR 2200 FEET IN FRONT OF N.B.C. TELEVISION. OVER FIVE MILLION PEOPLE CAME TO SEE THE GREAT ANTONIO IN TOKYO.

The Great Antonio, a Montrealer, was considerate enough to enclose an idea for a feature film with his letter.

BY THE GREAT ANTONIO MOTION PICTURE STORY —
NO. 1

The Great Antonio is very popular and impression the whole world.
1. Antonio pulling 4 buses 70 tons – World Record.

2. Hold with his hands 10 horses.
3. Pull by his hair 400 people.
4. One Championship Wrestling match.
5. Also Love Story drama with an actress.
6. Reconciliation.
7. Finish with big parade in front of millions and millions of people. Downtown mainstreet of Tokyo, New York, also Rio de Janeiro, Paris, London, Rome, Montreal, and all major cities in the world.

The Great Antonio arouses the curiosity of the whole world. The film will be big record success because all the people of the world like to see The Great Antonio. The film will cost one hundred million dollars, and will take two years to make. It will bring in between five and ten billion dollars. Everybody in the world wants to see The Great Antonio with his mysterious strength. The Great Antonio is invincible. The Great Antonio write the story and will direct The Great Antonio film.

THE GREAT ANTONIO REAL GOLDEN MINE.

Totally Unnecessary Productions Ltd.
1300 Sherbrooke St. West
Montreal, QUE H3G 1J4 Canada
Oct. 5, 1995

From the Desk of Barney Panofsky

Dear Great Antonio,

It is with deep sorrow that I must turn down your block-buster idea, the most exciting I've seen in years, but ours is too modest a production company to do justice to it, and it would be selfish of us to hold you up. However, I have had a word with my good friend Bobby Tarlis, of the Amigos Three Company in Toronto, and I have never heard him so enthusi-astic about a project before.

In the fond hope that I can be a midwife to this amazing venture, I am enclosing a cheque for $600 to cover your return airfare to Toronto, and other incidental expenses. The Amigos Three address in Toronto is 33 Yonge St. Don't bother to phone ahead. Bobby is expecting you. The sooner the better, he said. Oh, and I'm going to let you in on a little secret. Bobby is the former Hungarian amateur wrestling champion, and he has bet me a considerable sum that he can take you two falls out of three. I'm betting on you, Antonio, so don't fail me. Immediately you enter his office, try him on a drop-kick. He'd love that. Good luck.

Respectfully,
Barney Panofsky

At five p.m. I looked in at Dink's and lingered too long at the bar, moving on with Hughes-McNoughton and Zack Keeler, the *Gazette* columnist, to Jumbo's and, in the early morning hours, to a blind pig that Zack knew. Sean O'Hearne once told me, "In the old days, when we wanted to know where the illegal booze boxes were, we used to sit in our unmarked car waiting for Zack to stumble out of Jumbo's, and then we'd follow him to wherever he was heading. Bastard always had a nice bit of stuff with him. How does he do it, eh?"

"He does it," I said, "by being an uncommonly attractive man. Astute. Witty. Things beyond your grasp."

But that evening Zack, just back from a quick trip to Toronto, a gig on CBC-TV, got on my nerves. He had run into Miriam and Blair at a party. "You'd have us believe Blair's an unredeemed bore. Okay, levity is not his problem. But I liked him. If he was such a nerd, what would a woman like Miriam be doing with him?"

"How was she?"

"In terrific form. You know, very funny in that understated way of hers. But she isn't wild about Saul's new girlfriend. 'He's drinking out of a used cup,' she said. And she even worries about you. Your children say you're drinking too much. Shame on you."

It must have been four a.m. when I got home, two hands required to fit my apartment key in the lock, but I woke up early all the same, adjudging Tuesday a write-off. So I decided to show the Daddy flag, devoting my day to doing a round-up of the Panofsky progeny. I started with Mike. His secretary said the family had gone to Normandy for the weekend. The weekend? It was only Tuesday. A long weekend, she said. A British weekend. Next I rang Saul.

"Oh, my God, it's not even noon yet. I knew it had to be you. Call back later, please, Daddy."

"I recognize that gruff smoker's voice. You've been out late drinking again, haven't you?"

"Coming from you – "

"Now look here, I'm no prude. I have never objected to drinking, *but in moderation.*"

"I was up late last night reading the autobiography of Geronimo. Hey, the Apaches may be one of the lost tribes. Geronimo never ate bacon or pork. A tribal taboo. When his father died, the Apaches slew his horse and gave away all his other property. The Apaches never keep any of the riches of a dead relative. Their unwritten tribal law forbids it, because they fear that otherwise the children of a wealthy man might be glad when their father died. Give away the kid and kaboodle, Daddy. It would drive Caroline crazy."

"Saul, I hate to be a nag, but have you spoken to Kate recently?"

"So that she could subtly suggest what a failure I am, living as I do?"

"She adores you."

"Yeah, sure. Incidentally I'm not sending Mike any more of my articles. Months go by and he still hasn't got round to reading them. He pretends to be a vegetarian, if only to please her ladyship, but when he was in New York last week, and went out to dinner, it had to be the Palm, where he could dig into a huge steak. And he went out of his way to bait Aviva."

"Aviva?"

"She's an Israeli. Writes for the *Jerusalem Post* now that it's no longer an apologist for Arafat. So naturally he went on compulsively about how much he contributes to Peace Now, and the plight of the Palestinians. Never mind that her brother had been killed in a terrorist attack."

"Is that who you're living with these days?"

"I was listening to Glenn Gould's recording of 'The Goldberg Variations' yesterday and she starts filing her nails. She'd get up early and clip things she needed out of my copy of the *Times,* and when I finally got to the breakfast table, there were all these windows in the paper. So I had to kick her out. Say, when are you coming down here to spend a few days with me again?"

"Hey, last time we really had fun, didn't we?"

"Come clean. You adore Mike but consider me inadequate, and the sub-text of your always asking me who I'm living with – "

"You drink out of too many used cups, kid."

" – is that I'm not capable of a mature relationship."

"Would you really like me to visit again?"

"Yeah. And I did speak to Kate last week. We quarrelled. I just happen to know Mom had them to dinner the night before and Kate was gratuitously rude to Blair."

"Why, that's terrible. I won't have any of you taking sides. Blair may be a bit young for your mother, but he makes her happy and that ought to be good enough for the rest of us. He also happens to be a man devoted to many good causes. Like Greenpeace."

"Come off it, Daddy. You hate his guts. What did you think of my latest piece in the *American Spectator*?"

"I thought it was misinformed and bigoted, but, hey, you sure can put a spin on words."

"That's my old man. Sorry. Got to run now. Natasha is taking me to lunch at the Union Square Café."

"Natasha?"

"Why don't you marry Solange?"

"I'm too fond of her to do that. Besides, you know what the American courts have ordained? Two strikes and you're out.[2] Would you really like me to come to New York again soon?"

"Yes. Oh, something I forgot to mention. The *Washington Times* has sent me *Of Time and Fevers* for review."

"You mean somebody is actually going to publish McIver's crap in New York?"

"Easy now."

"Don't misunderstand. I wouldn't stoop to trying to influence you. Go ahead and review it. Praise it to the skies. It's your reputation, not mine. Goodbye now."

My first-born son thinks nothing of giving away a box of Cohibas I brought him and now Saul is willing to betray me for maybe $250. Some family I nourished. After I had calmed down with a couple of fingers of Cardhu, I lit a Montecristo and phoned Kate. "Am I calling at the wrong time?" I asked.

---

[2] Three strikes.

"Daddy, I was just about to phone you."

"Kate, it has been reported to me that your mother had you and Gavin to dinner recently and you went out of your way to be rude to Blair."

"Oh, he's always touching her at the table. It makes me want to puke."

"Darling, I know how you feel, but you mustn't do anything to hurt your mother. Besides, Blair has always been good to you and the boys. Obviously he was incapable of having children of his own, which could have something to do with it. *Touching her where at the table?*"

"Oh, you know. Holding her hand. Stroking her arm. Kissing her cheek when he gets up to refill her wine glass. Icky stuff like that."

"Now I'm going to tell you something, but you must never repeat it. Poor Blair is one of those men who has always felt insecure about his masculinity, and that's why he feels obliged to make public displays of his affection for your mother."

"I suppose Mom complained to Saul, who was always her pet – "

"I think he reminds her of me, when I was still young enough for her."

" – and he blabbed to you. Oh, I'm so angry with Saul. We had words."

"Saul adores you. He insists I come to New York again soon. How about that?"

"You come to see us first. Please, Daddy. Gavin will take you to a hockey game."

"*The Maple Leafs?*"

"You ought to hire him to handle your taxes, he's such a whiz, and he wouldn't charge you. What will you do if the separatists win the referendum?

"They won't. So there's no need for you to worry."

"Oh, you can be so condescending. When we were kids you could talk politics with the boys for hours, but never with me."

"That's not true."

" 'There's no need for you to worry.' I'm not stupid, you know."

"Of course you're not. All I meant is that you've probably got enough problems of your own to cope with."

Kate taught Eng. lit. at a school for gifted children, and one night a week she helped immigrants with their English in a church basement. She was constantly badgering me to finance a film about the mother of all Canadian suffragettes, the admirable Nellie McClung.

"Soon it will be Christmas and we'll be expected for dinner at Mom's. A tree and a menorah lamp. Mike and Caroline will fly over with the kids, and Saul will be there, and he and Mike will start shoving it to each other the minute they come through the door. Last year I couldn't stop crying. I love you, Daddy."

"I love you too, Kate."

"We used to be some family. I can't forgive Mom for leaving you."

"But it's my fault that I lost her."

"I'm going to hang up now. Before I start to blubber."

The tension between Miriam and Kate had almost always been there, smouldering. I couldn't understand it. After all, it was Miriam, not me, who had read stories to Kate every night, taught her how to read, and took her to all those museums and on theatrical binges in New York. My parental role had largely been confined to providing a good life, teasing the kids at the table, leaving Miriam to settle disputes and, oh yes, putting together those libraries after I had consulted Miriam. "When a child is born," I once explained to the kids, "some dads lay down bottles of wine for them that will mature when they grow up into ungrateful adults. Instead, what you're going to get from me, as each of you turns sixteen, is a library of the one hundred books that gave me the most pleasure when I was a know-nothing adolescent."

Late one afternoon when Kate was in her last year at Miss Edgar's and Miss Cramp's, she came home to discover a harassed Miriam, one eye on the kitchen clock, preparing two ducks for the oven. Perfectionist that Miriam was, she was plucking the last, barely visible, feather needles with an eyebrow tweezer. There were pots steaming on every gas jet. Bread waiting to be baked. Wine glasses, just out of the dishwasher, were lined up to be inspected against the light and to be washed again if necessary. A mound of strawberries in a glass bowl had yet to be hulled. A sullen Kate went directly to the fridge, pulled out a yoghurt, cleared a space for herself at the counter, and sat down to read *Middlemarch* where she had left off the day before.

"Kate, you could be a good goose and remove the stalks from those berries for me and then plump up the cushions in the living room."

No answer.

"Kate, we've got six people coming for dinner at 7.30 and I haven't even showered or changed yet."

"Why can't the boys help?"

"They're not here."

"When I grow up I'm not going to end up a housewife. Like you."

"*What?*"

"I'll bet they're not even your friends coming, but his."

"Are you going to do those berries for me, or not?"

"When I finish this chapter," she said, quitting the kitchen.

As luck would have it, when Miriam swept into our bedroom, I was holding out the arm of my clean shirt helplessly. "I don't know how many times I've asked you to switch laundries. Don't say it. I know. Mr. Hejaz has seven children. But he mashed one of my buttons again. Could you sew it on for me, please?"

"Do it yourself."

"What's wrong?"

"Nothing."

I attempted to take her in my arms, but she braced herself against me, sniffing. "Shit," she exclaimed, "my bread." And she raced into the kitchen, me trailing after.

"It's ruined," she said, tears sliding down her cheeks.

"No, it isn't. It's just well baked," I said, picking up a knife, prepared to start scraping.

"I'm certainly not serving it like this."

"I'll send Kate to the Bagel Factory."

"You'll find your daughter in her bedroom reading *Middlemarch*," she said, her manner abrasive.

"Boy, are you ever in a mood. Would you rather she was reading *Cosmopolitan*?"

"You are not to send her out on an errand. She dislikes me enough already."

"How could you even think such a thing?"

"Oh, Barney, you understand nothing about your own children. Mike's sick with worry because his girlfriend is three weeks late and Saul's dealing in drugs."

"Miriam, we can't discuss this right now. It's ten after seven and you haven't even changed yet."

Once Miriam had retreated back into our bedroom, I went to see Kate and found out what had happened. "Look here, Kate, your mother gave up a serious career in broadcasting to marry me and I honestly don't know what I would have done had she turned me down. She has made I can't say how many sacrifices for you and the boys. Furthermore, housewife or not, she is the most intelligent person I know. So you are to go into our bedroom at once and apologize."

"You know what the kids feel? We're always in the wrong, no matter what, because you're always sticking up for each other."

"You heard me," I said, taking her book from her.

"It makes me sick the way she's always catering to you."

"I like to think we cater to each other."

"She's been cooking up a storm since early this morning and when your friends get here they'll drink themselves stupid before they even sit down to the table, and then they'll zip through dinner the quicker to get into the cognac and cigars, and all her effort will have been for nothing."

"You are to go and apologize right now."

She did, but Miriam wasn't grateful for my intervention. "You have a remarkable gift for making matters worse, Barney. Did you take her book away from her?"

"No. Yes. I forget."

But it was still in my hands.

"Return it to her right now, please."

"Shit. Shit. Shit. There goes the doorbell."

Anticipating a disaster, given Miriam's state, I drank heavily before dinner, but once more she amazed me. Instead of graciously accommodating the most boring person at the table, as she usually did, simulating fascination with their banalities, Miriam was in one of her rare take-no-prisoners moods. Nate Gold's wife was the first to be stung, but she brought it on herself. She shouldn't have thrust her roast duck away from her, reached into the saddle bag slung over her chair, and fished out a bunch of green grapes from a cellophane bag. "The duck looks very tasty," she sang out, turning her portion over with a fork, probing it for fat, "but I'm on a diet." Nate, filling the silence that ensued, allowed that he had been to lunch with his esteemed friend, the secretary of state responsible for culture, in Ottawa earlier in the week. "And you know what," said Nate, "he has never read a book by Northrop Frye."

"But neither have I," said Nate's wife, adding to the mound of green-grape seeds on her dinner plate.

"No pictures," said Miriam.

Poor, vulnerable Zack Keeler was the next to be chastised. He was uncharacteristically morose to begin with, because he had been to Al Mackie's funeral that afternoon. Mackie, a sports writer of our acquaintance, had usually staggered on from Jumbo's or Friday's, both of which closed at two a.m., to the Press Club, which remained open until four. Zack was distressed because Al's widow, he said, seemed disconcertingly composed as her husband's coffin was lowered into its grave.

"That should come as no surprise," said Miriam. "It must be the first time in twenty years she knew exactly where her husband could be found after ten at night."

To do him credit, Zack's spirits revived at once. "You're too good for him," he said, kissing Miriam's hand.

TWELVE

THE morning I brought Clara home from the hospital, we had to pause on each of the five landings, enabling her to catch her breath. Clara immediately stripped down to her bulky, red-stained panties, and complicated arrangement of belts. "Your guarantee of chastity," she said. She arranged her collection of medicine bottles on the bedside table, popped a sleeping pill into her mouth, got right into bed, turned her face to the wall, and went to sleep. I settled into the kitchen with a bottle of vodka and a sense of descending gloom. Hours later I heard her stirring and brought her a tray with tea and toast. "So," she said, "what happens now?"

"You've got to get better before we can talk."

Shuffling off to the toilet, slippers slapping, she peered into the tiny room that was to have been the nursery. "Poor little Sambo," she said, and then she saw that I had made up a bed for myself out of the sofa pillows. "Why don't you send out for a red hot brand," she asked, "and burn an A into the flesh between my leaky tits?"

"I bought some veal chops for dinner. Will you want to eat in bed or in the kitchen with me?"

"I suppose you won't know what to do about me until Boogie gets back from Amsterdam and gives you your marching orders."

But a stoned Boogie was no help. I brought him up to date and then asked, "What were you doing in Amsterdam?"

"Shopping."

Yossel said, "Every time I see you you're drunk. I've got a lawyer for you. A landsman. Somebody who won't overcharge. Maître Moishe Tannenbaum."

"Not yet."

"You think it will be easier a month from now?"

Swimming in vodka starting at breakfast, necessarily brain dead, I don't remember too much about the following week, but I do recall that we were given to exchanging niceties. Barbed niceties.

"Feeling better, Clara?"

"Why would you care, Dr. Prudestein?" Another time, "I've been a neglectful wifey. I suppose I should ask how are things in the cheese business? Is Camembert moving better than Bresse bleu?"

"Charming."

"Poor Barney. His wifey a whore and his best friend a junkie. *Oy vey.* Such a sad fate for a nicely brought up Jewish boy."

One evening Clara, chain-smoking, pacing up and down our living room while I was reading on the sofa, ostentatiously ignoring her, suddenly whirled about and snatched my book from my hands. It was Austryn Wainhouse's translation of Beckett's *Molloy*.[1] "How can you read such boring shit?" she demanded.

This enabled me to put her down, quoting one of her favourite poets back at her. "William Blake once wrote a letter to a guy who had commissioned four watercolours from him, but deplored the

---

[1] Patrick Bowles was the translator of *Molloy*. Wainhouse translated de Sade and was the author of *Hedyphagetica. A Romantic Argument after certain Old Models. Scenes of Anthropophagy, and Assortment of Heroes.*

result. '. . . that What is Grand is necessarily Obscure to Weak Men,' he wrote. Or women, he might have added. 'That which can be made Explicit to the Idiot is not worth my care.' So just possibly it's not Beckett, but you who is inadequate."

She began to stay up late again, writing in her notebooks, drawing. Or she would sit for hours before her mirror, trying on different shocking shades of lipstick and nail polish, eye shadow with built-in sparkles. Then she would pop a sleeping pill or two, and not stir again until late the next day. One afternoon she disappeared, only to return three hours later with her hair dyed purple and streaked with orange. "Jesus Christ," I said.

"Oh, my honey," she said, eyelashes fluttering, a hand held to her heart, "you noticed?"

"Yeah."

"I suppose you preferred it shit-coloured?"

Other days she would quit the apartment early in the afternoon and not return until midnight or later.

"Did you manage to get laid while you were out?"

"Even a *clochard* wouldn't want me like I am now."

"If you're still bleeding badly, I should take you to see a doctor."

She blew me a kiss. "I'm ready to talk now. What about you, Prince Charmingbaum?"

"Sure. If not now, when?"

"Happy Chanukah. Merry Passover. You can have a divorce, if you want it."

"I do."

"But I should tell you that I've been to see a lawyer and she says if you divorce me I'm entitled to something like half of your income for the rest of your life. Thank God you're so healthy."

"Clara, you amaze me. I never suspected you had such a practical streak."

"One thing you can say about Jewish husbands. They're excellent providers. I learnt that on my mother's knee."

"I'm going home. Back to Canada," I said, surprised at myself, because I made that decision right there and then.

"I thought I was the crazy one here. What will you do in Canada?"

"Snow-shoe. Hunt beaver. Boil maple syrup in the spring."

"I'm not a pig, in spite of what you think. I'll settle for a year's rent on this dump and an allowance of fifty dollars a week. Oh, look at you, the colour's back in your cheeks."

"I'll move out tomorrow morning."

"You do that. And then I'm going to have the locks changed. I don't want you barging in when I could be enjoying a proper fuck. Now you get the hell out of here, please," she shrieked, tears flying. "Leave me alone, you righteous bastard." Her hollering pursued me down the stairs. "Why couldn't we start over again? Answer me that."

On Monday I found a room in a hotel on the rue de Nesle, and the next afternoon, while she was out, I filled a suitcase with essentials, and packed my books and records into cardboard cartons to be claimed later. But when I returned for them on Thursday, the apartment door locks not yet changed, I found the kitchen table set for a candlelight dinner for two. Maybe she's cooking up some soul food for Cedric, I thought. Certainly the apartment smelled vile, which I first attributed to the smoking gas stove and the charred chicken in the oven. Mouldy deposits had formed in the bowl of grated potatoes on the counter. Who in the hell was she intending to make latkes for? Something she would never do for me, pronouncing it greasy jewfood. By candlelight yet. I switched off the gas and whacked the kitchen window open. But the stench emanated from the bedroom, where I discovered Clara stone-cold dead, an empty bottle of sleeping pills on the bedside table.

Obviously some hanky-panky had been anticipated, because my bride died wearing her most alluring, all but diaphanous, black chiffon nightgown, a gift from me. There was no note. I poured myself a huge vodka, gulped it down straight, and then called the police and the American Embassy. Clara's body was removed to be stored in the morgue until Mr. and Mrs. Chambers of Gramercy Park and Newport, could fly over to take possession.

On my return to the Hotel de Nesle, the concierge rapped on the window of her tiny cubicle and slid open the slot. "Ah, Monsieur Panofsky."

"Oui."

A thousand apologies. A *pneumatique* had come for me on Wednesday, but she had forgotten to tell me. It was from Clara, insisting that I come to dinner. It was important that we talked. I sat down on the stairs and wept.

Finally practical considerations intruded. Could a suicide, even an unintended one, be buried in a Protestant cemetery? I had no idea.

Damn damn damn.

Then I remembered the story, possibly apocryphal, that Boogie had told me about Heine. Even as he lay on his deathbed, wasted, in a morphine-induced trance, a friend urged him to make his peace with God. Heine is supposed to have replied, "*Dieu me pardonnera. C'est son métier.*"

But I didn't count on it in my case. Still don't.

THIRTEEN

TOSSING and turning in bed last night, I was finally able to conjure up the luscious Mrs. Ogilvy of cherished memory, in a stimulating fantasy of my own invention. Here's how it goes:

An outraged Mrs. O. rebukes me in front of the class, clipping me on the head with a rolled copy of the Illustrated London News. *"You will report to me in the medical room immediately after classes."*

A visit to the dreaded, tiny medical room, equipped with a cot, usually means a strapping. Ten of the best on each hand. I turn up promptly at 3.35 p.m. and a seemingly irate Mrs. Ogilvy locks the door behind me. "What have you got to say for yourself?" she demands.

"I don't know why I'm here. Honestly."

She slashes the cellophane wrapper off a package of Player's Mild with a flick of a long red fingernail, pulls out a cigarette, and lights up. She exhales. She rids her lips of a tobacco particle with a slow movement of her wet tongue, and then glares at me. "I sat down on my desk top and began to read aloud the opening pages of Tom Brown's School Days, *and that's when you dropped your pencil on the floor, accidentally on purpose, so that you could peek up my skirt."*

"That's not true."

"Then, as if that weren't sufficiently disgusting on your part, you began to rub your roger right in the middle of my Highroads to Reading class."

"I did not, Mrs. Ogilvy."

"I swear," she says, flinging her cigarette to the floor and rubbing her heel into it, "I shall never grow accustomed to how they persist in overheating rooms in the dominions." She unbuttons her blouse and sheds it. She is wearing a filagreed black bra. "Come here, boy."

"Yes, Mrs. Ogilvy."

"And you're absolutely bursting with filthy thoughts right this very minute."

"I am not."

"Oh, yes you are, young man. The proof's in the pudding." And she undoes the buttons of my fly and reaches inside for me with incredibly cool fingers. "Just look at your roger now. Obviously you have no respect for your social superiors. Are you ashamed, Barney?"

"Yes, Mrs. Ogilvy."

She continues to rake me with those long red fingernails and I start to leak just a little.

"Now if this was a lolly," she says, "I might be tempted to give it a darling little lick. Oh well, waste not, want not." She clears the crown with a flick of her tongue, and immediately another little blob bubbles out. "Oh dear," says Mrs. Ogilvy, regarding me severely, "we don't want the train to leave the station prematurely, do we?" Then she steps out of her skirt and panties. "I want you to now rub that against me right down here. Mais, attendez un instant, s'il vous plaît. The motion should not be from side to side, but up and down, actually."

I attempt to oblige.

"You haven't got it quite right yet, damn you. Like you were having trouble striking a match. Do you understand?"

"Yes."

Suddenly she begins to shudder. And then, grabbing me by the back of the head, she lowers both of us on to the cot. "Now you

can pop it inside me, like a good boy, and up and down you ride.
Like a piston. Ready! Steady! Go!"

Actually these three pages represent my first and only attempt at writing fiction, my brief creative flowering prompted by Boogie, who was convinced I was capable of churning out what our bunch used to call a DB[1] for the Traveller's Companion series. Boogie wheeled me into Maurice Girodias's office on the rue de Nesle one afternoon. "You are looking at the next Marcus Van Heller," he said. "He's got two terrific ideas. One is called *Teacher's Pet*," he said, improvising, "and the other *The Rabbi's Daughter.*"

Girodias was intrigued. "I'll have to see twenty pages before I can commission you," he said. But I never got beyond page three.

I LINGERED LATE in bed this morning until I was wakened by the postman.

Registered letter.

I can count on hearing from The Second Mrs. Panofsky by registered mail at least twice a year: once, on the anniversary of Boogie's disappearance, and again, today, on the anniversary of my discharge by the court, adjudged innocent, but guilty as hell in her mind. This morning's missive was admirably succinct for a change. It read in its entirety:

> TO NONE WILL WE SELL, TO NONE
> DENY OR DELAY, RIGHT OR JUSTICE.
> Clause 40,
> Magna Carta, 1215.

Inevitably, I run into The Second Mrs. Panofsky from time to time. Once I caught sight of her in the lingerie department of Holt Renfrew, where I like to browse. On another occasion, at the take-out counter in The Brown Derby, where she was loading up on sufficient quantities of kishka, roast brisket, chopped liver, and potato salad to feed a bar mitzvah party, but which I knew was for herself alone. Most recently, I encountered her in the Ritz dining

---

[1] Dirty Book.

room where, to jump ahead in my story, I had taken Ms. Morgan to dinner, if only to continue our discussion of those committed, possibly not irretrievably, to the Sapphic persuasion. The Second Mrs. Panofsky was with her cousin, the notary, and his wife. Her own plate wiped clean of gravy with chunks of bread, she now picked up her fork and began to spear morsels of meat and potatoes off their plates. She glared at us, of course, taking note of the bottle of Dom Pérignon floating in a bucket at our tableside. Their bill settled, she contrived to pass by our table, where she stopped, smiled menacingly at Ms. Morgan, then turned to me and inquired, "And how are your grandchildren these days?"

"Don't look back," I said, "or you might turn into a pillar of salt."

The Second Mrs. Panofsky, while never svelte, even as a bride, but once pleasingly zaftig to give her her due, had taken long ago to alleviating her continuing sorrow at the table. Out of necessity, she now wears tent-like kaftans to accommodate a girth that would do credit to a sumo wrestler. She walks with difficulty, breathing hard, favouring a cane. She puts me in mind of Garrick's description of Sam Johnson's Tetty at fifty: " . . . very fat, with a bosom of more than ordinary protuberance, with swelled cheeks, of florid red, produced by thick painting, and increased by liberal use of cordials; flaring and fantastic in her dress, and affected in both her speech and general behaviour." I'm told she has few friends left, but does enjoy an intimate relationship with her TV set. I like to visualize her in the Hampstead mansion I paid for, supine on the sofa, devouring Belgian chocolates out of a bucket as she watches one soap opera or another, dozing before she settles into dinner, using a shovel rather than a knife and fork, and then sinks to the sofa again before her TV set.

AT BREAKFAST, I dutifully went through the *Gazette* and the *Globe and Mail*, doing my best to keep up with the comedy we're living through in Canada's one and only "distinct society."

Such is the panic here these days that those prescient, young, middle-class Jewish couples who decamped to Toronto in the eighties, escaping not only endless tribal hassle but also overbearing, intrusive parents, are now at risk. Many of them are getting urgent phonecalls from their ageing mammas and papas. "Herky, I know she isn't crazy about us, your wonderful wife, the shopper, but thank God you have that spare bedroom, because we're moving in next Wednesday until we can find an apartment in your neighbourhood. Remember, Mama can't stand rock music, you'll have to speak to your children, God bless them, and if you must smoke while we're there, it will have to be on the back porch. But we won't get in anybody's way. Herky, are you there? Herky, say something."

The latest opinion polls indicating a dead heat in the referendum, Dink's now reverberates with whistling-past-the-graveyard banter. One of the regulars, Cy Tepperman, a clothing manufacturer, anticipating a boycott of his goods in the rest of Canada, has said, "I'm seriously thinking of having 'Made in Ontario' labels sewn into my jeans, just in case those bastards win." Zack Keeler, the *Gazette* columnist, can be counted on, as usual, for puerile jokes. "Have you heard that the Newfies are for the Yes side? They think it will take two-and-a-half hours less to drive to Ontario if Quebec separates."

Ms. Morgan, of "Dykes on Mikes," told me on the morning of her first visit to my apartment that she intended to vote in favour of independence. "They're entitled to their own country. They *do* form a distinct society."

"I could take you to lunch."

"You're old enough to be my grandfather."

"Next question, please."

"Had the baby Clara miscarried been born white, would you still have abandoned her?"

"Divorced her, you mean. Well now, that's an interesting question. I might have been foolish enough to think it was mine."

"But you are deeply prejudiced against Afro-Americans."

"The hell I am."

"I have been in touch with Ismail ben Yussef, who you knew under his slave name, Cédric Richardson, and he claims you have taken to sending him abusive letters."

"I'm willing to swear on the heads of my grandchildren that he's lying."

She reached into a folder and passed me a Xerox of a letter, which was an appeal on behalf of something called The Elders of Zion Foundation to establish mugging fellowships for black brothers. "This is absolutely disgraceful," I said. "It's in the worst possible taste."

"But isn't that your signature at the bottom of the page?"

"No."

She sighed heavily.

"For years now Terry McIver – that racist – that *misogynist* – has been sending people abusive letters and signing my name to them."

"Come off it."

"And if you want respectable men not to stare at your charming bosom, why don't you wear a bra, so that your nipples don't protrude. It's disconcerting, to say the least."

"Now look here, Mr. Panofsky, I've already been pinched or grabbed by enough men tripping on penis power, so cut out the funny stuff right now. The reason why gay women frighten you is because you are terrified of what this would mean to the quote, normal, unquote patriarchal, authoritarian system based on women's submission to men."

"I don't mean to pry," I said, "but what do your parents think about your being a lesbian?"

"I prefer to think of myself as a humansexual."

"Then we have something in common."

"Did you agree to this interview just to poke fun at me?"

"Why don't we continue this discussion at lunch?"

"You can go straight to hell," she said, gathering her things together. "If not for you, Clara would be alive today. Terry McIver told me that."

FOURTEEN

PARIS 1952. Grudgingly surfacing from yet another vodka stupor only a few days after Clara's death, unsure of my whereabouts, it seemed that I was being summoned by something between a scratching and a knocking at my door, wherever it was. Go away, I thought. But the knocker persisted. Boogie again, perhaps. Or Yossel. My well-intentioned nurses. Go away, I thought, turning to the wall.

"Mr. Panofsky. Mr. Panofsky, please," pleaded a voice unfamiliar to me. A supplicant's voice.

"Fuck off, whoever you are. I'm not well."

"Please," came the whiney voice again. "I will stand here until you open the door."

Five p.m. I rose from the sofa, broken springs twanging, stumbled into the bathroom, and splashed cold water on my face. Maybe it was somebody who wanted to take the apartment off my hands. I had advertised it in the *International Herald-Tribune*. So I hastily gathered up soiled laundry, empty bottles, and plates with uneaten frankfurters or egg remnants on them, and dumped them into the nearest drawer. Careful not to trip over packed cartons containing her things, I opened the door to a small, tubby stranger, with a salt-and-pepper Vandyke beard, wearing horn-rimmed glasses that magnified his sad brown spaniel's eyes. I took him to be in his early fifties. He wore a woollen winter coat with a Persian lamb collar and a homburg, which he promptly removed to reveal a black yarmulke fastened to his flowing grey hair with a bobbypin. His coat was unbuttoned and I saw that the fat of his tie had been neatly rent with scissors. "What do you want here?" I asked.

"What do I want here? But I'm Charnofsky," he said. "Chaim Charnofsky," he repeated, as if that explained everything.

Charnofsky? Her first husband. I shook my pounding head, trying, unavailingly, to clear it of the jackhammer within. "The art teacher?" I asked, baffled.

"The art teacher? You understand Yiddish, may I be so bold to inquire?"

"Some."

"I'm your *machuten*. Clara's father. May I come in?"

"Yes. Certainly. Excuse me a minute, will you?"

I splashed my face with water once more, and emerged to discover I wasn't hallucinating. Mr. Charnofsky was still there. Hands clasped behind his back, he was studying the ink drawings that still hung on the wall. "I take it you are an artist, Mr. Panofsky."

"Clara's," I said.

"Clara's. Why would she buy such disgusting things?"

"She made them."

"She made them. I couldn't help noticing in that little room there, a crib. There is a child?"

"We lost him."

"So you lost a son and I lost a daughter. May there be no more mourning in your house or mine."

"Would you care for some coffee?"

"It gives me gas. Especially the frenchy kind they serve here. But a cup of tea would be nice, if you don't mind?"

He cleared a space for himself at the table, ostentatiously brushing it free of crumbs, and sweeping aside a half-filled mug in which several Gauloise butts floated. He inspected his teaspoon and wiped it on the edge of the tablecloth. "Lemon, you've got some?" he asked.

"Sorry. I'm out."

"He's out," said Mr. Charnofsky, shrugging. And then, sucking on a sugar cube, sipping tea, he told me he was the cantor of the B'nai Jacob Synagogue in Brighton Beach. "It's not a princely living," he said, "but they provide us with an apartment, the building belongs to the synagogue's president, he would die before he would agree to a paint job, never mind fix a leaky toilet bowl, his wife's barren, it's a shame, so who will he leave his fortune to? His problem. I have plenty of my own. Gall-bladder stones, you shouldn't live to see the day. I also suffer from sinus trouble, varicose veins, and corns on my feet. It's from standing so much in the synagogue. Listen here, cancer it isn't, right? And, oh yes, there is the pittance I earn from performing at weddings and funerals, they slip you fifty dollars they want a tax receipt, and I preside over seders every Pesach at Finestone's Strictly Kosher Hotel in the Catskills. Every year sold out because of me. My voice. A gift from the Almighty, Blessed be He. But where does Finestone put me up, he's so grateful for the money he's raking in? In a room the size of a cupboard behind the kitchen, the fridge and the larder locked up at night in case I might steal a Coca-Cola or a tin of sardines. I have to walk a mile to do my business. Anyway I sent Clara whatever I could spare care of the American Express, which is the only address I had for her."

Mr. Charnofsky had two children. There was Solly, an accountant, an alrightnik, married, blessed with two lovely kids. Rank-one scholars, both of them. He showed me photographs. "You're their uncle now. Milton was born on February 18th and Arty on June 28th, if you care to write that down for future reference." And of course there was also Clara. "*Alav-ha-sholem*," he said. "You look, *epes*, surprised to see me."

"I need time to take this in."

"Time he needs. And what about me, mister? Did I even know she was married, my own daughter?" he asked, his ingratiating manner yielding to anger. "You did say my Clara drew these filthy pictures?"

"Yes."

Obviously the condition of our apartment had emboldened Mr. Charnofsky. Mind you, to his Brighton Beach eyes it had to appear a dump, not the prize that had cost me a good deal of key money. He pulled a white linen handkerchief out of a trouser pocket and dabbed his forehead with it. "And she never told you about us, it goes without saying?"

"I'm afraid not."

"He's afraid not. Well, for my part, I'm certainly surprised Miss Cat's Meow married a Jewish boy. A nigger would have been more like it. She adored them."

"I don't like anybody calling them 'niggers,' if you don't mind?"

"If I don't mind. Be my guest. Call them what you like," said Mr. Charnofsky, sniffing the stale air, his nose wrinkling. "If you were willing to open a window, I wouldn't say no."

I did as he asked.

"If you are not an artist, Mr. Panofsky, do you mind if I ask what, exactly, is your field of endeavour?"

"I'm an exporter."

"He's an exporter. But business can't be so hot. To live like this. Five flights up and no elevator. No fridge. No dishwasher."

"We managed."

"You think I'm being unfair. But if your son, your own flesh and blood, *alav-ha-sholem*, had lived and grew up and was ashamed of you, how would you feel?"

I got up, found the cognac, and poured some into my coffee. Mr. Charnofsky clacked his tongue. He sighed. "Is that schnapps I see?"

"Cognac."

"Cognac. Honour thy father and thy mother. That's a commandment. Do you do that at least?"

"My mother's a problem."

"And your father, what may I ask does he do for a living?"

"He's a cop."

"A cop. Oh ho. Where are you from, Mr. Panofsky?"

"Montreal."

"Montreal. Ah. Then perhaps you know the Kramers? A fine family. Or Cantor Labish Zabitsky?"

"Sorry. No."

"But Cantor Zabitsky is well known. We have performed in concerts together in Grossinger's. People had to book early. Are you sure you never heard of him?"

"I don't come from an observant family."

"But you're not ashamed of being Jewish," he cried, a burst furuncle. "Like her. Like Clara."

"*Alav-ha-sholem*," I said, reaching for the cognac bottle again.

"She was twelve years old and she began to tear her hair out in clumps for a how-do-you-do. 'Dr. Kaplan,' I said, he's an honoured member of our congregation, a big contributor, 'what should I do?' 'Have her periods started yet?' he asked. Feh! How should I know a thing like that? 'Send her to see me,' he said. So you think Clara was grateful, he didn't even charge me. 'He felt up my tits,' she said. *A twelve year old. Language like that. From the gutter.* Mrs. Charnofsky held her down and I washed her mouth out with soap.

"Then it started. What am I talking? It had already started. The craziness. 'You're not my parents,' she said. We should be so lucky. 'I'm adopted,' she said. 'And I want to know who my real parents are.' 'Sure,' I said. 'You're the daughter of Czar Nicholas. Or maybe it's King George of England. I forget which.' 'I'm not Jewish,' she said. 'I know that much. So I want you to tell me who my real parents are.' Until we told her she said she wouldn't eat. So eventually we had to force open her mouth, and she was a biter let me tell you, pouring chicken soup into her mouth through a funnel. And then she would vomit all over me on purpose. My good suit. It was positively disgusting.

"Next I would find filthy books under her mattress. *Translated from the French. Nina* or *Nana* or some such. Poetry by that bastard Heine, he was also ashamed of being a Jew. Sholem Aleichem wasn't good enough for Miss Hotzenklotz. And she started to go to Greenwich Village and could be gone for two days. That's when I started locking her into her room at night. Too late, I found out. Because she was no longer a virgin. Going out on the street dressed like a whore. Our street. People were talking. I could lose my position in the synagogue, and then what? I'd have to sing on street corners. Listen here, that's how Eddie Cantor got started, and look at him today, with such a thin voice and those popping eyes. I'll bet he isn't even five feet tall. But he's a millionaire yet, so they look up to him, the goyim.

"It got to be too much. Her tantrums. The filth she talked. Sometimes not coming out of her room for ten days, sitting there, staring at nothing. Thank God for Dr. Kaplan, he arranged for a mental hospital. Expert care she got, never mind the expense. We did without. They gave her electro-shock therapy, the latest thing in modern medicine. She comes home she slits her wrists in the bathtub for a thank you. The ambulance sits outside. Everybody is peeking through their curtains. Mrs. Charnofsky was so ashamed she wouldn't leave the apartment for a week. On top of all my other duties I have to do the shopping or come home to tuna sandwiches.

"I want you to know, Mr. Panofsky, you shouldn't blame yourself, because it wasn't the first time she tried suicide. Or the second. Dr. Kaplan tells me it's a cry for help. She wants help she can ask. Am I deaf? A bad father? Nonsense. Mr. Panofsky you're still a youngster," he said, hauling out his immense handkerchief to blow his nose. "Exporting is a top-notch line of business and you should do better at it if you work hard. You should marry again. Have children. All those cartons on the floor. Are you moving out of here, I wouldn't blame you?"

"They're her things. Leave me your address and I'll have them shipped to you."

"What things, for example?"

"Clothes. Her notebooks. Poems. Diaries. Her ink drawings."

"What would I need them for?"

"There are people who think highly of her work. You should have a publisher look at it."

"Diaries you said. Full of lies about us I'll bet. Filth. Making us out for monsters."

"Maybe it would be better if I handled this."

"No. Ship them. I'll leave you my card. My nephew should

look at it. He's a professor of literature at NYU. Highly thought of. He used to encourage her."

"Like you did."

"Like I did. Oh, very nice. Thank you I'm sure. After all Mrs. Charnofsky and I suffered. The shame she brought on us."

"Electro-shock therapy. My God."

"What if I told you those times she wouldn't come out of her room for ten days, maybe two weeks, we left food for her outside the door. Once Mrs. Charnofsky goes to pick up the empty plate, she lets out a shriek, I thought somebody had died. And you know what was on that plate? You should pardon me, her number two. Yes, mister. That's what she did. At the hospital they recommended that operation. What do you call it? A frontal laboratory. But my nephew, the professor, said no. I mustn't allow it. Do you think I did wrong to listen to my nephew?"

"Oh, you did wrong, Mr. Charnofsky. Bloody wrong. But not about that, you damn fool."

"You damn fool. Is that a way to talk to an older man, I just lost a daughter?"

"Get out of here, Mr. Charnofsky."

"Get out of here. Did you think I was going to invite myself to dinner in such a dump?"

"Get out of here before I throw you on the floor and wash your mouth out with soap."

I grabbed him, frogmarched him out of the door, and slammed it shut. Then he started to pound on the door. "I want my homburg," he said.

I retrieved it, whacked open the door, and thrust it at him.

"You couldn't have made her so happy," said Mr. Charnofsky, "if that's what my Clara did to herself."

"You know, Mr. Charnofsky, I'm quite capable of literally throwing you down the stairs."

"Pish pish."

I took a step toward him.

"The man at the embassy told me she was dead two days[1] when you found her on Thursday. But the table was set for dinner for two.

---

[1] Not much more than twenty-four hours. See page 136.

There was a burnt chicken in the oven. So, I ask myself, where were you that night, Mr. Panofsky?"

I took another step toward him. He started down the stairs, stopped in mid-flight, shook his fist at me, and hollered, "Murderer. *Oysvorf. Mamzer.* I wish *makkes* on you and your unborn children. Plagues. Deformities. Phew," he said, spitting on the floor, and turning to flee once I started after him again.

FIFTEEN

Paris. Nov. 7, 1952. Now that she has fecundated, I cogitated that the thickening Clara would be less promiscuous, if not precisely celibate.[1] But this afternoon she brought me her latest poem, accepting my corrections commingled with encouragement, and then she subjected me to those ministrations at which she is so gratifyingly proficient, with that serpent's tongue, and then smearing my sperm on her face afterward. Good for her complexion, she said.

P— must suspect that he is a cuckold. Friday night, ambling down the boulevard Saint-Germain, something made me turn around. My third eye, Clara would say. And there he was, loping along less than a block behind, and when he caught my reproving glance, he stopped at a bookshop window, pretending he hadn't seen me. *Et voilà*, last night there he was again, trailing along behind me on the Boul' Mich. I think he has taken to following me in the hope of discovering us together. Increasingly, he turns up uninvited at my door, pretending to be concerned about me, taking me to lunch at that appalling restaurant on the rue du Dragon, expecting me to be grateful.

---

[1]The original handwritten entry in McIver's journal, lodged in the Special Collections Library, University of Calgary, reads: " ... if not precisely celibate, which would go against her otiose nature. But this afternoon, interrupting me at work again, she was back to subject me ..." See Notebook 112, page 42.

"I'm worried about Clara," he says, watching me closely. But I decline the trap he is setting for me.

670 words today.

Paris, Nov. 21, 1952. Another letter from my father in which I discover three split infinitives, two dangling participles, as well as the usual lapse into pleonasms here and there. Mother has taken a turn for the worse and longs to see me before she expires, but I have no wish to endure her opprobrium. I cannot put my manuscript aside, or risk the angst that such a visit would entail. The quarrels. The migraines. And her inevitable attempt to ·extract a deathbed pledge from me to stay on in Montreal to look after my father, whose health is also failing. I doubt, given my father's uxorious nature, that he will survive her for long. They were high-school sweethearts, having met, appropriately enough, at a Young Communist League picnic.

Nothing written today. Not a word.

SIXTEEN

MY mood vile, after Ms. Morgan had spurned my luncheon invitation and stormed out of my apartment, I attempted to calm my nerves by donning my straw boater, reaching for my silver-topped antique cane, and slipping into my tap-dance shoes. Accompanied by a King Oliver CD, I warmed up with some rhythm tap, managed a passable Shim Sham Shimmy and a neat Pulling the Trenches, but it failed to settle me down. I was in a state because the resoundingly silly but delectable Ms. Morgan was the recipient of a grant from The Clara Charnofsky Foundation for Wimyn, having been awarded $2,500 to help her complete her M.A. thesis, "On Wimyn as Victims in the Québécois Novel."

Mea culpa yet again. *Mea maxima culpa.*

You see, it was Clara's cousin, the highly thought of NYU professor, who would lovingly sort out her manuscripts and drawings and feed them to publishers and art dealers as they increased incrementally in value over the years. But he first insisted on seeing me in New York, an encounter I agreed to with dread, anticipating a difficult meeting with an academic drudge, prejudging, as I am wont to do. "You do realize," Hymie Mintzbaum once said, coming off a session with one or another of his shrinks, "that it's a defence mechanism. You're convinced that anybody who meets you for the first time will consider you a shit, so you take preventive action. Relax, boychick. When they get to know you better they will realize that they were right. You are a shit."

Norman Charnofsky turned out to be a gentle if naïve man, and a stranger to avarice. A *guten neshuma*, as my grandmother used to say. A good soul. A clear and present danger to himself and others. Having heard from his abominable Uncle Chaim that I was a boozer, Norman thoughtfully suggested we get together in the lobby of the Algonquin, where I was staying, and immediately reinforced my preconceived prejudice against him by ordering a Perrier for himself. An unprepossessing little man he was, with pewter hair, thick glasses, a bulbous nose, his tie gravy-stained, and his corduroy suit salted with dandruff round the shoulders and worn thin at the knees. The ancient schoolboy's satchel he set down beside him was overloaded to the point of bursting. "I should begin," he said, "by thanking you for taking the time to see me, and apologizing for my Uncle Chaim, who had no idea that the child Clara miscarried wasn't yours, while you were too considerate to point that out to him."

"So you've read her diaries."

"Indeed I have."

"Including the last entry about the dinner I failed to attend."

"My Uncle Chaim's surprising visit to your flat couldn't have been easy for either of you."

I shrugged.

"Please don't misunderstand me. I have an enormous regard for my Uncle Chaim. He is an embittered man, yes, but with cause, and many have reason to be grateful to him. Myself foremost. Chaim was the first of the Charnofskys to come to America from Poland, and from the very beginning he denied himself, pinching pennies, and sending for relatives. If not for his devotion my parents would have remained in Lodz, where I would have been born, and Auschwitz would have been the end of our story, as it was for too many Charnofskys. But the children of many of those who Chaim brought over here, men and women who have prospered in America, now regard him as an embarrassment. An atavism. A ghetto Jew. And they don't want him putting on his *talis* and *davenen* in their living room in the morning, which makes their children giggle, or sunning that pale body, but wearing his yarmulke, in their gardens out on Long Island, or in Florida, lest he compromise them before their neighbours. Okay. Enough. I talk too much. Ask my wife. And I'd have to agree he is a narrow man, obdurate, intolerant, but you see he is still baffled by what has become of the Jews in America. And from your point of view, I have no doubt, he was unpardonably cruel to Clara. But how could he be expected to comprehend such a precocious and wilful child in his house? She was so difficult. Such a troubled spirit. Oh poor Clara," he said, biting his lip, "when she was only twelve years old she would lie on the floor of our parlor, surrounded by books, sketching, her skinny legs swinging away, crossed at the ankles. I loved Clara and deeply regret I didn't do more to shelter her from what? From the world, that's what."

"Was it you, then, who came to Paris looking for her?"

"It was me. Then she wrote, pleading with me to stay away, not to worry, she had met a good man, you Mr. Panofsky, and he was going to marry her."

Norman taught a remedial-reading course one night a week in Harlem. He belonged to a group that collected clothes to be mailed to Jews in Russia, he was a blood donor, and had once stood as a Socialist Party candidate for the state legislature. His wife, Flora, had given up her job as a grade-school teacher to care for their only child, a boy who suffered from Down's syndrome. "Flora would be so pleased if you came to dinner one night."

"Another time, maybe."

"If Flora were here she would say stop kvetching and come to the point. I brought you here because I have found a publisher for Clara's poetry and a gallery that is interested in her drawings. But let me assure you, even if there was somebody who wanted them, it goes without saying that Clara's diaries could not be published in the lifetime of my Uncle Chaim or Aunt Gitel."

"Or mine?" I asked, my smile tentative.

"But if you read between the lines," he protested, "she was more than grateful for your devotion. I think she loved you."

"In her fashion."

"Look here, this could all come to nothing. But it is my duty to tell you that it could also turn out that her work has substantial financial value, and if that were the case it is you who is entitled to benefit from the income."

"Oh come on, Norman, you're talking nonsense."

"I have a proposal to make, which I want you to think over carefully. I'm crazy. Ask anybody. But just in case money should come in, I wish to establish a foundation in her name to help women of artistic or academic bent, because it continues to be exceedingly difficult for them," and he went on to run numbers at me of how few women at NYU or Columbia achieved tenure, or were appointed professors, and how they had to manage on smaller salaries and deal with male condescension. "I have brought some papers for you to look at," he said, reaching into his bulging satchel. "Waivers. Releases. Take them with you. Consult a lawyer. Consider the matter carefully."

Instead, eager for Norman's approval, I signed the papers in triplicate right there. Better my right hand should have been cut off. Go know I was setting in motion events that would lead to the ruin of one of the few truly good men I ever met.

II

THE SECOND MRS. PANOFSKY
1958–1960

ONE

IMISS the old days at Totally Unnecessary Productions when I could be yanked out of a boring production meeting in our boardroom because Miriam, her visit unexpected, was waiting for me in reception. Balancing Saul on her hip, holding Mike by her other hand. Her shoulder bag weighed down with a baby's bottle, diapers, a colouring book and crayons, at least three matchbox cars, a paperback Yeats or Berryman and the latest issue of the *New York Review of Books*. An apologetic Miriam shepherding a stray she had discovered panhandling on Greene Avenue or shivering in a doorway on Atwater. One morning it was a cadaverous teenager, shoulders hunched against anticipated blows, his smile at once both ingratiating and sly. "This is Timothy Hobbs," she said. "He's from Edmonton."

"Hi, Tim."

"'lo."

"I promised Tim that you had a job for him."

"Doing what?"

"Tim's been sleeping rough in Central Station, so I'm afraid he's going to need a week's salary in advance."

I put Tim to work running messages and managing our Xerox machine, even as he wiped his nose with a quick swipe of his sleeve. He was gone by the end of the week along with our receptionist's handbag, a calculating machine, an IBM typewriter, a bottle of Macallan, and my recently filled humidor.

Another morning Miriam brought in a runaway young girl, who was being wasted as a waitress in a greasy spoon, suffering a boss who, she said, could never pass her in the kitchen without fondling her breasts. "Marylou," she said, "is willing to take a computer course."

Next thing I knew, quitting my office at noon, I would run into a flotilla of courier-service motorcycles and bicycles parked outside. Marylou, it turned out, was servicing guys in what had become our office building's celebrated freight elevator. There were complaints and I had to let her go.

Nowadays I understand Miriam holds open house for Blair's students in their apartment on Friday evenings, comforting the troubled or those who are far from home. She has seen young women through their abortions and testified on behalf of young men appearing in court on drug possession charges.

I avoided the offices of Totally Unnecessary Productions this morning and, instead, lingered late in bed. Tuned into "By Special Request," eyes shut, adrift, and pretended Miriam was tucked under the duvet with me, warming my old bones. I know that voice's every nuance. *There's something wrong.* Playing that tape back at night, I was sure of it. Miriam is troubled. She's quarrelled on the phone with Kate again. Or, still better, with Blair. Possibly the time has come for the adorable old Panofsky to make his move. "Of course you can come home, my darling. If I start out right now I can be at your front door in Toronto first thing in the morning. No, you mustn't worry about me on the road. I've given up drinking. You're right. It makes for unfortunate changes in my personality. Yes, I love you too."

Emboldened by another stiff drink, I actually dialled her number in Toronto, but no sooner did she say hello in that distinctive voice of hers than I thought my heart would break. So I slammed down the receiver. Now you've gone and done it, I thought. Blair could be out somewhere hugging trees or pasting Animal Rights stickers on fur-shop windows. Miriam could be home alone, in her negligee, and think that a burglar was checking out her place. Or a heavy breather. I had frightened her. But I didn't dare call her back to reassure her. Instead, I freshened my drink and sensed that I was now in for one of those old fart's nights, rewinding the spool of my wasted life, wondering how I got from there to here. From the sweet teenager reading *The Waste Land* aloud in bed to the misanthropic, ageing purveyor of TV dreck, with only a lost love and pride in his children to sustain him.

BOSWELL: "But is not the fear of death natural to man?"

JOHNSON: "So much so, Sir, that the whole of life is but keeping away thoughts of it."

My first job, a harbinger of sins against good taste to come, was in vaudeville, or what the odious Terry McIver would surely call "*commedia dell'arte*, where P— was initiated in mimeticism." Put plainly, I was hired to sell ice cream and chocolate bars and peanuts in the Gayety Theatre, patrolling the aisles with my tray. Then Slapsy Maxsy Peel came to MC the show that starred Lili St. Cyr; and I got my first break. "Hey, peckerhead," said Maxsy, "how would you like to earn two bucks a performance?"

So, whenever Slapsy Maxsy was scheduled to make his first appearance of the show on stage, I would zip up to the balcony and, before he could get a word out, cup my hands to my mouth and holler, "Hello, shmuck."

Seemingly startled, Slapsy Maxsy would glare at the balcony and shout back, "Hey, kid, why don't you put your hands in your pockets and get a grip on life?" Then, responding to the guffaws in the orchestra seats, he would move on to lambaste people in the first row.

Morty Herscovitch checked me out last week and was delighted to proclaim, "You've shrunk almost half an inch since last year." Next he blew me a kiss and rammed his gloved finger up my arse.

"You won't find any truffles there," I said.

"We're going to have to get it trimmed one of these days. The sooner the better. Remember Myer Labovitch?"

"No."

"Sure you do. Room 39. Big in the A.Z.A. First guy to come to school wearing a zoot suit. He flew to Zurich yesterday. Kidney transplant. They buy them in Pakistan. Costs a fortune, but what the hell? You know what's coming soon to your neighbourhood health center? Heart transplants from pigs. They're working on it in Houston right now. Now tell me what will the Lubavitcher Rebbe say to that, eh, Barney?"

I was Morty's last patient of the day, but even as we retired to his office, shmoozing, a raging Duddy Kravitz whacked open the door and burst in on us, shedding his cashmere top coat and white silk scarf, revealing a snazzy tux. Dismissing me with a perfunctory nod, he turned on Morty. "I need a disease."

"I beg your pardon?"

"It's for my wife. Look, I'm in a terrible hurry and she's waiting in my car. It's a Jag. Latest model. You ought to get one, Barney. You pay cash you can knock them down. She's in tears."

"Because she hasn't got a disease?"

Duddy explained that his millions notwithstanding, never mind his donations to the Montreal Symphony Orchestra, the art museum, the Montreal General Hospital, McGill, and his whopper of an annual cheque to Centraid, he was still unable to crack Westmount society to his wife's satisfaction. But tonight, en route to the museum's Strawberry and Champagne Ball, "They usually seat us at a table in the bleachers," he said, "I had a brainwave. There has to be a disease out there not yet spoken for, something for which I could register a charitable foundation, organize a ball at the Ritz, fly in some big-name ballet dancer or opera singer to perform, who cares the cost, and everybody would have to turn out. But it's a tough call. Don't tell me. I know. Multiple sclerosis has already been nabbed. So has cancer. Parkinson's. Alzheimer's. Liver and heart diseases. Arthritis. You name it, it's gone. So what I need is some disease still out there, something sexy I could start a charity for, and appoint the governor general, or some other prick, honorary patron. You know, like Sister Kenny, or was it Mrs. Roosevelt, and the March of Dimes. Polio was terrific. Something kids get tugs at the heartstrings. People are suckers for it."

"What about AIDS?" I suggested.

"Where have you been living? That's long gone. Now there's that thing that women get, you know, they eat like pigs, then stick two fingers down their throat and vomit it out, what's that called?"

"Bulimia."

"It's disgusting, but if Princess Diana has got it, it could have lots of appeal for Westmount types. Goddamn it," said Duddy, glancing at his watch. "Come on, Morty. I'm running late. Any minute now she starts her blowing-on-the-horn routine. She's driving me crazy. Hit me with something."

"Crohn's Disease."

"Never heard of it. Is it big?"

"Maybe two hundred thousand Canadians suffer from it."

"Good. Now you're talking. So tell me about it."

"It's also known as ileitis or ulcerative colitis."

"Explain it to me in laymen's terms, please."

"It leads to gas, diarrhoea, rectal bleeding, fever, weight loss. You suffer from it you could have fifteen bowel movements a day."

"Oh, great! Wonderful! I phone Wayne Gretzky, I say, how would you like to be a patron for a charity for farters? Mr. Trudeau, this is DK speaking, and I've got just the thing to improve your image. How would you like to join the board of a charity my wife is organizing for people who shit day and night? Hey there everybody, you are invited to my wife's annual Diarrhoea Ball. Listen, for my wife it has to have some class. I want you to come up with a winner by nine o'clock tomorrow morning, Morty. Good to see you, Barney. Sorry your wife left you. Is it true it was for a younger guy?"

"Yes."

"They're into that now. The libbers. One night you help them with the dishes and the next they go back to college to get a degree and soon enough they're being *shtupped* by some kid. Barney, you want hockey or baseball tickets, I'm your man. Call me and we'll have lunch. There she goes. Beep beep beep."

I had just finished my drink, and was heading for bed, when Irv Nussbaum phoned to ask if I'd seen the latest opinion poll on the referendum. "We're sliding," he said.

"Yeah. I know."

All the same, Irv was euphoric. "But there are bound to be more anti-Semitic incidents any day now. I feel it in my bones. Terrific!" Irv had just returned from one of those United Jewish Appeal feel-good tours to Israel. "I met this guy named Pinsky there who claimed he knew you in Paris when you didn't have a pot to piss in. He said you did some deals together. Hey, if that's the case I'll bet they weren't so kosher."

"They weren't. What's Yossel up to these days?"

"Something to do with diamonds. I ran into him at Ocean, maybe the most expensive restaurant in Jerusalem. He was swilling champagne with one of those new young Russian immigrants. Some tootsie she was. A blondie. And he drove off in a BMW, so he has to be earning a living. Oh, he said to ask if some guy you both used to know – Biggie or Boogie, I forget – owed you as much money as he owed him."

"Had he heard from Boogie recently?"

"Not for donkey's years he said. He gave me his card. He'd like to hear from you."

Couldn't sleep. Consumed with guilt because I had lost contact with Yossel years ago. Was it that he was no longer useful? Is that the kind of shit I had become?

Damn damn damn. Had I suspected I would survive to such an advanced age, sixty-seven, I would prefer to have earned a reputation as a gentleman, rather than a ruffian who had made his fortune producing crap for TV. I would like to have become a man like Nathan Borenstein, the retired G.P. Dr. Borenstein must be in his late seventies now, what my daughter, Kate, calls a cotton top, round-shouldered, wearing trifocals, and seldom seen without the silvery-haired, petite Mrs. Borenstein, probably the same age, on his arm. I have arranged to sit immediately behind them at the symphony concert series at Place des Arts, the seat next to mine empty these days but held onto, just in case. When the house lights dim, he links arms with Mrs. Borenstein, ever so discreetly, and later he frees himself, opens his copy of the score, and follows the performance with the benefit of a pocket flashlight, nodding pleasurably or biting his lips as the occasion demands. The last time I saw them together was at the Montreal Opera Company's presentation of *The Magic Flute*. As usual, I kept an eye on Borenstein, applauding an aria when he did and abstaining when he did.

Overdressed, bejewelled women, who have benefited from rhinoplasty, ultrapulse carbon-dioxide laser treatment, abdominoplasty or lipo-suction, prevail at Place des Arts. These days, according to Morty Herscovitch, some of them also go in for soyaoil breast implants. You nibble a nipple and what do you get? Salad dressing.

I collect little snippets of information about the Borensteins. Her eyesight, I have heard, is failing, so he reads aloud to her after dinner. They have three children. The oldest son, a doctor, is with Médecins Sans Frontières, serving in Africa, wherever the fly-bitten children with bloated bellies can be found. There is a daughter, who is a violinist with the Toronto Symphony Orchestra, and a son who is a physicist at the – the – not Tel Aviv, but the other city in Israel. Not Jerusalem either. At the something institute in the not Tel Aviv nor Jerusalem city. It's on the tip of my tongue. It begins with an H. The Herzl Institute.[1] No. But something like that. What does it matter?

Once, following a concert at Place des Arts, I dared to approach the Borensteins. They were standing outside, seemingly irresolute. It was pouring. Thunder. Lightning. A flash summer storm. "Sorry to intrude, doctor," I said, "but I'm just going to fetch my car out of the garage. May I offer you a lift?"

"Why, that's very kind of you, Mr. . . .?"

"Panofsky. Barney Panofsky."

Then I saw Mrs. Borenstein stiffen and squeeze her husband's arm. "We've already ordered a taxi," she said.

"Yes," he said, embarrassed.

On the first page of this ill-starred manuscript, I suggested that I was a social pariah because of the scandal I would carry to my grave like a humpback. But, to come clean, following my acquittal there were men, Waspy types, reeking of old money, once given to dismissing me with the most cursory of nods, who now stood me drinks at the Ritz. "Good for you, Panofsky." Or slapped me on the back and sat down, uninvited, at my table in the Beaver Club. "In my humble opinion, you struck a blow for the good guys." Or asked me to join them for a game of noonday squash at the M.A.A.A. "And I'm not your only admirer there."

Some of their haughty wives, who had hitherto found me disagreeable, coarse, a sour and unattractive man, now got a charge out of my presence. They flirted shamelessly, my mean origins forgiven. Imagine. A kike with a passion for something else but money. A real murderer moving amongst us. "You mustn't take offence, Barney, but I associate your people with white-collar crime, not acts of, well, you know." I found these women were most aroused when I acknowledged rather than denied the heinous deed. I learned a good deal about Upper Westmount civilization and its discontents. The wife of a partner in McDougal, Blakestone, Corey, Frame and Marois, told me, "I could walk into the Ritz nude and Angus wouldn't even blink. 'You're late,' is all he would say. Oh, incidentally, Angus will be in Ottawa overnight on Tuesday, if that suits you, and I'm game for anything but the missionary position. I've

---

[1] The Weizmann Institute in Haifa.

read about the alternatives, of course. I'm a member of the Book-of-
the-Month Club."

But I was, and remain, anathema to the quality. Fortunately,
they are few in number in Montreal.

The Borensteins attend the Shakespearean festival in Stratford,
Ontario, every summer, and I was once seated not too far from
them in The Church restaurant. Mrs. Borenstein was flushed, and
I'm willing to swear the old man, his hand under the table, was
flirting with his wife of something like fifty years. I summoned the
waiter and asked him to send them a bottle of Dom Pérignon, but
only after I had left, and not to say where it came from. Then I
strolled out into the rain, feeling deeply sorry for myself and cursing
Miriam who had abandoned me.

I dislike most people I have ever met, but not nearly so much
as I am disgusted by the Rt. Dishonourable Barney Panofsky.
Miriam understood. Once, following an all-too-characteristic
drunken rage on my part, which led, inevitably, to my seeking sustenance from a bottle of Macallan, she said, "You hate those TV
shows you produce, and you're filled with contempt for just about
everybody who works on them. Why don't you give it up before it
gives you cancer?"

"And what would I do then? I'm not even fifty yet."

"Open a bookshop."

"That wouldn't keep me in Havanas and XO cognac and first-
class travel to Europe for the two of us. Or pay college fees. Or
leave anything for the children."

"I don't want to end my days with a sour old man, full of regrets
for a wasted life."

And, in the end, she didn't, did she? Instead, she is wasting
herself on Herr Doktor Professor Save-the-Whales, Stop-the-Seal-
Hunt, Wipe-Only-With-Recycled-Paper, Hopper né Hauptman,
who has dropped the second 'n' in his original family name lest
people discover he was related to the Lindbergh kidnapper, and
possibly even Adolf Eichmann, if you scrutinized his family history.

Enough.

Dr. Borenstein is the subject of today's sermon. Given that he is
a gentleman of impeccable taste, imagine my consternation when I
saw him, and Mrs. Borenstein, sitting in the fourth row for Terry
McIver's reading from *Of Time and Fevers* in the Leacock Audi-

torium last Wednesday night. I had to be there, hiding in the last row. I hadn't heard that pretentious fraud read from his work since that disastrous evening, on the other side of the moon, in George Whitman's bookshop. But what was such a cultured couple doing there among all those CanCult groupies?

Terry was introduced by Professor Lucas Bellamy, author of *Northern Rites: Essays on Culture and Place in Post-Colonial Canada*, who began his halting, ten-minute panegyric by saying Terry McIver needed no introduction. Terry's prizes were cited. The Governor General's Award for Literature. The Canadian Authors' Association Medal of Merit. His Order of Canada. "And," the professor concluded, "if there is any justice, the Nobel Prize in the not too distant future. For the truth is, if Terry McIver weren't a Canadian he would be internationally celebrated instead of overlooked by the cultural imperialists in New York and the snobs who rule the London literary roost."

Before launching into the reading, Terry announced that he had, along with a number of other writers, endorsed a statement opposing the use of clear-cutting and supporting the protection of British Columbia's Clayoquot Sound. Clear-cut logging, he said, led to species loss. It was estimated that one hundred species a day go extinct because of human impact on the environment, which also contributes to global warming – a prospect I would have thought was to be welcomed as a blessing in our country. "Biodiversity is our living legacy," he proclaimed to applause, and then he asked everybody to sign a petition that the ushers would pass around. I had come with Solange, my regular companion now, who would soon be joining me in the pensioners' ranks, but continued to wear short dresses more appropriate to a woman of Chantal's age. I feared they made her look foolish, which grieved me as I held her in such high regard, but I didn't dare say a word. Solange had done me proud as a TV director, but still longed to be on camera, playing romantic leads. I didn't allow her to stay on for the book signing, hurrying her out of the hall and taking her to dinner at L'Express. "Why did you sign that dumb petition they were passing around?" I asked.

"It wasn't dumb. Animal life *is* threatened everywhere."

"Yours and mine, too. But you know something? You're right.

I worry, in particular, about the possible loss of hyenas, jackals, cockroaches, deadly snakes, and sewer rats."

"Couldn't you wait until I finished my dinner?"

"What if, due to our negligence, they all went the way of the dinosaurs?"

"Like you?" she asked, and then I began to drift, fighting tears. I used to come here with Miriam. Miriam, my heart's desire. What was troubling her this morning? Maybe Kate had reproached her on the phone for leaving me? How dare Kate. *Oh yeah? Go for it, my darling. Remind her of what she's missing. No, don't.*

"Hello, hello, I'm still here," said Solange, waving her hand in front of my face.

"Are you going to buy his book?"

"Yes."

"But Solange, my dear, there are no pictures."

"If this is going to be one of your endearing all-actresses-are-idiots nights, go ahead, be my guest."

"Sorry. I shouldn't have said that. You see, I knew McIver in Paris and have seen something of him since."

"But you've already told me that more than once," she said, troubled.

"We don't like each other."

"What are you most jealous of, Barney, his talent or his good looks?"

"Oh, you are clever. But that will require some thought. Now, tell me, speaking as a *bona fide* pepper, a *pure laine* frog, probably descended from *les filles du roi*, how are you going to vote in the referendum?"

"I'm seriously thinking of voting Yes this time. There are some in the PQ who are really racist, which is abhorrent to me, but for more than a hundred years this country has exhausted itself, and been held back trying to fit a square peg into a round hole. Of course it's risky, and it won't be easy, but why shouldn't we have our own country?"

"Because it would destroy mine. Your ancestors were stupid. They should have sold Quebec and kept Louisiana."

"Barney, you're a mess. Drinking the way you do at your age. Pretending that Miriam will come back."

"And what about you? After all these years you still haven't thrown out Roger's clothes. That's sick, you know."

"Chantal says your behaviour in the office is more objectionable than ever. People dread the days you turn up. And Barney," she said, reaching for my lizardy hand, "you're coming to a time of life when it could be dangerous for you to be living alone."

"What's eating you, Solange? Spit it out."

"Chantal says that last Thursday you dictated a letter to be sent to Amigos Three and when you came in on Monday you dictated the same letter all over again."

"So I was forgetful once. I was probably hung-over."

"More than once."

"Morty Herscovitch checks me out once a year. I'm shrinking, he says. If I live to be ninety you'll be able to carry me around in your handbag."

"Chantal and I have talked it over, and should your health deteriorate you can always move in with us. We'll close off a section of the apartment with a steel mesh fence, the way people do for pet dogs they carry in the back of their station wagons. And we'll throw you the occasional latke."

"I'll move in with Kate first."

"Don't you dare even think of that, you bastard. She's had her troubles and now she's happily married. The last thing in the world she needs is you."

"It would be foolish of you to vote Yes. I don't want you to do it."

"You don't want me to? How dare you! What would you do if you were young and French-Canadian?"

"Why, I'd vote Yes of course. But neither of us is young and stupid any more."

When I dropped her off at her apartment on Côte des Neiges, Solange lingered at the car door. "Please don't carry on drinking now. Go straight home to bed."

"That's exactly what I'm going to do."

"Oh, sure, and you're willing to swear to it on the heads of your grandchildren."

"Honestly, Solange."

But, unable to face my empty apartment, my bed without Miriam, I drove on to Jumbo's, hoping to run into maître John

Hughes-McNoughton, or Zack. Instead, I was lumbered with Sean O'Hearne, who settled heavily onto the bar stool next to mine, his eyes bright with drunken malice. "Bring Mr. P. a drink," he said, between wheezes.

"You know something, Sean? I've been looking for you. Got something that might interest you."

"Yeah yeah yeah."

"Your guys dug up my garden, you sent divers down into the lake again and again, you took samples of everything in the cottage, looking for traces of blood, just like you'd seen cops do on TV. But dimwit that you are you never asked how come my chain-saw was missing."

"Bullshit. You never had one, Mr. P. Because if there was any hard labour to be done on your estate, you hired goys like me to do it. That's how it's always been with your lot."

"Then how come there was an empty hook on my garage wall?"

"Empty hook my ass. You can't take the piss out of me, Mr. P."

"What if I told you I went through a trunk of old tax papers in the cottage last weekend and found a bill for one chain-saw, dated July 4, 1959?"

"I'd say you were a fucken liar."

The others in the bar were watching the late news on TV. The daily referendum round-up. They guffawed when The Weasel filled the screen, indulging in death-rattle jokes that were now the common lot of anglophones.

"So where is that chain-saw now?"

"Where I dropped it. Four hundred feet deep somewhere, rusting, and of no use to you after all these years."

"You trying to tell me you had the guts to cut him up?"

"Sean, now that you're so thick with The Second Mrs. Panofsky, why don't you marry her? I'll continue the alimony payments. I'm even willing to provide a dowry."

"No way a guy like you could butcher a man. And there was no blood anywhere. So stop fucking with me, asshole."

"Sure there was no blood, because I could have butchered him far out in the woods. Don't forget I had a day alone at the cottage before you pricks had the good sense to charge me."

"You've got a sick sense of humour, you know that, Mr. P? Hey, look, there he is. Their fucken saviour."

It was a seething Dollard Redux who was filling the screen now. Don't be intimidated by threats, he said. No matter what they say today, after a Yes vote the rest of Canada will come to the table on bended knees.

"I suppose," said O'Hearne, "that you and the rest of your tribe will be moving to Toronto the day after. But what about guys like me? Stuck here."

"As a matter of fact, I'm now thinking of voting Yes myself."

"Yeah yeah yeah."

"For more than a hundred years this country has been held back trying to fit a square peg into a round hole. Are you prepared for another century of adolescent bickering, or should we settle the matter once and for all?"

I still wasn't ready to contend with my bed without Miriam, so I left my car where it was, turned my coat collar up against the punishing wind, a harbinger of the six months of winter to come, and began to wander the once vibrant downtown streets of the dying city I still cherished. Past boarded up stores. Signs in foundering Crescent Street boutiques that read CLOSING DOWN SALE or EVERYTHING MUST GO. Squatters had appropriated the crumbling building that had once been the art-deco York Theatre. Some lout had spray-painted "FUCK YOU, ENGLISH" on the window of a second-hand bookshop. Every lamp-post on St. Catherine Street was adorned with both OUI and NON placards. Scruffy, shivering teenagers with sleeping-bags were camped outside the Forum, where the tickets would go on sale in the morning for a Bon Jovi concert. A greasy, bearded old man, wild-eyed, muttering to himself, and wheeling a supermarket cart before him, was rummaging through a waste-bin, searching for empty cans that could be redeemed. A plump rat skittered out of the lane behind an Indian restaurant.

MacBarney hath murdered sleep.

Back in my bed, I tried one remedy after another, unavailingly. Tonight when I reached for Mrs. Ogilvy, sliding my hands under her sweater, attempting to unhook her filagreed bra, she whacked me a good one across the face. "How dare you," she said.

"Then why did you rub your tits against my back in the kitchen?"

"Why, I never. Do you think I'm so frustrated, a ravishing woman like me – getting it every afternoon in the gym from Mr. Stuart, Mr. Kent, and Mr. Abercorn, though not necessarily in that order – that I'd stoop to seducing a little Jeanne Mance jewboy wanker with dirty fingernails?"

"You left your bedroom door open."

"Yes. And you couldn't control your bladder even then. Had to make peepee. Only fourteen years old and already suffering from prostate problems. Probably cancer."

And still sleep wouldn't come. So I set the spool of my life on rewind, editing out embarrassments, reshooting them in my mind's eye . . . and that Monday afternoon in 1952 as I entered my hotel on the rue de Nesle, the concierge rapped on her cubicle window, slid open the glass, and sang out: "*Il y a un pneumatique pour vous, Monsieur Panofsky.*"

Clara was expecting me for dinner. Well, why not? I stopped at the nearest Nicolas and bought a bottle of St. Emilion, a favourite of hers. Discovering her in a deep sleep on our bed, an empty bottle of sleeping pills on the floor, I immediately propped her upright, supporting her, walking her up and down, until the ambulance came. After they had pumped out her stomach, I sat by her bedside, stroking her hand. "You saved my life," she said.

"Your hero."

"Yes."

Then her putrefying corpse floated up at me, the eye sockets empty, worms feeding on her bosom, and Cantor Charnofsky pounded on my door again. "You going to piss in bed at your age?" he asked.

Roused, I recognized it was time for one of my pinch-it-trickle-and-shake-it pees, and then padded back to bed.

Four-thirty a.m. Sinking, my eyes lit with joy at the sight of Boogie looming large before me. "I knew you'd turn up eventually," I said, "but where have you been all these years?"

"Petra. New Delhi. Samarra. Babylon. Papua. Alexandria. Transylvania."

"I can't begin to tell you the trouble you've caused me. Never mind. Miriam, the Boogie-man is here. Would you set another place at the table, please?"

"How can I? I don't live here any more. I left you."

"No, you didn't."

"Don't you remember?"

"*You're spoiling my dream.*"

Then I made a bad turn. And The Second Mrs. Panofsky intruded. Running for her Honda again, tears flying, shrieking, "What are you going to do?"

"I'm going to kill him is what I'm going to do."

O Lord, I have so much to answer for, but not yet. Please. Pretty please.

Which is when the phone began to ring. Ring and ring and ring. *Something bad has happened. Miriam. The kids.* But it was a tearful Solange. "Serge has been beaten up by a bunch of goddamn gay-bashers."

"Oh, no."

"He was cruising in Parc Lafontaine. He needs stitches. I think his arm is broken."

"Where is he?"

"Here."

"Why isn't Peter looking after him?"

Peter, a talented set designer, was Serge Lacroix's companion. They shared a converted loft in Old Montreal, and I joined them there for dinner on occasion. Walls painted purple. Mirrors everywhere. I don't know how many Persian cats on the prowl.

"If Peter had been here this never would have happened. He's on a film location in British Columbia."

"I'm coming right over." I hung up and dialled Morty Herscovitch's home number. "Morty, I'm sorry to waken you, but my ace director has been hurt in an accident. I'm going to take him to the General, but I don't want him waiting in emergency for two hours, only to be finally looked at by some intern who hasn't been to sleep for the last thirty-six hours."

"Not the General. I'll meet you at the Queen Elizabeth in half an hour."

Rather than drive, I took a taxi to Solange's apartment. Serge's scalp was torn, his swollen left eye was all but closed, and he was cradling a clearly broken wrist.

"What were you doing whoring in that park at your age? You know how dangerous it is."

"I thought you came here to be helpful," said Solange.

Morty, who was waiting for us at the Queen Elizabeth, sewed eighteen stitches into his scalp, had him X-rayed, and attended to his wrist cast. Then he took me aside, "I want him to have a blood test while he's here, but he says no."

"Leave it to me."

Later I took Solange and Serge back to my apartment. I put Serge to bed in my spare bedroom. "Now are you going to be a good boy or do I have to lock my bedroom door before I go to sleep?"

He smiled and squeezed my hand, and I retreated to the kitchen and cracked open a bottle of champagne for Solange. "I want you to stop fooling around with Chantal," she said.

"You're imagining things."

"She doesn't understand what a hooligan you are. And she is easily hurt."

I opened the fridge. "We have a choice. There's a tub of chopped liver. I could heat up some kasha knishes. Or I could grudgingly share this tin of caviar with you."

TWO

SHADES of Mrs. Ogilvy.

Story in this morning's *Gazette* about a pretty music teacher in Manchester, now forty-one years old, who has been charged, twelve years after the fact, with seducing boys, aged thirteen to fifteen, in a youth orchestra. An alleged victim, whose memory was enhanced after attending a two-day child-abuse workshop, told the judge how he had been taken advantage of after a violin lesson, when he was a mere fourteen years old. "Penelope lay down on her bed and pulled me down beside her. She unbuttoned her blouse and invited me to fondle her breasts. I undid her jeans. She was wearing red satin knickers. She put her hand inside my trousers. I had oral sex with her for twenty minutes. Afterward she served me tea, with chocolate digestives, and told me, 'You are a naughty boy.' "

In a separate incident, following a Christmas drinks party,

another allegedly abused boy said, "Penelope took off her knickers at the edge of the bed. She lay back, undid her shirt, closed her eyes, and there was a free-for-all."

The judge ruled that it would be unfair to proceed with a trial, because the alleged incidents had taken place so long ago, and it would be difficult to trace witnesses and evidence that would back up the teacher's denial of the charges. He ordained that it was clear that the boys had not suffered psychological damage but had been willing participants and had "thoroughly enjoyed the activities." However, he stopped short of noting that, on balance, Penelope had surely done more than Yehudi Menuhin to encourage musical appreciation among the young. Penelope lost interest in the boys once they reached the age of fifteen. Unfortunately this also proved to be the case with Mrs. Ogilvy. That cruel blow was only somewhat mollified by my new relationship with Dorothy Horowitz. Dorothy, who was my age, would never allow me to venture beyond groping on the family's plastic-covered sofa, or on a bench in Outremont Park, and even this activity was blighted by forcibly proscribed zoning laws. Dorothy would withdraw her hand, as if touched by fire, when I directed it to the pulsating root of my ardour, considerately unbuttoned, and popping like Punch out of its box.

1943 that was. Field Marshal von Paulus's army had already been decimated at Stalingrad, the Americans had taken Guadalcanal, and I had that pin-up of Chili Williams in a two-piece polkadot bathing-suit tacked to my bedroom wall. My mother had begun to mail jokes to Bob Hope and Jack Benny, as well as one-liners to Walter Winchell, and my father was already a uniformed member of Montreal's finest. Izzy Panofsky, the only Jew on the police force. The pride of Jeanne Mance Street.

In the here and now in my apartment in the Lord Byng Manor I zipped through breakfast, and decided to take advantage of the fact that the family living in the apartment immediately downstairs from me, the McKays, were at their weekend cottage on Lake Memphremagog. I rolled back my living-room carpet and pulled the curtain that hid my embarrassing but necessary full-length mirror. Next I donned my top hat, tails, and trusty Capezio taps, and shoved Louis Armstrong's rendition of "Bye Bye Blackbird" into my CD player. Remembering to tip my topper to the good folks in the balcony, resting my cane on my shoulder, I loosened up with a Round-the-

Clock Shuffle, eased into a satisfying Brush, followed by a really swell Cahito, before I risked a Shim Sham, and collapsed in the nearest chair, panting. ·

Hello, shmuck, I thought. And I resolved yet again to cut back on Montecristos, medium-fats on rye, single malts, that delicious beef-marrow[1] *hors d'oeuvre* they serve at L'Express, XO cognac, marbled rib steaks at Moishe's, caffeine, and everything else that was bad for me now that I could afford it.

Where was I? 1956. Long back from Paris. Clara dead but not yet an icon; Terry McIver's first novel published, when literature would have been better served had he been interrupted in mid-flight by a gentleman from Porlock; and Boogie, high on horse more often than not, writing to me whenever his need was dire. I didn't begrudge him the money, but it was a hardship, as I had just begun to test the polluted waters of TV production, struggling, never settling a bill until Final Notice. Compounding my troubles at the time, I had stupidly resumed my affair with Abigail, and oh my God she was now hinting at leaving Arnie for me, maybe bringing their two kids along with her.

Hold the phone. Somewhere in my Noter's Write Book I've got something very apropos to that time and the problem I fumbled so badly. It was written by Dr. Johnson in 1772, when he was sixty-three years old: "My mind is unsettled and my memory confused. I have of late turned my thoughts with very useless earnestness upon past incidents. I have yet got no command over my thoughts; an unpleasing incident is almost certain to hinder my rest."

What follows is an unpleasing incident, and how it began. One day, my accountant, the vile, ineffable Hugh Ryan, sent Arnie to the head office of the Bank of Montreal with a sealed envelope that he said contained a certified cheque for fifty thousand dollars. But when the bank manager opened the envelope he found photographs of naked boys and an invitation to a candlelit dinner at Arnie's place. A distraught Arnie came to see me at Dink's. "There's something you don't know. Every morning before I report for work I stop at the men's room to vomit. I'm suffering from shingles now. Abigail and I are watching 'Bonanza' on TV and suddenly I begin to sob. It's nothing, I say. Yeah. Some nothing. Barney, I'm your friend, and

---

[1] It's veal marrow.

he isn't. We go way back, you and me. When you couldn't do your trigonometry exam, who passed you the answers? I was a whiz at maths even then. I've been jiggling numbers for you for how many years now? I could go to prison for it, do I mind? *Fire the son of a bitch. I could do his job with one hand tied behind my back.*"

"Arnie, I don't doubt your abilities. But do you go salmon fishing on the Restigouche with Mackenzie of the Bank of Montreal?"

"I could never put a worm on a hook, it disgusts me."

"Do you know how much I've got at risk in development deals? I could go under just like that. Arnie, I've got to hold onto him for another year. Max."

"I shout at my kids. The phone rings I jump like somebody was shooting a gun at me. I wake up at three o'clock in the morning from imaginary quarrels with that Jew-baiter. I'm so restless in bed poor Abigail can't get any sleep, so one night a week she has to catch up. Wednesdays she cooks up a storm and takes it with her to a girlfriend's house in Ville St. Laurent. She spends the night with Rifka Ornstein. I don't blame her. She comes home refreshed."

"How much do I pay you, Arnie?"

"Twenty-five thousand."

"Starting next week I'm going to make it thirty."

When Abigail arrived promptly at eight Wednesday night I delivered my rehearsed speech. "Of course it was never like this for me before, but we must sacrifice ourselves for the sake of Arnie and the children. I couldn't live with myself knowing that I had hurt them and neither could a woman of your rare beauty and intelligence and integrity. We will always have our memories. You know, like Celia Johnson and Trevor Howard in *Brief Encounter.*"

"I never go to British movies. It's their funny accents. Who can understand how they speak English?"

"Nobody can take away the magic we shared, but we must be brave."

"You know something? If my hands were free, I'd clap. But I made you braised brisket and kasha. Here," she said, shoving it at me. "Choke on it."

Once she had gone, slamming the door, I heated up the brisket, which was wonderfully moist if a tad too salty. But the kasha was perfect. What, I wondered, if we cut out the fucking and she continued to cook for me? Naw. She wouldn't buy that.

Later that guilt-ridden night, pulling on a Montecristo, I surprised myself, resolving to finally do right by Arnie, and put an end to his office miseries. I woke up the next morning bent on self-sacrifice, a determined man glowing with virtue. Slipping into a soft-shoe shuffle, I belted out, "Blueberry Hill." Then, immediately following a long liquid lunch at Dink's, which served to bolster my resolve, I summoned Arnie to my office.

"What's wrong?" he asked, his lower lip trembling.

"Sit down, Arnie, old pal of mine," I said, beaming beneficently. "I've got news for you."

Arnie lowered himself onto the edge of a chair. Rigid. Sweaty. Treating me to a whiff of the stench of fear. "I've thought over our problems here," I said, "and I've come to the only possible conclusion. Fasten your seat belt, Arnie, I'm firing Hugh."

"Like hell you are," he hollered, shooting out of his chair, spittle beginning to fly. "I quit."

"Arnie, you don't understand. I'm –"

"Oh yeah? Well wipe that smirk off your face. You've made your choice, and me, I've got my pride, I've made mine."

"Arnie, listen to me, please."

"Don't think for a minute I don't know what's behind all this. Judas. You propositioned my wife. You tried to make it with the mother of my children. She didn't stay the night with Rifka yesterday, but came home before midnight and confessed it to me. You caught her by surprise *in my kitchen, at Craig's bar mitzvah party,* for Christ's sake, and rubbed against her, you bastard. She wouldn't have you and now I'm paying the price. You're laughing. You find that funny?"

"Sorry. I couldn't help myself," I said, my giggles uncontrollable now.

"You're in need of a laugh? Good. Because I've got a real hee-haw for you. There isn't a person here who isn't looking for a job somewhere else. Big shot. Whoremaster. You think you're David Selznick, but they call you Hitler and sometimes Dean Martin behind your back. Not because of your good looks – don't worry, you're so fucken ugly – but because you're a drunkard like him. What are you anyway? Nothing squared. Your father is a cop on the take and your mother was a laughing stock from day one. She got that letter from Hedda Hopper that time, with the autographed photo – *it was printed, her signature* – but your mother showed it to everybody on the street, they didn't know where to look."

"You're digging yourself a deep hole, Arnie."

"Francine once went to deliver some documents to you and she says she caught you wearing a silly straw hat, dressed like the Jack of Hearts, she said, wearing tap-dance shoes. Ha, ha, ha. Fred Astaire look to your laurels. Whoop-de-do, here comes Gene Kelly Panofsky. Boy, did we ever have a laugh at your expense! So up yours, you putz from way back, I can't tell you how glad I am to be finished here." And he was gone.

Charging out of my office in a rage, in pursuit of Arnie, I all but collided with Hugh Ryan. "This is all your fault, Hugh. You're fired. You're finished here today."

"I have no idea what you're burbling about, but methinks somebody has had one too many."

"I won't have you tormenting Arnie any more. Clean out your desk and get out."

"What about my contract?"

"You'll get six months' salary, and that's it. *Bonjour la visite.*"

"In that case, you'll be hearing from my lawyer."

Shit shit shit. What had I done? I could manage without Arnie, that peckerhead, but I couldn't do without my prized goyishe bank connection. In my mind's eye, I saw demand notes surfacing on my desk first thing in the morning. Loans being called in. Maybe government auditors sent for to rake through my files. "What's everybody staring at?" I demanded.

Heads lowered.

"Hitler here is thinking of cutting staff. Downsizing.[2] So if anybody here wants a job elsewhere, now's the time to make your

---

[2] Actually, "downsizing" did not enter the idiom until September 1975 when *U.S. News & World Report* informed its readers, " 'Longer, lower, wider' is out. 'Small, smaller, smallest' is in. Detroit's engineers call the current trend 'downsizing.' " Six years later, when the recession struck in 1981, and companies began to lay off workers by the thousands, "downsizing" made the leap to its current meaning.

move. You're dispensable. Every last one of you. Like Kleenex. Have a nice day."

Feeling wretched, deeply embarrassed by my unforgivable outburst, I made straight for Dink's, in search of sustenance.

"Hard day at the office, darling?" asked John Hughes-McNoughton.

"You know something, John? You're not nearly as witty as you think. Especially when you've been boozing all day. Like now," I said, and moved on to the Ritz bar.

It must have been eight o'clock when I staggered out of there, slid into a taxi, and drove to Arnie's apartment in the wilds of Chomedy. Abigail answered the door. "You dare to come here?" she hissed, aghast.

"To see him, not you," I said, brushing past her.

"It's shit-face, Arnie. For you."

Arnie switched off the TV. "I went to see my lawyer this afternoon and anything you have to say should be said to him. Because in Lazar's opinion, I have a good case for damages. Unfair dismissal."

"But you quit."

"You fired him first," said Abigail. "He's got that in his notes."

"Anybody mind if I sit down?"

"Sit."

"Arnie, I did not fire you today. I called you in to say I was firing Hugh," I said, emphasizing the H.

"Oh, my God," said Arnie, rocking his head in his hands.

"Don't start your snivelling. This has already been too long a day for me."

"Did you?"

"What?"

"Fire Hugh?"

"Yes."

"About time," said Abigail.

"Have you got anything to drink here?"

Arnie hurried over to a cupboard. "We've got some peach brandy left over from Craig's bar mitzvah. Wait. There's something left in this bottle of Chivas."

"He doesn't drink Chivas. He drinks – How would I know? I'm all mixed up. I don't know what I'm saying. I'll get you a glass."

"So what happens now?" asked Arnie, rocking, his hands squeezed between his legs.

"Well, you said some very harsh things to me today."

"But I was going crazy in there. I take it back. Everything. I want you to know I've always admired you for the great things you've accomplished. You're my mentor."

"I'm going to die," said Abigail.

"Arnie," I said, gulping down the heel of the Chivas left in the bottle, "you can now do one of two things. You can quit with a year's salary or come back to work tomorrow morning. Discuss it with the mother of your children."

"Tell him you want Hugh's job and Hugh's salary."

"I want Hugh's job and his salary."

"I heard her. The answer is no."

"Why?"

"Arnie, you've heard my offer. Discuss it with Abigail and then let me know," I said, getting up.

"You shouldn't drive in your condition," said Arnie. "Wait one minute. I'll drive you."

"I came in a taxi. You could call me another one right now, Arnie, please."

No sooner did Arnie disappear into the kitchen than Abigail said, "*My casserole. The Pyrex dish.* If he finds them missing he'll blame our cleaning lady."

"But I haven't finished the kasha yet," I said.

THREE

Oct. 23, 1995
Dear Barney,

To each his own albatross.

From the day of your arrival in Paris, touchingly gauche, ill-educated, pushy, it was abundantly clear to me (and others I could name) that you were consumed with envy for my talent. Nay, obsessed is what you were, ingratiating yourself by feigning friendship. I was not fooled. But I took pity on you and watched, amused, as you wormed your way into the affections of The Motley Crew, not too proud to fill the office of unpaid factotum. Clara's meal-ticket. Boogie's poodle. With hindsight, of course, I reproach myself for having been so indulgent, because, had I not introduced you around, poor Clara Charnofsky would be alive today, and so would Boogie, the latter, alas, a larger loss to drug dealers than the world of letters. Since then, as an observer of *la condition humaine*, I have sometimes wondered how you continued to function after being responsible for two untimely deaths. Sleep cannot come easy.

I have heard that your maternal grandfather was a junk dealer, so it strikes me as altogether fitting, a symmetry of sorts, that you have subsequently become wealthy as a purveyor of TV trash to the hoi-polloi. I was not surprised, given your vengeful nature, that you considered it droll to title an especially prurient series, "McIver of the RCMP." Neither was I astonished to see you suffering at the Leacock Auditorium when I recently read to a sell-out audience. But, fool that I am, I believed that there was some calumny that even you would not stoop to. Congratulations, Barney. Your latest maledictory gesture caught me unawares. Which is to say I have read your son's vicious attack on *Of Time and Fevers* in the *Washington Times*. Poor sclerotic Barney Panofsky. So depraved in the years of his decrepitude that he has to enlist his son where he fears to tread.

Although I never deign to respond to, or even read, reviews of my work (most of them flattering, I might point out), I did feel obliged to write to the literary editor of the *Washington Times* to point out that Saul Panofsky's diatribe had been inspired by his father's personal animus.

Sincerely,
Terry McIver

FOUR

WHAT follows appears to be yet another digression. It isn't. I'm making a point. Mr. Lewis, our class master in Room 43, F.F.H.S. delighted in reciting Henry Newbolt's stirring *Drake's Drum* to us.

If the Dons sight Devon, I'll quit the port o'Heaven,
An' drum them up the Channel as we drummed them long ago.

However, according to today's *New York Times*, Newbolt (surprise, surprise) was a phony. He scribbled patriotic doggerel, yes, but avoided military service in the Boer War, protesting that it was his role to boost national morale at home. The legend of Drake's drum was fraudulent, his invention. Actually, the poet, self-advertised as the embodiment of Victorian virtues, enjoyed a lifelong relationship with his wife and her cousin, screwing his wife in London and her cousin on alternate nights in the country. W.H. Auden once wrote:

> Time that is intolerant
> Of the brave and innocent,
> And indifferent in a week
> To a beautiful physique,
>
> Worships language and forgives
> Everyone by whom it lives;
> Pardons cowardice, conceit,
> Lays its honors at their feet.

Well maybe yes and maybe no. But I've never known a writer or a painter anywhere who wasn't a self-promoter, a braggart, and a paid liar of a coward, driven by avarice and desperate for fame.

Hemingway, that bully, his built-in shit-detector notwithstanding, concocted his First World War record on his typewriter. That old sweetie, Lewis Carroll, beloved by generations of children, wasn't the guy you wanted to babysit your ten-year-old daughter. Comrade Picasso sucked up to the Nazis during the occupation of Paris. If Simenon actually screwed 10,000 women, I'll eat my straw boater. Odets ratted on old friends to the House Un-American Activities Committee. Malraux was a thief. Lillian Hellman lied outrageously. Lovable old Robert Frost was actually one mean son of a bitch. Mencken was a rabid anti-Semite but not as bad as that notorious plagiarist, T.S. Eliot, or many more I could name. Evelyn Waugh was a social climber and Frank Harris probably died a virgin. Jean-Paul Sartre's Resistance record was iffy and later he became an apologist for the Gulag. Edmund Wilson was a tax cheat and Stanley Spencer a boor. T.E. Lawrence did not read every book in the Bodleian. The closest Marco Polo ever got to The Middle Kingdom was most likely the Piazza San Marco. Why, if the facts were known, I'll bet it would turn out old Homer had 20/20 vision.

I had lit out for the cultural territories, going to Paris, hoping to be enriched by associating with the pure of heart, "the unacknowledged legislators of the world," and came home determined not to have anything to do with writers or painters again.

Except for Boogie.

Following my departure, the Boogie-man was reported to have been seen in Istanbul, Tangier, and that island off the coast of Spain. Not Majorca, but the other one. Crete? Don't be stupid. The one that was ruined by the hippies.[1] Anyway the first letter I got from Boogie, in 1954, two years after I returned to Montreal, came from a Buddhist monastery in what used to be called Formosa,[2] but is now named something else, just like Coke has been reborn Coke Classic. Fuck it. At my age, I'm not obliged to keep up any more. I scan the movie ads, promoting films starring this or that surly toy boy and tit-enhanced starlet, each one scoffing $10-million a shot, and I have no idea who they are. Fact. Once women, who had become stars of the silver screen, had to don dark glasses and a headscarf in order to pass unrecognized on the street, but now all they have to do is get dressed. While I'm at it, I have no idea what

---

[1] Ibiza.

[2] In fact, this letter from Boogie was written in 1957, mailed from New York, not Taiwan, after Boogie had been to his first rock'n'roll concert.

"snogging" means, or "whingeing," or why young trendies started the grazing shtick in restaurants. I'm not on-line and never will be.

Boogie wrote:

Mankind, manifestly imperfect, is still riding the evolutionary cycle. In the far future, if only for the sake of convenience, the genitals of both men and women will rise to where our heads are now, and our increasingly redundant noggins will sink to where our genitals once rested. This will enable young and old to lock into each other without tiresome romantic foreplay or the inevitable struggle with buttons or zippers. They will be able to "only connect," as Forster wrote, while waiting for a traffic light to change, or lining up before the supermarket cashier, or on a synagogue bench or church pew. "Fucking," or the more genteel "love-making," will be known as "a header," as in, "Walking down Fifth Avenue, I sniffed this fetching chick, and threw her a header."

The flip side of this cultural refinement is that the brothel, or cathouse, will yield to the library as the forbidden place where sinners meet to tryst (unzipping or lowering panties, to converse grammatically) under constant threat of closure by the anti-literacy squad. And the new social disease will be intelligence. Remember, you read it here first.

Terry returned to Montreal a year after I did to wind up his father's estate, the old man's bookshop becoming a pizza parlor, and – this is amazing, truly amazing – the first time we ran into each other, on Stanley Street, we actually embraced, delighted by our chance encounter, and retreated to the Tour Eiffel for a celebratory drink, fostering the illusion that we had once been bosom buddies, survivors of those two loosy-goosy years together on the Left Bank. We shared an hour or more of remember this and, damn it, don't forget that. The evening we all went to that Charles Trenet concert and ended up eating onion soup in Les Halles. Or, hey, how about the time Boogie sat down to the piano in that bar in Montmartre, letting on that he was Cole Porter, and earning all of us rounds of free drinks. Then we got into *de haut en bas* riffs about the provincial city we had deigned to return to, and how St. Catherine Street, Montreal's main stem which we now recognized as all but total sleaze, had once seemed a crossroads of the world to us. My God, I thought, I never realized what a good fellow McIver was, and I'm sure he felt the same about me that afternoon. I promised to call him, if not tomorrow then the day after, and he assured me he would do the same. But he didn't, and I didn't. Too bad. Because had either of us come through I think we could have become friends. It was a road not taken. But not the only one in my life. Hell, no.

Onwards. Leo Bishinsky was back in New York, established in a Village loft, and already the subject of unreadable reviews in *recherché* art journals. And Cedric Richardson's splendid first novel had been published to ecstatic reviews. I sent him an unabashed fan letter, which he did not acknowledge. That hurt. Considering that we had once been more than friends. That we shared a bond of sorts.

"You people, he said to me. You people. Brandishing that poor, wizened dead thing at me as if it had slid out of a sewer."

Next thing I knew, Cedric's photograph was on the front page of the *New York Times*. Bloody, his nose broken, he was being held by two smirking, fat-assed Kentucky state troopers. He had taken part in an attempt to register twelve black children in an all-white school and had been caught up in the flying bricks and fisticuffs that ensued. Ten whites had also been arrested in the riot.

As for me, following my retreat from Paris and the artistic wankers I had wasted my time with there, I resolved to make a fresh start in life. What was it Clara had once said? "When you go home, it will be to make money, which is inevitable, given your character, and you'll marry a nice Jewish girl, somebody who shops . . ." Well, I'll satisfy her ghost, I thought. From now on it was going to be the bourgeois life for Barney Panofsky. Country club. Cartoons scissored out of the *New Yorker* pasted up on my bathroom walls. *Time* magazine subscription. American Express card. Synagogue membership. Attaché case with combination lock. Et cetera et cetera.

Four years had passed, and I had graduated from dealing in cheese, olive oil, antiquated DC-3s, and stolen Egyptian artifacts, but was still brooding about Clara, guilt-ridden one day, defiant the next. I went out and bought myself a house in the Montreal suburb of Hampstead. It was perfection. Replete with living-room conversation pit, fieldstone fireplace, eye-level kitchen oven, indirect lighting, air-conditioning, heated toilet seats and towel racks, basement wet bar, aluminum siding, attached two-car garage, and living-room picture window. Admiring my acquisition from the outside, satisfied that it would make Clara spin in her grave, I saw what was wrong, and immediately went out and bought a basketball net and screwed it into place over the garage double-doors. Now all that was missing was a wifey and a dog called Rover. By this juncture, sitting on $250,000 in the bank, I sold off my agencies, netting even more *mezuma*, registered the name Totally Unnecessary Productions Ltd., and rented offices downtown. Then I set out in quest of the missing piece in my spiteful middle-class equation, the jewel in reb Panofsky's crown, so to speak. After all, it is a truth universally acknowledged that a single man in possession of a good fortune must be in want of a wife. Yes. But, in order to acquire Mrs. Right, I had first of all to prove myself a straight arrow.

So I decided to infiltrate the Jewish establishment, set on qualifying as a pillar or at least a cornice. For openers, I volunteered to work as a fund-raiser for United Jewish Appeal, which explains how late one afternoon I actually found myself sitting in the office of a suspicious but hot-to-trot clothing manufacturer. Certainly I had come to the right place. A Man-of-the-Year plaque hung on the wall behind tubby, good-natured Irv Nussbaum's desk. So did a pair of bronzed baby shoes. There was an inscribed photograph of Golda Meir. In another photograph Irv was shown presenting a Doctor of Letters scroll to Mr. Bernard Gursky on behalf of Friends of the Ben-Gurion University of the Negev. A model of an eighteen-foot yacht that Irv maintained in Florida was mounted on a pedestal: the good ship *Queen Esther*, after Irv's wife, not the Biblical Miss Persia. And photographs of Irv's obnoxious children were here, there, and everywhere. "You're kind of young for this," said Irv. "Usually our fund-raisers are, well, you know, more mature men."

"A guy can't be too young to want to do his bit for Israel."

"Care for a drink?"

"A Coke would be nice. Or a soda water."

"How about a Scotch?"

"Darn it. It's too early in the day for me, but you go right ahead, please."

Irv grinned. Obviously, contrary to reports, I wasn't a boozer. I had passed a test. So now I submitted to a crash course of do's and don'ts.

"I'm going to trust you with just a few cards to begin with," said Irv. "But listen up. Rules of the game. You must never visit your target in his office, where he is king shit and you're just another shmuck looking for a handout. If you run into him in the synagogue, you can butter him up with Israel's needs, but it's no good putting the touch on him there. Bad taste. Money-changers in the temple. Use the phone to schedule a meeting, but the time of day you get together is of the utmost importance. Breakfasts are out, because maybe his wife wouldn't let him bang her last night, or he didn't sleep because of heartburn. The ideal time is lunch. Pick a small restaurant. Tables far apart. Some place you don't have to shout. Make it eyeball to eyeball. Shit. We've got a problem this year. There's been a decline in the number of anti-Semitic outrages."

"Yeah. Isn't that a shame," I said.

"Don't get me wrong. I'm against anti-Semitism. But every time some asshole daubs a swastika on a synagogue wall or knocks over a stone in one of our cemeteries, our guys get so nervous they phone me with pledges. So, things being how they are this year, what you've got to do is slam-dunk your target about the Holocaust. Shove Auschwitz at him. Buchenwald. War criminals thriving in Canada to this day. Tell him, 'Can you be sure it won't happen again, even here, and then where will you go?' Israel is your insurance policy, you say.

"We will provide you with the inside info on your target's annual income, and if he starts to cry, saying he's had a bad year, you say bullshit and read him numbers. Not the numbers on his tax returns. The real numbers. You tell him now that we've got that fucker Nasser to contend with, his pledge has to be bigger this year. And if he turns out to be a hard nut, a *kvetcher*, you slip in that everybody at Elmridge, or whatever country club he belongs to, will know exactly how much he pledged, and that his order books could suffer if he turns out a piker. Hey, I understand you've gone into television production. You need help with casting, Irv's your man."

Help with casting? A babe in the show-biz woods that swarmed with ferrets, conmen, and poisonous snakes, I even needed help tying my shoelaces in those days. I was bleeding, no, haemorrhaging money. My first pilot, the idea sold to me by a hustler who claimed he had a co-credit on a Perry Mason episode, was for a projected series about a private eye "with his own code of honour." A sort of Canadian son of Sam Spade. The pilot, directed by a National Film Board hack, starred a Toronto actor (our Olivier, his agent said, who turned down Hollywood offers on principle) who could be counted on to be drunk before breakfast, while the woman cast as his Girl Friday was, unbeknownst to me, a former mistress of his who broke into sobs whenever they had to do a scene together. The result was so unbelievably awful, I didn't dare show it to anybody, but I've got it on a cassette now and play it back for laughs whenever I'm feeling depressed.

I proved to be such an adroit fund-raiser that Irv invited me to his twenty-fifth wedding anniversary party, a dinner dance for the quality held in private rooms at Ruby Foo's, black tie, everybody there except me good for a minimum twenty-thousand-dollars-a-year UJA bite, never mind the bond drive, and other community appeals for vigorish. And that's where I met the virago who would become my second wife. Damn damn damn. Here I am, sixty-seven years old, a shrinking man with a cock that trickles, and I still don't know how to account for my second marriage, which now sets me back ten thousand dollars a month before adjustments for inflation, and to think that her father, that pompous old bore, once feared *me* as the fortune-hunter. Looking back, in search of anything that would justify my idiocy, pardon my sins, I must say I was not the real me in those days but an impersonator. Pretending to be the go-getter Clara had damned. Guilt-ridden. Drinking alone in the early-morning hours, fearful of sleep, which was invaded by visions of Clara in her coffin. The coffin, as ordained by Jewish law, was made of pine, holes drilled into it, so that the worms might fatten on that too-young corpse as soon as possible. Six feet under. Her breasts rotting. " . . . you'll be able to entertain guys at the United Jewish Appeal dinner with stories about the days you lived with the outrageous Clara." Bingeing on respectability, I was now determined to prove to Clara's ghost that I could play the nice middle-class Jewish boy better than she had ever dreamed. Hey, I used to stand back, observing myself, as it were, sometimes tempted to burst into applause in celebration of my own hypocrisy. There was the night, for instance, when I was still caught up in the lightning one-month courtship of the time-bomb who would become The Second Mrs. Panofsky, taking her to dinner at the Ritz, drinking far too much as she continued to yammer about how she would do up my Hampstead respectability trap with the help of an interior decorator she knew. "Will you be able to drive me home," she asked, " . . . in your condition?"

"Why," I said, bussing her on the cheek, and improvising on a script that could only have been produced by Totally Unnecessary Productions Ltd., "I could never forgive myself if you were hurt in an accident, because of my 'condition.' You're far too precious to me. We'll leave my car here and take a taxi."

"Oh, Barney," she gushed.

I shouldn't have written " 'Oh, Barney,' she gushed." That was rotten of me. A lie. The truth is I was an emotional cripple when I met her, drunk more often than not, punishing myself for doing things that went against my nature, but The Second Mrs. Panofsky had sufficient vitality for the two of us, and a comedic flair, or sparkle, all her own. Like that old whore Hymie Mintzbaum of blessed memory, she possessed that quality I most admire in other people – an appetite for life. No, more. In those days a determi-nation to devour all matters cultural, even as she could now wolf her way through the counter in the Brown Derby without pause. The Second Mrs. Panofsky didn't read for pleasure, but to keep up. Sunday mornings she sat down to the *New York Times Book Review*, like an exam that had been set for her, noting only those books likely to be discussed at dinner parties, ordering them promptly, and careering through them at breakneck speed: *Dr. Zhivago*, *The Affluent Society*, *The Assistant*, *By Love Possessed*. The deadliest sin, so far as she was concerned, was time-wasting, and I was accused of it again and again, squandering hours on nobodys encountered in bars. Shooting the breeze with superannuated hockey players, boozy sports columnists, and small-time conmen.

On a three-day junket to New York we stayed at the Algonquin, booked into separate bedrooms, which I insisted on, eager to play by what I took to be the rules. I could have happily passed that interlude wandering aimlessly, drifting in and out of bookshops and bars, but she was locked into a schedule that would have required a fortnight for a normal person to fill. Plays to be monitored afternoon and evening: *Two for the Seesaw, Sunrise at Campobello, The World of Suzie Wong, The Entertainer.* Between times her check-list included forced marches to out-of-the-way craft shops and jewellery designers recommended by *Vogue*. Footsore, she was still among the first through the doors of Bergdorf-Goodman when it opened in the morning, hurrying on to Saks, and those places on Canal Street, known only to the cognoscenti, where Givenchy's new "bag" dresses could be bought on the cheap. Flying down to New York, she wore an old outfit that could be dumped into her hotel-room wastepaper basket as soon as she acquired her first new one. Then, on the morning of our scheduled flight home, she tore up incriminating sales receipts, retaining only those that obliging sales-ladies had fabricated for her, say a bill for $39.99 for a $150 sweater. Boarding the plane, she wore only God knows how many sets of underwear, and one blouse over another, and then she clowned her passage past the Montreal customs inspector, flirting with him *en français*.

Yes, The Second Mrs. Panofsky was an exemplar of that much-maligned group, the Jewish-American Princesses, but she succeeded in fanning my then dying embers into something resembling life. When we met she had already served a season on a kibbutz and graduated from McGill, majoring in psychology, and was working with disturbed children at the Jewish General Hospital. They adored her. She made them laugh. The Second Mrs. Panofsky was not a bad person. Had she not fallen into my hands but instead married a real, rather than a pretend, straight arrow, she would be a model wife and mother today. She would not be an embittered, grossly overweight hag, given to diddling with New Age crystals and consulting trance-channellers. Miriam once said to me, Krishna was licensed to destroy, but not you, Barney. Okay, okay. The truth, then.

"You're far too precious to me," I gushed. "We'll leave my car here and take a taxi."

"Oh, Barney," she said, "are you ever full of shit tonight."

Oh, Barney, you bastard. When I try to reconstruct those days failing memory is an enormous blessing. Vignettes wash over me. Embarrassing incidents. Twinges of regret. Boogie flew in from Las

Vegas, moderately successful at the tables for once, to be my best man. He met my bride a couple of days before the ceremony was to take place and the two of us went out to dinner, on a night I should have been at Maple Leaf Gardens in Toronto, watching the Canadiens beat the Leafs 3–2, taking a 3–1 lead in the Stanley Cup Finals. Some game I missed. Down one-zip going into the third period, the *bleu, blanc, et rouge* potted three goals in just over six minutes: Backstrom, McDonald and Geoffrion.

"Don't go through with it, Barney, please," said Boogie. "We could drive to the airport as soon as we finish our cognacs and catch the first plane to Mexico or Spain or wherever."

"Aw, come on," I said.

"I can see that she's attractive. A luscious lady. Have an affair. We could be in Madrid tomorrow. Tapas on those narrow streets running off the Plaza Mayor. *Cochinillo asado* at Casa Botín."

"Goddamn it, Boogie, I can't leave town during the Stanley Cup Finals." And, with a heavy heart, I went on to show him my two tickets in the reds for the next game in Montreal. *The game that was being played on my wedding night.* If the Canadiens won, it would mean our fourth straight Stanley Cup, and, just this once, I was hoping that they'd lose, so that I could postpone our honeymoon and take in what would surely be the final and winning game. "Do you think she'd mind," I asked, "if, after the dinner, I slipped out for an hour and maybe caught the third period in the Forum?"

"Brides tend to be touchy about things like that," he said.

"Yeah, I guess so. My luck, eh?"

Irv Nussbaum had radiated joy at his anniversary-dinner dance.

"Seen this morning's *Gazette*? Some guys shat on the front steps of the B'nai Jacob Synagogue. My phone's been ringing all day. Terrific, eh?" This was followed by a wink and an elbow nudge. "You dance any closer with her and I'm going to have to book you a room here."

Saucy, voluptuous, smelling of everything nice, my future bride did not withdraw from my embrace on the dance floor. Instead, she said, "My father is watching us," pressing even harder against me.

Seemingly polished bald head. Waxed moustache. Gold-rimmed glasses. Bushy eyebrows. Small beady brown eyes. Jowly. Cummerbund squeezing prosperity belly. Foolish rosebud mouth. And no warmth in that measured smile as he descended on our table. He was a property developer. A builder of biscuit-box office blocks and bee-hive apartment buildings, owner of an engineering degree from McGill. "We haven't met," he said.

"His name's Barney Panofsky, Daddy."

I accepted the offer of a damp limp little hand. "Panofsky? Panofsky? Do I know your father?"

"Not unless you've ever been booked for anything, Daddy, and didn't tell me."

"My father's a detective-inspector."

"I say. Is he, indeed? And how do you earn your daily bread?"

"I'm in television production."

"You know that commercial for Molson's beer, it's such a scream? The one that makes you laugh? Barney produced it."

"Well, well, well. Mr. Bernard's son is sitting with us, and he would like to dance with you, precious, but he's too shy to ask," he said, taking her firmly by the arm. "Do you know the Gurskys, Mr. . . .?"

"Panofsky."

"We're good friends of theirs. Come, my sweet."

"No," she said, yanking her arm free, tugging me out of my chair, and leading me back onto the dance floor.

You've heard of mock turtle soup? Well, the father of the bride turned out to be the ultimate mock Wasp Jew. From the points of his waxed moustache to the toes of his Oxford wingtip shoes. Most days he fancied a pin-stripe suit, his canary-yellow waistcoat enhanced by a gold pocket-watch chain and fob. For sojourns in the countryside, he carried a malacca walking stick and, out for an afternoon of golf with Harvey Schwartz, he wore plus fours. But for dinner parties at his Westmount manse, he favoured a magenta velvet *smoking* with matching slippers, and was forever stroking his wet lips with his forefinger, as if lost in contemplation of weighty philosophical problems. His insufferable wife, who wore pince-nez, jiggled a tiny bell each time the company was ready for another course. The first time I dined there, she corrected the way I wielded my soup-spoon. Demonstrating the proper manner, she said, "Ships sail out to sea."

Naturally the ladies took their coffee in the living room, while the chaps, lingering at the table, were offered port, the decanter passed to the left, as Mr. Mock Wasp announced a subject worthy of debate: "George Bernard Shaw once said..." or "H.G. Wells would have us believe... Now what do you say to that, gentlemen?"

The old fool objected to me, of course. But, to be fair, he was one of those possessive fathers who would have been outraged by the thought of even a Gursky screwing Daddy's girl, not that we had gone that far yet. Complaining to her, he said, "He talks with his hands." An attribute he considered compromising. *Très* Jewy. "I don't want you to see him again."

"Oh, yeah? Well in that case I'm moving out. I'm going to rent an apartment."

Where, in his mind's eye, the poor man visualized his precious one being ravished morning, noon, and night. "No," he protested. "You will not move out. I won't stop you seeing him. But it is my fatherly duty to warn you that you are making a bad mistake. He comes from another *monde*."

As things turned out, he was right to object to his daughter marrying such a scamp, but he did not intervene, for fear of losing her entirely. Summoning me into his library, he said, "I can't pretend this match delights me. You come from no family, you have no education, and you are engaged in a vulgar business. But once the two of you are wed it will be contingent upon my good wife and me to accept you as one of our own, if only for the sake of our beloved daughter."

"Why, you couldn't have put it more graciously," I said.

"Be that as it may, I do have one request. My good wife, as you know, was one of the first Jewish women to graduate from McGill. Class of '22. She is a past-president of Hadassah and has had her name entered in the mayor's golden book. She has been commended by our prime minister for the work she did with British children who were evacuated here during the last global conflict – "

Yes, but only after he had written to the prime minister's office, pleading for that letter of appreciation, which was now framed and hung in their living room.

" – She is a most fastidious lady, and I would be grateful if, in the future, you would refrain from garnishing your conversation with expletives at our dining-room table. Surely this is not too large an imposition to impose on your good self."

With hindsight, there were things to be said in the old boy's favour. He had served in the Tank Corps during the Second World War, a captain twice mentioned in dispatches. Look at it this way. The sour truth is that many people whom liberals like me poke fun at – army colonels, dim private-school boys, suburban golfers, banal-tongued mediocrities, tiresome stuffed shirts – were the ones who went to war in 1939 and saved Western civilization, while Auden, ostensibly an anti-Fascist commando, fled to America when the barbarians were at the gate.[3]

My father-in-law's business reputation was impeccable. He was a constant husband, and a loving father to The Second Mrs. Panofsky. Stricken with cancer only a year after we married, he behaved with dignity during his last wasting months, as stoic as any of the G.A. Henty heroes he so admired. Unfortunately, my relationship with both Mr. and Mrs. Mock Wasp got off to a rocky start. There was, for instance, my first meeting with my future mother-in-law, a lunch *à trois* in the Ritz Gardens, arranged by my apprehensive bride who coached me for hours the night before. "You are not to order more than one drink at the table before lunch."

"Right."

---

[3] As I was going through my father's manuscript, limiting myself to correcting facts and filling in names, places, or dates, where memory had failed him, I also happened to be reading Peter Vansittart's memoir of post-war London, *In the Fifties* (John Murray, London, 1995), and came upon the following passage on page 29:

> In 1938, a mildewed colonel about whom we gibed that he had lost one leg at Mons, another at Ypres, a third on the Marne, and the last of his wits on the Somme, had barked at me: "Your Mr. Auden's no great lover of Herr Hitler, but will he be joining me to fight the bugger?" Many whom Auden derided – colonels, retarded public school boys, suburban golfers, trite-tongued mediocrities, romantic but goofy stuffed shirts – saved Western civilization. My vision of Auden as anti-Fascist commando could not be maintained when, with the barbarians at the gate, he departed to America.

I can't add plagiarism to the many sins my father has to answer for. Rather, I prefer to think Kate was right when she insisted that this had to be an innocent error. "No doubt," she said, "shuffling through his index cards, Daddy mistakenly took a thought of Vansittart's that he had transcribed for one of his own."

"And, whatever you do, no whistling at the table. *Absolutely no whistling at the table*. She can't stand it."

"But I've never whistled at the table in my life."

Things started badly, Mrs. Mock Wasp disapproving of our table. "I should have had my husband make the reservation," she said.

It was an effort to begin with, the conversation halting, Mrs. Mock Wasp infuriating me by demanding answers to direct questions about my family background, my past, my health, and my prospects, before I eased us into safer territory: the death of Cecil B. De Mille, how enjoyable Cary Grant was in *North by Northwest*, and the coming Bolshoi Ballet tour. In fact, my behaviour was four-star exemplary until she told me how she had adored *Exodus*, by Leon Uris, and, all at once, I began to whistle "Dixie."

"*He's whistling at the table*."

"Who?" I asked.

"You."

"But I never. Shit, was I?"

"He didn't mean to, Mother."

"I apologize," I said, but when the coffee came I was so nervous, I found myself suddenly whistling "Lipstick on Your Collar," one of that year's hit numbers, stopping abruptly. "I don't know what's got into me."

"I would like to contribute my share of the bill," said my future mother-in-law, rising from the table.

"Barney wouldn't hear of it."

"We come here often. They know us. My husband always tips twelve-and-a-half per cent."

Next there came the dreaded day I was obliged to introduce my father to my future in-laws. My mother was already out of it by this time (not that she was ever deeply into it), wasting in a nursing home, her mind adrift. The walls of her bedroom were plastered with signed photographs of George Jessel, Ishkabibble, Walter Winchell, Jack Benny, Charlie McCarthy, Milton Berle, and the Marx Brothers: Groucho, Harpo, and, you know, the other one.[4] It's on the tip of my tongue. Never mind. The last time I had been to

---

[4] Chico. But there was also a fourth brother, Zeppo, who appeared in many of the films.

see my mother she had told me that a male orderly had tried to rape her. She called me Shloime, her dead brother's name, and I fed her chocolate ice cream out of a tub, her favourite, assuring her that it wasn't poisoned. Dr. Bernstein said she was suffering from Alzheimer's, but I mustn't worry, it needn't be hereditary.

In preparation for the visit of Mr. and Mrs. Mock Wasp to my house, I drew a "W" with a ballpoint on my right hand, a reminder not to whistle. I purchased appropriate books and left them lying about: the latest Harry Golden, a biography of Herzl, the new Herman Wouk, a photobook on Israel. I bought a chocolate cake at Aux Délices. Filled the fruit bowl. Hid the liquor. Unpacked a box of hideous china cups and saucers I had acquired only that morning and set five places with linen napkins. I vacuumed. Plumped up the sofa cushions. And anticipating that her mother would find an excuse to look into my bedroom, I checked it out inch by inch for hairs that did not belong to me. Then I brushed my teeth for the third time, hoping to kill the Scotch smell. Mr. and Mrs. Mock Wasp, as well as their daughter, were already seated in the living room when my father finally arrived. Izzy was impeccably dressed in the clothes I had chosen for him at Holt Renfrew, but, as a small act of rebellion, he had added a touch distinctively his own. He was wearing his snappy soft felt fedora with that ridiculous, multi-coloured brush in the brim large enough to serve as a duster. He also reeked of Old Spice and was in a mood to reminisce about his old days on the beat in Chinatown. "We was young fellers, pretty smart, and we soon learned us a few words of China. We watched from the rooftops when they made their trades. Then you could tell if they was smoking, because they always hung wet blankets on the street, due to the smell. Barney, would you pour me a Scotch, please," he said, pushing away his teacup.

"I don't know if I have any," I hissed, glaring at him.

"Yeah, and there's no coal in Newcastle," he said, pronouncing the 't,' "or snow in the Yukon."

So I fetched him a bottle and a glass.

"What about you? Aren't you drinking this afternoon?"

"No."

"L'chaim," said Izzy, belting one down, my own throat dry. "There was girls involved, you know. Oh yes, it was – Christ – now you take the average French-Canadian family, I don't know about today but years ago they had ten or fifteen kids, so you know, they had nothing to eat, so they used to send the girls down there and one would bring another and you come in, you raid some place, you know, and you found four-five Chinamen with four-five girls, Christ, they'd even give them dope, you know. There was a lot of opium then. I'm talking 1932 when, you know, our entire detective force had only one automobile, a two-seater Ford." Izzy paused to slap his knee. "If we catch us two crooks, you know, we'd just throw them across the hood and put the handcuffs on, and vroom-vroom, off we go. They'd be laying there like deer, you know, when you go hunting, they just lay on the hood."

"But the engine was under it," said my future bride. "Wasn't it hot?"

"We weren't going very far. Just to headquarters. And anyways I didn't feel it," said Izzy, chuckling. "*They* was on there."

"On second thought," I said, not daring to look at my future in-laws, "I just might have a wee drink myself." And I reached for the bottle.

"Are you sure, darling?"

"I feel a cold coming on."

Izzy now cleared his throat, and shot a wad of snot into one of my new linen napkins. Bull's-eye. I sneaked a glance at my future mother-in-law, attracted by her rattling teacup.

"We'd arrest a guy, we'd take him downstairs to open him up, if you know what I mean?"

"You weren't gratuitously violent with suspected felons, were you, Inspector Panofsky?"

Izzy looked pained. "Gratuitously?"

"Unnecessarily," I said.

"No fucken way, mister. I condoned it. Absolutely. But, you know, it's human nature, when a feller is young, you give him authority, he likes to push people around. But when I was young I didn't, because I knew my name was Panofsky."

"But how did *you* get suspects to talk, Inspector?" asked my future father-in-law, looking directly at his daughter, as if to say, are you prepared to marry into such a family?

"I got my ways and means how."

"How time flies," I said, glancing pointedly at my wristwatch. "It's almost six o'clock."

"You lay down the law to them. They don't want to talk, you take them down below."

"Then what transpires, Inspector?"

"Well, we get this feller in the room, we slam the bloody door and then we start to throw chairs around. You know, scare the shit out of them. Maybe I step on his toes. *Come clean*, I shout."

"What happens if, perchance, it's a woman you take downstairs?"

"Well I never remember – I'm sincere when I tell you about this – I never remember beating a woman, we never had occasion to, but if you get a tough guy, in many instances I could tell you . . ."

"Dad, may I have the bottle back, please?"

"Darling, should you?"

"Let me give you another for instance. In 1951 this was, I found those bearded rabbinical students were being beaten up outside their school on Park Avenue by all those punks. Just because they were Jews. Well, those punks they see you and I, well they doubt a little bit because we may not look too much like Jews, and we don't act it, but when they see a guy all dressed up, you know . . . Anyways their leader, this Hungarian roughneck, just off the boat, was caught, and I drove him to Station seventeen to have a look at him. He's got those boots on, you know those big boots, rough as hell, I shut the door. What's your name, I says? I don't care about anybody, he says in that accent they have. His English is terrible. So I slammed him good, mister. Down he goes. He passes out. Jesus Christ. I thought he would die. I tried to give him first aid. You know what passed through my mind? Just imagine . . . JEW POLICE OFFICER KILLS . . . if the guy died. So I rushed up an ambulance and we get him to come to . . ."

Then, even as Izzy wiped his mouth with the back of his hand, and was about to embark on another for instance, I was driven to take a desperate measure. I started to whistle. But this time, in deference to my future mother-in-law, something cultural, the "La donna è mobile" aria from *Rigoletto*. That succeeded in clearing the house of both my future in-laws and my bride. Following their hasty departure, Izzy said, "Hey, congrats. They're very nice people. Warm. Intelligent. I enjoyed talking to them. How'd I do?"

"I think you made an unforgettable impression."

"I'm glad you brought me here to look them over. I'm not a cop all these years for nothing. They're loaded. I could tell. Demand a dowry, kid."

FIVE

HEY, nonny-nonny, here's a hot one, plucked from this morning's *Globe and Mail*:

PROBATION FOR "DEVOTED"
WIFE WHO KILLED HUSBAND
Caring for sick man "intolerable burden"
after 49 years' marriage

A devoted 75-year-old wife who killed her seriously ill husband shortly before the couple's golden wedding anniversary walked free from the High Court in Edinburgh yesterday.

The poor dear was placed on probation for two years after she admitted that she had suffocated her husband with a pillow in their home last June before trying to commit suicide with a drug overdose. The court heard that she and her husband had been a "devoted and loving couple" for forty-nine years. But after hubbie, that inconsiderate boor, suffered a massive heart attack and had chronic kidney failure, the burden of nursing him had become too much for his wife, and made her suffer from depression. Tch-tch. The lawyer[1] said that caring for her husband had become "an increasingly intolerable burden." The night of the killing, he said, the husband had been getting out of bed and she ordered him to return to it, but he refused. She slapped him and, after he fell, put the pillow over his face and smothered him. The Lord Justice Clerk said he was satisfied it would not be appropriate to impose a prison sentence. "This is a truly tragic case," he said. "You find yourself

---

[1] In Scotland, an advocate or, following recent legislation, a solicitor-advocate, would have pleaded her case.

facing a situation with which you could not cope. It is clear that you committed this crime at a time when you were suffering from the mental illness of depression under considerable strain."

This poignant tale of true love gone awry among the senior-boppers put me in mind of one of my few surviving septuagenarian buddies, and so that afternoon I bought a box of handmade Belgian chocolates in Westmount Square, and went to visit Irv Nussbaum, now seventy-nine years old, yet frisky as ever, and still active in community affairs. Irv, bless him, was angst-ridden about the fate of our people, but uppermost in his mind was the coming referendum. Only yesterday The Weasel's most rabid pointman had warned *les autres* that if we voted No massively we would be punished. "That's good news," said Irv, "because that prick must have started at least another thousand nervy Jews packing. I'm grateful. Now if only they'd opt for Tel Aviv rather than Toronto or Vancouver."

"Irv, what's to be done with you, you're a terrible old man."

"Remember how when we were young the pepsis[2] marched down the Main chanting, 'Death to the Jews,' and *Le Devoir* read like it got its ideas from Julius Streicher? Do you recall how in those days there were all those restricted hotels in the Laurentians, and a Jew couldn't even get a job as a cashier in one of the banks here, never mind marry out. Like damn fools we complained about it. We fought discrimination bitterly. But, with hindsight, it was a blessing, anti-Semitism, if you feel as deeply as I do about Israel and Jewish survival."

"Do you think we ought to bring back pogroms?"

"Ho ho ho. I kid you not. Now we're accepted, even welcomed just about everywhere, and the young think nothing of marrying a *shiksa*. Look around, will you. These days there are Jews serving on the boards of banks, in the supreme court, and even in the cabinet in Ottawa. That Gursky suck-hole Harvey Schwartz sits in the senate. The lasting problem with the Holocaust is that it made anti-Semitism unfashionable. Ah, the whole world's gone topsy-turvy. I mean you're a drunk today, what is it? A disease. You murder your parents, sneaking up behind them with shotguns and blasting their heads off, like those two kids in California, what do you need? Understanding.

---

[2]"Pepsi" is pejorative. Slang for French-Canadians who were reputed to drink Pepsi-Colas for breakfast.

You slit your wife's throat and you walk because you're black. Excuse me, African-American. You're a homosexual now and you expect to be married by a rabbi. Once that was the love that dared not speak its name, but you know what mustn't show its face today? Anti-Semitism. Listen here, my old friend, we didn't survive Hitler so that our children could assimilate and the Jewish people disappear. Tell me something. Do you think Duddy Kravitz will beat the charges this time?"

"Insider trading is difficult to prove."

The last time I ran into Duddy, attended by a bimbo of a secretary, was at the airport in Toronto. "Hey, Panofsky, you going to London, let's sit together."

"Actually, I'm flying to New York, where I'm going to pick up the Concorde," I said, hastily adding that it was not me, but MCA, that was paying for the ticket.

"You think I can't afford the Concorde? Shmuck. I've done it and I don't like it. You fly the Concorde everybody on it is worth millions. DK likes to go first class on a 747 flying out of Montreal, so that I can stroll back through club and economy and all those shits who used to look down their nose at me can see how well I'm doing and choke on it."

Irv went on to say, "I even hope their fucken Parti Québécois wins the referendum this time and scares the hell out of the Jews who still remain here. Only I want them going to Tel Aviv, Haifa, or Jerusalem this time. Yes. Before Israel is overwhelmed by Ethiopian blacks or those new Russian immigrants, most of whom are not even Jewish. How about that? Seven hundred and fifty thousand Russian immigrants. Israel itself could soon become just another goyishe country. But, for all that, the Israelis are now the only anti-Semites we can still count on. Let's face it, they hate diaspora Jews. You speak a word of Yiddish there they want to flush you down the toilet. 'Oh, you must be one of those ghetto Jews.' After all these years of fund-raising, and I must be personally responsible for at least fifty million squeezed out of here over the years, and I go over there and they tell me I'm a bad Jew because my children haven't settled there and don't serve on the front lines."

Entry in Panofsky's Ledger of Ironies:

My first wife, Clara, had no time for other women and is enjoying an afterlife as a feminist icon, but it is The Second Mrs.

Panofsky, that *yenta* still bent on my imprisonment for murder, who is now the militant feminist. I keep tabs on her, and I have learned that every Passover she joins six other rejected wives, latter-day Boadiceas, for a women's seder. They begin by toasting the Shekinah, which is the female aspect of God, according to the Kabbala. Lifting the plate with the matzohs, they chant:

> This is the Seder plate.
> The plate is flat. Woman is flat, like a plate,
> flat in the relief of history ...

They go on to chant:

> Why have our mothers on this night
> been bitter?
> Because they did the preparation but
> not the ritual. They did the serving but
> not the conducting. They read of their
> fathers but not of their mothers.

According to the women warriors who composed this travesty of the Haggadah, Miriam, the sister of Moses, never got a fair shake. Where in Exodus, for instance, was the story of Miriam's well? On the cutting-room floor, that's where. But, according to rabbinical legend, it was in Miriam's honour that a well of sweet water followed the children of Israel through the desert. And when Miriam died, the well dried up and disappeared.

The daughter of Rabbi Gamaliel said: "There is anger in our heritage. In the desert Miriam and Aaron asked, 'Is Moses the only one with whom the Lord has spoken? Has he not spoken with us as well?' The Lord passed among them and left Miriam white with leprosy but Aaron unharmed. Miriam was treated like the wicked daughter whose father spat in her face and sent her from the tent for seven days until she was forgiven."

Miriam, Miriam, my heart's desire. I spit in Blair's face, never yours.

Miriam's birthday today. Her sixtieth. Were she still with me, she would have been served breakfast in bed. Roederer Crystal champagne, Beluga caviar, not to mention sixty long-stemmed roses, and gifts of silk lingerie, elegant but naughty. Maybe that over-priced pearl choker I saw at Birk's. Instead, I imagine Herr Doktor Professor Hopper would splurge on an air-pollution testing kit. Or perhaps a pair of sensible shoes with no animal leather content. No, I've got it. He's giving her a record of whale music. Har, har, har.

I was supposed to be meeting somebody for lunch, but I couldn't remember where or with whom, and I didn't dare phone Chantal to check it out as she was already sufficiently suspicious of my occasional memory lapses, which are nothing to worry about. It's common to people of my age. So I phoned Le Mas des Oliviers to find out if I had a reservation there. No. Neither had I booked L'Express nor the Ritz. Then Chantal phoned. "I'm calling to remind you that you have a date for lunch today. Do you remember where?"

"Of course I do. Don't be impertinent."

"Or with whom?"

"Chantal, I could fire you just like that."

"It's with Norman Freedman and you're supposed to meet him at Moishe's at one. Or I could be lying, and it's with my mother at Chez Gauthier. But since you remember anyway, no problem. Bye bye now."

Norman Freedman had been among the more than two hundred guests who came to my wedding at the Ritz-Carlton Hotel. Black tie, evening gowns. Boogie stoned and me blasted, my mood vile, as I longed to be in my seat in the reds in the Forum. Damn damn damn. The Canadiens could clinch their fourth Stanley Cup in a row in my absence. But there was nothing to be done, because by the time I had discovered that I was double-booked it was too late to postpone the wedding. And, remember, the 1959 *Club de hockey canadien* was one of the greatest teams of all time. Consider the line-up: Jacques Plante in the nets, Doug Harvey, Tom Johnson, and Jean-Guy Talbot minding the blue line, and, up front, Maurice and Henri Richard, Bernie Geoffrion, Dickie Moore, Phil Goyette, Ab McDonald, and Ralph Backstrom. But, alas, the Canadiens were without their best playmaker for the cup finals. Big Jean Beliveau had taken a bad fall in the third game against Chicago in the semi-finals, and was out for the rest of the season.

Immediately we were pronounced man and wife, I kissed the bride, and made straight for the bar. "What's the score?"

"Mahovlich went off for cross-checking a couple of minutes ago and Backstrom[3] scored. So it's one-zip, but it's still early in the first period. They're missing Beliveau bad," said the bartender.

I was thoroughly ill at ease among so many strangers at the Ritz, my mood unspeakable, until everything changed. Then and forever. Across the crowded room, as Howard Keel once belted out,[4] there stood the most enchanting woman I had ever seen. Long hair black as a raven's wing, striking blue eyes, ivory skin, slender, wearing a layered blue chiffon cocktail dress, and moving about with the most astonishing grace. Oh, that face of incomparable beauty. Those bare shoulders. My heart ached at the sight of her. "Who is that woman being talked at by Myer Cohen?" I asked Irv.

"Shame on you. Don't tell me you've only been married for an hour and you've already got eyes for another woman."

"Don't be ridiculous. I'm curious, that's all."

"I forget her first name," said Irv, "but I do know that Harry Kastner tried it on with her, maybe a half-hour ago, and whatever she said it made him turn pale. She's got a sharp tongue, that one. She lives in Toronto since her parents died."

Absolutely exquisite, she stood alone but alert now. Myer Cohen dismissed, another suitor had gone to fetch her a glass of champagne. When she caught me staring, and saw me starting toward her, she averted those blue eyes to die for, retreating, turning her back to join a group that included that bastard Terry McIver. I wasn't the only one watching. Skinny, bony-backed and girdled butterball wives were looking her up and down disapprovingly. Then The Second Mrs. Panofsky was with me, having just finished a dance with Boogie. "Your friend is such a melancholy man, so vulnerable," she said. "I wish we could do something for him."

"There's nothing to be done."

---

[3] Backstrom scored at 4:12, assisted by Geoffrion and Moore.

[4] Actually, it was Ezio Pinza in *South Pacific*, which ran 4 years 9 months on Broadway.

"I think you should go over and talk to your friend McIver. He seems lost here."

"Fuck him."

"Ssh. *That's my grandfather at the table right behind us.* Didn't you invite McIver?"

"Terry comes to all my weddings."

"Oh, nice. Very nice. Why don't you have another drink? Your father has already had too much, and if he starts on one of his stories my mother will die of shame."

"Now tell me who is that woman bloody Gordon Lipschitz is coming on to?"

"Oh, that one. Forget it, Mr. Love-Bucket. You're not good enough for her. Now will you please do something about your father. Slip this into your pocket."

"What is it?"

"A cheque for five hundred dollars from Lou Singer. I hate to nag, but I think you've already had enough to drink."

"What do you mean I'm not good enough for her?"

"Because if I knew she was going to honour us with her presence, I would have laid out a red carpet. Don't tell me you find her attractive?"

"Certainly not, my darling."

"I'll bet she wears a size nine-and-a-half shoe and, even at that, it squeezes her toes. Her name's Miriam Greenberg. We were at McGill together, she had a scholarship, a good thing too because the fees would have been difficult. Her father was a cutter and her mother took in sewing from a dressmaker. She comes on so grand, tell me about it, but she was brought up in one of those cold-water flats on Rachel. My Uncle Fred used to own a bunch of them and he said it would have been easier to draw water from a stone than collect the rent from some of those types. They could do a flit in the middle of the night. Sue? There was no point. Uncle Fred adored me. I'm going to kidnap you, he used to say. The fraternity guys wanted Miriam Greenberg to be Winter Carnival Queen. God knows she's not that attractive, those feet, but it would have been the first time for a Jewish girl. She said no. Miss America was good enough for Bess Myerson, but of course Bess wasn't, ahem ahem, an intellectual. She didn't shlep *Partisan Review* or the *New Republic* with her to classes, so that everybody could see what she was reading. Yeah, sure. I'll bet if you checked out her room she also took *Cosmopolitan*. Some young pianist, nobody ever heard of him, would be making his debut at Moyse Hall, and she would stand there on stage in that same black dress, it couldn't have cost more than $29.99 off the rack at Eaton's, turning the pages for him. Big deal. Now she's moved to Toronto to look for work in radio. Some hope with that voice. Your father's back at the bar again. He's talking to Dr. Mendelsohn. *Do something.*"

"Miriam Who did you say?"

"Greenberg. You want me to introduce you?"

"No. Let's dance."

"The bartender is trying to catch your eye."

"Oh, yeah, I told him if he had any problems to – Excuse me. I won't be a minute."

"First period's over," he said, "and we're now up three-zip. Geoffrion[5] and Johnson[6] have both scored. Bower looks shaky in their nets."

"Yeah, but now they'll lay back and let the Leafs come to them. Mahovlich or Duff can still do a lot of damage."

Wheeling my bride onto the floor, I contrived to lead her in the direction of Miriam, who was dancing with McIver. I came close enough to sniff her subtle scent, memorizing it. A soupçon of Joy. applied to her temples, the backs of her knees, and the hem of her skirt, as I would eventually learn. Once, years later, lying in bed with Miriam, emptying my cognac snifter onto her breasts and lapping it up, I said, "You know if you had really, really been intent on entrapping me on my wedding night, you wicked woman, you would not have dabbed yourself with Joy, but in Essence of Smoked Meat. A maddening aphrodisiac, made from spices available in Schwartz's delicatessen. I'd call it Nectar of Judea and copyright the name." But on my wedding night, I said, "Excuse me," to Miriam, having bumped against her, and then The Second Mrs. Panofsky said, "I don't want to hear you've been checking out the latest hockey score with that bartender again. This is our wedding night. It's insulting."

"I won't do it again," I lied.

"Your father has moved to the rabbi's table. Oh my God," she

---

[5]Geoffrion scored at 13:42, assisted by Backstrom and Harvey.

[6]Johnson scored at 16:26, assisted by Backstrom.

said, thrusting me in that direction. But it was already too late. Including the rabbi and his wife, the Hubermans, Jenny Roth, Dr. and Mrs. Mendelsohn, and some others I didn't know, there were twelve stunned people gathered at the long table, a sodden Izzy Panofsky in full flow. "It was when I was on morality," he said, "that I learned to appreciate the madams. Parisian ladies some of them, and very nice. There was always from fifteen to twenty-five girls there, and as soon as you came in the madam would open a door and say, 'Les dames au salon,' see, and they'd all come in and you pick out who you want."

"May I remind you there are ladies present at this table," said the rabbi in his mellifluous voice.

"Yeah, so? They all look over twenty-one to me. At least. Only joking, girls. Nobody stayed the night, the turnover was too much, you know what I mean? Some of them whorehouses was elegantly furnished."

"Daddy, I'd like to have a word with you."

"Clean? Rabbi, you could eat off the floor. And, oh, they had beautiful beds and everything was systematically . . . you know what I mean? . . . You get a big pitcher in the room and as soon as you'd come in they wash it for you."

"Daddy, my bride is waiting to dance with you."

"You're interrupting."

"Excuse me," said the rabbi's wife, rising from the table, grudgingly followed by two more ladies.

"Well, in them days it was a dollar a shot, and the girls had to pay for the soap, for the towel, and by the time she's finished she'd have to pay to work there half the time. Then they had all kinds of peddlers going in there, Hebes, smart, selling them goods on time. Hey, doc, didn't you say your name was Mendelsohn?"

"Bessie, would you care to dance?"

"Hold your horses, doc. Shmul Mendelsohn. We used to call him 'Grabby,' because, well, do I have to draw a map?" asked my father, winking. "The peddler. Was he your old man?"

"I'm coming," said Bessie.

Finally I was able to hoist my father out of his chair and propel him to the bar, where I immediately asked the bartender for the second-period scores.

"Geoffrion[7] popped another one between Bower's legs and then Bonin[8] banged one in."

"Hey, that has to be his tenth in the playoffs."

"You got it. But when Doug Harvey went off for tripping, Pulford got one back. So now it's 5–2 for the good guys."

"I thought they'd all be snobby here," said my father, "but they're very friendly it turns out. Boy, am I ever having a good time. What are you laughing at?"

"Come here," I said, and I gave Izzy a hug. He wiggled his eyebrows, took my hand and pressed it against the service revolver he wore on his hip. The revolver that would eventually be my ruin. Almost. "I don't go anywheres naked any more," he said. "Somebody gives you trouble, you tell me, and I'll fucken air-condition him."

That settled, we laid our glasses on the bar, father and son, and demanded more sustenance. The bartender scratched the back of his head. He winced. "I'm afraid, sir, that your wife and father-in-law were just here and said neither of you were to have any more."

My father dug out his wallet and flashed his badge at the bartender. "You're talking to the law," he said.

I leaned over and reached for the nearest bottle of Johnnie Walker Black and poured us both stiff drinks. "Where is that pompous bastard?" I asked.

"I'm having such a good time," said my father. "Don't embarrass me."

I found my father-in-law pontificating at a table for eight. "Lord, what fools we mortals be, Shakespeare once wrote, and how right he was, the Bard of Avon. Here we are, gentlemen, gathered together in civil discourse, ruminating on the human condition, our brief passage in this world of woes, exchanging ideas, surrounded by family and old companions. Even as we sit here, consuming the fruits of the vine with commendable restraint, there are some seventeen thousand souls howling in their seats in the Forum, their tiny minds totally engaged by the progress of a little black rubber disc that is being passed up and down the ice, its possession disputed by

---

[7,8] In fact it was Pulford who scored first, at 4:27, assisted by Armstrong and Brewer. Bonin scored at 9:56, assisted by Henri Richard and Harvey, and Geoffrion scored at 19:26, assisted by Backstrom and Johnson.

men who have never read Tolstoy or listened to Beethoven. It's enough to make you despair of humankind, don't you think?"

"Excuse me. There must be some mistake," I said. "The bartender says you instructed him not to serve my father or me anything more to drink."

"It's no mistake, young man. My daughter is in tears. *On her wedding night.* And your esteemed father, young man, has deeply upset the rabbi's wife, and because of him my good friends, the Mendelsohns, have left early."

"Dr. Mendelsohn's father was a peddler who used to feel up the girls in whorehouses."

"So say you. Mrs. Mendelsohn, I'll have you know, is a Gursky. Somebody should take your father home before he tells more disgusting stories, or falls flat on his face."

"If anybody takes my father home, I go with him."

"How could you impose such – such – very well, I'll say it – such hooligans on my family and friends? That young man there," he said, pointing at McIver seated alone at a table, scribbling, "talks to my guests and then retires to make notes. And that one over there," he said, indicating Boogie, "was found sitting at a dressing-table in the ladies' powder room, sucking some substance into his nose with a straw. The ladies' powder room, mark you."

More reproaches followed, but I was no longer listening, for there was Miriam, besieged by admirers again, and I started toward her, beaming foolishly. As the ballroom began to tilt and sway, I gathered my sea-legs under me and sailed right over to her, waving off her admirers with a glowing cigar that threatened to do damage. "We haven't been introduced," I said.

"I've been remiss. You're the groom. *Mazel tov.*"

"Yeah. Possibly."

"I think you had better sit down," she said, helping me into the nearest chair.

"You too."

"Briefly. It's late. I understand you're in television."

"Totally Unnecessary Productions."

"That's harsh."

"It's what I call my company."

"You don't," she said.

And oh my oh my I had earned a small smile. Oh, the dimple in her cheek. Those blue eyes to die for. Those bare shoulders. "Do you mind if I ask you a personal question?"

"Like what?"

"What size shoe do you wear?"

"Eight. Why?"

"I get to Toronto often. Could we go out to dinner together one evening?"

"I think not."

"I'd like that."

"It's not a good idea," she said, attempting to slip away. But I restrained her, grabbing her elbow. "I've got two tickets for tomorrow's flight to Paris in my jacket pocket. Come with me."

"Would we pause to wave goodbye to your bride first?"

"You're the most beautiful woman I've ever seen."

"Your father-in-law is staring at us."

"Tuesday we could lunch at the Brasserie Lipp. I'll rent a car and we'll drive to Chartres. Have you ever been to Madrid?"

"No."

"We could stop for tapas on those narrow streets running off the Plaza Mayor and order *cochinillo asado* at Casa Botín."

"I'm going to do you a favour and pretend this conversation never took place."

" 'Come live with me and be my love.' Please, Miriam."

"If I don't leave now I could miss my train."

"I'll divorce her as soon as we get back. Anything you want. Just say yes, please. We won't even take any luggage. We'll buy everything we need there."

"Excuse me," she said, sliding away, silky things rustling.

Crushed, I moved over to the table where my father was now holding court, surrounded by enthralled young couples. "Oh, you mean the one on Ontario Street," he said. "We were right across from it, in Station 4. They was raided from time to time, the whorehouses. So you know you're working on morality, naturally being a young feller when we went on raids the officer would be downstairs and we'd sneak up, you see, before we'd disturb them, you know what I mean? You want to see a show . . ."

Miriam was still in the ballroom, but she had her coat on, chatting with Boogie at the door, handing him something. Then Boogie came to our table, even as my father started on another story, and slipped me a folded piece of paper, which I promptly lowered on to my lap and read under the shelter of the tablecloth:

Final score. Canadiens 5, Toronto 3.[9]
Congratulations.

"Boogie," I said, "I'm in love. For the first time in my life I am truly, seriously, irretrievably in love."

Of course I hadn't realized at the time that The Second Mrs. Panofsky was standing directly behind me, and now she embraced me, rocking my head. "And so am I, honey," she said. "And so am I."

With guilt my heart was laden. Yes. But, all the same, I slipped out of the Ritz ballroom a couple of minutes later and got into the first taxi waiting in the queue outside.

SIX

"WINDSOR Station, please," I said to the driver, "and hurry." I had only minutes to spare, but, shit shit shit, the traffic was being tied up by Stanley Cup merrymakers. Cars, crawling along, honking their horns. Bugles blowing. Drunks, cavorting in the middle of the street, shouting, "We're number one! We're number one!"

My heart thudding, I did manage to get to the station in time to buy a sleeper on the overnight train to Toronto. I found Miriam in the third car, deep into *Goodbye, Columbus*, and collapsed into the seat beside her, grinning goofily, just as the train jerked to a start. "Hi," I said.

"I don't believe this," she said, banging her book shut.

"Neither do I, but here I am."

---

[9] Toronto scored twice in the third period. Mahovlich, at 12:07, assisted by Harris and Ehman, and Olmstead, at 16:19, on a power play, assisted by Ehman.

"If you don't get off this train when we stop at Montreal West, I will."

"I'm in love with you."

"Don't be ridiculous. You don't even know me. Montreal West. You or me. Make up your mind right now."

"If you get off there, so will I."

"How could you do such a thing on your wedding night?"

"I did."

"You're blind drunk. I'm going to call the conductor."

I showed her my ticket.

"Please, Barney, don't embarrass me any further. Get off the train at Montreal West."

"If I do, will you agree to have dinner with me in Toronto?"

"No," she said, leaping up and grabbing a bag from the over-head rack. "Now I'm going to my sleeper and I'm locking the door. Good night."

"You're not being awfully friendly, considering the trouble I've gone to."

"You're crazy. Good night."

I did stagger off the train at Montreal West,[1] and stood on the platform, swaying, watching it chug out of the station. And then, lo and behold, Miriam waved from her window and I could swear she was laughing. My heart soared. Encouraged, I began to run after the train, trying to board it again. I stumbled and fell, ripping my

---

[1] My doubts about the chronology of these events were confirmed when I discovered that the hockey game, on April 9, 1959, ended at 10:29, but the overnight train to Toronto left at 10:25 which meant that it would have been impossible for my father to learn the final score, and still have time to race to Windsor Station and board my mother's train. However, when I confronted my mother with these troubling details, her lower lip began to tremble. "It's true," she said, "it's true." And then she began to sob, and I thought it insensitive to pursue the matter further.

I do not doubt my father's veracity, or my mother's testament, but I do believe Barney muddled things. Miriam probably left the Ritz at the end of the second period, at 9:41, and my father's taxi was not tied up in Stanley Cup traffic until he returned from the Montreal West station. Another possibility is that the departure of the overnight train to Toronto was delayed. I have twice written to Canadian Pacific to ask for the departure time of the overnight train to Toronto, on April 9, 1959, but I am still waiting for a reply.

trousers and scraping my kneecap. Outside, I was lucky to find a taxi. "The Ritz," I said. "Hey, that was some game, eh?"

"Mon blood pressure est sky high," said the driver. "C'est le stress."

Knocking timorously on the door of our overnight suite in the Ritz, I braced myself, anticipating the worst, but to my amazement The Second Mrs. Panofsky greeted me with a hug, compounding my guilt. "Oh, thank God you're safe," she said. "I didn't know what to think."

"Needed some fresh air," I said, rocking her in my arms.

"I'm not surprised, but – "

"The Habs won without Beliveau and with the Rocket sitting on the bench. How about that, eh?"

" – couldn't you have told me? We've been worried sick."

Only then did I notice her father fulminating in a chair. "She wanted me to call the police to see if there had been an accident. I thought it might be more prescient to check out the neighbourhood bars instead."

"Oh, my God. Look at your knees. I'll get a wet towel."

"Don't fuss, please." Then, beaming at her father, I said, "Would you care to join us in a nightcap before you leave?"

"I have imbibed quite enough tonight, young man, and so, most assuredly, have you."

"Well, toodleloo then."

"Am I to credit that you were walking the streets for an hour and a half?"

"Daddy, he's safe and sound and that's all that matters."

No sooner had he left than The Second Mrs. Panofsky lowered me into a chair, wet a towel in the bathroom, and returned to dab my scraped kneecap. "Tell me if it hurts, honeybunch, and I'll stop."

"You deserve a better man than I am."

"But it's too late now, isn't it?"

"I have behaved badly," I said, unbidden tears streaming down my cheeks. "If you want a divorce, I will not stand in your way."

"Oh, you're such a scream," she said, kneeling to remove my shoes and socks. "What you need is some sleep."

"On our wedding night?"

"I won't tell."

"Oh, no," I said, beginning to fondle her breasts, and then, apparently, I slumped back in the chair and began to snore.

SEVEN

I ONCE dared to hope that Miriam and I, into our nineties, would expire simultaneously, like Philemon and Baucis. Then a beneficent Zeus, with a gentle stroke of his caduceus, would transmogrify us into two trees, whose branches would fondle each other in winter, our leaves intermingling in the spring.

Trees remind me of the afternoon Sean O'Hearne sat with me and Miriam on the wraparound porch of our cottage in the Laurentians, looking down at the lake, where police divers had once searched for Boogie. Boogie who, if I were to be believed, had last been seen zig-zagging down the hill, racing across the dock and, dodging my bullet, plunging into the water. Revealing a surprising poetic streak, O'Hearne, eyeing me closely, indicated the trees and ventured, "I wonder what those elms would say, if they could talk."

"Why, that's easy, O'Hearne," said Miriam. "They would say, 'We are maples.' "

In the years since Boogie's disappearance, I don't know how many times I've sat on that dock, willing him to emerge safely out of the waters. Why, only the other night I dreamt that Boogie, sobered by his long swim, did in fact heave himself onto the dock. Hopping up and down on one leg, trying to shake water out of his ear.

– Boogie, I didn't mean it. Not one word. I don't know what got into me.

– Hey, we're buddies from way back, he says, embracing me. Good thing you're such a bad shot.

– Right.

Back to the real world. Knee-slapper of a story in this morning's Gazoo that I must clip and mail to the enchanting Ms. Morgan of "Dykes on Mikes."

FEMINIST OUTRAGE AT
CHAIN GANGS FOR WOMEN

Male convicts in Alabama, who were put in leg irons last year, manacled together to put in twelve-hour shifts on the highways, cutting and trimming the roadsides, had petitioned the governor to say that their punishment amounts to sexual discrimination. In response, The Alabama Corrections Commissioner said, "There's no real defence for not doing the females." He has instructed the warden of the Julia Tutwiler State Prison for Women at Wetumpka, near Montgomery, to start a chain gang for women within three weeks. But they will not labour on the highways. Instead they will work on prison property, planting vegetable gardens, mowing grass, and picking up litter.

Still guilt-ridden after all these years, the subject I've been trying to avoid until now is my disastrous honeymoon in Paris with The Second Mrs. Panofsky, its cafés haunted for me by memories of Clara, my mood tainted by my longing for Miriam. Compounding matters, a photograph of Clara was on display in the window of La Hune. She was shown seated at a table in the Mabillon and, if you looked closely, the group included Boogie, Leo Bishinsky, Hymie Mintzbaum, George Plimpton, Sinbad Vail, Cedric Richardson, and me. Only a year later Cedric joined students from Agricultural and Technical College in a sit-in at a lunch counter in a variety store in Greensboro, North Carolina. Then, in 1963 I think it was, Cedric quit Martin Luther King in favour of Malcolm X, and was next rumoured to have gone to ground somewhere in Chicago, not yet accompanied everywhere by his Fruits of the Loom[1] body-guards, or whatever the Prophet Elijah's thugs were called. I'm running ahead of myself again.

The photograph in La Hune was mounted atop a pile of Clara's recently translated poems which, if memory serves for once, had already gone into its sixth edition in the United States. By this juncture, The Virago's Verse Book had been published in sixteen other languages and, to my astonishment, the foundation created by Norman Charnofsky was coining it in. And then, honouring Clara's

---

[1] They are called Fruits of Islam.

proclivities, Norman appointed a couple of black feminists to the board of directors, setting the seeds of his ruin in place.

I had suspected a small Left Bank hotel might not suit The Second Mrs. Panofsky, so I booked us into the Crillon instead. A good thing, too, because she was still brooding about our fiasco of a wedding night, understandably so.

I should point out that, prior to our honeymoon, the only time The Second Mrs. Panofsky and I had spent together were those three frenetic days in New York when I hardly saw her as she flitted from here to there. We had yet to get beyond groping each other, until, squirming free, she'd call, "Time out," settling her breasts back into her bra and tugging her skirt back over her knees. "Whew! That was close." We made love for the first time on our bed in the Crillon, where I was surprised to discover she was not a virgin.

Taking The Second Mrs. Panofsky to Paris was a mistake. True, I was now able to afford all those fine restaurants I used to pass in 1951: Le Grand Véfour, Lapérouse, La Tour d'Argent, La Closerie des Lilas. But seated on the terrace of the Café de Flore, my bride in her finery and me in my good suit, watching the unkempt young stroll past hand in hand, I felt too much like the rich tourists Clara and I used to poke fun at when we were together. It made me ill-tempered. "Couldn't you put that damn guidebook away while we sit here?"

"I'm embarrassing you?"

"Yes."

"Like with the bidet?"

"You didn't have to ask the maid. I could have told you what it was for."

"Can you speak Hebrew?"

"No."

"Have you got an M.A. from McGill?"

"No."

"Am I embarrassed?"

I began to growl.

"We've already been sitting here for maybe an hour and I think you've said maybe eight words to me. I don't want to appear ungrateful for so much attention, but how much longer do we sit here?"

"One more drink."

"That makes eleven words. I didn't come here to mourn the death of your first wife."

"Neither did I."

"You keep saying my father is such a snob, but you think I'm a lesser person because I thought it was a footbath. Look at yourself in the mirror, why don't you?"

"I don't dare."

"Well, I'm not going to sit here any longer, watching you stare into space, because we've only got four more days here, and I've still got lots to do," she said, pulling those cards out of her handbag, with a check-list divided into three categories: Must Do's, Optionals, and If There's Time. "I'll meet you back at the hotel at seven. And it would be nice if you were still sober when we went to dinner. Let's just say it would be a welcome change."

As our hotel room filled with her purchases, I began to feel like a character in that play by the Romanian, you know who I mean.[2] He wrote one in which Zero Mostel turned into an elephant.[3] No, a hippopotamus. The play was called *Chairs*, yes, that's it, and the author's first name was the same as that guy who managed the Expos in their early years. Gene Mauch it was. The baseball manager, not the playwright. *A Romanian called Gene?* Oh, what does it matter? In the play, the set fills up with furniture, until there is no room for the characters, and so it seemed in our obstacle course of a hotel room.

I watched, bemused, as our dresser top became covered end to end with bottles of perfume, eau de cologne, shampoos, and body oils; lipsticks lined up like bullets; cartons of variously scented soaps; boxes containing sprays, bath salts, and powders; a sea sponge; jars of restorative creams and tubes of mysterious ointments; eyebrow pencils; compacts and compact fillers. Here, there, and everywhere, I stumbled over boxes and bags from shops on the boulevard de la Madeleine, the Faubourg Saint-Honoré, the rue de Rivoli, the Avenue George-V, and the boulevard des Capucines. Outfits, with matching accessories, acquired at Courrèges, Cardin,

---

[2] Eugene Ionesco (1912–) Romanian-French dramatist of the Theatre of the Absurd, author of *The Bald Prima Donna, The Lesson*, and other plays.
[3] *Rhinoceros*.

Nina Ricci. An evening bag from Lanvin. And not for nothing was
The Second Mrs. Panofsky a McGill M.A. Long after I had gone to
bed, she sat up carefully razoring out tell-tale couturier labels to be
mailed home, and sewing in labels from Eaton's, Ogilvy's, and Holt
Renfrew that she had brought with her from Montreal.

We did do the Louvre, the Jeu de Paume, the Musée Rodin,
where, forearmed with a list of the major works, she would have a
quick glance, check it off her list, and move on to the next. We had
only been in Paris for four days when, to her delight, we were able
to start in on Optionals.

I'm an impulsive man, a guy who believes in making his own
mistakes rather than regretting things not done, and one of the
worst was my lightning courtship and marriage to The Second
Mrs. Panofsky, which doesn't excuse my atrocious behaviour on our
honeymoon. She had to be confused, as I vacillated between being
morose and then, prompted by guilt, attentive beyond compare,
resolved to make our union work. One night, simulating
enthusiasm for her latest acquisition from Dior or Lanvin, which
she had modelled for me in our room, I took her to dinner at one of
the restaurants on her list, and then slyly inquired about relatives
of hers I had met at our wedding, monied alrightniks I hoped
never to see again, feigning interest in her garrulous responses, and,
finally, as an afterthought, I said, "Oh yeah, and then it seems to me
there was that girl, I forget her name, wearing a layered blue chiffon
cocktail dress, who obviously considered herself quite a number, not
that I did."

"Miriam Greenberg?"

"Yeah, I think that was her name. Is she also a relative?"

"Hardly. She wasn't even invited."

"You mean she had the audacity to crash our – ? Now I find
that awfully pushy."

"My cousin Seymour brought her."

Managing a yawn, I asked, "Is he her boyfriend?"

"How would I know?"

"Ah, what does it matter? Let's move on to the Mabillon for a
nightcap."

"If you haven't already had enough to drink, I'd rather we went
to Harry's Bar."

My lady of the lists had done her homework, poring over sex

manuals not available in The Jewish Public Library, and making notes and diagrams on index cards. To my astonishment, she knew all about *feuille de rose, gamahuche, pompoir, postillonage, soixante-neuf, saxonus,* and even *the Viennese oyster,* and every night I begged off attempting one or another. The Second Mrs. Panofsky went about her pleasures relentlessly. Life, for her, was an exam to be passed.

"What could she see in your cousin Seymour?"

"Are we finished now?" she asked, wiping her mouth with the bed sheet.

"You set the agenda here, not me."

"Feh. I can't imagine what people see in it." She brushed her teeth. She gargled. Then she was back. "Now what was it that was so important?"

"It's of no importance whatsoever, but I was just wondering what she could see in your cousin Seymour, he's such a prick."

"Who?"

"Oh, I can never remember her name. The girl in the layered blue chiffon dress."

"Ah ha. Ah ha." Glaring at me, she demanded, "I want you to tell me what I wore to lunch today?"

"A dress."

"Yeah, sure. A dress. Not my nightgown. *What colour was it?*"

"Oh, come on."

"Have you got Miriam Greenberg on the brain or something?"

"Calm down. I was just wondering what she could see in Seymour."

"He drives an Austin-Healey. He keeps his sailboat, it sleeps six, in the West Indies somewhere. He's going to inherit like a block of Sherbrooke Street and I don't know how many shopping centers. Some prick."

"Are you saying she's a fortune-hunter?"

"You know how many times I've seen her in that same layered blue dress you can't get out of your head, it's maybe ten years old, prêt-à-porter, probably picked up in a January sale in Macy's. Why shouldn't she be interested in bettering herself?"

Then there were her daily phonecalls to her mother.

"I've got to be brief, we're just on our way out. No, not for dinner, it's only seven o'clock here. *Apéritifs,* my dear. A café in Montparnasse. The Dôme I think it's called. Yes, I remember what

Aunt Sophie said, and I only drink the bottled water. Last night? Oh, we had dinner at this terrific restaurant called La Tour d'Argent, you'd love it, they take you up in an elevator, and you look out and see Notre-Dame all lit up, I thought Charles Laughton would be swinging from one of the gargoyles any minute. Only kidding. Their specialty is pressed duck, and each one is numbered and they give you a postcard with your number on it, and I'm going to mail it to you this morning. You know who was sitting there, only two tables away from us. Audrey Hepburn. Yes, I know Jewel is a big fan, but I've already got something for her. *I couldn't*. It would have embarrassed him. I'm not even allowed to ask for a menu for a souvenir. I never lived in Paris on ten cents a day, so to his way of looking I'm like a war criminal, maybe worse. Only joking. No, Mom, we're getting on fine. What? Oh, I was wearing my new Givenchy, you just wait till you see me in it, and do give Daddy a big hug and tell him thank you a thousand times. What? Oh, it's a simple black silk and wool, with a bow marking the high waist and the hem raised just to cover the knee. No, the 'sack' is out. Finished. But don't you say a word to Pearl or Arlene, let them find out on their own now they've spent so much on what's now really last year's *shmatas. Will you stop worrying, please*. When we come in every night, no matter how late, they lock up my pearls for me in their safe. Yes yes yes. The camera too, I remember how expensive it was. In fact, I leave the camera there. He won't let me walk down the street with it, somebody might mistake us for tourists. Oh, let me see. I started with the smoked salmon, it was mouth-watering. No, they don't serve it with cream cheese here. No, Barney had the snails in their shells. Yes, I know. But he likes them. No, I wouldn't. Or the oysters, honestly. I had to tell him to move the bread away from me or I'd eat the whole basket and the butter, it's from Normandy, and it melts in your mouth. Then we both had the duck, and crêpes for dessert. Oh, I don't know, but it was red and cost him plenty, not that he'd complain about it, but he sure impressed the wine waiter who looked at us at first like he'd smelled something bad. Yes, with his coffee and cigar. Cognac, a special one, no two. They wheel over this huge wagon full of bottles. No, they don't heat the snifters here. Yes, but Ruby Foo's isn't the be-all and end-all, and nowhere I've been in Paris do they heat the glasses. Yes, two is what he had, I said. What? Yeah, I'll tell him, but it's not like he had to drive us home and we are on our honeymoon. Enjoy? Right. It can lead to what in middle-age? Gwan. Dr. Seligman told you that? Really? Well, that's certainly not his problem so far, knock wood. What do you mean, you're offended? I'm a married woman now. It's allowed. Yes, Mom. Sure. Well, I shook him awake at seven, then I brushed my teeth and washed my hair and, guess what, we showered together, don't tell Daddy, he'd be shocked. And I'll bet you're blushing right now. Only kidding. You should see the bathrobes we've got here, and the soaps are from Lanvin. Yeah, sure I will. In fact I've already stuffed three bars for you into one of my suitcases, which reminds me I'd better buy another one today for my new things. Mom, I know Uncle Herky could get it for me wholesale, but I happen to need it here and now. I'm not being impatient. I'm not raising my voice. You're imagining. What? Yes, the waist is back and I've still got mine. *I am not being snarky.* How many times do I have to tell you that you have a terrific figure for a mature woman. It's from Dior. Yeah, I wore it this morning. Boy, did I ever turn lots of heads. It's pale blue shantung pleats with a cape collar, and over it I wore my new coat, it's a Chanel, a cardigan, nubby beige wool piped with navy blue silk. I'll wear it to the temple on Rosh Hashonna, Arlene will die on the spot. And wait till you see my shoes and the handbag that goes with. You tell Daddy he's spoiling me rotten, but I'm not complaining. Don't say a word, but I bought him a silk foulard at Hermès and pearl cufflinks and a shirt at Cardin, and I'm not saying what I got you, but I think you'll be pleased. *Mom, I swear I'm not being sarcastic about your figure.* I'm sure most women your age envy you. No, I didn't forget Jewel or Irving. That wouldn't be 'just like me.' I'm getting everything on your list. Mom, stop it. Nobody will be sending photographs to Rabbi Hornstein. Of course we lock the door before we get into the shower together, but it's not a criminal offence in this day and age. There's nothing wrong with taking pleasure in our bodies. Yes yes yes. I know you have my best interests at heart, but let's not get into that one, please. *I did not accuse you of nagging.* What do you mean it's in my tone of voice? Don't start. Oh, Mom, Barney saw an item in the *Herald-Tribune* that the Canadiens might be trading Doug Harvey, and he wants to know if it's true. *I know you never read the sports pages,* but it wouldn't hurt you to look it up. Mom, I can't tell you how beautiful it is here. What? That's not true. I am not suggesting that Montreal is ugly.

Boy, are you ever touchy today. If I didn't know better, I'd say you were getting your period. *I am not being snide.* I know it will happen to me too one day, and when it does, I hope I will be more accepting than you are. There you go again. It's the only voice I have, and if you don't care for the tone I guess I'd better hang up right now. Okay, okay. I apologize. No, he hates shopping, but of course we met for lunch. What? It's called the Brasserie Lipp. He had the choucroute, they're famous for it. No, wait, he started with oysters. *Mom, I didn't.* But, to be honest, it wasn't on religious principle. I had the hard-boiled egg with mayonnaise and the salmon with french fried potatoes. No, he had a beer and I drank white wine. Mom, it was only a glass. I won't be joining the A.A. when I get home. Oh, he went back to the hotel for his nap. Good thing he didn't know I was going shopping for bras and lingerie, because that's the only time he'll come with me. They get him a chair, and he sits there smiling like the cat who swallowed the canary, watching the women come and go. *Mom, would you rather he was like your poor cousin Cyril?* No, he's not a homosexual. How could he be? A member of our esteemed family. He's just a fifty-five-year-old bachelor, who still lives with his mother and subscribes to every body-building magazine in print, and was asked to stop hanging around the Y.M.H.A. swimming pool when all those schoolkids were there. I beg your pardon. Okay, he wasn't asked. That was gossip. He simply stopped going. But, in my opinion, we've all done him enormous psychological damage by making him pretend he's something he isn't. No, you're wrong there. Barney thinks he's very witty. He happens to like him. They've been out to dinner together more than once. How about that? Tonight? There's a tap-dancer appearing at a club in Pigalle who Barney wants to see. Yes, Mom. He's a hockey fan and he likes tap-dancing, do you think I should get a divorce? Now I really, really have to hang up, we're just on our way out. Barney sends love to you and Daddy. No, I'm not making it up. He asked me to say that. We'll talk again tomorrow."

EIGHT

"CANADIAN Broadcasting Corporation. Radio-Canada. Can I help you?"

"Please connect me with *Artsworld*."

"*Artsworld* here. Beth Roberts speaking."

"I'd like to talk to Miriam Greenberg."

"Hello."

"Hi, Miriam. It's Barney Panofsky. Remember me?"

"Oh."

"I just happen to be in Toronto and I was wondering if you were free for lunch tomorrow?"

"Sorry, no."

"Dinner, then?"

"I'm busy."

"I heard your interview with Mailer and I think you put all the right questions to him."

"Thanks."

"Say, what about drinks at five o'clock?"

"Barney, I don't go out with married men."

"Drinks, for Christ's sake. It's not a federal offence. I just happen to be right across the street in the bar at the Four Seasons Motor Hotel."

"Please don't be difficult."

"Some other time, then?"

"Sure. Maybe. No. But thanks for calling."

"Don't mention it."

I'm writing this on a Sunday afternoon at my desk in my cottage in the Laurentians, where the night before I watched an old black-and-white movie on TV with a brooding, more than somewhat prickly Chantal for company. *Operation Hellfire*, directed by Hymie Mintzbaum in 1947, starred John Payne, Yvonne de Carlo, Dan Duryea, and George Macready. The story opens two weeks before D-Day on an American army camp in England. Major Dan Duryea, a graduate of the school of hard knocks, is fed up with Sergeant John Payne, a lazy playboy heir to a department-store fortune, and orders him parachuted into occupied France to contact a group of partisans led by somebody code-named Hellfire. Hellfire turns out to be Yvonne de Carlo, and she and Payne take an instant dislike to each other. Everything changes, however, after Payne, shooting from the hip, rescues her from the torture cellars of Gestapo man George Macready, who has just ripped off her blouse. Together, on D-Day Plus Two, sweethearts Payne and de Carlo blow up a troop train bound for the beaches of Normandy. And when Duryea and his battle-weary troops march into St.-Pierre-sur-mer, prepared for another costly struggle, they find it has already been liberated by Payne, who is swilling champagne with de Carlo on the village square, surrounded by admiring peasants. "I thought you'd never get here," says Payne with a wink for de Carlo. The end.

I want to make something absolutely clear. I did not invite Chantal out for the weekend. She took me by surprise, arriving in time for dinner on Saturday, laden with goodies she had picked up at the Pâtisserie Belge on Laurier Avenue: pâté de foie gras, thick slices of baked ham, a quiche lorraine, containers of beet and potato salads, cheeses, a baguette and croissants for breakfast. I was careful to greet her with no more than an avuncular peck on both cheeks after I had relieved her of her overnight bag.

"Hey, aren't you glad to see me?" she asked.

"Of course I am."

But I pointedly did not open a bottle of champagne. Instead, I fetched a glass of Aligoté.

"I'll set the table," she said.

I explained that a movie directed by an old friend of mine would start on TV at eight, and I wanted to eat in front of the set. "Oh, how charming," she said. "I'll try not to talk."

I resisted joining her on the sofa, but settled into an easy chair at a safe distance with a bottle of Macallan and a Montecristo number four. Afterwards, I heard myself saying, "Chantal, I'm really glad to have you here, but I want you to sleep in one of the upstairs bedrooms tonight."

"Has my mother spoken to you about us?"

"Certainly not."

"Because I'm no longer a child and this is none of her business."

"Chantal, my dear, this isn't right. I'm a grandfather and you're not even thirty yet."

"I just happen to be thirty-two years old."

She looked so glowingly young, so fetching, that I decided if she refused to sleep upstairs and slid into bed with me instead, I would not protest. I'm weak. I could do so much and no more. She glowered at me and then disappeared upstairs, and the next thing I heard was the slam of her door. Damn damn damn. When King David was old he was warmed in his bed by nubile young women, so why wasn't I entitled as well? Pouring myself a hefty drink, I thought, possibly I should go upstairs to comfort her. But I didn't do it, proud of myself for once, and anticipating praise from Solange. I didn't get to sleep until four a.m., and when I got up at noon Chantal had already driven off without leaving me a note. And that evening Solange phoned: "She gave up her weekend to drive all the way out to your place to help you with next month's budgets and all you wanted to do was watch TV and booze. What did you say to her, you bastard? She hasn't stopped crying since she got here and she doesn't want to work for you any more."

"You know something, Solange. I've had it up to here with women. Including you. Especially you. And now I'm seriously thinking of moving in with Serge."

"I want to know what you said to hurt her."

"You just tell her I expect her in my office at ten o'clock tomorrow morning."

NINE

I LAST saw Hymie Mintzbaum on my most recent trip to Hollywood, only a few months ago. There to peddle a pilot, I was suddenly overcome by the itch to try my liver-spotted hand at screenplay writing again. So I stupidly went to pitch a screwy idea of mine to the young squirt who now runs the studio. Shelley Katz, a grandson of one of the founding fathers, passes for a maverick in Beverly Hills. Instead of tooling up and down the canyons in a Rolls or Mercedes, his birthright, Shelley's signature is a souped-up 1979

Ford pickup truck, its creatively dented fenders, I suspect, the work of somebody in the studio art department. Shelley would probably have said to him, "What I'm after is a realistic redneck type look as in a story set in some pisspoor town in, say, northern Vermont. Some rust would be a nice touch. Good man. I want you to know your work is appreciated. We're a family."

Parking valets at the Dôme and Spago's earn fifties for reporting the Ford pickup's arrival in the lot to a number of relevant agents and producers ("It's here, and he's inside, just. No, I'm not phoning anybody else. Honestly"), enabling them to hurry over to pay obeisance, maybe earn a chance to shmooze a little, plug a project.

"Our hero," I said to Shelley, "is a latter-day Candide figure."

"Candide?"

"You know, Voltaire."

"Which is it?"

This is not to suggest that Shelley is a functional illiterate, but, rather, one of the industry's new *wunderkinder*. Had I dropped the name of Superman, Batman, Wonder Woman, or the Submariner, he would have nodded knowledgeably, allowing that we were both scholarly types. The young today. Christ Almighty. Privileged beyond compare. Born too late to remember the Battle of Stalingrad, D-Day, Rita Hayworth peeling off that elbow-length glove in *Gilda*, Maurice Richard charging over the blue line, the siege of Jerusalem, Jackie Robinson breaking in with the Montreal Royals, Brando in *A Streetcar Named Desire*, or a beaming Harry Truman holding up the front page of the *Chicago Tribune* with the banner headline DEWEY DEFEATS TRUMAN. "Our protagonist," I continued, "is an innocent. A kid. My story opens in 1912, he's on the *Titanic*, the maiden voyage, everybody in the audience is waiting for the icebergs to hit – "

"You know what Lew Grade said about his *Raising the Titanic*, a real stinker? 'It would have been cheaper to lower the Atlantic Ocean.' "

"But, lo and behold," I went on to say, "the ship docks safely in New York, where the innocent kid is met by a sexy reporter, a Lauren Bacall type, who – "

"Lauren Bacall," he said. "You've got to be kidding, unless she's playing somebody's mother."

"A Demi Basinger type, I mean, who asks him what the trip was like? Boring, he says, and then – "

"Demi Basinger? That's some wicked sense of humour you've still got there, Mr. Panofsky. I want you to know I do appreciate this window of opportunity to strategize with somebody who used to be a player, but I'm afraid I'm going to have to pass on this one. Hey, I'm married to Hymie Mintzbaum's granddaughter. Fiona. I love her. We've been blessed with two children."

"And do you love them too?"

"Absolutely."

"Imagine that."

Then the phone rang. "Speak of the – . I almost said the you-know-who. It's my wife. Excuse me."

"Certainly."

"Uh huh. Uh huh. Now you calm down, darling, and apologize to Miss O'Hara and tell her it's okay. I think I've just solved the problem. Honestly. Yeah. No. I can't explain right now." Hanging up, he beamed at me. "When Fiona told Hymie you were coming in to dialogue with me, he asked would you like to join him for dinner tonight at Hillcrest. Keep the limo. My pleasure."

Enough time had passed, as well as my sense of betrayal, since our brawl in London, so I was inordinately pleased that Hymie wanted to patch things up. There would be so much to talk about. Before starting out for Hillcrest, I stopped at Brentano's, and bought Hymie the latest novel by Beryl Bainbridge, a writer I admired. Then I called for my limo.

I would not have recognized Hymie had not a waiter led me to the table in the Hillcrest dining room where he sat, dozing, in his motorized wheelchair. His crown of tight curly black hair had been reduced to random white balls of fluff, fragile as dandelion heads at risk in the slightest breeze. The linebacker's body had diminished to a near-empty sack of projecting bones. The waiter, who had thoughtfully provided Hymie with a bib, now shook him awake. "Your guest has arrived, Mr. Mintzbaum."

"Flush glish mmerm," said a roused Hymie, reaching out for me with an unsteady twig of a hand, the one that still worked.

"Just say you're glad to see him too," said the waiter, winking at me.

Hymie's eyes were rheumy, and his mouth was tugged down on

one side, yanked by an invisible wire. Spittle trickled down his chin.
He smiled, or tried to, the result a rictus, and pointed at my glass.

"Would you care for a drink?" asked the waiter.

"Make it a Springbank. Straight up."

"And the usual for Mr. Mintzbaum, no doubt," he said, moving
off.

His head bobbing up and down, Hymie began to whimper. He
reached out for me again, taking my hand, the pressure feeble.

"It's okay, Hymie," I said, and I wiped his eyes and then his chin
with his bib.

The waiter brought me my Springbank and poured Hymie an
Evian. "Floshui beshuga shlup," said Hymie, his eyes bulging with
effort, as he knocked over his Evian and pointed at my glass.

"You're being naughty, Mr. Mintzbaum."

"Don't talk to him like that," I said, "and bring him a Springbank, please."

"He's not allowed."

"At once," I said.

"Providing you tell her it was you who insisted on it."

"Her?"

"His granddaughter. Mrs. Katz."

"Fetch."

"I know what Mr. Mintzbaum is having," said the waiter,
passing me a menu, "but what about you," and he paused before
adding, "sir?"

"And just what is Mr. Mintzbaum having?"

"Some steamed vegetables topped with a poached egg. No
salt."

"Not tonight he isn't. We both want roast brisket and latkes.
And don't forget the horseradish."

"Cryta fishum," said Hymie, rocking with delight.

"And we'd like a bottle of Beaujolais. And, oh dear, I see that
Mr. Mintzbaum hasn't got a wine glass. Bring him one."

"Mrs. Katz is going to hit the roof."

"Just do as you're told and I'll handle Mrs. Katz when she gets
here."

"Your funeral."

Hymie stabbed at his gaping mouth with his fork, his eyes
raging.

"Don't even try to talk, Hymie. I can't understand a word you're saying."

The waiter brought him his Springbank. I clicked glasses with him and we both drank. "Here's to us," I said, "and the good times we had together that nobody can take away from us."

He sipped his drink. I wiped his chin with his bib.

"And here's to the Eighth Army Air Force," I said, "and Duke Snider and Mozart and Kafka and Jelly Roll and Dr. Johnson and Sandy Koufax and Jane Austen and Billie Holiday."

"Flugit," said Hymie, weeping softly.

Pushing my chair closer to him, I helped Hymie cut up his brisket and latkes. When the waiter approached our table again, Hymie began to splutter and gesture. "Okey-doke. Gotcha," said the waiter, and he brought Hymie a pad and a pencil.

It took Hymie a while, concentrating, writing something, ripping out a page, starting again, ripping again, breathing hard, drooling, before he finally handed me what he had managed to print:

And now we were both drunk, but, fortunately, our compromising plates had been cleared by the time Fiona Darling swept into the dining room, Shelley trailing after her like a spoor, the two of them working the tables, raining blessings on those who were still A-list, while those not entitled to callbacks were dismissed with a nod. Finally they got to us. Stubby Fiona Darling, bejewelled, shrink-wrapped into a chiffon evening gown that bulged in the wrong places, her black velvet cape secured by a diamond-studded clasp. Shelley wore a tux, one of those purple ruffled shirts that always reminded me of a washboard, a string tie with a Navajo pendant, and hand-tooled cowboy boots, proof against snake bite when he risked crossing Rodeo Drive. "I'll bet you two old rascals had plenty to talk about," said Fiona Darling, crinkling her cute, surgically sculpted nose, and impressing a scarlet lipstick stain on

Hymie's all but bald pate. "I hear you guys had some life-style when you were in Gay Paree together in the old days."

"Why in the hell didn't Shelley warn me that he couldn't speak?"

"Now now. That's not nice. You sure are lacking in empathicity. Hymie is just difficult to understand at times. Isn't that so, Gramps?"

The rest was confusion, but I do remember that the waiter took Fiona Darling aside, and then she turned on me: "Did you let him drink hard liquor and eat red meat with wine?"

Hymie, his eyes popping, struggled to be heard. "Fluga pshit."

"He's incontinent," said Fiona Darling. "Would you like to be the one to clean up after him at three o'clock in the morning?"

"Don't tell me you do it?"

"It just happens to be Miss O'Hara's night off tonight."

I remember Hymie reversing his wheelchair back from the table, stopping, then propelling himself at a shrieking Fiona Darling, Shelley pulling her out of harm's way in time. Or maybe that didn't happen and it's just a case of my tinkering with memory, fine-tuning reality. Next I think a frustrated Hymie, who had always abhorred squealers, rode off in pursuit of the waiter, intent on ramming him, but attempting too sharp a turn at speed and colliding with a woman at another table. But possibly I only wished that had happened. Dining out on a story I tend to put a spin on it. To come clean, I'm a natural-born burnisher. But, then, what's a writer, even a first-timer like me?

In any event, I recall angry words were exchanged. An increasingly screechy Fiona Darling called me an irresponsible drunk. Then I inquired, icy polite, if her breasts were her own or had been artificially enhanced, as to my expert eye they appeared to be of unequal thrust and density. This prompted Shelley to threaten to punch me out. Responding to that challenge, I coughed out my dentures and slid them into a jacket pocket before raising my fists. Fiona Darling rolled her heavily made-up eyes heavenwards. "Oh, isn't he disgusting," she said. "Let's get out of here." And she wheeled Hymie out of the dining room, even as he continued to jabber incoherently.

When I went to claim my limo, Shelley's pleasure, the doorman explained that Mrs. Katz had told the driver to go home. "In that case," I said, my shirt stained with Beaujolais, Fiona Darling's parting shot, "I'm going to need a taxi."

"Where are you going, sir?"

"The Beverly Wilshire."

The doorman summoned a blond, muscle-bound car jockey. "Clint will drive you there for twenty-five bucks," said the doorman, "gratuity not included."

Clint eased somebody else's Rolls-Royce out of the parking lot and deposited me at the Beverly Wilshire in style. Agitated, grieving, I made right for Fernando's Hideaway, settling into a bar stool and ordering a Courvoisier XO, which was foolish of me, as I had already had more than enough to drink and could no longer handle cognac late at night.

"And what happened to you, you bad boy?" asked the young woman seated next to me, indicating my shirt.

An attractive redhead she was, endearingly freckled, her smile saucy, and her tight jersey scooped low. She also wore an ankle-length skirt, a slit riding high up one side. "May I offer you a drink?" I asked.

"I'll have a glass of French champagne."

Petula (Pet for short, but not for long, she said) and I began to exchange banalities, even my most feeble wisecracks rewarded with a gentle squeeze of my knee. I signalled the bartender for another round.

"Lookee," she said, "if we're going to go on like interfacing together, you know, and why not, it's a free country, why don't we grab that little table in the corner, you know, before somebody else like beats us to it?"

Sucking in my stomach, I accepted her hand and trailed after her to the table, shlepping her inordinately heavy handbag, my delight enhanced because it seemed to me, in my sodden state, that other men in the room, younger men who had dismissed me as past it, the prerogative of the callow, were now regarding me with envy. Then it began to ring. *Her handbag, for Christ's sake.* Startled, I thrust it at her. She dug into it and pulled out a cellular phone. "Yeah. Uh huh. No, like I'm with somebody. Tell them like I said howdy and he'll adore Brenda," she said, replacing the phone.

Two middle-aged men, both wearing Los Angeles Kings swea-ters and blue jeans, huddled at the next table. "Is it true," asked the one sporting number 99, whispering the name of a studio, "that the sale to the Japs is going through?"

"Just between you and I, I've seen the paperwork," said his companion. "All that remains to be done is to cross the 't's' and slant the 'i's'."

"Don't tell me," said Petula, stroking my knee, "you're a producer. Not that I'm like looking for work, you know, so don't worry. Like guess my age."

"Twenty-eight."

"You kidder you. Like I'm thirty-four, you know, my body clock going tickety-tick-tock even as we eyeball each other here. And let me look at you. Like I'd say you were like fifty-four years old, you know. Am I right?"

Unwilling to dip into my breast pocket for my compromising reading glasses, I pretended to study the wine list, a total blur, and ordered a bottle of Veuve Cliquot and a Courvoisier XO.

"You're positively evil," she said, nudging me.

The brisket and latkes got to me, still sitting there, a stone, and I was hard-pressed to contain what I feared would be a resounding fart. Then, happily, she had to go to "the little girl's room," enabling me to let rip a sneaker, sighing with relief, but looking absolutely innocent when the man, downwind a table to my right, glowered at me, his wife ostentatiously fanning herself with her menu.

Petula, sashaying back my way, was stopped briefly by the young man with an earring seated alone at a table. I didn't care for the look of him. "What did he want?" I asked.

"Speaking frankly," she said, shooting me her *Weltschmerz* look, "what do all men want?"

As we worked through the champagne, mine laced with cognac, I dipped into my grab-bag of self-serving anecdotes and began to shamelessly drop names. But she had never heard of Christopher Plummer or Jean Beliveau; and Pierre Elliott Trudeau, whom I had been introduced to once, lit the wrong fire.

"Oh, you like tell him for me that I just love *Doonesbury*." Suppressing a yawn, she added, "Like why don't we drink up now and go to your room? But you do understand, you know, like I'm a professional escort, don't you?"

"Ah."

"Don't look so glum, baby," she said, even as she unclicked the clasp of her immense handbag and allowed me a peek at her credit-card machine. "My agency accepts all credit cards, except for American Express."

"As a matter of interest, what do you charge?"

"It's not a charge, it's like an honorarium, and that depends on the menu, you know, and the time factor involved." Then she reached into her handbag again and retrieved a card, encased in plastic, that testified that she was AIDS-free.

"Petula, this has been a very long day for me. Why don't we just finish our drinks and say good night here? No harm done."

"Well, thanks for wasting my time, gramps," she said, sweeping up her glass and heading right for the table where her pimp with the earring sat alone. I signed the bill and rose unsteadily, doubting that I managed to look dignified as I tottered out of the bar. Back in my room, I was too angry with Miriam to sleep. Look at me now, I thought, flirting mindlessly with a hooker at my age, all because you abandoned me. I got into bed with Boswell's *The Life of Samuel Johnson*, the book I always travel with because I want them to find it at my bedside should I expire during the night, and I read: "I'm afraid, however, that by associating with Savage, who was habituated to the dissipation and licentiousness of the town, Johnson, though his good principles remained steady, did not entirely preserve that conduct, for which, in days of greater simplicity, he was remarked by his friend Mr. Hector; but was imperceptibly led into some indulgences which occasioned much distress to his virtuous mind." Then the print began to leap on the page, and I had to set the book aside.

I could now compound my humiliation, but find a modicum of relief, I thought, by flicking on whatever adult movie was available on TV, but I decided against it. Instead, my heart pounding, I called upon good old reliable Mrs. Ogilvy in my mind's eye. Mrs. Ogilvy, who had come to us from Kent, where her father owned a draper's shop, or what we colonials, corrupted by Americanisms, as she put it, called a dry-goods store. Once more I blundered into her bedroom, surprising her, catching her in a posture to die for: Mrs. Ogilvy, stalwart of the St. James United Church choir, in panties and garter belt, bending forward, pensive, to trap her breasts and fasten her bra. No, no. Too soon for that. I willed my personal soft-core memory video into fast-track reverse, starting with my arrival at her apartment that morning.

The luscious Mrs. Ogilvy, who took our French and literature classes, often reading aloud to us from *John O'London's Weekly,* was all of twenty-nine, impossibly inaccessible, I thought. Then there was that Saturday she had recruited me to help paint her one-bedroom apartment. "Provided you prove to be a good worker," she said, "I'll treat you to dinner. *En français, s'il vous plaît.*"

"I beg your pardon, Mrs. Ogilvy."

"Worker?"

"*Ouvrier.*"

"*Très bien.*"

We started in the tiny kitchen, and that morning, excruciating beyond belief, we inevitably bumped into each other several times in that provocatively constricted space. Twice the backs of my hands accidentally brushed against her breasts, and I feared they would catch fire. Then she climbed the ladder, taking her turn at the ceiling. Wow. "Help me down now, dear," she said.

Losing her balance, she tumbled briefly into my arms. "Whoops," she said.

"Sorry," I said, steadying her.

"Sorry isn't frightfully flattering," she said, ruffling my hair.

At noon we sat down to eat fishpaste smeared on white bread, seated on stools at the kitchen counter. She also opened a can of tomatoes, plopping one on my plate, and taking another for herself. "Let's not be idle while we sit here. Exams are due in a fortnight, don't you know? Now I want you to tell me the proper name for what Americans, as well as you people in this copycat dominion, call a baby carriage."

"A perambulator."

"Good lad. And the King's English for the wee bird known as a chickadee here?"

"I don't know."

"A tit."

"Aw, come on," I said, just about choking on my fishpaste.

"Oh yes, we do call them tits, but I know what you're thinking, you naughty boy. Now the origin of the word 'alibi,' please."

"Latin."

"Well done."

That's when she noticed the white paint smudge on her skirt. She got up, dipped a rag in turpentine, and raised her skirt, flattening it over a stool to rub the stain. Pleated brown it was, the skirt.[1] I can see it now. I thought my thudding heart would burst right out of my chest and fly through the window. Then, rotating her hips, she wriggled her skirt back into place. "Oh dear. Now I'm damp in unmentionable places. I'd better change. Excuse me, dear," she said, brushing past me, the feathery touch of her breasts surely leaving a permanent burn on my back, as she disappeared into her bedroom.

I lit a cigarette, smoked it, and she still wasn't back. I needed to pee desperately, but would have to pass through her bedroom to reach the toilet. The kitchen sink, I thought. No. What if she came in and discovered me at it? Unable to bear it any longer, I drifted into the living room and saw that her bedroom door was ajar. The hell with it, I thought, such was my agony. I stepped into the bedroom, and there she stood in her panties and garter belt, bending forward, pensive, to fasten her bra. "I'm so sorry," I said, flushing. "I had no idea . . ."

"What does it matter?"

"It's just that I had to go to the toilet."

"Well, do go ahead then," she said, her voice surprisingly harsh.

When I emerged, dizzy with desire, she was already dressed. She flicked on the radio and somebody sang "Mr. Five by Five."[2]

That's when I finally summoned up the courage to reach out for her, sliding my hands under her sweater to unhook her bra. She didn't resist. Instead, both terrifying and delighting me, she kicked off her shoes. "I don't know what's come over me," she said. Then she wiggled out of her skirt and I yanked at her panties.

"You're so impatient. Such an eager puppy. *Attendez un instant.* Now tell me what a gentleman is never in . . .?"

Fuck fuck fuck.

"Don't you remember?" she asked, sending her tongue darting into my ear. "A gentleman is never in . . ."

"A hurry," I shot back triumphantly.

---

[1] Described as "a tartan skirt" on page 13.
[2] The song was "Mairzy Doats" on page 13.

"Bang on. Now give me your hand. There! Like that! Oh yes, *s'il vous plaît!*"

Which is exactly when, alone in my hotel room, my dentures soaking in a glass on my bedside table, I reached down to grab myself. At my decrepit age, the only answer is usually self-service. Certainly it would ease me into sleep at last, but it wasn't to be the case. No sir. For at that moment, in my mind's eye, Mrs. Ogilvy slapped my hand away. "And just what do you think you're doing? Insidious street urchin. Presumptuous jewboy. You get right back into your smelly clothes, which I'm sure you bought wholesale, and get out of here."

"What have I done wrong this time?"

"Dirty old man. Did you mistake me for a common tart who could be picked up in a bar? What if Miriam had walked in right then and seen what had become of you in your dotage? Or one of your grandchildren? *Dégoûtant* is what you are. *Méchant.* Tonight you will memorize Keats's 'Ode to the West Wind' and recite it for me in class first thing Monday morning."

"It was Shelley."

"Stuff and nonsense."

MIRIAM CAME TO me in my dreams, armed with one of her charge sheets: "You'd like to think you were being kind to Hymie, standing up for his rights, but I know you so well. Too well!"

"Please, Miriam."

"The truth is you fed him all that food and drink because you never forgave him for not telling you that it was Boogie's original story. You were being vengeful as always."

"No."

"You never forgave anybody anything."

"And you," I hollered, wakening. "And you?"

I ROSE EARLY, as I am wont to do no matter what time I fall asleep, suffering from the previous night's sins: head throbbing, eyes scratchy, sinuses blocked, throat raw, lungs hot, limbs underwater heavy. I made the usual resolutions, showered, slipped my mint-fresh chompers into place, if only to restore the shape of my collapsible jaw before shaving, and then dialled room service, using that foolproof technique for having a hotel breakfast brought up in a hurry. Something I had learned from Duddy Kravitz.

"Good morning, Mr. Panofsky."

"What's so good about it? I ordered breakfast three-quarters of an hour ago and you gave me your word I would have it within twenty minutes."

"Who took your order, sir?"

"How in the hell would I remember who took my order, but it was for a freshly squeezed orange juice, poached eggs, rye toast, prunes, the *New York Times* and the *Wall Street Journal*."

A pause, then she said, "I can't find a record of your order, sir."

"I'll bet you're all illegal immigrants down there."

"Give me ten minutes."

"Just see I don't have to call down again for a third time."

Twelve minutes later my breakfast order was there, the waiter offering profuse apologies for the delay. I knocked back my orange juice with my garlic, blood pressure, cholesterol, anti-inflammatory, enjoy-a-good-daily-dump, and Vitamin-C pills, and then checked out my stocks in the *Journal.* Merck was up a point-and-a-half, Schlumberger was holding steady, American Home Products had slipped a notch, Royal Dutch had gained two points, and the rest were idling. The *New York Times* obit page yielded neither friend nor foe. Then the phone rang. It was that smarmy BBC-TV producer, who collected blank receipts from taxi drivers and probably pocketed all the mini jam jars at his hotel breakfast table. Calling from the lobby. Christ, I had forgotten all about him. "I thought you said 10:30," I said.

"No. 8:30, actually."

I had run into him a couple of days earlier in the Polo Lounge, where he told me he was making a documentary about the Hollywood blacklist. In a mood to bullshit, I had bragged about all the blacklisted types I had met through Hymie in London in 1961, and I agreed to be interviewed in the hope that Mike might see it. No, because I liked the idea of being asked to pontificate.

Seated under the hot lights, squinting, simulating deep thought, I said, "Senator McCarthy was an unprincipled drunk. A clown. True enough; but now that the witch hunt is long past, I do believe he can be seen, with hindsight, as the most perspicacious and influential film critic ever. Never mind Agee." Then, remembering to pause for effect, I dropped my sandbag. "He certainly cleaned out the stables, as it were."

"I daresay," said the Beeb's presenter. "I've never heard it put quite like that before."

Seemingly groping for words, obviously troubled, I hesitated before I ventured, "My problem is I had considerable respect for The Hollywood Ten as people, but not as writers of even the second rank. That driven bunch invested so much integrity in their foolish, guilt-ridden politics that they had none left for their work. Tell me, did Franz Kafka need a swimming pool?"

That won me a tight little laugh.

"I don't like saying it, but for the BBC, *veritas*. The truth is much as I detested Evelyn Waugh's politics, I would happily take one of his novels to bed rather than watch a rerun of one of their sentimental, knee-jerk liberal films on late-night TV."

Gabble, gabble, gabble. Then, pausing to light my first Montecristo of the day, pulling on it, removing my reading glasses, I looked directly into the camera, and said, "Let me leave you with a couple of pertinent lines from W.B. Yeats. 'The best lack all conviction, while the worst/are full of passionate intensity.' So it was, I fear, in those days."

My shtick done, the grateful producer thanked me for my original thoughts. "Super stuff," he said.

TEN

THE phone rang, which startled me, because nobody knew I had driven out to the cottage the day before. It was Kate, of course. "How did you know I was here?" I asked.

"Intuition. A hunch. But when we talked Wednesday night you didn't say a thing about going away. Then I phoned Solange and she also had no idea where you were. The doorman – "

"Kate, I'm sorry."

" – had to let her into your apartment. I was going crazy with worry here."

"I should have phoned. You're right."

"You shouldn't be moping around there anyway. It's no good for you."

"I'll be the judge of that, darling."

"There's nothing for you in Montreal any more. Michael's in London. Saul's in New York. It's not like you're King Lear and none of your children will have you. You could move in with us tomorrow. I'd take care of you."

"I'm afraid I'm too set in my ways to answer to anybody. Even you, Kate. Besides, my friends are still here. However, I promise to come for a visit soon. Maybe next weekend."

But then I would be obliged to sit through one of Gavin's endless perorations on the need for income tax reform. He would tell me the plot of the last movie he had seen. Following Kate's instructions, he would take me to a game at Maple Leaf Gardens, simulating enthusiasm.

"Hey, you know what I found in a drawer here? An exercise book with some of your grade five compositions."

"Sell the cottage, Daddy."

"I can't, Kate. Not yet."

The truth is I retreat to the cottage in the Laurentians, the scene of my alleged crime, from time to time, wandering, drink in hand, through empty rooms that once resonated with Miriam's laughter and the happy squeals of our children. I go through photo albums, sniffling like an old fool. Miriam and I on the Ponte Vecchio in Florence. Or on the terrace of the Colombe d'Or, where I told her about that time with Boogie and Hymie Mintzbaum. Miriam seated on our bed, serene, nursing Saul. I play her favourite Mozart. I sit here, tears sliding down my cheeks, coddling her old garden shoes. Or sniffing that nightgown of hers I hid when she was packing. Imagining that this is how they will find me. An abandoned husband. Dead of heartbreak. Her nightie pressed to my schnozz.

"What's that the old Jew is clutching," asks Professor Blair Hopper né Hauptman, "the number of his Swiss bank account, written on an old rag?"

"Oh, my poor love, forgive me," she pleads, sinking to her knees, holding my cold hand to her cheek. "You were right. He's a shmuck."

Then I rise from the dead, like what's-her-name, that sexpot,[1] ostensibly drowned in the bathtub, in that movie with Kirk Douglas's son, the boy as ugly as the father, only I'm not wielding a knife. *Final Attraction*.[2] Rising, my voice quavering, I say, "I forgive you, my darling."

Don't knock self-pity. There's a lot to be said for it. Certainly I enjoy it. But, on occasion, the accusatory voice of The Second Mrs. Panofsky, who also lived with me here, intrudes on my reveries:

"I don't please you, do I, Barney?"

Looking up from my book, frowning, clearly indicating that I have been interrupted, I say, "Of course you do."

"You despise my parents, who never did you any harm. It was you, wasn't it?"

"It was me what?"

"Who sent my poor mother that letter on Buckingham Palace stationery, I don't know how you got it, saying she was being considered for an OBE on the New Year's Honours List, for her charitable good works."

"I did no such thing."

"She waited by the window for the postman every morning and finally had to cancel the party she had planned in her honour. I hope you were pleased to humiliate her like that."

"It wasn't me. I swear."

"Barney, I want you to give us a chance. I want you to tell me what I could do to make you happy."

"ImhappyImhappy."

"Then why don't you ever talk to me?"

"Correct me if I'm wrong. But isn't that what we're doing right now? Talking."

"I'm talking, you're listening, sort of. You haven't even put down your book."

"There. It's down. Now what?"

"Oh, go to hell, why don't you?"

I had hoped for some solitude here, but, after I was charged, cars used to park outside, and people would get out to stare at the

---

[1] Glenn Close.

[2] *Fatal Attraction*, co-starring Michael Douglas. Released in 1987 by Paramount. Its North American box office gross was $156,645,693.

murderer's house. Powerboats would cut their outboards offshore, and bastards would stand up to snap photographs. But in the early days of my second marriage, I did, in fact, manage the occasional escape from my wife.

"Darling, I don't think you want to come up this weekend. The black flies are at their worst. Never mind the mosquitoes after this rain. You go to the Silverman wedding. Make my apologies, and I'll get Benoit to come to attend to the leaky roof."

My father, recently obliged to retire from the Montreal police force, intruded on the odd weekend. "I could get a job in security somewheres with my topnotch experience, but those *chazerim* took away my gun licence."

"Why did they do that?"

"Why? Why? Because my name is Panofsky, that's why."

So Izzy phoned the high-ranking officer in the Quebec Provincial Police who had once been his driver. "Weeks went by and I couldn't get him on the phone. But finally I swung it, eh? Finally I knew how to get him, you know. I had a girlfriend call up, you see, I made her say she's the operator, long distance from Los Angeles, and human curiosity, you know, you're not expecting it, well he answered. I said, listen, you goddamn horse's ass, you know if I call the Pope, I says, I can get him quicker than you. Oh, he says, Panofsky, you know, I'm busy. I says don't give me that horseshit, you weren't busy when I knew you. I says I don't want no favours. But look, every greaseball in town's got a permit, and I'm looking for a job in security and I'd feel naked without a gun. So he comes through for me. So now it's okay, I kept two revolvers, my favourites. I got a snub nose, beautiful, and a Tiger. I got that and I got two automatics, and I'm leaving one here for you in the drawer of your bedside table, eh?"

"What in the hell for?"

"Somebody breaks in, you're in the middle of nowheres here, you fucken air-condition him."

Most weekends, rather than endure my silence, The Second Mrs. Panofsky would invite her parents out, or other undesirables. So, in self-defence, I established some summer rituals. I would disappear for an hour or two with my snorkel and flippers, plunging into the lake and swimming underwater, searching for schools of perch. Protesting that I never got any exercise and was putting on too much flab, every Saturday morning, rain or shine, I filled my backpack with a couple of salami sandwiches, some fruit, a bottle of Macallan, a Thermos of coffee, and a book, and set out in my spruce[3] canoe, a latter-day *voyageur*, for the mountain on the opposite shore, belting out "Mairzy-doats" or "Bongo, bongo, bongo, I don't want to leave the Congo . . ."

The mountain, still listed on the map as Eagle Head in those days, has long since been renamed Mont Groulx, after the rabidly racist Abbé Lionel Groulx, who is such a hero to the separatists here. Climbing to a clearing on the top, I would settle into the shade of the little lean-to I had built, wash down my lunch with Macallan, and read until I fell asleep.

On my return to the cottage, usually nicely sodden, I sometimes managed to avoid the dinner party, as well as the games of charades or Scrabble that followed, pleading a headache. Because joining the family at the table I would inevitably quarrel with my father-in-law who would announce, for example, that Richard Nixon had done himself credit in his kitchen debate with Nikita Khrushchev in Moscow.

"Daddy would like to put you up for membership at Elmridge."

"Why, that's awfully good of him, but the gesture would be wasted on me. I don't golf."

"Frankly speaking," said my mother-in-law, "it's the social connections you could make there, seeing as you never enjoyed the advantages we take for granted. Mr. Bernard's son is a member and so is Harvey Schwartz."

"We often make up a threesome," said my father-in-law.

"Look what it's done for Maxim Gold, and he doesn't golf either. When he came over from Hungary as a boy he could hardly speak a word of English."

The odious Gold, incomparably rich now, ran a drug company, plasma its hottest seller. "Frankly speaking," I said, "I would not want to belong to a club that has accepted the likes of Maxim Gold, who buys and sells blood for a profit. And furthermore," I added, smiling my most gracious smile at my father-in-law, "I fail to understand grown men, otherwise mature, wasting an afternoon trying to

---

[3]Cedar.

hit a little white ball into a hole. It's enough to make you despair of humankind, don't you think?"

"He's kidding you, Daddy."

"Well now, I can take a jest as well as the next chap. But at least, out there in the fresh air – "

"Unpolluted by cigar smoke," said my mother-in-law, fanning herself.

" – savouring what Mother Nature Bountiful has bestowed on us, we don't indulge in fisticuffs as do the hooligans who play hockey. What say you to that, Barney?"

I am emotionally tied to this cottage, which resonates with so many memories. Take this one, for instance.

One summer night only two years ago, there I was, seated on my rocking chair on the wraparound balcony. Pulling on a Monte-cristo, sipping cognac, I was luxuriating in the remembrance of family good times past, when I was disturbed by the crunching of tires on the gravel approach road. It's Miriam, I thought, my heart leaping. Miriam come home. Then a Mercedes-Benz sports car jolted to a stop immediately before me, and out stumbled a *GQ* fashion-plate, his smile tentative. A scrawny little old man, seemingly unaware of how ridiculous he looked. It was a distraught Norman Charnofsky, long since retired from NYU, what was left of his once pewter hair no longer to be seen. Norman was sporting a toupee. "Well I'll be goddamned," was all I could manage.

"I came here because I want you to hear my side of the story. I feel I owe you that much."

Poor, innocent, sweet-natured Norman, shrunken now but still unable to control his crying jags as it turned out. His incongruous lounge-lizard outfit was redeemed by a meat gravy stain on his trousers.

"Before you start," I said, "I want you to know that I've been in touch with your wife." And then I invited him into the living room.

"You've been in touch with Flora. You think I don't worry about her?"

Norman began by reminding me of our meeting at the Algonquin all those years ago, on the other side of the moon, when I signed over the rights to Clara's work which we had both considered to be without commercial value. But to Norman's astonishment and mine, as Clara's reputation soared, that coffee-table book of her ink drawings began to sell in the thousands year after year, and her widely translated *The Virago's Verse Book* was reprinted again and again. The Clara Charnofsky Foundation, inaugurated as a loving but seemingly futile gesture, started to bank millions. To begin with, its office was that tiny den in Norman's apartment where, seated under a bare light bulb, he answered correspondence on his portable typewriter in the early-morning hours, maintaining scrupulous records of money spent on stationery, postage, type-writer ribbons, paper clips, and carbon paper. Yes, carbon paper, if any of you out there are old enough to remember what that was. Why, in those days we not only used carbon paper but when you phoned somebody you actually got an answer from a human being on the other end, not an answering machine with a ho ho ho message. In those olden times you didn't have to be a space scientist to manage the gadget that flicked your TV on and off, that ridicu-lous thingumabob that now comes with twenty push buttons, God knows what for. Doctors made house-calls. Rabbis were guys. Kids were raised by their moms instead of in child-care pens like piglets. Software meant haberdashery. There wasn't a different dentist for gums, molars, fillings, and extractions – one nerd managed the lot. If a waiter spilled hot soup on your date, the manager offered to pay her cleaning bill and sent over drinks, and she didn't sue for a kazillion dollars, claiming "loss of enjoyment of life." If the res-taurant was Italian it still served something called spaghetti, often with meatballs. It was not yet pasta with smoked salmon, or linguine in all the colours of the rainbow, or penne topped with a vegetarian steaming pile that looked like dog sick. I'm ranting again. Digressing. Sorry about that.

The foundation's office, once an airless den, had yielded years ago to a five-room suite on Lexington Avenue, with a staff of eight, not counting legal advisers, or its portfolio manager who had per-formed stock-market miracles. Millions were accumulated not only by dint of royalties and shrewd investments, but also through endowments left to the foundation. After it all became too much for Norman to handle, he had appointed two African-American feminists to the board of directors: Jessica Peters, whose poetry was published in both the *New Yorker* and the *Nation*, and Dr. Shirley Wade, who lectured on "cultural studies" at Princeton. The two formidable sisters brought in an abrasive historian, Doris Mandel-baum, author of *Herstory from Boadicia to Madonna*.

It was Ms. Mandelbaum who led the initial boardroom rebel-lion, pointing out that it was a typical male power move, some might even say "an oxymoron, gender-wise," that the chairperson of the board of a feminist foundation should be a man, of the nuclear family persuasion, his only claim to that office that he was a relative of Clara's, herself a martyr to male chauvinist insentience. An embarrassed Norman readily agreed to step down as chairperson, and was replaced by Dr. Shirley Wade. But Norman continued to keep an eye on things, sifting through the foundation's accounts. At a 1992 board meeting, his manner characteristically timorous, he nevertheless questioned a junket the sisters had made to a literary conference in Nairobi, with a stopover in Paris, charging it to the foundation.

"I suppose if we had gone to Tel Aviv, you wouldn't have ques-tioned the trip."

Next Norman had the audacity to query the legitimacy of lunches at The Four Seasons, Le Cirque, Lutèce, and The Russian Tea Room, also charged to the foundation.

"But I imagine it would have been kosher, so to speak, if we had met to discuss foundation business over chitlins in some greasy spoon in Harlem."

"Please," said Norman, flushing.

"We've had enough of your tripping on penis-power here, Norm."

"The truth is we're all weary of your patronizing manner – "

" – and your sexual hang-ups – "

" – and your racism."

"How can you accuse me of – Didn't I appoint you and Shirley to the board?"

"*Oy vey*, bubbelle, but it made you feel good inside, didn't it? It warmed your kishkas."

"You could go home and tell your wifey, we've got *schvartzes* on the board now."

As a consequence of an emergency board meeting, held in Norman's absence at La Côte Basque two years later, he was sent a registered letter dismissing him from the board of the Clara Charnofsky Foundation, which would now be known as The Clara Charnofsky Foundation for Wimyn.

"Goddamn it, Norman, why didn't you get a lawyer and throw the lot of them out?"

"Sure, and then they would write a letter to the *Times* condemning me as a racist."

"So what?"

"So they would have been right, don't you see? I've discovered that I am a racist, and so are you, only I acknowledge it now, they did that much for me. I'm also sexually prejudiced. A hypocrite. I used to wear an AIDS ribbon on my jacket lapel to classes in NYU, but you know what? I stopped going to that Italian restaurant on 9th Street – Flora and I were regulars for years; some of the waiters are gay, suddenly very gaunt, and what if one of them cut his finger peeling potatoes in the kitchen, and thought nothing of it?

"Those women forced me to take a good look at myself. I had to admit it did make me feel good inside, noble even, to appoint two African-Americans to the board, and deep down what I expected from them was gratitude. You know I once told them Shamir was an abomination to me, and I was for a Palestinian state, and it's true, but was that the real reason, or was I intent on ingratiating myself with them? Hey, Charnofsky is a nice Jew. He doesn't break the arms of Arab kids on the West Bank. Jessica once taunted me at a board meeting, come clean, she said, if I saw her three sons walking toward me on, say, 46th Street, wouldn't I cross to the other side of the street for fear of being mugged? They've all got those flat-top haircuts, but one of them has a scholarship to Julliard, and the other two are at Harvard. It's raining, they hail a taxi, it shoots right past them. And if I were driving a taxi maybe I'd do the same. You too. Jesse Jackson cracks a joke about Hymietown and everybody has a fit, but I've heard you call them *schvartzes*, and I'll bet had your daughter married one you wouldn't have cracked open a bottle of champagne. I also have to say that both Jessica Peters and Shirley Wade are far more intelligent than I am. But instead of being pleased – There I go again. *Being pleased*," he said, banging his fists against his forehead. "What right have I to react like that to an African-American's superior intelligence? None whatsoever. But at the time I was secretly resentful. After all these years I was still only an associate professor at NYU, I said to myself, but Shirley's a full professor at Princeton only because of 'affirmative action.' Yeah, sure. But Shirley and Jessica are both witty and fast. I hardly dared open my mouth at board meetings, I was so intimidated, they could cut you down with a quip just like that.

"Listen to this. When they voted themselves an annual retainer of thirty thousand dollars for attending board meetings and other duties, I fought it like crazy, but boy oh boy was I ever thrilled. I could taste it. The money. But Jessica, with that smile of hers, she says, why, Norman, if you're so offended, you could always waive your retainer. No, I couldn't do that, I said, terrified, because it would appear I was being critical of my respected colleagues. It might be interpreted as a moral judgment.

"You want to hear something even more shameful about me? Jessica is not only brilliant, but she is also a beauty, and has a reputation for sleeping around. Now I have never made love to a black woman. What am I talking about? I'm sixty-three years old and I'd never done it with anybody but Flora. I could die and I wouldn't know if I was missing out because it was a lot better with somebody else. Anyway, at board meetings I would catch myself sneaking glances at Jessica's breasts, or her crossed legs, and she knew, you bet your life she knew. She would be sitting there in that short skirt, if it ended any higher, never mind, expounding brilliantly about Henry James or Twain, doing riffs, throwing out ideas I hadn't been able to come up with in thirty years of teaching, and I would have an erection. I used to order lunch for those board meetings from the restaurant downstairs, and one day it's chicken pieces and potato salad, and Shirley is about to serve me a quarter of breast when Jessica stays her hand, and says, I think it's the dark meat that Norman fancies, and the two of them are into those belly laughs, and I'm red in the face. Oh, I'm so ashamed. I'm such a pig. And Doris, yes Doris, I couldn't stand her teasing, but she was right about me. I wouldn't want my daughter moving in with another woman. The truth is I don't really feel comfortable even sitting in a room with a lesbian or homosexual. Why? I'll tell you. Like Doris said, I'm insecure about my masculinity. If I were lying in bed with my eyes closed, and it was a man who was sucking me off – pardon me for talking like this – but would I know the difference? Wouldn't I come just the same? I think something like that and I'm just about sick to my stomach with fear. But I'll bet it would be the same for you, if it were a man doing it, and that's why you make jokes about fags, but not me any more.

"Okay. Enough of that. No more stalling, Norman. What you are really dying to ask is why I, quote, stole, unquote, the money. Well, it wasn't stealing, it was taking what I deserved. No. Less than I deserved. Look here, if not for me who ever would have heard of Clara Charnofsky? Did you publish her poems at your own expense? Did you shlepp that privately printed book from publisher to publisher, in those days I was like dirt to them, and wasn't I the one who wrote all those begging letters to book reviewers? What would an agent have charged? Ten per cent I think it is, or maybe fifteen. The foundation was my idea, nobody else's. Millions sitting there, earning interest day in and day out, all because of me. And every year we fork out hundreds of thousands of dollars in grants, fellowships, you name it, and do you think I ever once had a thank-you note? Forget it. So I added up all the hours I had put in over the years, and I reckoned I was worth $50 an hour, which is less than a fucking plumber charges these days, never mind a lawyer, and it came to $750,000. They can call it stealing, or embezzlement, or fraud, I don't give a shit, I was entitled. Hey, you want a laugh? I'll give you one. Pour me another drink."

"I think you've had quite enough, Norman."

"He thinks I've had quite enough. Coming from you, that's a hot one," he said, holding out his glass.

I poured him a short one and added lots of water.

"I went to Lutèce for lunch. They fit me in, the table next to where the waiters were coming and going, and I didn't know what to order or which wine with what. You like caviar? I've been reading about it for years in novels, but it's so salty. I don't understand the fuss. Can you tell I'm wearing a toupee, if you didn't know me from before, I mean?"

"Would you like to stay the night, Norman?"

"I've already booked into a motel."

"That was hardly necessary."

"One, I couldn't be sure you'd be here, or that you'd be welcoming. Two, I'm travelling with a young woman, you wouldn't care for her, but it's my business, if you don't mind?" Then his tears yielded to giggles. "Doreen reads Archie comics. She listens to rock music in the car and pops her bubble gum. It drives me crazy. We have to book into a motel with a TV 6:30 prompt every evening so that she can catch "Jeopardy." I'm ashamed to undress in front of her, a skinny old man like me. Pardon me for asking, but do you have varicose veins yet?"

"Some."

"Barney, Barney, I don't know who I am or what I'm doing any more. I sit on the toilet weeping and I turn on the taps so she won't hear me. I'm worried sick about Flora, my daughter must hate me, and one day they'll catch up with me, and I'll end up in prison with common criminals. So how are you these days, I haven't even asked?"

"Have you spent all the money?"

"I think two hundred thousand dollars so far, possibly less. What does it matter?"

"Are you willing to return what's left?"

"I took only what was rightfully mine."

"Answer my question."

"Answer his question. I'm not going to prison."

"If you were willing to return what's left, I could go to New York and talk to the board. I'll offer to make good whatever is missing, providing they agree to drop any charges, which I'm sure they would do."

"How could I let you do such a thing?"

"I'm rich, Norman."

"He's rich. Maybe I should have gone into TV, producing crap for the unwashed."

"Norman, you're beginning to sound like your Uncle Chaim, *alav-ha-sholem.*"

"I appreciate your offer. Honestly I do. But Flora would never have me back. How can I blame her? And I wouldn't dare show my face to old friends again," he said, rising abruptly from his chair. "Say, you wouldn't happen to have any nibbles here you could spare? Cashews or chocolates, or whatever? I promised to bring her something, but now everything will be closed."

"Sorry. No. Norman, I want you to come back here for breakfast, and we can talk some more. I'm serious about making up the missing money. I could also talk to Flora."

"Peanut butter maybe? Some sliced bread?"

"Sorry, I don't come here that often any more. Hey, I could do with some fresh air. Why don't you leave your car here and I'll drive you back to the motel."

"It's only a couple of miles from here, maybe three. I'm perfectly capable."

I should have insisted.

ELEVEN

Jeremy Katz
Chairperson
CRAP
PO Box 124
Montreal, Quebec

May 18, 1994

The Clara Charnofsky
Foundation for Wimyn,
615 Lexington Ave.
New York, N.Y.
U.S.A.

Dear Personhoods,

Hi, there. I'm writing to apply for a grant on behalf of CRAP (Chaps Resolutely Against Prejudice), but, before I get into that, I should tell you something about our organization, little me, and my significant other.

My resource person, Georgina, of whom I am very proud, is the only female member of the Montreal Police Force SWAT team. A position she attained in spite of being situationally disadvantaged, the subject of whistles, ogling, and other gender-based harassment. Only last week, in fact, as she left Station 10 in her civvies (a bodyform jersey, micro-skirt, black mesh pantyhose, and stiletto heel shoes), the duty officer wiggled his eyebrows and exclaimed, "Hey, do you ever look great tonight, Georgy."

I am the one who keeps the home fires burning, looking after our two children, Oscar and Radclyffe. I adore Georgina but she can be a trial on occasion. After work Georgina can meet somebody at Sappho's Cellar, her favourite watering hole, and invite her home to dinner without phoning me first. I really don't mind but I do dislike being surprised in my frumpy housecleaning clothes. I would appreciate a warning phonecall and an opportunity to change into something more *soigné*, never mind not to be caught with *paper napkins* on our table.

Late yesterday afternoon, Georgina phoned to say she wouldn't be home for dinner. It seemed that two wimyn patrol-persons at Station 10, Brunhilde Mueller and Helene Dionne, had decided to tie the knot, setting up a household together. So all the wimyn at the station had organized a doe party, having booked a couple of tables at COX, a male strip joint in the East End. And so I sat down to enjoy a rare treat, *the morning newspaper*. And there, on the front page of the sports section, was a photograph of Mike Tyson, the convicted rapist, who would soon be in pursuit of the heavyweight boxing crown again, and that's what gave me my brainwave.

The next morning I set out my best Irish linen tablecloth, and invited all of the CRAP executive to my kitchen for tea and sugar-free cookies.

I hate to toot my own horn, but the truth is they greeted my brainwave with squeals of enthusiasm. So there it is. Put plainly, wouldn't it be simply magnifico if Mike Tyson, that violator of womankind, that embarrassment to visible minority persons everywhere, *could be challenged and beaten for the heavy-weight title by a womyn contender.* Surely, this would be a LANDMARK in HERSTORY. With this in mind, CRAP is willing to undertake a coast-to-coast search for just such a womyn contender. But our financial resources are limited, and that's why we are applying to the Clara Charnofsky Foundation for Wimyn for a $50,000 grant, to add to whatever we earn through bake sales and bingo nights. You can share in creating the first Womyn Heavyweight Boxing Champion of the World. How about that?

CRAP eagerly awaits your response.

Sincerely yours,
Jeremy Katz
for CRAP

TWELVE

BORED, I picked up my office phone in time to hear our receptionist say, "Good afternoon. Totally Unnecessary Productions Limited."

"May I speak to Barney Panofsky, please?"

"Who's calling?"

"Miriam Greenberg."

"If you are an actress, Mr. Panofsky prefers that you send a letter."

"Will you just tell him that Miriam Greenberg is on the line, please?"

"I will see if he's available."

"Miriam, are you in Montreal?"

"Toronto."

"What a coincidence. I'm going to be in Toronto tomorrow. How about dinner?"

"You're impossible, Barney. I'm calling because your gift arrived yesterday."

"Oh."

"How dare you be so familiar."

"You're right. I shouldn't have done it. But I happened to see it in Holt Renfrew's window and I thought of you immediately."

"I've sent it back."

"Oh, to my office?"

"Don't worry."

"I said I apologize."

"This has got to stop. It's not as if I've ever done anything to encourage you."

"I think we should meet and talk this over."

"There's nothing to talk about."

"You needn't be so angry."

"What sort of woman do you think I am?"

"Oh, you'd be amazed. Miriam, Miriam, the truth is I think about you all the time."

"Well stop. I happen to be going out with someone."

"You're not living together, are you?"

"What business could that be of yours?"

"I'm being a nuisance. I realize that. So why don't we meet for lunch and – "

"I've already told you – "

" – Wait. Lunch. Just once. And if you decide you don't want to see me again, well, that's it."

"Honestly?"

"I swear."

"When?"

"You tell me and I'll be there."

"Wednesday. We can have a meal-in-a-bowl on the Park Plaza Roof."

"No. Downstairs. The Prince Arthur Room."

THIRTEEN

LAST night I made a big mistake. I reread some of the crap I've written in what I've come to grandly consider my very own *Apologia pro vita sua*, with a tip of my chapeau to Cardinal Newman. Digressions, or what I prefer to think of as Barney Panofsky's table talk, abound. But Laurence Sterne got away with it, so why not me? Count your blessings. Readers don't have to wait until the end of volume three before I'm even born. Something else. It doesn't take me six pages to cross a field, as it would if this had been written by Thomas Hardy. I rein in my metaphors, unlike John Updike. I am admirably succinct when it comes to descriptive passages, unlike P.D. James, a writer I happen to admire. A P.D. James character can enter a room with dynamite news, but it is not to be revealed until we have learned the colour and material of the drapes, the pedigree of the carpet, the shade of the wallpaper, the quality and content of the pictures, the number and design of the chairs, whether the side tables are bona fide antique, acquired in Pimlico, or copycat from Heal's. P.D. James is not only gifted, but obviously a real *baleboosteh*, or chatelaine. She is also endearing, which is not my problem, and brings me to yet another digression. Or character flaw acknowledged.

Lying on my lonely sofa at night, boozing as I channel surf, I keep a pair of binoculars within easy reach on my coffee table. I need them as I watch "probing" CBC-TV interviews with yacky political pundits, economists, newspaper editors, sociology or psychology mavins, and other certified idiots. Why? Because these interviews are usually conducted in what purports to be a library, the shelves behind the blabber laden with books. Say it's the celebrated author of that seminal study of five thousand Canadians that has revealed (hello, hello) that the rich are happier than the poor, and less prone to suffer from malnutrition. Or, still better, a sexologist, whatever that is, who ventures that serial rapists are often loners who were sexually abused as children or at least come from dysfunctional families. Whichever, I immediately whip out my binocs to study the titles on the bookshelves. If there's anything there by Terry McIver, I flick off my TV and sit down to compose a letter to the CBC questioning their expert's intelligence and taste.

Slept badly last night, wakened at five a.m., and had to wait until six-thirty for my morning newspapers.

Good one in today's *Globe and Mail*. Eldfriede Blauensteiner, a Viennese widow, is in deep doo-doo. Seems she used to run regular ads in the lovelorn columns of the Austrian press:

> Widow, 64, 1 metre 65cm, would like to share the quiet autumn of her life with a widower. I am a housewife, gardener, nurse, and a faithful companion.

The Kraut Mrs. Lonelyhearts is also a bleached blonde who wears blue-tinted glasses, and was hooked on the roulette wheels and blackjack tables of Baden. Lots of lonely old guys, mostly pensioners, answered her ads, and she screened them for their assets. The police say her earnings from bank accounts, property, and cash left to her in altered wills ran into millions. Her favoured *modus operandi* was to add a soupçon of diabetic medicine to her victim's food and drink over a period of months. This inevitably led to death, ostensibly from natural causes. So far honeybunch has confessed to four murders, but the police suspect there are more skeletons in her closet, so to speak. I am reminded of the character

Charlie Chaplin played in that last film of his, Monsieur What's-his-name,[1] wherein he wasted all those widows, and I wonder if Eldfriede was inspired by the same idiotic reasoning. Namely, what do a few useless old lives matter compared to the world's horrors?

In my favour, I never seriously considered accidentally drowning, or poisoning, The Second Mrs. Panofsky, although our breakfasts together were descents into hell. Thoughtful beyond compare, my gabby missus habitually shared what she could remember of her last night's dreams, which was plenty, with our morning coffee. One morning in particular is imprinted on my sometimes iffy memory now and forevermore. To recap. The night before, two tickets to the hockey game riding in my breast pocket, I met John Hughes-McNoughton, who was to be my companion, at Dink's. John was already blasted, and Zack Keeler was there, also well into it: "Hey, Barney, do you know why Scotsmen wear kilts?"

"I'm not interested."

"It's because the sheep can hear the sound of a fly being unzipped."

Saul, whose opprobium I am obliged to suffer, takes a dim view of my being a hockey nut. "At your age," he said recently, "it is no longer appropriate for you to still be a jock-sniffer."

But I never got to the game. And when Dink's closed at two a.m., John, Zack, and I stepped into the ear-tingling cold, snow swirling in the wind, not a taxi in sight, and shuffled on to a blind pig on McTavish Street, our overcoats steaming in the sudden gust of warmth.

Understandably, I was in agony the next morning when The Second Mrs. Panofsky joined me at the breakfast table in her quilted pink dressing-gown. Ducking behind the *Gazette*, opening it at the sports section, I read: *Big Jean Beliveau led the –*

"I had the most troubling dream about you last night."

– the Canadiens to a –

"Yoo hoo. I said I had the – "

"I heard you."

– to a convincing 5 to –

---

[1]*Monsieur Verdoux* (Universal, 1947) was not Chaplin's last film. His last film was *A Countess from Hong Kong* (Charles Chaplin, 1967), and it starred Marlon Brando.

"I was sixteen years old again, but I can't understand how come in my dream I was still wearing my hair in a pigtail, tied with that velvet ribbon from Saks Fifth Avenue my Aunt Sarah gave me maybe a month before she had to go in to be scraped out, you know, for her hysterectomy. They cut out the poor woman's uterus, and the next thing you know she's hired a private detective to follow Uncle Sam everywhere. The worst she found out was that when he was supposed to be at Rabbi Teitelbaum's Talmud class, he was actually playing pinocle in the back room of the Broadway Barbershop on St. Viateur. You know, next door to where Reuben's Best Kosher Butchershop used to be, my mother swore by his chickens. Reuben was such a card. My mother would take me with her, I was only ten, he would say, 'How come a beauty like you isn't married yet?' Anyway it was certainly incongruous, my still wearing a pigtail in my dream, and I haven't figured it out yet, but at that age I was already going to a hairdresser, Mr. Mario's Salon, on Sherbrooke near Victoria. That reminds me, did you pick up the lampshade at Grunwald's yesterday? It's only the third time I asked you and you promised. You forgot again? You had more important things to think of? Yeah, sure. But if I said there was no single malt whisky left in the house, *fat chance*, you would have dropped everything and shot down to the liquor commission. I was Mr. Mario's favourite. Such beautiful natural curls, he used to say, I ought to pay *you* for doing your hair. He died three years ago, no four, cancer of the testicles is how it started."

With a trembly hand, I lowered my coffee cup and lit a Montecristo Number Four.

"Have you ever heard of emphysema, I wonder?"

"You were saying?"

"It must be worse than a hysterectomy, for a man I mean, losing his testicles, never mind what it meant to Gina, his wife, poor dear. You name a Verdi aria and Gina could sing it for you word perfect while she washed your hair. It had already spread, the testicle cancer, and they opened up Mr. Mario's stomach and sewed it up again, nothing to be done. He left behind Gina and two children. The daughter now works at the Lanvin perfume counter in Holt Renfrew, which is why I never go there any more, she's too familiar. I don't care for that. I don't need her squealing out my first name, as if we were best friends, you can hear it from one end of the floor to

the other. But the youngest, Miguel, is the chef and I think part-
owner of Michelangelo's on Monkland. You know, just down the
street from The Monkland. I saw *Forever Amber* there when I was
just a kid, my father would have died had he known. With Linda
Darnell and Cornel Wilde, and George Sanders, remember him, I
used to think he was terrific. We ought to try Michelangelo's one of
these days. The Silvermans were there last week and they said it was
both inexpensive and delicious with a decent space between the
tables. Not like one of your St. Denis Street bistros, because they
remind you of Paris, you go there and it's like you invited the
Frenchies on either side of you to join you for dinner, and you start
talking loud in English, looking for trouble as usual. Oh, I know
how much you enjoy it. Pretending, just because they're eavesdrop-
ping, that you have a big fat bank account in Switzerland, and can't
understand the menu as it's written in French. What in the hell is
pâté you bellowed that time, pronouncing it like it rhymed with
wait. You were lucky not to be punched out that night. The guy at
the next table was fuming. Herb had the pasta e fagioli and then the
lasagne Sorrento style. He doesn't worry about his weight that one,
you'd think he would, he climbs one flight of stairs and it's like he
had run the Boston Marathon. He suffers from boils. Some of them
in the genital area. It's a turn-off, Marsha told me, especially if one
pops. Marsha had the antipasto and the veal cutlets Milanese, never
mind with those gaps between her teeth, she would never put up
with braces when we were in Young Judea together, little bits get
lodged there and I don't know where to look. I was thoughtful
enough to whisper to her about it once, we were on a double-date,
dinner at Miss Montreal, I was with Sonny Applebaum, he wanted
to marry me and today, you know what, I could be looking after a
guy with Parkinson's. I whispered to her about it and, boy, if looks
could kill, so I never mentioned it to her again. But she shouldn't
talk with her mouth open. Oh, excuse me. I do beg your pardon. In
your eyes she can do no wrong. You danced with her again and
again at the Rothstein wedding, I couldn't have slipped a hair
between your bodies. Don't think everybody didn't notice the two
of you were nowhere to be seen for an hour. I know. Don't tell me
again. She was feeling a little dizzy and you took her for a stroll
down to the water. Yeah, yeah. But look here, Sir Galahad, Norma
Fleischer – it's not the eating that makes her so fat, it's glandular –

could faint on the dance floor and you wouldn't lift a finger. Down for a stroll. You took Marsha to the boat-house. It wouldn't be the first time for her, anybody wearing pants for that one, so don't count yourself so special. She ought to give you guys postcards, like they do for the ducks in that restaurant you took me to in Paris, the Tour d'Argent."

— 5 to 2, but it could turn out to be a costly —

"Am I boring you?"

"No."

"Then put your paper down, if you don't mind."

"It's down."

— to a costly win, because Phil Goyette was cross-checked by Mikita —

"You're reading again."

"You started to tell me about your dream."

"I know exactly what I started to tell you about, and I'll get to the point in my own good time. I didn't know we were in such a hurry here. Boy, did you ever make a racket when you finally got in last night. That hockey game must have gone on for eighteen periods instead of the usual three, judging by the time you got in, and how did you tear your shirt I'd like to know. No. I'd rather not know. But that reminds me, your behaviour, there's something I have to ask you. We're going to my parents for Shabbat dinner on Friday night, you're not getting out of it this time. Oh, I know it's a big imposition, you have to wear a suit, but my father always has the very best single malts there just to please you. Oh, I forgot. The new maid served it with ice in your glass last time you came. Off with her head, eh? The truth is I could cut out my tongue, because I was once foolish enough to tell you my mother simply cannot stand whistling at the table. You don't do it here or anywhere else. *Never, never.* But sit down at our family table on a Friday night and before we have even finished the gefilte fish, you could be auditioning for the 'Ed Sullivan Show' or something. So this Friday at the table will you please, please, please not whistle 'Mairzy-doats' or 'Bongo, Bongo, Bongo, I Don't Want to Leave the Congo,' or some idiot tune by Spike Jones. You find that funny? Something to laugh about? Well, fuck you. My father is still waiting for the results of that biopsy, and if it comes back positive I don't know what I'll do, I think I'll die. Where was I?"

"Sixteen is where you were, with a pigtail."

"That was the year of my Sweet Sixteen dinner dance at the temple. I wore a white taffeta dress from Bergdorf-Goodman, with matching gloves and silk stockings, and high-heeled shoes. My father took one look and his eyes filled with tears. Mr. Bernard and his wife came to the dinner, and so did the Bernsteins and the Katanskys and – "

"What did they serve?" I asked, my smile menacing.

"*Are you being sarcastic?*"

"I'm interested."

"In anything that means something to me? Yeah, sure. And you never laid a hand on one of your *shiksa* so-called actresses and you didn't drink a drop last night. Right? Wrong. Well, for your information, it was catered by Monsieur Henri, no expense spared. He was a Sephardic Jew from Morocco, but not one of your greasy ones. He was extremely polite. Very sophisticated. Introduce him to a lady and he would kiss her hand, without actually touching it. Then it turned out his only son was an epileptic, and it broke his heart. He began to drink and his business went downhill. *Don't give me that look. Spare me.* I know it doesn't interfere with your work. Not yet anyway. In fact, in your case, I would say it's your work that interferes with your drinking. No reaction? What do I have to do to get you to crack a smile? Stand on my head? Take off my panties in Eaton's window? Something that young actress you're so fond of, that Solange woman, could never do. I'm told she doesn't wear any and I'm looking at the guy who I'm sure could confirm that one way or another. Yes? No? Never mind. Back in those days Monsieur Henri's business was burgeoning and he catered a lot of affairs that weren't even Jewish. Old families in Westmount who wouldn't have a Jew, even one as cultured as my father, in one of their clubs booked him for their daughters' coming-out parties and all sorts of events that make the social column in the *Gazette*. Oh, look at you. Impatient already. I'd better stick to the point, eh? Or you'll soon tell me you have to go to the toilet urgently, *taking your newspaper with you*, but I happen to know you've already been this morning, *and how*. So next time would you remember to spray, that's what it's for, you know. Look at it like this. Not every bottle is to drink from. No smile as per usual. No ha ha ha. You don't think that was witty. Only you can make jokes. Okay, okay. Tara-tara-tara. The menu. We started with *foie de poulet*, served in a cucumber canoe, and surrounded by sour-pickle slivers and flower petals. My Aunt Fanny didn't know what they were, and ate them all, it became a family joke for years. My father would take us to dinner at the Café Martin, there would be a vase with flowers in the middle of the table, and he would wink and say, 'It's a good thing Aunt Fanny isn't here.'

"At my Sweet Sixteen boys dressed like bedouins went from table to table with baskets of chocolate-chip and cinnamon and raspberry and lemon bagels, which nobody had ever seen before. It was Monsieur Henri's invention. The soup was some kind of bouillon, but ooh so fragrant, with itsy-bitsy heart-shaped balls of minced veal, wrapped in paper-thin dough, floating in it. Then everybody was served a little peppermint sherbet to clear the palate, and some of the older guests began to mutter, they thought the meal was over, they weren't going to get a main course. The main course was rack of spring lamb, sitting on a bed of couscous, and garnished with apple fritters. Afterwards there were date squares and pecan fingers and quartered fresh figs and strawberries dipped in chocolate, everything spilling out of a biscuit crust shaped like a hunter's horn.

— by Stan Mikita early in the first period —

"My father gave me an onyx ring and a pearl necklace with matching bracelet and earrings. I had it valued at Birk's, don't look at me like that, I'm not mercenary, I had to, for the insurance, and it was worth $1,500 altogether, and I'm talking 1947, never mind now. He also gave me a sterling silver vanity set from Mappin and Webb that still sits on my dressing-table, and would you please not put down your whisky glasses there any more, it leaves rings on the antique leather, not that you care. My grandmother gave me my first mink jacket with matching muff, who wears them now, eh? But I wouldn't part with it for anything. You're reading again."

"I am not."

"Then why did you move your coffee cup just now?"

"Because I spilled some."

"Tell me something. You go to a hockey game on Thursday night, you see what's going on, you know who scored the goals, but first thing the next morning you turn to the sports pages. Why? You think the score is going to be different in the *Gazette*?"

"You were going to tell me about your dream."

"You're not interested in my dream."

"Of course I am."

"Because it was about you?"

"I didn't bring it up, for Christ's sake."

"I'll tell you what I'm interested in. Sylvia Hornstein saw you in the lingerie department of Holt Renfrew two weeks ago, and says she saw you buy a silk negligee, and had it gift-wrapped, and then – and this I found interesting – had it wrapped over again in brown paper – as if it was going to be mailed to somebody. So obviously it wasn't for me. Who for, then?"

"As a matter of fact – "

"Oh boy, is this ever going to be good!"

" – Irv Nussbaum's anniversary is coming up, and he phoned me from Calgary and asked me to get it for his wife and mail it to her here."

"Liar, liar, liar."

"This is outrageous."

"Which of your so-called actresses wore it for you last night, you didn't get in until four a.m."

"As it happens, I was out with John and Zack last night, and you can check that out if you like."

"You can go straight to hell," she said, leaping up.

– it was the fire-wagon Habs taking the play to the Hawks. First it was Big Jean Beliveau feeding Dickie Moore in the slot, then it was Boom-Boom beating Glenn Hall on his glove side with a forty-footer the Hawk netminder would like to have back, and then Beliveau, taking a long pass from Doug Harvey, skated in all alone on Hall. Bang bang bang, 5–1 for the good guys.

FOURTEEN

THE Second Mrs. Panofsky pounded on my shower door. "It's the phone," she said. "Your father."

Izzy said, "You were going to take me to the hockey game tonight? Big treat. The fucken Rangers. Probably you couldn't find another customer. Well, I can't go. Neither can you." Then he paused to blow his nose. "It's over."

"What's over?"

"Your poor mother's suffering. She passed away in her sleep last night and I'm heartbroken."

"Don't give me that."

"Hey, show some respect. You should have seen her when we got hitched. She was a number. We had our little tiffs over the years, who doesn't, but she always kept a clean house. I had no complaints in that department."

But I had some complaints in mine. My father was seldom home when I was a boy. For supper I ate macaroni and cheese most nights, but on special occasions my mother boiled hot dogs served with lumpy mashed potato pyramids covered with corn flakes. She did do one thing for me, registering me for a tap-dance class with Mr. Jeepers Creepers, who had twice been charged with molesting boys. It was her fondest hope that I would appear on *Major Bowes' Amateur Hour*, and be discovered, but she lost interest when I bombed in audition for a local show. The closest I ever came to her was when she was already out of it in the hospital. I would shut the door to her room, don my straw boater, twirl my cane, and tap-dance round her bed, singing "Shoofly Pie and Apple Pan Dowdy" or "Ac-cent-tchu-ate the Positive," another of her favourites. She would squeal, and clap her hands, tears sliding down her cheeks, and my mood would see-saw from joy, for having reached my mother at last, to rage at her for being so damn stupid.

Izzy wept at the funeral, if only for the benefit of her two brothers and their wives, who had flown in from Winnipeg where my mother came from. My uncles, whom I hadn't seen since my bar mitzvah, were respectable people. Milty was a pediatrician and Eli a lawyer, and they both warmed to The Second Mrs. Panofsky immediately. "I understand," said Uncle Eli, "that your father is a good friend of Mr. Bernard's. He's going to speak at a fund-raiser in our synagogue next week. Tell your father if I can be of any help, I'm at Mr. Bernard's service."

The Second Mrs. Panofsky hastily explained that her parents were travelling in Europe, or of course they would have been at the funeral.

"Should business ever bring your father to Winnipeg, he has a friend there now. You tell him that."

My uncles had always disapproved of my father and been embarrassed by my mother, whom they took to be the family idiot. All the same, Uncle Milty asked my father, "Where will you be sitting shiva?"

"My own philosophy, speaking personally, is modern," said Izzy. "I don't go in for the religious hocus-pocus."

Relieved, my aunts and uncles made arrangements to fly home. I dropped off The Second Mrs. Panofsky at our house, and drove my father on to Dink's, where we could mourn together in Panofsky fashion. Only after we were well into it, did Izzy begin to sniffle, dabbing at his eyes with a filthy handkerchief. "I'm never going to marry again. Ever."

"Who in the hell would put up with an old fart like you?"

"You'd be surprised, kiddo. She loved you, you know. When she was pregnant, you were an accident, you know."

"Oh?"

"She was pregnant, worried about her figure, I said you want an abortion, I can arrange it. Naw, she said. She wanted to call you Skeezix, after the kid in "Gasoline Alley," but I put my foot down and we settled on Barney, after *Barney Google*."

"*You mean I'm named after a character in a comic strip?*"

"She hoped one day you would grow up to be a radio personality."

"Like Charlie McCarthy or Mortimer Snerd?"

"Come on. Those was dummies. Hey, even a spot on Canadian radio would have pleased her. She never missed a 'Happy Gang' show. Remember? Bert Pearl. Kay Stokes. That bunch."

"Do you need any money, Daddy?"

"I've got my health, you can't buy that with millions. What I need is a job. I went to see the mayor of Côte St.-Luc. How about it, I said? Izzy, he said, I'm a Jew and the alderman is a Jew. It wouldn't look good to have a Jewish cop too. The goyim would talk. You know how they are. He had a point. When I was a youngster, I discovered that they even used to resent Al Jolson. He's not a real nigger, they'd say. It's make-up."

"Daddy, I don't know what I'd do without you. You don't need a job. I'm going to tear apart our basement and turn it into a self-contained apartment for you."

"Yeah, sure. Your missus would really go for that."

As Izzy anticipated, The Second Mrs. Panofsky was furious when I told her I was going to convert the basement into a flat for him. "I won't have that animal here," she said.

"He's my father. I don't like to think of him all alone in a rented room at his age."

"How would you like it if mine moved in, he's so sick, a day goes by he doesn't see me, he's miserable."

The move from a seedy rooming-house on Dorchester to a squeaky clean, all mod con flat on a tree-lined street in suburban Hampstead did not intimidate my father. He made himself at home at once. Within weeks his planned kitchen reeked of stale farts and White Owl cigars and Chinese take-out food mouldering on abandoned paper plates. No sitting-room chair was without its stack of magazines and newspapers (*True Detective*, the *National Enquirer*, the *Police Gazette*, *Playboy*[1]), the magazine cover corners unfailingly ripped off, having served as makeshift toothpicks while he watched "Perry Mason" or "Have Gun, Will Travel." His bed was perpetually unmade and orange peels and sunflower seeds and chunks of sour pickle and cigar butts filled ashtrays to the overflow. Empty rye and beer bottles rode every surface.

I adamantly refused The Second Mrs. Panofsky's request to attach a lock to the kitchen door that opened on to an interior staircase to my father's flat. Poor Izzy. The intrepid cop who had wrestled second-storey men to the ground, chased bank robbers down lanes, flattened drug dealers with his left hook, and cracked the skulls of muggers with his revolver butt, feared The Second Mrs. P. as he had no lawbreaker. Only if he heard me moving about solo would Izzy mount the stairs tippytoe, open the kitchen door tentatively, and ask, "Is the coast clear, kid?"

"She's out."

Grabbing a glass, Izzy would make straight for the liquor cabinet in the dining room.

"Careful, Daddy. She marks the level of each bottle with a pencil."

---

[1] Actually, the first issue of *Playboy* did not appear until December 1963.

"Hey, you're talking to a detective."

"So these days I pour myself a single malt," I said, looking him in the eye, "there's no need to add water. It's already been done for me."

"It's the new maid. Boy, is she ever a prude."

"Goddamn it, Daddy, you haven't – "

"I never laid a hand on her, I don't care what she says."

Izzy especially enjoyed Wednesdays, the night The Second Mrs. Panofsky went to visit her parents in order to avoid my weekly poker game. I would usually be joined by Marv Guttman, Sid Cooper, Jerry Feigelman, Hershey Stein and Nate Gold. I remember one Wednesday in particular, the one where Irv Nussbaum filled in for the absent Nate Gold. Shuffling the cards, Irv beamed at Marv. "Well now, did you and Sylvia enjoy yourselves in Israel?"

"It's unreal. We had a marvellous time. I tell you what they're doing there . . ."

"What they're doing there," said Irv, addressing the group as he began to deal, "is costing untold millions, and this year everyone, and I mean everyone, is going to have to get behind the bond drive as never before."

"It's been a lousy year for us," said Hershey.

"The worst," said Jerry.

"And with the cost of materials today," said Marv.

"And what," asked Irv, "about the cost of fighting the fedayeen, or absorbing our brothers from Yemen?"

Inviting Irv had been a mistake, I realized too late, as within an hour the game began to falter, the guys watching, indignant, as Irv pulled over a cut-crystal bowl filled with chips and began to stack them in piles, according to colour. The chips weren't his, but, on his insistence, represented ten per cent off the top of each pot, proceeds to the Ben-Gurion University of the Negev. Irv was a governor.

"He never rests," said Hershey, glaring at Irv.

"Neither," said Irv, "do our enemies."

By ten o'clock the fun had leaked out of our game. And, after one more round, awfully early by our standard, the guys decided to pack it in, digging into the goodies I had set out on platters on a side table: smoked meat, salami, chopped liver, potato salad, sour pickles, bagels, and sliced *kimmel* bread. Counting the chips in the cut-crystal bowl once more, Irv announced, "We've collected three hundred and seventy-five dollars for the Ben-Gurion University of the Negev. If we each chipped in another twenty bucks that would make five hundred even."[2]

Which was when Izzy, lured by the promise of food and drink, burst into the dining room, grinning as he brandished his snub-nosed revolver. "Don't anybody move," he hollered, assuming his gunfighter's stance. "This is a raid."

"Daddy, for Christ's sake, I'm really tired of that joke. It's asinine."

Snorting, his mouth clamped on a mushy White Owl, Izzy heaved himself into the chair closest to the food platters. "I keep three guns in the house." Avoiding my reproving look, he yanked the smoked-meat platter toward him and, reaching for a fork, began to stab at fat slices, flicking the lean cuts aside, as he began to stack meat on *kimmel* bread. "They're well-hidden, scattered, you know. Somebody comes in here, uninvited, boy, if he wants to I'll air-condition him, sure as hell." Then he started on one of his trips down memory lane. "During the Depression, you know what I earned? Twelve hundred bucks a year, that's all, and I'll bet some of you lost that much tonight. Could I live on it? Good question. Don't forget I had a free car. I was in the mood for a piece of tail, it was always compliments of the house," said Izzy. And then, carrying his wobbly sandwich with him, he drifted over to the liquor cabinet to pour himself a hefty shot of Crown Royal and ginger ale. "You'd go into places, everybody knows you're in the detective office, they're glad to see you, you know how it is? Butcher shops, especially the kosher ones, groceries, most of them are glad to see you. Specially they may need your help. So they load you down with free stuff. Clothing factories too, they may need you in an investigation, like you go inside to scare an employee for them who wants to start a union or shit like that. I didn't feel the Depression at all." And then, his immense sandwich balanced in one hand, his rye and ginger ale in another, a sour pickle clenched between his teeth, Izzy wiggled his eyebrows at me and retreated to his basement flat.

"He's something else," said Nate.

---

[2]$375 plus 6-times-$20 actually equals $495.

"Tell me, Marv," said Irv, "did you stop over in Europe on your way to Israel?"

"Paris."

"You shouldn't spend your dollars in Europe. France, specially. In 1943[3] they rounded up more Jewish kids for the gas chambers than even the Gestapo could cope with."

Sensing trouble, everybody hurried into their coats and fled. Standing at the top of the stairs to my father's flat, I shouted, "You're a pig, a *chazer*, and I can see through all your childish tricks."

Slippers flapped on the stairs, and my father ascended, his face ashen. There were times he looked fifty, his energy boundless, and other times, like now, he seemed old and crushed. "You all right, Daddy?" I asked.

"Heartburn."

"I'm not surprised, packing away a sandwich like that."

"Can I have an Alka-Seltzer, or has she locked that up?"

"Please don't start, Daddy. I'm tired," I pleaded, fixing him an Alka-Seltzer.

Izzy accepted the glass, gulped it down, and belched resoundingly. "Barney," he said, a quiver in his voice, "I love you." And suddenly, unaccountably, he was in tears.

"What is it, Daddy? Tell me, please. Maybe I can help."

"Nobody can help."

Cancer. "Here, Daddy."

My father accepted a Kleenex, blew his nose, and wiped the corners of his eyes. I stroked his hand and waited. Finally he raised his tear-streaked face and said, "You don't know what it's like not to be able to fuck regular any more."

Here we go again, I thought, angrily withdrawing my hand, as once more Izzy lamented the departure of Madame Langevin, our first maid. "Forty-eight years old," he said, grieving, "and she had

---

[3]On July 16, 1942, thousands of French police officers rounded up 13,000 Jews in Paris, invalids, pregnant women and 3,000 children among them. The Jews were locked into the winter Vélodrome without food or water to await deportation to an extermination camp. The round-up was part of an agreement Vichy's Pierre Laval had made with the Nazis, who were hard put to cope with the transportation of so many Jews at one go.

breasts," he reminded me again, rapping a tiled counter top with his knuckles, "hard as this."

Madame Langevin, once The Second Mrs. Panofsky had found out, had been sent packing over my objections. Our new maid, a West Indian, was not allowed into the basement flat unless Izzy was out.

"Daddy, will you go to bed now, please."

But he was back at the liquor cabinet, helping himself to another rye and ginger ale. "Your mother, may she rest in peace, suffered terribly from gas. What held her together during those last years? Wire and string. Stitches. All those operations. Shit. Her stomach was so criss-crossed, it looked like centre ice at the end of the third period."

"You're not being decent," I protested.

Izzy, drunker than I imagined, embraced me, kissing me on both cheeks, his eyes welling with tears again. "I want you to hang in there, Barney. Get as much as you can while the going is good."

"You're a disgusting old man," I said, disengaging myself.

Izzy shuffled over to his stairs, paused, and turned to me once more. "Jeez. The garage doors. It's her car. The Duchess of Outremont is back. See you around, kid."

Ten days later he died of a heart attack on a massage-parlour table.

FIFTEEN

ON a sweet summer evening in 1973 I was out to dinner with a radiant Miriam, by then the mother of our three children, and like everybody else in those days we were caught up in a heated discussion of the televised Watergate hearings, which we had watched all afternoon. "The tapes are going to do him in," she said. "He's going to have to resign."

"The hell he will. He's a survivor, that bastard."

Of course she was right, as usual. And I, as usual, brought her my office problems. "I never should have commissioned Marty Klein to write those scripts."

"I hate to say I told you so."

"But his wife's pregnant and he left the CBC to come to me. I can't fire him."

"Then promote him. Make him executive producer, or vice-president in charge of ashtrays. Anything. So long as he doesn't write."

"I couldn't do a thing like that," I protested.

It took me three days, as usual, to absorb Miriam's advice, and then I did exactly as she had suggested, pretending it was my idea. Other couples used to joke about us. We would go to a party and end up in a corner, or sitting together on the stairs, gabbing away, ignoring everybody else. Then some gossip wound its way back to Miriam. She was out to lunch with one of her so-called girlfriends, then embroiled in an ugly divorce action, and she was told, "I thought Barney had eyes only for you. At least that's what people say. Now please don't be angry with me, but, speaking from experience, I don't want you to be the last to know. Dorothy Weaver, you don't know her, saw him at the Johnsons' cocktail party last Wednesday. And there was your devoted husband coming on to a woman. Chatting her up. Whispering in her ear. Massaging her back. They left together."

"I know all about that."

"Thank God, because the last thing I want to do is upset you."

"Oh dear, I'm afraid that woman was me, and we went on to the Ritz from there, to drink champagne, and afterwards, now don't you repeat this, but I agreed to go home with him."

The two of us were out to dinner at La Sapinière in Sainte Adèle. As Miriam perused the menu, I brought a flush to her cheeks, sliding my hand under the table so stroke her silken thigh. Oh, happy days! Oh, nights of rapture! Leaning over to nibble her ear, I suddenly felt her stiffen. "Look out," she said.

Yankel Schneider, of all people, had just entered the restaurant with a couple of friends, only this time he didn't stop at our table to insult me, his anger justifiable. Nevertheless, he put Miriam and me in mind of our last encounter with him at our make-or-break lunch at the Park Plaza in Toronto. That lunch that had started out as a disaster. Me, making such a fool of myself. With hindsight, however, we were now able to laugh at what had since become a cherished part of our personal history. A story, albeit an edited version, our children had come to adore.

"And then what happened?" Saul might ask.

"Tell them, Miriam."

"Certainly not."

But that evening in Sainte Adèle, Yankel's presence still filled me with guilt. Sneaking glances at him, I did not see the man in his early forties, but, instead, the ten-year-old schoolboy whose life I had made such a misery. "I still don't understand why I tormented him like that. How I could behave so abominably?"

Sensing my distress, Miriam reached for my hand.

O, Miriam, Miriam, my heart's desire. Without her, I am not only alone, but incomplete. In our halcyon days I could share everything with her, even my most shameful moments, of which there are too many to haunt me in my dotage. Take this one, for instance. On that day that was ruined for me, because I had read in the *Gazette* that McIver had won the Governor General's Award for fiction, I sent him a note. *An anonymous note.* Some lines from Dr. Johnson's *The Vanity of Human Wishes*:[1]

"Toil on, dull crowd, in extacy," he cries,
"For wealth or title, perishable prize;
While I these *transitory* blessings scorn."
This thought once form'd, all counsel comes too late,
He plies the press, and hurries to his fate;
Swiftly he sees the imagin'd laurels spread,
He feels th' unfading wreath surround his head;
Warn'd by another's fate, vain youth, be wise,
These dreams were *Settle's* once and *Ogilby's*.[2]

Once I was not only an unredeemed sadist, given to ridiculing a classmate with a stammer, but on occasion a coward, and also a petty thief. When I was a boy one of my chores was to deliver and collect our sheets from the Chinese laundry on Fairmount Street. One

---

[1] In fact, the quotation is from *The Young Author*, written when Dr. Johnson was twenty years old.

[2] John Ogilby is long forgotten and so is Elkanah Settle, once the official "City Poet" of London.

afternoon the stooped old man ahead of me, bearded, wearing a yarmulke, didn't notice that he had dropped a five-dollar bill on the floor as he paid for his laundry. I covered it with my shoe immediately, retrieving it once he had shuffled out of the shop.

In fifth grade, I was the one who wrote FUCK YOU, MISS HARRISON on the blackboard, but it was Avie Fried who was expelled from school for a week as a consequence. Our principal, Mr. Langston, summoned me to his office. "I am obliged to strap you, young man, because I know you were aware Fried was the culprit. However, I do admire your pluck for declining to snitch on a classmate."

"Thank you, sir," I said, extending my hand, palm upward.

I have many more claims to obloquy. It was not an accident that at Sheila Ornstein's Sweet Sixteen party, up there in the higher reaches of Westmount, I knocked over a lampstand and shattered a Tiffany shade. I did it, because I detested them for being rich. Sure, but I was indignant when, maybe five years ago, ruffians broke into my Laurentian cottage and not only stole my TV set, among other movables, but also shat on my sofa. I am an impenitent rotter to this day, a malevolent man, exulting in the transgressions of my betters.

Case in point.

I understand why our most perspicacious men of letters object to the current trend in biography, its mean practitioners revelling in the carve-up of genius. But the truth is, nothing delights me more than a biography of one of the truly great that proves he or she was an absolute shit. I'm a sucker for studies of those who, like that friend of Auden's wrote (not MacNeice, not Isherwood, but the other guy), " ... travelled a short while toward the sun / And left the vivid air signed with their honour."[3] But took no prisoners en route, *now that the facts are known*. Say, the story of T.S. Eliot having his first wife locked up in the bin, possibly because she had written some of his best lines. Or a book that delivers the dirt on Thomas Jefferson, who kept slaves and provided the prettiest one with an unacknowledged child. ("How is it," asked Dr. Johnson, "that we hear the loudest yelps for liberty among the drivers of negroes?") Or reveals that Martin Luther King was a plagiarist and a compul-

---

[3]Stephen Spender. Lines from "The Truly Great," p. 30, *Collected Poems 1928–1985*. Random House, New York, 1986.

sive fucker of white women. Or that Admiral Byrd, one of my boyhood heroes, was actually a smooth-talking liar, a terrible navigator, an air traveller so frightened of flying that he was frequently drunk while others did the piloting, and a man who never hesitated to take unearned credit. Or tells how FDR cheated on Eleanor. Or that JFK didn't really write *Profiles in Courage*. Or how Bobby Clarke slashed Kharlamov across the ankles, taking out the better player in that first thriller of a hockey series against the incredible Russians. Or that Dylan Thomas was a *schnorrer* born. Or that Sigmund Freud faked some of his case-notes. I could go on, but I think you get the idea. And, in any event, my feelings are licensed by no less a moralist than Dr. Johnson, who once pronounced on the uses of biography to Edmond Malone, a Shakespearean scholar:

> If nothing but the bright side of characters should be shown, we should sit down in despondency, and think it utterly impossible to imitate them in *anything*. The sacred writers (he observed) related the vicious as well as the virtuous actions of men; which had this moral effect, that it kept mankind from *despair*.

In a nutshell, I am not unaware of my failings. Neither am I a stranger to irony. I realize that I – who took The Second Mrs. Panofsky's rambling conversation to be an abomination – have consumed hundreds of pages, piling digression upon digression, to avoid getting to that seminal weekend in the Laurentians that all but destroyed my life, rendering unto me my reputation as a murderer, which is believed by some to this day. So coming up at last, the lowdown. Exit Boogie. Enter Detective-Sergeant Sean O'Hearne. And I'm willing to swear that what follows is the truth. I am innocent. Honestly. So help me God, as they say.

SIXTEEN

WAIT. Not quite yet. I'll get to the cottage (Boogie, O'Hearne, Second Mrs. P., et cetera et cetera) in a jiffy. I promise. But right now it's time for "By Special Request." Miriam's hour. Damn. There seems to be something wrong with my radio. Weak what-do-you-call-thems maybe. You know, the thingumajigs that provide the juice. I can only hear her when I turn the volume way up. Everything's going on the blink here. Last night it was my TV. The volume fading in and out again. When I finally got it adjusted, I was interrupted by a pounding on the door. It was the downstairs neighbour's son. "Are you not answering your phone, Mr. Panofsky?"

"Of course I'm answering my phone. What's your problem, Harold?"

"My mother was wondering if you'd mind turning your TV down."

"Your mother must have very sensitive hearing, but, okay, I'll turn it down."

"Thank you."

"Oh, Harold. One minute."

"Yes, sir."

"Trick question. If your radio was going dead, what would you suspect was the problem? It's not a plug-in, but one of those you carry from room to room . . ."

"A portable."

"That's what I said, isn't it?"

"I guess you ought to check out your batteries."

Harold gone, I poured myself a couple of fingers of Cardhu, and looked into what late movies were available on TV. Burt Lancaster in *The Crimson Pirate*. *The Silver Chalice* with Paul Newman and Virginia Mayo. *FBI Girl* with Cesar Romero, George Brent, and Audrey Totter. No, thanks, but sleep wouldn't come. So I dredged up my trusty Mrs. Ogilvy out of the mists, recalling the Sunday she had borrowed somebody's Austin sedan and invited me to go on a picnic in the Laurentians. To my amazement, my mother had actually prepared food for us. Unspeakable concoctions of her own invention. Combination banana and oozy boiled-egg sandwiches and other two-deckers, these filled with sardines and peanut butter. "Remember, be a nice, polite boy," she said.

"Sure thing," I said, dumping the sandwiches in the back lane.

Mrs. Ogilvy, an iffy driver, managed to jump the sidewalk in her attempt to park. She was wearing that two-sizes-too-small, sleeveless summer dress that buttoned down the front. Tires squealing as she hit the brakes for red lights, stalling more than once, jolting to starts, we did eventually make it safely into the countryside. "Did you bring your bathing costume?" she asked.

"I forgot."

"My goodness, so did I."

She reached out to fondle me, the Austin swerving into the wrong lane.

"It's Mr. Smithers's car, don't you know? He lent it to me in the hope that I might acquiesce, and go for a drive with him some moonlit night, but nothing would entice me into the back seat for that one. He suffers from pyorrhoea."

We settled on a blanket in a clearing in the woods and she opened up her picnic hamper. Gentleman's relish. Fishpaste. Oxford marmalade. Scones. Two pork pies. "Now we're going to play a game. I want you to lean against that tree, with your *derrière* to me, and count to *vingt-cinq en français*. Then I'm going to hide some sweeties on me, bonne-bouche chockies with ambrosial centres, and then you can root for them, and lap them up. On your marks, get set, go. But no peeking."

As I anticipated, I turned around to find her spread nude on the blanket, the chocolates positioned exactly where I suspected. "Hurry. They're beginning to melt and it's getting très tickly."

Bracing myself as she began to buck and moan, gradually subsiding, I was finally able to pull back and wipe my mouth with my wrist. To my astonishment, she raised her legs, delivering a sharp blow to my chin with her knee. "You know, and I know, that none of this ever happened. Prevaricator. You made this up, you little wanker, sullying the good name of a perfectly respectable school teacher . . . born and bred in London, a survivor of the Blitz, our finest hour, only to be shipped to this callow dominion, this *tiefste Provinz*, where they use tea bags . . . You invented this because you

are suffering the *dégringolade* of old age, and hoped to rouse yourself
sufficiently to trickle a drop or two of spunk on your sheets. Crikey,
it's become so rare you ought to have it bottled. You fabricated this
picnic – "

"The hell I did. You took me on a – "

"Quite. But you got no further than groping me in your greedy,
inexperienced manner before that rustic – that *habitant* – speaking
that patois that passes for French here, came to say we were tres-
passing. You made up the rest, because no woman worth her salt
will even give you a look any more, you filthy-minded, shrinking,
liver-spotted, sunken-bellied old Jew, now almost a deaf-mute, if the
truth were known. You concocted this salacious story because you
are still procrastinating, and would scribble anything rather than get
to the truth of what happened at the cottage. Now out of bed with
you for one of your pathetic little pees that couldn't fill an eye-
dropper. Poor Boogie."

SEVENTEEN

I NEVER lost touch with Boogie, who would send me cryptic
little postcards from wherever he was. Marrakesh. Bangkok.
Kyoto. Havana. Cape Town. Las Vegas. Bogota. Varanasi:

> In the absence of a *mikva*, there is always the Ganges
> for purification. Read Chester, Alfred. Green, Henry. Also
> Roth, Joseph.

Or a note from that city in Kashmir, whatever it's called,[1] where
the druggies stop to refuel. When I was a boy, I had a map pinned to
my bedroom wall on which I traced the path of the Allied armies in
Europe after D-Day. Now I kept a globe in my office so that I could
follow the progress of my friend the latter-day pilgrim through his
own Slough of Despond. His short stories appeared infrequently in
the *Paris Review, Zero* and *Encounter*. Inevitably, Boogie settled into a

---

[1]Srinagar.

loft in the Village and became a regular at the San Remo and The Lion's Head. Women sought him out. Among them, to the amazement of onlookers one evening, Ava Gardner. He commanded the attention – no, something approaching reverence – of the young as well as beautiful women, by his silence, broken only when he made one of his rare pronouncements. One evening, for instance, when Jack Kerouac's name came up, he muttered, "Energy isn't enough."

"It's not writing," I said. "It's typing."[2]

Boogie was also disdainful of Allen Ginsberg. Once, when I just happened to be there, a beguiling young woman, out to make an impression, made the mistake of reciting the opening lines of *Howl* to him:

"I saw the best minds of my generation destroyed by madness, starving hysterical naked
dragging themselves through the negro streets looking for an angry fix . . ."

Boogie responded, "The best minds? Names, please."

"I don't understand."

"Isaiah Berlin? No, too old. Surely not Mr. Trocchi?"

Among Boogie's regular drinking companions were Seymour Krim and Anatole Broyard. He was the polar opposite of Hymie Mintzbaum, never dropping a name, but then a letter might turn up from Cuba, addressed to Boogie c/o The Lion's Head, and it was from Ernest Hemingway. Or John Cheever could come by and take him to lunch. Or Norman Mailer or William Styron might pass through, and they would sit with him or inquire about his whereabouts if he wasn't to be seen. Billie Holiday, after her disastrous last cabaret tour of France and Italy, turned up, looking for him. Mary McCarthy came. So did John Huston. His legend flowered after an excerpt from his novel-in-progress appeared in the *New American Review*, but I knew he had written it in Paris something like ten years earlier. All the same, Boogie gradually acquired a reputation as author of the greatest modern American novel yet to be written. The editors of some of the most distinguished publishing houses in

---

[2]Actually, this observation was first and famously made by Truman Capote.

New York came a-courting, armed with cheque books. One of them
once dispatched a limousine to drive Boogie to a meticulously engi-
neered dinner party in Southampton, only to discover that he had
gone to visit a girlfriend in Sag Harbor instead, the car arriving at
the publisher's dacha without him, adding to Boogie's mystique.
Another editor took him to lunch at The Russian Tea Room.
Oozing flattery, he asked, "Would it be possible to see more of your
novel?"

"That would be indiscreet," said Boogie, tending to his dripping nose. "I can't seem to shake this cold."

"Possibly we should talk to your agent?"

"I haven't got one."

His own best agent, Boogie was noncommittal, or changed the
subject, as generous contracts were proffered. The longer he
resisted cutting a deal with a publisher, the higher the figures flew.
Finally Boogie signed with Random House for an advance that ran
into six figures, not unusual today, but I'm talking 1958, the year the
Canadiens won their third Stanley Cup in a row, taking out
the Boston Bruins 5–3 in game five. Geoffrion and Maurice Richard
scored in the first period; Beliveau, and Geoffrion again, in the
second; and Doug Harvey, with a seeing-eye sizzler from forty feet
out, in the third. So there's nothing wrong with old Barney Panofsky's memory, is there? Spaghetti is strained with a colander. The
names of the Seven Dwarfs are Sleepy, Grumpy, Sneezy, Doc,
Happy, and the other two.[3] The Weizmann Institute is in Haifa.
Frederic Wakeman didn't write *The Man in the Grey Flannel Suit*, it
was the other guy.[4] Napoleon was defeated in that town Spike Jones
wrote that nonsense song about:

> She's the pearl diver's daughter,
> And she's nuts about the water,
> WATERLOO ...

Boogie is where I was at. He squandered some of the money at
blackjack and chemin de fer tables; and drank, sniffed, and main-
lined the rest into his arm, and when that vein hid from him,

---

[3]Dopey and Bashful.
[4]Sloan Wilson.

he stabbed his ankle and even his tongue. Then came the day he phoned me at my office. Had I been blessed with foresight, I would have hung up. I didn't.

"I'd like to crash at your place in the country for a while," he said. "I'm trying to kick. Can you put me up?"

"Sure."

"I'm going to need some methadone."

"My friend Morty Herscovitch will provide."

I picked up Boogie at the airport, unprepared for how gaunt he had become since I had last seen him, sweat beading his forehead and sliding down his cheeks in spite of the chill in the air, unseasonable for late June. "We're going to celebrate with a bang-up lunch at El Ritzo," I said, linking arms with him, "and then we'll drive out to the Laurentians," where, I told him, The Second Mrs. Panofsky was awaiting us.

"No, no, no," he said. "You've got to take me somewhere I can shoot up first."

"I thought you were here to kick?"

"Just one more time or I won't make it."

We drove to my house, where Boogie promptly shed his jacket, rolled up his shirtsleeves, knotted a tie round his arm, and then began to pump it like a windmill softball pitcher, trying to get that elusive vein to protrude, even as I heated up his stuff in a spoon. It took three bloody probes before he was finally able to drive the syringe into the vein. "I guess that's what Forster meant by 'only connect,'" I said.

" 'Do you mind my asking what the syringe is for?' the druggist asked. 'Why, I'm cooking a ham Southern style, injecting it with Jack Daniels.' "

"Shall we go and eat now?"

"I don't. Good to see you."

"You too."

"How many of those cigars do you smoke a day?"

"I never count."

"They're bad for you, you know. Say, whatever became of your friend McIver?"

"Nothing much."

"He showed some promise, I thought."

"Ah."

The Second Mrs. Panofsky was waiting for us on the porch, dressed in her finest, and looking attractive, even sexy, I am honour-bound to acknowledge. She had gone to a good deal of trouble, preparing a dinner by candlelight. But Boogie slid into sleep over the first course, split-pea soup, his head lolling and his body racked by sudden attacks of twitches. I led him into the room that had been prepared for him, dumped him onto the bed, and showed him where I had left his methadone supply. Then I returned to the dining-room table. "Sorry about that," I said.

"You would get him drunk before bringing him out here, never mind that I've been standing over the hot stove all day."

"It wasn't like that."

"Now you'll have to sit here and talk to me, pretending we were a real couple. Or should I get you a magazine?"

"He's awfully sick, you know."

"I don't want him smoking in bed. He could set the house on fire."

"He doesn't smoke. Bad for your health, he says."

"Where are you going? I haven't even served the lamb yet. Or are you not hungry either?"

"I was just going to pour myself a Scotch."

"Well, in that case, bring the bottle to the table, so you don't have to jump up every two minutes."

"Zowie, are we ever in for a few days of fun here."

"You don't know the half of it. I had to empty your pockets before I took your suit to the cleaners Tuesday and this is what I found."

Oy oy oy. A bill from Regal Florists for a dozen long-stemmed red roses. "Oh, that," I said, reaching for the bottle.

"I thought that was so sweet of you. I washed out a vase and I didn't dare leave here all day – *in case I missed the delivery.*"

"I guess they couldn't find the cottage."

"Your nose is getting longer by the minute."

"Are you suggesting that I'm a liar?"

"Suggesting? No, honeybunch. *I'm saying.*"

"That's outrageous."

"*Who were they for?*"

"As a matter of fact, the purchase was entirely innocent, but I refuse to be interrogated in this manner in my own home."

"Which one of your whores were the roses for?"

"You're going to be awfully embarrassed when those roses turn up here tomorrow morning."

"Only if you sneak out to the general store and put in an emergency phonecall for another dozen. *I want to know if you keep a whore in an apartment somewhere.*"

"Only one?"

"I'm waiting for you to answer my question."

"I could prove my innocence and answer your question just like that," I said, flicking my fingers, "but I don't care for your tone of voice, or your insults."

"I'm the one who's behaving badly?"

"Absolutely."

"*Now tell me who the roses were for.*"

"An actress we're trying to get to commit to a pilot I'm planning."

"Where does she live?"

"Somewhere in Outremont, I think. But how would I know? That's what I have a secretary for."

"Somewhere in Outremont?"

"Côte St.-Catherine Road, I think."

"You want to try again?"

"This is ridiculous. The lamb is delicious. Really excellent. Why can't we enjoy our dinner like two civilized people?"

"I phoned Regal Florists, pretending to be your secretary – "

"You had no business doing such a – "

" – and the guy there wanted to know if you wished to change your standing order. A dozen long-stemmed red roses once a week to an address in Toronto. No, I said, but I wanted to check the party's name. That must have made him suspicious, because he said, 'I'll have to look that up and call you back.' So I hung up. Now tell me the name of your whore in Toronto."

"I refuse to sit here any longer," I said, leaping up, my bottle of Macallan in hand, "and tolerate this manner of questioning."

"You're sleeping in the other spare bedroom tonight, and if your friend, the druggie, wants to know why, tell him to ask me. Does he know you're taking tap-dance lessons?"

"Tell him. I don't mind."

"I can't wait for him to see you in that straw hat and cane. You look like such a shmuck."

"I suppose I do," I said.

"My father saw right through you. If I had listened to him, may he rest in peace, I wouldn't be in this position."

"Married beneath yourself."

"I'm an attractive young woman by any standard," she said, her voice cracking, "intelligent, and well educated. *Why did you need somebody else?*"

"Let's get some sleep. We can talk in the morning."

But she had begun to weep. "Why did you marry me, Barney?"

"It was wrong of me."

"I came up behind you at our wedding, and you were saying to Boogie, 'I'm in love. For the first time in my life I am truly, seriously, irretrievably in love.' I can't tell you how touched I was. What I felt in my heart for you at that moment. And look at us now. We've hardly been together for more than a year, it's been months since you've made love to me, and I hate you in my bones for disgracing me."

"I want you to know," I said, laden with guilt, "that I haven't been unfaithful to you."

"Oh, I'm so ashamed. So broken. And you are such a liar. Such a street person. Such an animal. Go ahead. Finish your bottle. Good night."

I didn't quite finish the bottle, but almost, and wakened early to the sound of her on the phone to her mother. The Second Mrs. Panofsky's morning report. "It was leg of lamb. No, not New Zealand. Local. From Delaney's. Maw, I'm well aware it's cheaper at Atwater Market, but I didn't have the time and there's never a place to park. I remember. Certainly I'll check his bill. I always do. No, you were absolutely right to complain about the roast that time. It was tough. I was not embarrassed. I just preferred to wait outside. Maw, that's not fair. Not every Irish Catholic is an anti-Semite. It just happened to be a tough standing rib. I am not criticizing your cooking. What? Oh, split-pea soup, and afterward green salad and cheese. Yes, you gave me that recipe. I know Rabbi Hornstein is crazy for it, but Barney doesn't care for desserts. God knows he gets enough sugar out of the Scotch he drinks. I'll tell him, honestly, but he says he isn't interested in living to be a gibbering old idiot of eighty. I agree. That's not old any more. Please, he knows very well you have a degree from McGill, and that you review books for the ladies' reading group at the Temple. *He does not think you're stupid.* Correction. He thinks everybody is stupid. What? He said that to you? Well, to tell you the truth, I don't think he ever finished the seven volumes of Gibbon either. You don't have to prove anything to him. Maw, I think that Frank Harris is disgusting too, and he shouldn't have given it to you for Chanukah. It was a bad joke. What? Oh, he's a writer. An old friend of Barney's from his Paris days. Moscovitch. Bernard Moscovitch. No, not Canadian. He's a real writer. Maw, you're not the only one who hasn't heard of him. I beg your pardon, but I'm suggesting no such thing. I know you're very well read. *Maw, I'm not being condescending.* Let's not get into that. It's my natural tone of voice. I was born with it. But I couldn't yesterday. There was so much to do here. I didn't forget and I don't consider phoning you an obligation. I *do* love you and I appreciate how much you miss Daddy, and how I'm all you have left now. And, while I'm at it, I'd like you to know that I never suggested there was anything wrong with having your hair coloured, but I think the curls he does for you are a bit too girlish for a woman of your age. Maw, I know very well I'll be your age one day, and I only hope I will look as attractive as you do when my time comes. *I am not being critical.* You can't have it both ways. If I say something I'm being critical, if I don't, and somebody else mentions it, then I was too uncaring to warn you ahead of time. *I didn't say somebody else mentioned it.* Maw, please. Yes, of course we'll go to New York together next month. I can't tell you how much I look forward to our trips. But, Maw, please don't be offended, you're a fourteen now, and you must stop wasting time trying to squeeze into twelves. Hold it. Stop. You have never embarrassed me. At your age, I would be lucky to still have such a good figure. We could be sisters, isn't that what the saleswomen at Bloomingdale's thought? He said we could go to the showroom and have anything we wanted wholesale? No kidding. Hey, do you think Katz has his eye on you? *I am not being disrespectful.* Nobody could ever replace Daddy for me either. But, you know, there's a problem with Katz's outfits. It's not that they're *shmatas*, they aren't. They're excellent copies of what he saw in the Paris shows, if you don't mind the machine stitching. But you take something off one of his racks, you get all dolled up for a party, and there's bound to be at least one other woman wearing the same thing. What do you mean you weren't invited to the Ginsbergs' anniversary dinner party, you always were. Maw, you're imagining it. Old friends are not dropping you, because Daddy has passed away. It's not true that people don't feel good to have a widow at the table. Among your age group, it has to be a common experience. I'm sorry. I didn't mean to offend you. Maw, I'm not insensitive and I am not waiting for you to die. You are not a burden to me. But in your age group these things happen. That's life. *Maw, would you prefer me to censor my thoughts before I express them?* Can we no longer speak frankly? Is it now only safe for us to talk about the weather? Maw, you are not going to hang up on me in that mood. Maw, please. Stop at once. No sniffling. *I am not being impatient.* Call Malka, I'll bet she's as lonely as you are, and the two of you could go out to dinner, and then maybe pick up a couple of guys in a bar. Maw, it was a joke. I know very well you would never do such a thing. Okay, she never picks up a bill. So what? You're not exactly broke. What do you mean what do I mean by that? I meant nothing by that. *Maw, I never asked you how much he left and I don't want to hear it now.* Shit. If you think that, you can leave everything to the SPCA for all I care. That's a horrible thing to think of me. You know how I feel this very minute? *Degraded.* Now I've got to hang up and – Maw, it is absolutely sick on your part to suggest that I always manage to twist things round just before I hang up on you, so that I'm the one who has been hurt. What? Come on. I said *hurtful* things to *you*? Name one. Uh huh. Uh huh. Shit. If you think you look pretty in those Shirley Temple curls, keep them. And you know what? You're going to Florida with Malka next winter, get yourself a bikini. Handkerchief-size. But don't count on me coming down to visit you, if that's the case. Now I've got to hang up and – I am not having one of my tantrums. Maw, if we had a tape recording of this conversation I'd play it back to you, if only to prove I never suggested you suffered from cellulite deposits. You've still got great legs. Now I've really, really got to hang up and get busy here. Barney sends his love. No, I'm not just saying that. Goodbye now."

Following the previous night's quarrel, The Second Mrs. Panofsky and I were inordinately polite to each other all morning. I boiled and peeled the eggs for her salad Niçoise and she, appreciating my condition, made me a Bloody Mary. But the silence in the kitchen was choking, until she flicked on the radio, looking for relief from "CBC Sunday Morning Round-Up." A Toronto writer, who was being interviewed, said not one bookseller would give him a window display, because he wasn't American or British. Hell, he added, was the blank sheet of paper that confronted him in his typewriter every morning. The Second Mrs. Panofsky turned up the sound. "I don't believe it. He's being interviewed by Miriam Greenberg."

"Is that who it is?"

"I'd recognize that unfortunate voice anywhere. I can't explain it, unless she slept her way into that job. She had some reputation at McGill."

"Did she?"

"Would you open that tin of anchovies for me, please?"

"Certainly, darling."

Boogie, his sheets soaked, was too sick to come downstairs for lunch. I took a tray to his room, and then explained to The Second Mrs. Panofsky that I had to get to the office to sign some cheques, among other things that couldn't wait, but I promised to drive back in time for dinner. "Careful on the road," she said, offering her cheek for a kiss.

"Yes, certainly," I said, obliging. "Oh, anything you need from town?"

"I don't think so."

"I'll phone before I leave, dear, just in case."

A grumpy Hughes-McNoughton was waiting for me at Dink's. "What was so urgent?" he asked.

"I want a divorce."

"Like tomorrow morning?"

"Yes."

Quebec law is rooted in the Napoleonic Code, and in that church-ridden province, back in 1960, divorce was only possible through a private member's bill introduced in the House of Commons, and the grounds had to be adultery. "*Deo volente*," said Hughes-McNoughton, "she's having an affair, and you can prove it. What are you laughing at?"

"She'd never be unfaithful to me."

"Well then, will she agree to sue you for divorce?"

"We haven't discussed it yet."

"If she were amenable, the usual procedure is I hire a hooker, and the two of you are discovered *in flagrante delicto* in a squalid motel in Kingston, or wherever, by an alert private detective of impeccable honour."

"Let's go."

"Not so fast. She has to agree to the comedy first. And there is unfailingly a price tag. *Lex talionis*. The law of retribution. Her lawyer can take you for a mighty big chunk of your income now and forevermore. I speak from experience, my child."

"It's worth anything to me."

"That's what you say now. That's what they all say now. But five years down the road you will feel differently, and you will blame me. Now I don't mean to pry. But I take it there is such urgency because you are smitten with somebody else, you rotter. Is she with child?"

"No. And I'm not smitten. I'm in love."

"Which explains your stupid behaviour. Maybe if you talk to her first, and she is agreeable to subverting the law, then her lawyer and I can agree to a settlement in advance that will allow you to retain one chair and table, a bed, and a spare pair of socks."

"She's going to inherit scads of money."

"My God, Barney, you shouldn't be allowed out without a keeper. What's that got to do with it?"

"Shit, what time is it?"

"Going on eight. Why?"

"I promised to be back at the cottage in time for dinner."

"You can't drive in your condition. Besides, I just ordered another round."

I went to use the payphone in back.

"I knew once you got there you'd start drinking," she said. "Now what am I supposed to do? Entertain *your* guest? I hardly know him."

"He won't budge from his room in his condition. Honestly. Just bring a tray to his room. A couple of boiled eggs. Dry toast. A banana. Keep it simple."

"Go to hell."

"I'll be back in time for lunch tomorrow."

"Wait. Don't you dare hang up. I'm going crazy here. We go through the morning like a couple of robots, as if nothing happened. It's torture. I must know something. Are we going to try to make this marriage work, or not?"

"Of course we are, darling."

"That's what I thought," she said, hanging up.

Hughes-McNoughton had settled the bill. "Shall we move on to Jumbo's?" he asked.

"Why not?"

"Did you tell her you want a divorce."

"Yes."

"What did she say?"

"Good riddance."

"I've clocked our consultation at three hours and change so far. At $150 an hour, you owe me $450, and of course we are now moving into overtime."

It was stifling, the first evening of a heatwave that would last for days, and Jumbo's air-conditioning was on the blink. It was also jammed with singles, but we managed to find a quiet corner. "What happens if she won't cooperate?" I asked.

"I thought you said – "

"But what happens if?"

"It could take ages and be considerably more expensive. Barney, whatever you do, you mustn't admit you are in love with somebody else. Wives are surprisingly touchy about such things. Why, they can even be vengeful. The best strategy is for you to move out and let her think you are in no hurry for a divorce."

From Jumbo's we moved on to the Montreal Press Club, so it was later than three a.m. when I got home. But I wakened at six a.m. all the same. Depressed. Riding alternating waves of guilt and anxiety. Worried about Boogie. Convinced she would make me crawl before she agreed to sue me for divorce on harsh terms dictated by her mother and some cut-throat lawyer of their acquaintance. I shaved, showered, went through a pot of coffee, lit a Montecristo, and drove out to the cottage, rehearsing variations of my I-think-it-best-for-you-that-we-divorce speech, every one of which sounded disconcertingly farouche to me. The Second Mrs. Panofsky was not to be found in the kitchen, or in our bed, which had already been made up. Maybe, as troubled as I was, she had also risen early, and gone for a swim. Certainly it was already hot enough for that. What if I scrawled a note, saying I will agree to divorce you, left it on the kitchen table, and beat it. No, that would be cowardly, I thought. *So what, Barney? No, I mustn't.* I decided to waken Boogie and talk my problem over with him. And, lo and behold, there they were, my wife and best friend, snug in bed. I couldn't believe my good luck. "Well, well, well," I said, simulating outrage.

"Shit." The Second Mrs. Panofsky leaped out of bed, starkers, scrambled for her nightgown, and fled.

"It's your fault," said Boogie. "You were supposed to phone before you left town."

"I'll settle with you later, you bastard," I hollered, and then pursued The Second Mrs. Panofsky into our bedroom, where she was already dressing.

"I came back here hoping we could be reconciled," I said, "determined to make our marriage work, and I find you in bed with my best friend."

"It was an accident. Honestly, Barney."

Stacks of cliché-ridden TV scripts hadn't passed through my office for nothing, and now I began to crib from the worst of them. "You betrayed me," I said.

"I brought him a tray, like you asked," she said, between sobs, "and he was trembling, and his sheets were soaked, and I lay down beside him just to keep him warm, and he began to do things, and I was putty in his hands because you haven't touched me in months, and I'm only human, and one thing led to another. I hardly even knew what was happening until it was over."

"My wife and my best friend," I said.

She reached out to comfort me.

"Don't touch me," I said, hoping I wasn't overdoing it.

"We shouldn't talk about it now," she said, "when I'm so upset."

"You're so upset?"

Tears flying, she grabbed her purse, snatched her car keys off the dresser, and started down the stairs, me following after. "I'll be at my mother's," she said.

"Tell her we're getting divorced."

"You tell her. No, don't you dare. She has a dentist's appointment this afternoon. Root canal." She whirled to confront me in front of her car. "If you loved me, you never would have left me alone with a man like that."

"I trusted you."

"You have no morals, guys like you and Boogie. I'm so inexperienced and he's such a – I had no idea what was happening. He seemed so distraught, so sad, I thought his hand – that he didn't even know he was stroking me there – that it was by accident – I pretended it was – I didn't want to seem like a square – make a fuss. I – he's your best friend, I – then it was too – I still don't know how he got my nightie off. I – he – Oh, what's the use? Nothing I do is right, so far as you're concerned." She got into the car and lowered her window. "Shit. Now I've broken a fingernail. I hope you're happy. You haven't stopped yelling at me, but he was the one who started it, honest to God he was, your best friend, I'll bet he fucked your first wife too, a man like that. Some friend. So what are you going to do about him?"

"Oh, I'm going to kill him is what I'm going to do, and then maybe I'll come after you and your mother."

"My mother. Shit. I can't let her see me like – I forgot my make-up kit on my dressing-table. I want my eye-liner. I need my Valium."

"Go get it, then."

"Fuck you," she shrieked and, hitting the accelerator, she raced down the driveway, her rear tires spitting pebbles. Once she was safely out of sight, I slipped into a Hotch on the porch, bracing myself against the banister. I followed this up with a nifty Shim Sham and a Da-Pupple-Ca, and nearly got caught at it as she roared back up the driveway and lowered her window again. "You can keep a whore in Toronto, I'm not supposed to complain, you're a man and I'm not, that's life. Well, now you know that two can play at the same game. Tough shit, isn't it?"

"I married a fishwife."

"You want a divorce? Be my guest. But it will be on my terms, you bastard," she said, and off she went again, grinding gears, narrowly missing a tree.

Yabba dabba do. Barney Panofsky, you were born with a horseshoe up your ass. I decided to put off phoning Hughes-McNoughton until later, but I wasn't going to need a hooker or a private detective any more. Nosireebob. Composing myself, looking appropriately stern I hoped, I started inside to confront Boogie. He was already downstairs, unshaven, a scrawny sight in his boxer shorts, lifting a bottle of eighteen-year-old Macallan, and two glasses, out of the bar. "It's cooler down here, isn't it?"

"You screwed my wife, you son of a bitch."

"I think we should have a drink before we get into this."

"I haven't even had breakfast yet."

"It's too early to eat," he said, pouring both of us stiff ones.

"How could you do this to me?"

"I did it to her, not you. And if you had phoned before leaving Montreal, this embarrassing business could have been avoided. I think I'll go for a swim."

"Not yet you won't. So it's my fault, is it?"

"In a manner of speaking, yes. You've been shirking your conjugal duties. She said it was seven months since you last made love to her."

"She told you that?"

"Cheers," he said.

"Cheers."

"She came into my room with a tray," he said, pouring us another drink, "and sat down on my bed in that short nightie. Now it was already awfully humid, so I could hardly blame her, but I suspected there was a message in there somewhere. A sub-text. *Skol.*"

"*Skol.*"

"I laid my book aside. John Marquand's *Sincerely, Willis Wayde*. Now there's a novelist who is sadly underrated. Anyway, following a forced exchange of niceties (hot, isn't it? I've heard so much about you. It's so good of you to put up with me in my condition, et cetera et cetera), and an awkward silence or two – I'd really like to go for a swim. May I borrow your snorkel and flippers?"

"Goddamn it, Boogie."

He poured us another drink and we both lit up Montecristos. "I guess we're going to have to fix our own lunch today," he said. "*A votre santé.*"

"Sure. Now get on with it, please."

"And then, uninvited as it were, she began to tell me about the problems you two were having, hoping for some good advice. You preferred the bar-room companionship of losers to home most evenings, and on the rare occasions you deigned to come straight home from the office, you didn't talk to her but read a book at the table. Or the *Hockey News*, whatever that is. If she had other couples in to dinner, old friends of hers, you ambushed them. If they were of the right, you argued that it was the Soviets who had won World War II, and that one day Stalin would be recognized as the man of the century. But if they were of the left, you claimed there was scientific evidence to prove blacks were of inferior intelligence and too highly sexed; and you praised Nixon. Whenever you joined her parents for a sabbath dinner, you whistled at the table, an offence to her mother. She married you over the objections of her father, a distinguished intellectual, and then what? You neglect her in bed and she discovers that you are keeping a mistress in Toronto. Say, I happen to know there are some devilled eggs in the fridge. What do you think?"

So we moved to the kitchen table, taking the bottle and our glasses with us. "*L'chaim*," he said.

"*L'chaim.*"

"I must say, she is given to verbosity. In full flow, there was no stopping her, and I fear my mind had begun to drift. But the next thing I knew, she leaned over to remove my tray and I caught a glimpse of her pleasing bosom. She sat down on my bed again, and began to sniffle, and I felt obliged to take her in my arms to comfort her, and still she didn't stop her prattling. I began to stroke her here and then there, and her protests, a kind of cooing, struck me as an invitation. 'You mustn't.' 'We ought to stop right now.' 'Oh, please not there.' And then, pretending that she wasn't returning my caresses, she started in on a dream she had had the previous night, even as she voluntarily raised her arms so that I could ease her out of her nightie, and, man, I figured the only way to shut her up was to fuck her, and that's how it happened. I think this bottle is empty."

I went and fetched another.

"Chin-chin," he said, reaching for a dish towel to wipe the sweat off his chest. "Are all the windows open?"

"I ought to knock your teeth out, Boogie."

"Only after I've had a swim. Oh, she asked a lot of questions about Clara. You know, on reflection, I think I was no more than a convenient *deus ex machina*. She wanted to get even with you for that woman you're keeping in Toronto."

"One minute," I said. I hurried into our bedroom, and returned with my father's old service revolver, which I set down on the table between us. "Scared?" I asked.

"Couldn't that wait until after I've done some snorkelling?"

"You could do me a great service, Boogie."

"Anything."

"I want you to agree to be a co-respondent in my divorce. All you have to do is testify that I came home to my beloved wife and found you in bed with her."

"Why, you planned this, you bastard. Taking advantage of an old friend," he said, holding out his glass for a refill.

I scooped up the gun and aimed it at him. "Will you testify?" I demanded.

"I'll think it over on my swim," he said, rising shakily to fetch my snorkelling equipment and flippers.

"You're too drunk to swim, you damn fool," I said, following after him with that revolver still in hand.

"You come too," he said, starting down the steep grassy slope to the water. "It will do us both good. Ime-tay or-fay old oys-bay to et-gay ober-say."

"I'm going to lie down. So should you. Look at you. You can hardly walk in a straight line. Don't, Boogie."

"Last guy in the water does the washing up."

"Stop," I hollered, "or I'll shoot."

Boogie guffawed in appreciation of my jest. He paused to adjust his snorkelling gear, falling down twice, and then continued down the slope in his flippers. "Look out," I said, and I fired a shot well over his head.

Boogie's arms shot up in a gesture of surrender. "*Kamerad*," he called, "*kamerad. Nicht schiessen.*" Then he zig-zagged the rest of the way down the slope, raced across the dock, and plunged into the lake, disappearing underwater.

I retreated into the living room to lie down, and had just begun to drift off on the sofa when the phone rang.

"I am calling to inform you that my daughter will be staying with me for the foreseeable future. I am instructed that you are not to attempt to communicate with her, but may address any inquiries to Hyman Goldfarb, Q.C."

"Why, Goldilocks, that ain't very friendly."

"How dare you."

"And tell her for me that Miriam Greenberg hasn't got an unfortunate voice. It is a beautiful voice," I said, hanging up.

Big-mouth, I thought. Now you've gone and done it. Hughes-McNoughton will blow his top.

Getting down on all fours, I made it back to the sofa and fell instantly into a contented sleep. I had only been out for minutes, it seemed to me, when a roaring, like an airplane engine, shook the room, and I dreamt that my plane was going down. Shaking off my stupor, I was overwhelmed by confusion. Was I in Montreal? Miriam's apartment? The cottage? Scrambling slowly to my rubbery feet, I staggered outside, trying to locate the source of that roaring. It had been a passing airplane, but it was now so far away, I couldn't tell whether it was one of those NATO fighters out of Plattsburg or a trans-Atlantic jet. Then I saw that it was dusk. Glancing at my wristwatch, I was surprised to discover that I had been asleep for more than three hours. I slipped back into the cottage, splashed my face with cold water, and then stood at the foot of the stairs and called out, "Boogie."

No answer.

"Wakey, wakey, Boogieman."

He wasn't in his bedroom, or anywhere else in the cottage. Passed out on the dock, probably, I thought, but he wasn't there either. *Oh, my God, he's drowned. No, not Boogie. Please, God.* The lake is shallow and clear for forty feet out from our dock. I leaped into our boat, got the outboard motor to start, and began covering water, searching the bottom, increasingly frantic. Finally I climbed back up to the cottage and phoned the provincial police. They arrived two endless hours later and I gave them an edited version of what had happened. I didn't mention my quarrel with The Second Mrs. Panofsky, or even her earlier presence at the cottage. However, I did allow that Boogie and I had been drinking, and that I had pleaded with him not to swim.

Boogie's body had not yet floated to the surface, and a police motor boat launched at Merkin's Point, and covering the shoreline, could find nothing.

"Maybe he's tangled in weeds somewhere," I said.

"No."

Early the next afternoon the provincials were back,

accompanied by a detective. "My name's Sean O'Hearne," said the detective. "I think we should have a little chat."

BOOGIE PLUNGING into the lake was the last I ever saw of him. I'm willing to swear on the heads of my grandchildren that was exactly how it happened, but he had disappeared more than once before, and I have never given up hope. Not a day passes when I don't think there will be a postcard from Tashkent or Havana or Addis Ababa. Or, still better, that he will sneak up behind me at Dink's and say, "Boo."

Enough is enough. Boogie would be seventy-one years old now – no, seventy-two – and I can't understand why he won't appear to clear my name once and for all.

III

MIRIAM
1960–

ONE

LIKE I said, it started out as a disaster. Jumpy as a teenager, counting the days to what I took to be my make-or-break lunch with Miriam, I decided to fly to Toronto the night before, checking into the Park Plaza, resolved not to stir from my room or drink a drop. But I couldn't concentrate on the copy of *Rabbit, Run* that I had brought with me. The *New Republic*'s account of Senator Kennedy's triumph over Humphrey in the West Virginia primary did not thrill me. Remembering that bastard Joe Kennedy, I was suspicious of the son. Neither could I get excited by that front-page photograph in the *New York Times* of an exultant Nikita Khrushchev displaying some debris from the demolished U-2 spy plane. Flinging book, magazines, and newspapers aside, I switched off my bedside lamp. But sleep wouldn't come, and, inevitably, Mrs. Ogilvy materialized, running her tongue over her lips, beginning to unbutton that dress that was a size too small.[1] "That will do you no good, you condescending imperialist slut," I said. "I am not even unfaithful to Miriam with my wife, so why would I bother with you?"

I tossed. I turned. *Remember, look directly into those blue eyes to die for, but* DO NOT *stare at her breasts. Or her legs. Animal.* I polished anecdotes that might please, possibly rewarding me with that dimple in her cheek, and stories that inadvertently reflected well on me, and dismissed everything I could think of as self-serving horseshit. Hoping to calm my nerves, I smoked a Montecristo´ and then hurried into the bathroom to brush my teeth, and even my tongue, fearful of bad breath. On my route back to bed, as luck would have it, I was obliged to pass my mini-bar. It would do no harm, I thought, to check it out, maybe munch a few cashews. Well,

---

[1] Described as two sizes too small on page 273.

one quick snort wouldn't do any harm. But, at three a.m., I was shocked to be able to count a dozen little empty bottles of Scotch, vodka, and gin on the glass table. *Drunkard. Weakling.* Charged with self-hatred, I slid back into bed and conjured up a picture of Miriam at my wedding, wearing a layered blue chiffon cocktail dress, and moving about with astonishing grace. Those eyes. Those bare shoulders. *Oh my God, what if I stood up to greet her in the Prince Arthur Room and she could see that I had an erection?* I made a mental note to jack-off immediately before lunch, if only as a preventive measure. Then I slept, but only for a little while, literally leaping out of bed, cursing myself: *you've overslept, you idiot, and now you're going to be late.* I started to dress frantically and then had the good sense to look at my watch. It was six a.m. Damn damn damn. I undressed, showered and shaved, dressed again, and went out to tramp the streets until seven a.m., when the Prince Arthur Room would open for breakfast. "I booked a table for two for lunch," I told the maitre d', "and I want one by the window."

"I'm afraid they're already reserved, sir."

"That one," I said, slipping him a twenty.

Back in my room, I found the red light on my phone blinking. My heart began to thud. *She can't make it. She's changed her mind.* "I don't lunch with grown men who jerk-off in hotel-room toilets." But the call was from The Second Mrs. Panofsky. I rang home. "You forgot your wallet on the hall table," she said.

"I did not."

"I've got it right in my hand with all your credit cards."

"Count on you for good news."

"It's my fault, is it?"

"I'll think of something," I said, hanging up. And suddenly overcome by nausea, I fled to the toilet. Sinking to my knees, head hanging over the toilet bowl, I was sick again and again. *Congratulations, Barney, now you're going to smell like a sewer.* So I undressed again, showered again, just about brushed the enamel off my teeth, gargled, changed my shirt and socks and hit the street once more. I had only gone three blocks when I stopped short, remembering that I had asked the maitre d' to have a bottle of Dom Pérignon in a bucket beside our table at 12:55. *Show-off.* A woman of Miriam's quality was bound to consider that ostentatious. Pushy. As if I was out to seduce her. "Did you think that if you bought me a bottle of champagne, I'd leap into bed with you?" I certainly had no such impure notions. *Honestly.* So I doubled back to the hotel and cancelled the champagne. But what if, against all odds, she did agree to come back to my room with me? I do have some good points.

– *This is a multiple choice question, Panofsky. Tick off a minimum of three good character points out of the following ten.*

– *Fuck you.*

Checking out my room, just in case, I saw that the bed hadn't been made yet. I phoned housekeeping to complain, and room service to order a dozen red roses and a bottle of Dom Pérignon with two glasses.

"But, Mr. Panofsky, you cancelled your champagne order."

"I cancelled the bottle for the Prince Arthur Room, but now I want a bottle for my own room, properly chilled, no earlier than two p.m., if that's not too much trouble."

Footsore come noon, badly hung-over, weary, emotionally exhausted, I decided a cup of black coffee in the Roof Bar would be just the trick, but, on impulse, I ordered a Bloody Mary instead. Nursing it, I found I still had another three-quarters of an hour to kill when all that was left in my glass were ice-cubes. So I ordered another. Then dug into my pocket for that list of interesting conversational topics I had prepared. Had she seen *Psycho*? Read *Henderson the Rain King*? What did she think of Ben Gurion meeting Adenauer in New York? "Should Caryl Chessman have been executed?" Floating on new-found confidence after my third Bloody Mary, I glanced at my watch: 12:55. And was consumed by panic yet again. *Hell, I had forgotten to masturbate this morning, and now it was too late. My props.* I had forgotten them in my room. Her father had been a socialist, and so I had brought along the Penguin edition of Laski's *Liberty in the Modern State*, as well as the latest issue of the *New Statesman*. I made a dash for my room, shoved the *New Statesman* into my jacket pocket, and got to my table in the Prince Arthur Room at 1:02, and there she was, Miriam being directed to the table by the maitre d'. Rising to greet her, I managed to hide my compromising tumescence behind my linen napkin. O, how beautiful she appeared in her saucy black leather hat and black wool dress, her hair cut shorter than I remembered. I longed to compliment her on her appearance, but I feared she might consider that flirty. Gauche. "Great to see you," I said. "Care for a drink?"

"What about you?"

"Oh, a Perrier will do. Say, this is an occasion, don't you think? What about a bottle of champagne?"

"Well now . . ."

I summoned the waiter. "We'd like a bottle of Dom Pérignon, please."

"But you already can—"

"*Just bring it, if you don't mind?*"

Lighting one Gitane off another, I groped for one of the *bon mots* I had rehearsed, but all I could come up with was, "Hot today, isn't it?"

"I didn't think so."

"Neither did I."

"Oh."

"Haveyouseen*HendersontheRainKing*?"

"I beg your pardon?"

"*Henderson the* – I mean *Psycho*?"

"Not yet."

"I thought the shower scene – But what did you think of it?"

"I suppose I'd have to see it first."

"Oh, sure. Naturally. We could catch it tonight, if you – "

"But you've obviously seen it already."

"Oh yeah. That's right. I forgot." Shit, is he going all the way to Montreal to fetch that bottle of champagne? "In your opinion," I asked, beginning to slide in sweat, "should Ben Gurion have agreed to meet Eisenhower in New York?"

"I think you mean Adenauer."

"Of course I do."

"Did you invite me here to be interviewed?" she asked. And there it was, the dimple in her cheek. I'm going to die right here and go to heaven. *Don't you dare lower your gaze to her bosom. Keep it at eye level.* "Ah, there he is."

"Room service wants to know if you still want the other bottle in your – "

"Just pour, will you, please?"

We clicked glasses. "I can't tell you how glad I am you could make it today," I said.

"Well, it was good of you to fit me in between your business appointments."

"But I'm just here to see you."

"I thought you said – "

"Oh, sure. Business. Yes, I'm here on it."

"Are you drunk, Barney?"

"Certainly not. I think we should order. Ignore the prix fixe. Have whatever you want. They ought to air-condition this place," I said, loosening my tie.

"But it's not hot."

"Yes. I mean no, it isn't."

She ordered a pea soup to begin with and I, unaccountably, asked for the lobster bisque, a dish I hate. As the Prince Arthur Room began to tilt and sway, I groped for a witty remark, a knockout aphorism that would put Wilde to shame, and heard myself say, "Do you enjoy living in Toronto?"

"I like my job."

I counted to ten and then I said, "I'm getting a divorce."

"Oh, I'm so sorry."

"Wedonthavetodiscussitnow, butitmeansyou'llbeabletoseemea-gain, becauseI'llnolongerbeamarriedman."

"You're talking so fast I'm not sure I can make out – "

"Soon I'll no longer be a married man."

"Obviously, if you're getting a divorce. But I hope you're not doing this on my account."

"What can I do? I love you. Desperately."

"Barney, you hardly know me."

Then, as luck would have it, a fulminating Yankel Schneider, whom I hadn't seen since we had been ten-year-olds together in primary school, loomed over our table: not quite Banquo's ghost, but close enough. "You're the bastard who made my life a misery when we were children, imitating my stammer."

"I don't know what you're talking about."

"You're unfortunate enough to be his wife?"

"Not yet," I said.

"Please," said Miriam.

"Leave her out of this, if you don't mind?"

"He used to mock my stutter, and I would tear my hair out in bed, and my mother had to literally drag me kicking and screaming to school. *Why did you do it?*"

"I didn't, Miriam."

"What pleasure did it give you?"

"I'm not sure I even remember who in the hell you are."

"For years I used to dream I would be in my car, you would be crossing the street, and I would run you over. I put in eight years with an analyst before I decided you weren't worth it. You're filth, Barney," he said, and taking one last drag of his cigarette, he dropped it into my lobster bisque and strode off.

"Christ," I said.

"I thought you were going to hit him."

"Not with you here, Miriam."

"I'm told you have a vile temper, and that when you've had far too much to drink, like now, which is hardly flattering, you start looking for a fight."

"McIver?"

"I'm not saying."

"Don't feel well. Going to be sick."

"Can you make it to the toilet?"

"So embarrassed."

"Can you – "

"Got to lie down."

She helped me to my room, where I immediately fell to my knees, retching over the toilet bowl, farting resoundingly. *I wished myself buried alive. Or drawn and quartered. Pulled apart by horses. Anything.* She wet a towel and wiped my face and finally led me to my bed.

"This is so humiliating."

"Ssh," she said.

"You hate me and never want to see me again."

"Oh, shettup," she said, and she sponged me with that wet towel again, and made me drink a glass of water, supporting the back of my head with her cool hand. I resolved never to wash my hair again. Lying back, I closed my eyes, hoping to shut out the spinning room. "I'll be all right in five minutes. Please don't go."

"Try to sleep."

"I love you."

"Yes. Certainly."

"We're going to get married and have ten children," I said.

When I wakened, maybe a couple of hours later, she was sitting in the easy chair, her long legs crossed just so, reading *Rabbit, Run*. I didn't speak out immediately, but took advantage of her being so self-absorbed to feast on the sight of such beauty seated there. Tears slid down my cheeks. My heart ached. If time stopped now, forever, I thought, I would not complain. Finally, I said, "I know you never want to see me again. I don't blame you."

"I'm going to order some dry toast and coffee for you," she said, "and, if you don't mind, a tuna sandwich for me. I'm hungry."

"I must stink something awful. Will you not go if I have a quick shower?"

"I take it you find me predictable."

"How can you say such a thing?"

"You were expecting me to come to your room."

"Certainly not."

"Then who were the champagne and roses for?"

"Where?"

She pointed.

"Oh."

"Yes. Oh."

"I don't know what I'm doing today. I'm not myself. I'm a mess. I'll phone room service and have them take it away."

"No, you won't."

"I won't."

"Now what shall we talk about? *Psycho*, or Ben Gurion's meeting with Adenauer?"

"Miriam, I couldn't lie to you. Not now, or ever. Yankel was telling the truth."

"Yankel?"

"The man who came to our table. I would block his path on the playground and say, 'D-d-do you p-p-piss in b-b-bed, p-p-prick-face?' And if he stood up, terrified, obliged to answer a question in class, I would begin to giggle before he could get a word out, and he would collapse in tears. 'N-n-nice going, Y-y-yankel,' I'd say. Why did I do such dreadful things?"

"Surely you don't expect me to be able to answer that?"

"Oh, Miriam, if you only knew how I'm counting on you."

Then, all at once, I endured – no, enjoyed – something like the spring breakup of the ice crushing my soul. I began to jabber, incoherently, I fear, mixing misadventures of my childhood with tales of Paris. From an account of Boogie negotiating a heroin purchase, I doubled back into a story of my mother's indifference to me. I told her how Yossel Pinsky had survived Auschwitz and now passed his days cutting deals in a bar on Trumpeldor Street in Tel Aviv. I had once dealt in stolen Egyptian artifacts, I thought she should know that. I tap-danced. From a yarn about Izzy Panofsky's days on morality, I segued into the evening McIver had read in George Whitman's bookshop, and then slid into a riff on Hymie Mintzbaum. I told her about the *pneumatique* that had reached me too late, and how Clara had gone to an early grave unnecessarily, and that I still dreamt about her rotting in her coffin.

"So you're the Calibanovitch in that verse."

"Yes I am."

I explained that I had stumbled into marriage with The Second Mrs. Panofsky out of spite – no, guilt about Clara – no, out of anger at her judgment of me. But I swore that I had never been in love until I had espied Miriam at my wedding. Then I saw that it was dusk outside and that our bottle of champagne was empty. "Shall we go somewhere for dinner?" I asked.

- "Why don't we go for a walk first?"

"I'd like that."

Self-satisfied Toronto is not a city I ever warmed to. It's this country's counting house. But plunging into the rush-hour din on Avenue Road that warm evening in early May, a spring in my step, I was in a forgiving, happy-to-be-alive mood. After all, the trees were plump with buds. If the clusters of daisies on display in buckets outside fruit stores were spray-painted orange or purple, they were redeemed by pristine bunches of daffodils. Some of the office girls passing in pairs in their summer dresses were undeniably pretty. Such was my rapture that I guess I smiled too broadly at the young mother coming toward us, wheeling a toddler in a stroller, because in response she frowned and quickened her pace. For once, I didn't mind a sweaty jogger in shorts, running in place as he waited for a traffic light to change. "Wonderful evening, isn't it?" I sang out, and he immediately patted his back pocket to ensure that his wallet was still there. Possibly I shouldn't have paused to admire a brand new Alfa Romeo parked in front of an antique shop, as this propelled its owner to the front door, glaring at us. Somewhere, higher up, we came upon a small park and I thought we might rest a while on one of its benches, but the gate was padlocked, and a sign screwed into the railing read:

NO EATING

NO DRINKING

NO MUSIC

NO DOGS

Squeezing Miriam's hand, I said, "Sometimes I think what inspires this city, its very mainspring, is the haunting fear that someone, somewhere, may be happy."

"Oh, shame on you."

"Why?"

"You're quoting Mencken on puritanism. Unacknowledged."

"Am I?"

"Pretending it was yours. I thought you promised never to lie to me."

"Yes. Sorry. Starting now." ·

"I was brought up on lies, and I'll never put up with it again."

And then, a suddenly impassioned Miriam, told me about her father, the cutter, and union organizer. She had adored him, such an idealist, until she discovered that he was a compulsive womanizer. Having it off with factory girls in the can. Trolling sleazy dance halls and downtown bars on Saturday nights. It broke her mother's heart.

Why do you put up with him? Miriam asked.

What should I do? she answered, bent over her sewing machine.

Miriam's mother died a lingering death. Bowel cancer. "He gave it to her," said Miriam.

"That's a bit strong," I said.

"No, it isn't. And no man will ever do that to me."

I can't remember where or what we ate, somewhere on Yonge Street, seated side by side in a booth, thighs touching. "I had never seen anybody look so miserable at his own wedding. Every time I looked up you were staring at me."

"What if I had stayed on that train?"

"If you only knew how much I wanted you to."

"You did?"

"I had my hair done this morning, and I bought this outfit especially for our lunch, and you never once said that I looked nice."

"No. Yes. Honestly, you look wonderful."

It was getting on to two a.m. when we reached her apartment building on Eglinton Avenue. "Now I suppose you're going to pretend you don't want to come in," she said.

"No. Yes. Help, Miriam."

"I have to be up at seven."

"Oh. Well. I guess in that case . . ."

"Oh, come on," she said, tugging me by the hand.

TWO

NOW that I'm beginning to run out of it, time has begun to click past me fast as a hot taxi meter. I'm soon going to be sixty-eight, and Betty, who keeps track of these things, will want to arrange a lunch-time party at Dink's. Betty, a sentimental type, wants Zack, Hughes-McNoughton, me, and some of the others, cremated when we die so that she can mount us in urns over the bar to keep her company. Possibly, I shouldn't have told her what Flora Charnofsky has done. After Norman hit that power pole in his Mercedes-Benz sports car, dying instantly, she had him cremated and divvied up his ashes. The larger portion went into an hour-glass she had made, and the rest into an egg-timer. "Norm is always with me," she said.

I'm not going to Betty's party. There's nothing to celebrate. Besides, I'm now such an irascible old bastard, I don't trust myself. Yesterday afternoon I went to Downtown Video to return *The Bank Dick*, a W.C. Fields favourite of mine, and the young pony-tailed lout behind the counter, who now also wore a nose-ring, said, "Oh oh. There will be an additional three-dollar charge for us to do the rewind."

"Have you got a pen?"

Baffled, he handed me one, and I took the point and began to rewind the spool clockwise,[1] ignoring the five customers waiting behind me.

"What are you doing?"

"Rewinding."

"It will take ages."

"It's only three o'clock, sonnyboy, and this isn't due back until five."

"Give it to me, pops, and you can forget about the three bucks."

Ate breakfast late this morning, and then flicked on the radio, having decided to listen to Miriam live for a change. Hallelujah. I caught her just as she was reading a letter that purported to be from a listener in Calgary:

Dear Ms. Greenberg,

I'm one of those old codgers you read about, a guy who gave the best years of his life to a woman he loved, who then ran off with a younger man. I hope you can make out my handwriting, which ain't the same since I suffered my last little stroke. As you can surely tell I haven't had much education. Not compared to the listeners whose letters you usually read aloud. I'm a retired garbage collector or recycler ha! ha! ha! But I sure hope my grammar is good enough to get me on the airwaves. I still miss my wife and keep her photograph by my bedside in the Winnebago I live in out here. Today is Marylou's birthday and I'd like you to play a ditty that was playing in the dining room of The Highlander Inn, in Calgary, which I took her to when we were celebrating her thirtieth back in 1975.

I can remember a few words to the ditty (which fits my present condition like a glove), but not the title or the background music. The lyrics went:

> Full moon and empty arms,
> something something your charms . . .

And the music, as I recall, was mostly on the piano, and was written, she said, by a famous Polack. Wait. I think there was once a film about him, starring Cornel Wilde, and that he

---

[1] Counter-clockwise

suffered from TB, the piano player, not Cornel. I'd like you to play this number and dedicate it to Marylou, who I bear no grudge. Thanks a million.

Yours sincerely,
Wally Temple

P.S. I really enjoy classical music and I'm a big fan of your show. One of my favourite tapes, which I recommend highly to you, maybe to play another morning, is "Mozart's Greatest Hits."

Miriam paused, and then went on to say, "this letter comes from the same prankster who has also pretended to be Doreen Willis, among others."

Shit.

"I have read it aloud just to let the listener in question know that he hasn't fooled me. And, in appreciation of his efforts, I will now play a recording by Louis Lortie, of Chopin's 12 Etudes, Opus 10. This Chandos Record was produced in Suffolk, England, in April 1988."

The family bush telegraph, or disinformation highway, has recently gone into overload, and I've been able to piece together the following tidbits. Mike phoned Saul. "Hold on to your hat, Daddy is writing his memoirs."

"I knew he was up to something. Excuse me a minute. Nancy, you are putting that book on the wrong shelf. It has to go back precisely where it came from. Sorry about that, Mike. His memoirs. Damn, what if he can't find a publisher? It would break his heart."

"There's a market for anything about Clara Charnofsky these days and don't forget he knew a lot of other famous people."

"Say, didn't you say that Caroline's brother-in-law was a top orthopaedic surgeon?"

"Yes. So?"

"Nancy, no, that's not *precisely* where it came from. Shit shit shit. Sorry, Mike. I'd like a second opinion on something. If I mailed you my X-rays, would you pass them on to him?"

"It's bound to revive all that old business about the death, or what our Kate still calls the disappearance, of Bernard Moscovitch."

"I asked you a question."

"Yes. Sure. If you insist."

Then Saul phoned Kate. "Have you heard? Daddy's going to make us famous."

"What made you think you were the only writer in the family?"

"Has he shown you any of it?"

"Saul, you should hear him on the phone. Cracking up over old stories. Remembering hockey stars he saw in their prime. Daddy had an affair with his school teacher when he was only fourteen years old."

"Aw, he was having us on. I never believed that one."

"Remember how he used to lecture us about the dangers of drugs? Well, he smoked hashish day and night when he was in Paris. When he talks about the past he sheds years. The past is the only thing he's enthusiastic about these days."

Then Mike phoned me. "Daddy, you can write anything you like about me, but you are to please spare Caroline."

"Would you talk that way to Samuel Pepys or Jean Jacques Rousseau, not that you've ever read either one."

"I'm not joking, Daddy."

"You have nothing to worry about. How are the kids?"

"Jeremy has done brilliantly in his A-levels. Harold is writing you a letter even as we speak."

Saul rang at ten the next morning. "What are you doing up so early?" I asked.

"I've got an eleven o'clock with my dermatologist."

"Oh, my God. Leprosy. Hang up immediately."

"Are you really writing your memoirs?"

"Yup."

"I'd better have a look. Please, Daddy."

"Eventually, maybe. How's Nancy?"

"Oh, that one. She'd leave my CDs out to gather dust and she dog-earred my copy of *The Neo-Conservative Reader*. I sent you a copy, remember? Nancy's gone back to her husband."

The call that really unnerved me came from Miriam, whom I hadn't spoken to in some eighteen months. The sound of that voice speaking to me directly was sufficient to set my heart thundering.

"Barney, how are you?"

"I'm fine. Why do you ask?"

"People do when they haven't spoken to each other in such a long time."

"Right. Yeah. And you?"

"I'm fine, too."

"Well, I guess that just about covers it, doesn't it?"

"Barney, please."

"I hear your voice, you say my name, and my hands start to tremble, so don't please me no Barney pleases."

"We were together for more than thirty years –"

"Thirty-one."

" – Most of them wonderful. Shouldn't we be able to talk?"

"I want you to come home."

"I am home."

"You always prided yourself on being direct. So come to the point of this call, please."

"Solange phoned me."

"There's nothing between us. We're good friends, that's all."

"Barney, you don't owe me any explanations."

"Damn right I don't."

"You're no longer thirty –"

"Neither are –"

" – and you can't carry on drinking the way you do. She wants you to see a specialist. Please do as she says, Barney."

"Aw."

"I still care, you know. I think about you often. Saul says you're writing your memoirs."

"Oh, so that's it. Well now, I've decided to leave some footprints on the sands of time."

That earned me a throaty chuckle.

"You mustn't say anything hurtful about the children. Especially –"

"You know what Early Wynn once said?"

"Early Wynn?"

"Baseball pitcher. Hall-of-Famer. He was once asked if he would throw at his mother. 'It would depend on how well she was hitting,' he said."[2]

"Especially Saul. He's so damn sensitive."

"Or Professor Hopper, right, whom I made welcome in my home. Oh, excuse me. How is Blair?"

---

[2] I have been unable to trace this quote.

"He's taking early retirement. We're going to spend a year in London, where he can finally finish his biography of Keats."

"There have already been about six. What in the hell has he got to say that's new?"

"Barney, control your temper."

"I beg your pardon. Saul's the one with the hot temper, not me."

"Saul's your spitting image and that's why you're so rough on him."

"Yeah yeah yeah."

"Blair doesn't want you reminding anybody that he once wrote for the *American Exile in Canada*."

"Then why is he hiding behind your skirts? He could have phoned me himself."

"He doesn't know I'm making this call, and the real point of it, honestly Barney, is that I'm worried about you and want you to see a doctor."

"Give Blair a message for me. Another biography of Keats. Christ. Tell him I said there is absolutely no need for more books like artificially ripened tomatoes," I said, hanging up before I could embarrass myself further.

I DID NOT hear directly from Blair, but, soon enough, there came one of those WITHOUT PREJUDICE, registered letters from his lawyers in Toronto. Their client, Professor Blair Hopper, Ph.D., had learned, through an application made to the FBI, under the Freedom of Information Act, that, in 1994, an anonymous letter had been sent to the principal of Victoria College, University of Toronto, stating that the aforementioned Professor Hopper, a known sexual deviant, had been sent to Canada by the FBI in 1969, to spy and report on the activities of American draft dodgers. If this libel, totally without substance, were to be repeated in a forthcoming memoir, by Barney Panofsky, Professor Hopper reserved the right to sue the author and publisher. Enlisting the aid of Hughes-McNoughton, I wrote back, WITH PREJUDICE, to say I would never stoop to writing an anonymous letter, and if this vile accusation were repeated in public, I reserved the right to take legal action myself. I went out to register the letter and then had second thoughts. I took a taxi down to Notre Dame Street, bought a new typewriter, redid the letter, and registered it. Then I threw out my old machine, and the new one as well. I am not the son of a detective-inspector for nothing.

THREE

I'VE got a neighbour on the lake, one of an increasingly large number of TV pirates, who has installed a pizza-sized satellite dish that is against the law here because it picks up a hundred American channels not licensed in Canada. He manages to unscramble these channels by forking out thirty dollars for a decoder. I mention this only because in my present state of decline, I suffer long nights when I receive a veritable jumble of pictures out of my past, but lack the means to unscramble them. I have wakened more than once recently no longer certain of what really happened that day on the lake. Wondering if I had corrected the events of that day even as I have embellished other incidents in my life, enabling me to appear in a more favourable light. To come to the point, what if O'Hearne was right? What if, just as that bastard suspects, I did shoot Boogie through the heart? I need to think I am incapable of such brutality, but what if I were in fact a murderer?

One night last week I surfaced, badly shaken from a nightmare in which I shot Boogie and stood over him as he convulsed, blood pumping out of his chest. Freeing myself from sweat-drenched sheets, I dressed and drove out to my cottage, arriving at dawn. I wandered through the woods, hoping that the site would jog my memory, leading me to the scene of my alleged crime, in spite of how much growth there had been since Boogie had disappeared some thirty-something years ago. I got lost. I panicked. All at once, I didn't know where these woods were or what I was doing there. I must have sat on a fallen log for hours, pulling on a Montecristo, and then I heard music, far from celestial, coming from somewhere. I walked toward it until I found myself on my cottage lawn, where Benoit O'Neil had set up a ghetto blaster to keep him company as he raked leaves.

Hello, shmuck.

Arguably the days my memory functions perfectly are heavier to bear than those when it fails me. Or, put another way, as I continue to tour the labyrinth of my past there are some episodes I recall all too clearly. Take Blair, for instance.

Blair Hopper, né Hauptman, had entered my life, like an unwanted polyp, in the summer of 1969. He turned up at our cottage in the Laurentians (where Miriam, that bleeding heart, welcomed troubled kids, abused wives, and other flotsam) on a rainy evening, having found our address in the *Manual for Draft-Age Immigrants to Canada*:

> Even though circumstances, and not choice made Canada your haven, we are happy to welcome you. Those of us providing service to the Anti-Draft Programme assume that your opposition to the war in Vietnam stems from principle and therefore you are likely to become outstanding citizens.

(Oh, I should mention here that under the exigent terms of my liberation from The Second Mrs. Panofsky, she got the house with the conversation-pit in Hampstead, but I was able to retain the property in the Laurentians. My first instinct had been to get rid of the scene of my alleged crime, but on reflection this seemed to me as good as a confession of guilt. So, instead, before moving in with Miriam, I had the cottage torn apart, knocking down walls, putting in French doors and skylights, adding rooms for children and studios for both me and Miriam.)

Enter Blair. I would like to report that Max, our usually prescient German Shepherd who gave the children so much pleasure, had greeted that interloper with a growl, his teeth bared, but the truth is that treacherous hound loped right up to him, wagging his tail. Honour compels me to admit that Blair Hopper né Hauptman was a handsome young man in those days. No doubt about it. Closer to Miriam's age than mine, which is to say, some ten years my junior. He was tall, straw-haired, blue-eyed, and broad-shouldered. He would have looked nifty in an SS uniform. But in fact he was wearing a shirt, tie, seersucker suit, and loafers. He arrived bearing gifts: a tub of unpasteurized honey (made by a commune in Vermont, his first stop on the latter-day underground railway) and, hubba hubba, a pair of Indian bead moccasins. I was sipping a Macallan at the time and invited him to join me.

"I'd be grateful for some mineral water," he said, "but only if you have a bottle that is already opened."

We were fresh out. So Miriam fixed him a herbal tea. Rosehip I think it was. "Did you have any trouble at the border?" she asked.

"I came in as a tourist. Passing for a country-club Republican in my seersucker suit. And I was able to show the pigs plenty of travellers' cheques."

"I should warn you," I said, doing my icy polite bit, "that my father is a retired police officer. So we don't go in for that epithet in this house."

"I'm sure things are different in this country, sir," he said, his cheeks reddening, "and that the police here behave admirably."

"Well now, I don't know about that." And, as I was about to launch into an anecdote about the shenanigans of Detective-Inspector Izzy Panofsky, Miriam cut me off.

"How about a peanut butter sandwich?" she asked.

Blair had arrived on a Friday, and was with us for only ten days, but that first weekend he was already making himself useful, insisting on doing the washing-up, and mending the front gate that I had promised to get round to one of these days. When a hornet got into our kitchen, and I reached for a fly swatter, he called out, "Don't, please," and managed to release it through the screen door. Why, that devious bastard could open a child-proof, press-and-turn bottle of aspirins just like that, without struggling and muttering, "Shit. Shit. Shit." Something else. I didn't care for the way he had big eyes for Miriam and how she seemed to be amused by his attentions.

Sunday evening Miriam asked, "Must you drive back to town tonight?"

"Aw, I thought I'd take the week off," I said, as casually as I could manage.

"What about your Wednesday-night poker game?"

"They can do without me for once. And if anybody needs me at the office, they can phone me here."

Miriam, so naturally graceful, was adorably unaware of her spellbinding presence. I could have happily spent the rest of my life watching her, amazed at such beauty in my presence, not that I ever told her as much. And now, closing my eyes, fighting back tears of remorse, I can remember her nursing Saul, her eyes lowered, one hand cupping that throbbing vulnerable head. I can see her teaching Mike how to read, making a game of it, the two of them giggling. I can summon up a picture of her and Kate splashing each other in the bath. I can visualize her busy in the kitchen on a Saturday afternoon, listening to the Metropolitan Opera broadcast on the radio. Or asleep in our bed. Or seated in an armchair, reading, her long legs crossed just so. In our halcyon days if she was to meet me in the Ritz bar, the two of us bound for an evening out, I would choose to wait for her at a table all but hidden in a far corner, so that I could watch her drifting into the room, elegantly dressed, serene, commanding everybody's eye, and then blessing me with a tender smile and a kiss. Miriam, Miriam, my heart's desire.

Miriam was a demure dresser, indifferent to prevailing swank. She, who had no need to advertise, would never be seen in a mini-skirt, or a dress with a plunging neckline. But in our summer cottage on the lake she went native. Her long charcoal black hair caught in a bauble, she eschewed even minimal make-up, and favoured loose T-shirts embossed with David Levine caricatures of Mozart or Proust, cut-off jeans and bare feet, which was okay with me as long as we weren't entertaining a horny young draft-dodger with whom she had things in common. Neither of them, for instance, were old enough to remember the Second World War, and on Monday night, sparked by a newspaper story about Bomber Harris of British Bomber Command, they got into condemning the saturation bombing of German cities, the needless slaughter of innocent civilians. Naturally this put me in mind of the young Hymie Mintzbaum flying over the Ruhr. "One minute," I said, "what about Coventry?"

"I do understand," said Blair, "that it is different for your generation, but how can you justify the fire-bombing of Dresden?"

Later that night I caught Blair eyeing Miriam as she stooped to gather up the children's toys from the living-room floor. Tuesday afternoon, I wakened from my snooze to find the cottage empty. No wife. No kids. No *Übersturmführer* Blair Hopper né Hauptman. They were all in the vegetable garden. Blair, wearing a T-shirt with a Picasso dove emblazoned on it, was helping Miriam turn over the compost heap, another chore I had scheduled to attend to in the far future. From my vantage point, on our wraparound balcony, I saw Blair peeking down her loose T-shirt as she leaned over her spade. Bastard. Sauntering down to the vegetable garden, I asked, "Can I help?"

"Oh, go read a book," said Miriam. "Or pour yourself a drink, darling. You'll only be in the way." ·

But before leaving the vegetable garden, I pulled my wife to me, clasping her bottom with both hands, and kissed her hard. "Oh, my," she said, blushing.

Later that afternoon I caught up with that Peeping Tom in the garage, where he was sharpening our lawn-mower blades. I had brought along a couple of beers and handed him one. "Care for a cigar as well?" I asked.

"No, thank you, sir."

"But you don't mind if I light up?" I asked, sitting down on an overturned rain barrel.

"Certainly not, sir."

"Drop the 'sir,' will you, for Christ's sake?"

"Sorry about that."

"Blair, I worry about you. Maybe you made a mistake running away to Canada. Why didn't you simply tell your draft board that you were queer?"

"But I'm not."

"Exactly what I told Miriam."

"You mean to say she thinks – "

"Of course not. Even I wasn't suggesting for a minute that you were. I guess it's just the way you walk."

"What's the matter with the way I walk?"

"Look here, the last thing I want to do is make you self-conscious. There's nothing in it. Forget it. But you could have pretended to be queer. Now that you've come here you'll never be able to go home again."

"My father wouldn't want me back in any event. He campaigned for Nixon last year."

"What will you do here?"

"I hope to complete my post-grad studies in Toronto and then teach."

"Were you at Columbia?"

"Princeton."

"I want you to know if I were your age, and American, I would have been out there last year, Clean for Gene. I believe James Baldwin was right on when he called your country 'The Fourth Reich.' But one thing about the student occupation of Columbia bothered me. I read somewhere that a student shat in the top drawer of a dean's desk. Now don't get me wrong. I realize he was making an anti-fascist statement. But all the same, you know . . ."

"They sent in the p— the cops, lots of them in plainclothes, and beat the hell out of those students. More than a hundred ended up in the hospital."

Mr. Mary Poppins ingratiated himself with our kids, teaching them goyishe stunts, like how to tie different sailors' knots, how to coax a chipmunk to pluck a nut out of the palm of your hand, and how to tend to a flooded outboard motor, which I coped with by cursing and yanking the cord until it came off in my hands. Late one afternoon, rising from my nap, looking to pour myself a drink downstairs and maybe horse around with Mike and Saul (Kate wasn't born yet), I discovered yet again that they were nowhere to be seen. "Blair took them strawberry picking," said Miriam.

"You shouldn't have allowed him to take them out unchaperoned. He could be a paedophile."

"Barney, did you suggest to Blair that I thought he was gay?"

"On the contrary. I assured him you thought no such thing. He tends to distort matters."

"You're not jealous, are you?"

"Of that drip-dry lefty? Certainly not. Besides, I trust you implicitly."

"Then if I were you, I'd stop baiting him. He's far more intelligent than you think, but he's too polite to be rude to you."

"I feel invaded."

"Because he's so kind?"

"Intrusively so."

Blair was contaminating my Yasnaya Polyana. Our ten lakeside acres. After crazy Clara, following the crap I went through with The Second Mrs. Panofsky, my trial and subsequent disgrace, the dipshit TV business I hated but that continued to earn me big bucks, Miriam was my winning lottery ticket. My redeemer. My MVP award. Imagine, if you can, the Boston Red Sox actually winning a

World Series, or Danielle Steele taking the Nobel Prize, and you'll have some idea of how I felt when Miriam agreed, against all odds, to marry me. But my epiphany was tainted by fear. Surely the gods on Olympus had taken down my number for remedial action.

– Get Panofsky. Crash his next Air Canada flight.

– Hmmm.

– Or what would you say to testicular cancer? Snip, snip. Off with his balls.

Having avoided Morty Herscovitch for years, I now went for annual check-ups, lest I be blindsided by lesions in my lungs. Hoping to placate the vengeful Jehovah, I became a big contributor to charities, tempted to wave my receipts heavenwards whenever we were threatened by thunder or lightning. I started to secretly fast on Yom Kippur. I expected my children to be born deaf and dumb, with no arms, or Down's Syndrome, and when this turned out not to be the case, it only served to heighten my forebodings. Something creepy-crawly was waiting for me out there. I knew it. I counted on it. Unknown to Miriam, I had five thousand dollars in cash socked away in a locked drawer. Money I would use to pay off drug-crazed burglars who could break into our place any night of the week.

Once school was out, I packed Miriam and the kids off to our cottage on the lake, and I would join them on weekends and sleep over on Tuesday nights. Driving out however late on a Tuesday or Friday night, I knew all the cottage lights would be blazing. Miriam would be waiting on the balcony, Saul snoozing in her arms and Mike playing with his Lego at her feet. They would all come running as I opened the car door, Miriam to be embraced and the kids to be flung into the air, squealing, caught just in the nick of time.

Mornings when I was in attendance, Miriam was free to plunge into the lake before breakfast and swim to the far shore of the bay. I would sit on the balcony with the kids, sipping black coffee, delighted in how proficient she was at the crawl, watching her swim back toward me, *coming home*. I would meet her on the shore with a towel, rubbing her dry, lingering in places permissible only to Barney Panofsky, Esq. But now Blair, an even more expert swimmer, joined her. Once on the far shore, he would scramble to the crest of the highest projecting rock to dive back into the lake, not doing a belly flop à la Panofsky, but barely raising a ripple.

Wednesday night I took an urgent call from Serge Lacroix, that *Cahiers du Cinéma* aficionado who was directing a "McIver of the RCMP" episode for me. Serge's notion of art was to cross-cut from our bare-chested male lead sinking to a polar bear rug with his lady love ... to a close shot of a tumescent jack-hammer breaking concrete ... or, God help us ... to a gasoline pump ejaculating into a car's tank. Watching his rushes made me heave with laughter, but his call meant I would have to spend Thursday in town.

Now when I started on this true story of my wasted life, I resolved to tell even those things that were still deeply embarrassing to me years later, so here goes. I contrived to set a trap for my ostensibly faithful, but possibly smitten, wife and her handsome SS admirer. Wednesday night I announced that I was going to take the kids with me to Montreal, assuring a dubious Miriam that they would not be a nuisance, but would have fun hanging out with me on the set. Then, early Thursday morning, as Miriam and Blair Hopper né Hauptman, surely related to war criminals, were enjoying their morning swim, I grabbed Miriam's delicate kitchen scale off a counter, scooted upstairs, fished her tube of vaginal jelly out of our bathroom cupboard, set it on the scale, and noted its exact weight. Still in my James Bond mode, I plucked a hair out of my head and laid it on the container that held her diaphragm. At the breakfast table downstairs, I sang out: "I'm not sure what time I'll get back tonight, but I promise to phone just before I leave town in case you need anything."

Sent for by an hysterical Serge to pronounce on budgetary dilemmas, and to settle down a troubled cast, I was so ill-tempered that I only exacerbated the problems. Our *soi-disant* male lead did not take kindly to my telling him in front of the crew, which was unforgivable, that unless he stopped camping on camera he would be replaced. Then I told that no-talent bimbo who was our female lead that there was more to acting, even in such a piece of shit, than jiggling her tits, and she fled the set in tears.

As I continued to lash out boorishly on all sides, I visualized a sweat-soaked Miriam and Blair experimenting with positions never dreamed of in the *Kama Sutra*. I was overcome by dread. *Déjà vu* all over again, as Yogi Berra once put it. Well, not quite. Same cottage, but a different cast. And this time, fortunately, I lacked a gun. Finally, at six p.m., I called the cottage. I counted fourteen rings before Miriam, obviously loath to be roused from a post-coital nap, or interrupted while posing for yet another pornographic photograph, answered the phone. "We won't be able to leave here for another hour," I said.

"You sound awful. What's wrong, darling?"

"Be there eight-thirty the earliest," I said, hanging up. Then I rounded up the kids and started for the cottage immediately. If they were intending to shower together, I planned to catch them in the act.

Animals.

Mike and Saul, sensitive to my mood, were moxy enough to pretend to doze all the way back to the lake. "You're to tell Mummy you had a terrific time. Right?"

"Yes, Daddy."

No sooner did I pull up, bounding out of the car, ready for mayhem, than Miriam was at my side, glowing, greeting me with a hug. "You'll never guess what we've done," she said.

Brazen bitch. Whore of Babylon. Jezebel.

Taking me by the hand, she led me to my tractor parked in the back. "Remember you were going to pay Jean-Claude to cart it to the dump and buy a new one?"

"Yeah. So?"

She made me sit in the saddle and handed me the key, Blair smiling his modest aw shucks smile all the while. I turned the key, pumped the pedal, and the motor hummed.

"Blair worked on it all afternoon. He cleaned the spark plugs, changed the oil filter, and did God knows what else, and just listen to it now."

"You must be careful not to flood it in the future, Mr. Panofsky."

"Well, yeah. Thank you. But I really must go to the john now. Excuse me."

Locking our bathroom door, I opened the cupboard under the sink and found my hair still in place on her diaphragm container. And there was no detectable weight loss in Miriam's tube of vaginal jelly. *But what if he had jumped her, and she didn't use either, and I was now going to be the father of his child. Probably a vegetarian. Certainly a subscriber to* Consumer's Report. No, no. Still troubled, but also more than somewhat guilt-ridden, I replaced the kitchen scale, lifted a bottle of champagne out of the kitchen fridge, and brought it to the dining-room table.

"What's the occasion?" asked Miriam.

"The redemption of my tractor. Blair, I don't know how we ever got on without you."

With hindsight, I guess I shouldn't have uncorked a second bottle, and a bottle of Châteauneuf to go with Miriam's *osso bucco*, and then the cognac. Refusing the cognac, Blair primly covered the proffered snifter with his hand. "Aw, come on," I said.

"I hope I'm not failing a test of my masculinity," he said. "The truth is I'd be sick if I had another drop to drink."

Then, inevitably, he launched into his daily Vietnam sermon, excoriating Nixon, Kissinger, and Westmorland. In no mood to acknowledge that I had no time for that bunch either, I said, "Sure it's a dirty war, but Blair, don't you feel just a wee bit guilty, a man of conscience like you, allowing this war to be fought largely by blacks and rednecks and working-class kids out of the inner cities, while your middle-class ass is safe in Canada?"

"Do you think it's my duty to be out there napalming babies?"

Miriam changed the subject, and then a real imbroglio threatened. Blair's sister, it turned out, a storefront lawyer in Boston, also headed an organization that sought employment for the deaf, the blind, and the wheelchair-bound. Rather than allow that this was truly admirable, I protested, "Yeah, but they would be doing able-bodied men out of jobs. I can see it now. Our house is on fire and they can't find it because they're blind. Or I'm in intensive care, whimpering, 'Help, help! Nurse, nurse! I'm dying.' But she can't hear me because she's a deaf-mute."

His last night with us, "Uncle" Blair built my enchanted kids a bonfire, and I sat on the porch fulminating, nursing a Remy Martin and pulling on a Montecristo. Watching them out there on the shore, toasting hot dogs and marshmallows, I hoped that sparks would start a forest fire and that Blair, wanted as a pyromaniac in "The Fourth Reich," would be led away in handcuffs. No such luck. Strumming on that bloody guitar of his, Blair was teaching my kids Woody Guthrie ballads ("This land is your land," and other lefty daydreams), Miriam joining in. My family, the *mishpocheh* Panofsky, only two generations removed from the *shtetl*, transmogrified into an old Norman Rockwell *Saturday Evening Post* cover. Shit. Shit. Shit.

Blair was gone before I came down for breakfast the next morning and that, I figured, would be the last I'd ever see of him. But then the postcards began to trickle in from Toronto, individual cards addressed to Mike and Saul, inviting them to become pen-pals. Picking them up at the village post office, my first thought was to dump them in a rubbish bin, but I feared Miriam might find out. So I produced them at the dining-room table to cries of delight from my treacherous children. Quislings, both of them. And those of you too young to know who Quisling was can look it up under – under – you know the country next to Sweden. Not Denmark, the other one.[1] "Of course you must answer him, kids," I said. "But the cost of the postage stamps will come out of your allowances."

"I don't believe what I'm hearing," said Miriam.

"I haven't finished yet. Tonight I'm taking everybody to Giorgio's for dinner."

"And tell me, Père Goriot, will the kids have to pay for their own burgers and fries, and eat up at record speed, so that you can get home in time to catch the first inning of the ball game?"

Then Blair sent Miriam a copy of an article he had written for the *American Exile in Canada*, which she attempted, unavailingly, to hide from me, as even she was embarrassed.

Suppose Canada, Blair ventured, was forced by the masses of its people to assert independence "by nationalizing U.$. owned industry and ending the free reign of U.$. investment. The inevitable U.$. invasion would be tough, brutal, and blood-letting." But, Blair figured, Canada would win:

> The important thing to remember in the eventuality of a Yanqui invasion is that the mass of Canadians would fight the pigs. Guerrilla and partisan struggle would decimate the Yanqui invaders. The mass of Canadians would support the partisan defenders, aid them, feed them, hide them, adopt them as their brothers. We must learn from the Vietnamese how to struggle against Yanqui invasion . . .

[1] Norway.

Didn't that prick know that the last time the Americans had descended on Montreal, Lt.-Gov. Guy Carleton had fled, the city had capitulated, and a spokesman for the *habitants*, Valentin Juatard, had greeted the Yanqui pigs as brothers, saying, "Our hearts have always desired union and we have always received the troops of the Union as our own."

FOUR

Zipporah Ben Yehudah
Dimonah
Negev
Eretz Yisroel
Tishri 22, 5754

The Clara Charnofsky
Foundation for Wimyn,
615 Lexington Ave.
New York, N.Y.
U.S.A.

Attention Chavera Jessica Peters and Dr. Shirley Wade

Shalom Sisters,

I was born Jemima (after the eldest of Job's three daughters) Fraser in Chicago thirty-five years ago, but since I came to the town of Dimonah in the Negev four years ago I pass by the name of Zipporah Ben Yehudah. I am a Black Hebrew, a follower of Ben Ammi, the former Illinois state wrestling champion who taught us we were the true Israelites. Yes. A Black people dispersed by the Romans to Africa, and then brought as slaves to America. Our bros include the South African Lemba who also call themselves Israelites even if they don't keep glatt kosher any more. In the year 1966 of the Christian Era, Ben Ammi, still preaching in Chicago's South Side, had a vision that came to him in the fire-bombing of a liquor store. Rapping with Jehovah, he learned it was time for the true children of Israel to make *aliyah*. Three hundred and fifty cool cats took part in the Great Exodus, and now *Gott zedank* we number 1,500 but continue to suffer like the slings and arrows of the anti-Semitism of the white Jewish usurpers.

Let me tell you being a Black Jew in Eretz Yisroel is no bowl of cherries. There are golf clubs in Caesaria that won't have us and restaurants in Tel Aviv and Jerusalem that are fully booked if we turn up. The Israelis of pallor disapprove of some of our rituals, especially polygamy *which is based on a true reading of the Five Books of Moses*. We shame them, perhaps, because we are more observant than they are. We fast for the entire Shabbat. We are strict vegetarians, avoiding even milk and cheese. And we don't wear synthetic clothing. In a nutshell, we have returned to the true faith, before it was corrupted by "Euro-gentile" civilization, so called.

We are patriots. We don't dig Muslims because they were the main slavers. And we are against a Palestinian state. Our community is rigidly disciplined, far removed from the Black street culture of Chicago. In spite of what you might have read in the *Jerusalem Post* we don't do drugs. Our children bow slightly when greeting adults and our women defer totally to their husbands. The ultimate word in all matters belongs to Ben Ammi our Messiah whom we call "Abba Gadol" Great Father.

Our *mishpocheh*, made up of seven "soul" bands, is feared, because bigots see us as the vanguard of a huge Black migration under the Law of Return. But, according to our *Abba Gadol*, there are at most 100,000 American Blacks who are of Israelite descent. True, Israelite tribes in Africa may number some five million, but we don't expect more than half a million to join us here.

I wish to disown what one of our teenagers allegedly told a white reporter from *Jerusalem Report*:

"In the year 2,000 gonna be a big apocalypse. Volcanoes and everything. You gonna see Blacks comin' in from all over the place back to Israel. Then we gonna run the country."

Sisters, the reason why I'm writing to you is I am in need of a grant, say $10,000, so my bunch can begin work on composing a rap Haggadah, inspired by the poetry of Iced T. This would be our gift to Eretz Yisroel. Sort of a latter-day Sixth Book of Mo.

Thanking you in advance I remain,

Respectfully yours,
Zipporah Ben Yehudah

FIVE

"MY name's Sean O'Hearne," said the detective, who turned up a day after Boogie's disappearance, extending his hand. "I think we should have us a little chat."

His more than firm handshake was sufficient to put my finger bones at risk, and then he suddenly flipped over my throbbing hand as if he meant to read my palm. "Those are some blisters you've got there."

O'Hearne, not yet gone to fat, or balding, or cursed with wet cough seizures that made his eyes bulge, wore a straw fedora and a racing-green gabardine jacket and tartan slacks. As he settled into a bamboo chair on my porch, I caught a glimpse of his two-tone golf shoes with tasselled tongues. He intended to spend the afternoon on the links. "That Arnold Palmer is something else," he said. "I caught him once at the Canadian Open and figured to go home and make a bonfire of my clubs. What's your handicap?"

"I don't golf."

"Oh, more fool me. I figured that's how you got those blisters."

"I've been digging a trench for an asparagus patch. Have you guys found Boogie yet?"

"They say no news is good news, but maybe not in this case, eh? The police launch and divers have both come up empty and, so far as we know, nobody has picked up a hitchhiker wearing a bathing suit and flippers."

O'Hearne had arrived in an unmarked car, followed by two Sûreté du Québec cars. And now four young cops, feigning boredom, started to wander over the grounds, obviously looking for signs of freshly dug earth. "You're damn lucky not to be stuck in the city in this heat," said O'Hearne, removing his straw fedora and wiping his brow with a handkerchief.

"Your guys are wasting their time out there."

"I had me a place once on Lake Echo. Not as grand as this, just a little shack. But I remember how you always got to worry about ants and field mice. So before leaving every weekend you got to clean up and bag the rubbish. Do you drive yours to a dump?"

"I leave it outside the kitchen door and Benoit O'Neil collects it. You want to go through it, be my guest."

"You know I can't understand your not telling the first officers who came round – "

"They didn't come round. I sent for them."

" – what transpired here, given how upset you must have been, losing your friend like that, thinking he was drowned."

"He's not drowned. He's broken into somebody's cottage and he won't be heard from until he's finished every bottle of booze he can find."

"Uh huh. Uh huh. But there have been no break-ins reported."

"I fully expect a sobered Boogie to turn up here later today or tomorrow."

"Hey, maybe Mr. Moscovitch is still somewhere out there in the woods in his bathing trunks. God, the mosquitoes must be driving him crazy. I'll bet he's getting hungry too. What do you think?"

"I think you should be covering every cottage on the lake until you find him."

"That's your considered opinion, eh?"

"I've got nothing to hide."

"Nobody suggested you did. But maybe you could help me fill in some of the boring details, just for the record."

"Would you care for a drink?"

"I wouldn't say no to a cold beer."

So we moved inside. I fetched O'Hearne a Molson and poured myself a Scotch. O'Hearne whistled. "I've never seen so many books outside of a library." He stood close to a small ink drawing hanging on the wall. Beelzebub & Co. ravishing a nude young woman. "Hey, somebody has a real sicko imagination."

"It's by my first wife, not that it's any of your business."

"Divorced, eh?"

"She committed suicide."

"*Here?*"

"In Paris. That's in France, in case you didn't know."

I was on the floor, my head ringing, before I even realized that I had been hit. Startled, I scrambled to my feet on rubbery legs.

"Wipe your mouth with something. You don't want to get blood on that shirt, eh? I'll bet it comes from Holt Renfrew. Or Brisson et Brisson. Where that bastard Trudeau[1] shops. Your wife's been in touch with us. Correct me if I'm wrong, but according to her there was a misunderstanding here early Wednesday morning, and you thought you had reason to be angry with her and Mr. Moscovitch." Flipping open his little black notebook, he continued, "According to her, you drove in from Montreal, arriving unexpectedly early, and surprised the two of them in bed, and thought they had been, well, fornicating. But, and I'm quoting her again, the truth is your buddy was a very sick man. She brought him breakfast on a tray, and he was trembling so bad, chilled in spite of the heat, his teeth chattering like crazy, that she got into bed to hold him, just like a nurse might, and that's when you barged in, sore as hell, jumping to conclusions."

"You are such a prick, O'Hearne."

This time he surprised me with a quick punch to my stomach. I reeled, sucking air, and slid to the floor again. I should have stayed put, because no sooner did I get up, lunging at him, than he slapped me hard across the face with his left, and then walloped the other cheek with his right. I ran my tongue against my teeth, probing for loose ones.

"Now I don't buy it lock, stock, and barrel either. Not the whole *bobbe-myseh*, eh? I know some Yiddish. I was brought up on the Main. You're looking at a professional *shabbes goy*. I used to earn nickels and dimes Friday nights, lighting fires for religious Jews, and I never knew a finer, law-abiding bunch. I think you ought to wipe your chin again."

"You were saying?"

---

[1] Pierre Elliott Trudeau was still largely unknown in 1960. 1968 was the year of Trudeaumania, and his election as prime minister.

"Hey, it must have knocked you for a loop. Your wife and your best buddy in the sack together."

"Let's say I wasn't pleased."

"I don't blame you. Nobody would. Say, where did Mr. Moscovitch sleep?"

"Upstairs."

"Mind if I take a peek? It's my job, eh?"

"Have you got a search warrant?"

"Ah, come on. Don't be like that. Like you said. You've got nothing to hide."

"First bedroom to your right."

Fighting anger, commingled with fear, I went to the kitchen window and saw one of the cops moving into the woods. The other one had emptied my garbage pail and was going through the contents. Then O'Hearne returned, one hand held behind his back. "Damn peculiar. He left his clothes behind. His wallet. His passport. Say, that Moscovitch has sure done a lot of travelling."

"He'll be coming back for his things."

He dug into a jacket pocket. "You're fucking with me, Panofsky. If I didn't know better, I'd say this was marijuana."

"But it's not mine."

"Oh, I almost forgot," he said, finally bringing his other hand round from behind his back. "Look what I found."

Damn damn damn. It was my father's service revolver.

"You got a permit?"

That's when panic got the better of me and I blew it. "I never saw it before. It must be Boogie's."

"Like the marijuana?"

"Yeah."

"Only I found it on your bedside table."

"I have no idea how it got there."

"Hey, you're some sucker for punishment, aren't you?" he said, slapping me so hard I lost my balance again. "Now let's get serious."

"Oh, I remember now. It's my father's. He left it behind one weekend. He was a detective-inspector with the Montreal police force."

"Well, I'll be damned. You're fucken Israel Panofsky's son."

"Yes."

"That makes us *mishpocheh* sort of. Isn't that what you jokers call family? There's an empty chamber in the gun."

"He never could load a gun properly."

"Your dad?"

"Yeah."

"I'm going to let you in on a little secret. Just like your dad, I've put more than one suspect into the hospital. 'Resisting arrest,' you know."

"I fired it."

"Now we're getting somewhere. Like recently?"

"Boogie and I had a lot to drink after my wife drove off."

"Sure thing. You must have been furious with him. I know I would have been. Screwing your wife behind your back. Biff bam boom. A guy with your hot temper."

"What do you mean my hot temper?"

"You were brought into Station Number Ten once, I've got the date here somewhere, for fighting in a bar. Another time a waiter in Ruby Foo's had you charged with assault. I hope you didn't think I was a *goyisher kop*. We guys may not own big lakeside properties, but we sure do our homework, eh?"

"I pleaded with Boogie not to go for a swim in his condition. And when he started down the slope, I fired a warning shot over his head."

"You just happened to have the gun in your hands?"

"We had begun to horse around by that point," I said, beginning to sweat under my shirt.

"And you fired a shot over his head for a hee-haw? You fucken liar," he said, giving me a shove. "Let's get serious here."

"I'm telling you the truth."

"You're lying through your teeth, while you've still got them. Because it would be fucken embarrassing if you fell and lost some, wouldn't it?"

"I don't give a damn how it looks. That's how it happened."

"So he went for a swim and then what?"

"I was feeling a bit woozy myself. So I went to lie down on the sofa, and I wakened from a nightmare in what I took to be only a few minutes later. I dreamt I was in an airplane about to crash into the Atlantic."

"Oh, you poor dear."

"I had actually been asleep for something like three hours. I went off in search of Boogie, but couldn't find him anywhere in the house. I feared he had drowned. So I phoned the police, and asked them to come over as soon as possible, which I clearly would not have done had I anything to hide."

"Or if you were too smart for your own good. You know something? I'm an Agatha Christie fan. I'll bet if she wrote this one up she'd call it *The Case of the Missing Swimmer*. You should have turned in this weapon after your father died."

"I forgot it was here."

"You forgot it was here, but you had it in your hand, and fired a shot over his head for a laugh?"

"No, I got him right through the heart, and then I buried him out there in the woods, where those pricks are searching right now."

"Now we're getting somewhere."

"Are you a total stranger to irony, O'Hearne?"

"Unless I'm hard of hearing, what you said is, 'I got him right through the heart, and then I – '"

"Fuck you, O'Hearne. If you're here to charge me with anything, let's hear it. If not, the three of you can bugger off right now."

"Boy, that's some temper you've got there. I hope you're not going to hit me. I mean I'm sure glad it wasn't me you found in the sack with your wife."

"Here's something else for your notebook. But I'm afraid it weakens your case. I wasn't the least bit upset with Boogie. I was delighted. Happier than I've been in ages. Because I wanted a divorce and now I had grounds. Boogie had agreed to be my co-respondent. I needed his testimony. So why should I kill him?"

"Hold your horses. I never suggested any such thing," said O'Hearne. Then he wet his tongue and flipped over several pages of his notebook. "According to your wife, just before she drove off, because she had reason to be afraid of your violent temper – "

"I have not got a violent temper."

"I'm only quoting her. She asked, 'What are you going to do about Boogie?' and you said, quote, I'm going to kill him, unquote, and went on to threaten her and her recently widowed mother."

"It was a figure of speech."

"You don't deny it?"

"Goddamn it, you idiot. I had no intention of harming Boogie. I needed him."

"You've got a girl in Toronto?"

"That's none of your business."

"A nice piece of ass called Miriam Somebody?"

"You fucking keep her name out of this, you boor. She wasn't even here. What could she have to do with it?"

"Okay. Gotcha. Now I will have to take this illegal gun with me, but I will leave you a receipt."

"Let me know if you need any help with the spelling."

"Hey, you're a card."

"Do you wish to charge me with anything?"

"Bad manners, maybe."

"In parting, then, let me wish you an afternoon of joy on the golf course. May you be hit on the head with somebody else's drive, not that anybody would be able to tell the difference afterward," I said, grabbing him by the jacket lapels and beginning to shake him. He didn't resist. He merely smiled. "*Bobbe-myseh. Shabbes goy. Mishpocheh.* Don't you dare patronize me with your pidgin Yiddish, you functionally illiterate prick. Agatha Christie. *The Case of the Missing Swimmer.* I'll bet the last book you read was your Dick and Jane reader, and you're probably still trying to work out the plot. Where did you learn how to question a suspect? Watching 'Dragnet'? Reading *True Detective*? No, I would have known. Your lips would still be chapped."

Smirking, O'Hearne released himself from my grip with a neat chop of his hand, making me wince again. Then he cupped the back of my neck with his other hand, yanked my head forward, and drove a knee into my groin. My mouth agape, I was bent over double only briefly, because next he raised his joined fists like a sledgehammer and caught me under the chin, sending me sprawling backward to the floor, arms windmilling. "Panofsky, do yourself a favour," he said. "We know you did it and sooner or later we'll find wherever you buried the poor bastard. Asparagus bed my ass. So save us time and effort. Show some *rachmones* for hard-working officers of the law. That means pity in your lingo, which I'm willing to bet I speak better than you. Come clean. Lead us to the body. We give points for that. I'll swear in court you were a real sweetheart, cooperative, filled with remorse. You hire yourself a smart Jew lawyer and you are charged with manslaughter, or some shit like that, because there was a struggle and the gun went off by accident. Or it was self-defence. Or, good heavens, you didn't even know it was loaded. Judge and jury will be understanding. Your wife. Your best friend. Holy mackerel it had to be temporary insanity. Worse case you get three years and you're home-free after eighteen months. Hey, you might even get off with a suspended sentence. A poor, deceived husband like you. But if you insist upon that *bobbe-myseh* you're spinning us, and I testify in court that you hit me, nobody will believe your story and maybe you get life, which is at least ten years, and while you're rotting in jail eating dog food, getting the shit beat out of you by bad guys who don't like Jews, your hot number in Toronto will be spreading her legs for somebody else, eh? I mean you finally get out you'll be a broken old man. So what do you say?"

Nothing is what I said, because I couldn't stop retching.

"Jesus, look what you're doing to your carpet. Where can I find a basin to bring you?"

O'Hearne leaned over and offered a hand to raise me off the floor, but I shook my head, no, fearful of another pummelling. "The only thing for that carpet now is a shampoo. Well, *merci beaucoup* for the beer."

I groaned.

"And if and when your buddy, the long-distance swimmer, turns up, do be good enough to give us a call, eh?"

On his way out, O'Hearne managed to step on my hand. "Whoops. Sorry."

I lay on the floor for an hour, maybe longer, after O'Hearne and his minions drove off, then I managed to pour myself another Laphroaig, bolting it down, and rang John Hughes-McNoughton. He wasn't at home or in his office. I found him at Dink's and told him that the cops had paid me a visit. "Your voice sounds funny," he said.

"O'Hearne beat the shit out of me. I want him charged."

"I hope you didn't answer any questions."

I thought it was best to tell John everything, including O'Hearne's discovery of my father's revolver, and my speaking harshly to him before we parted.

"You grabbed him by the lapels and shook him?"

"I think so. But only after he hit me."

"I want you to do me a favour, Barney. I've still got a few bucks in the bank. It's yours. But I want you to find another lawyer."

"I'm also going to need you for my divorce. But, hey, we no longer need a hooker and a private detective. I caught her in the act. Boogie will be my witness."

"Only he's probably dead."

"He'll turn up. Oh, there's something else I should mention. She knows about Miriam."

"How come?"

"How would I know? People talk. Maybe we were seen together. *She never should have said that about Miriam's voice.*"

"What are you talking about now?"

"I blabbed. Okay, I shouldn't have. But I did. Look, John, I can't go to prison. I'm in love."

"We never met. I don't know you. That's final. Where are you phoning from?"

"My cottage."

"Hang up."

"You're paranoid. That would be illegal."

"*Hang up right now.*"

Shit. Shit. Shit.

EARLY THE next morning in Montreal I was wakened by the doorbell. It was O'Hearne with a warrant for my arrest for murder. And it was Lemieux who put the cuffs on me.

SIX

THE children never tired of stories about my courtship of Miriam, rejoicing in our naughtiness, constantly pressing for more details.

"You mean he ran from his own wedding and followed you onto the train to Toronto?"

"He did."

"You're bad, Daddy," said Kate.

A solemn Saul looked up from his book and said, "I wasn't born yet."

"What time did the train leave for Toronto?" asked Michael for the umpteenth time.

"Around ten o'clock," said Miriam.

"If the hockey game ended at, say, ten-thirty, and the train left at approximately ten, I don't see how – "

"Michael, we've been through this before. It must have been a late departure."

"And you made him get off at – "

"I still don't see how – "

"I have not yet come to the end of my sentence," said Kate.

"Oh, you're such a pain in the – "

"You may speak only when I have come to the end of a sentence. And you made him get off at Montreal West. Period."

"Actually she was secretly miffed that I didn't ride all the way to Toronto with her."

"It was his wedding night, dear."

"He was pissed," said Saul.

"Daddy, were you. Question mark."

"Certainly not."

"But it's true, isn't it, that you couldn't stop staring at her, comma, even though it was your wedding night. Period."

"He never even asked me to dance."

"Mummy thought he was just a bit goofy. Period."

"If you were staring, tell me what she was wearing at the time."

"A layered blue chiffon off-the-shoulder cocktail dress. Ha, ha, ha."

"And is it true, comma, that the first time he took you to lunch he was sick all over the place, question mark."

"I wasn't born until three years later."

"Yeah, and I'm surprised they didn't declare it a national holiday. Like Queen Victoria's birthday."

"Children, please."

"You went with him to his hotel room on your first date, question mark. Shame on you. Period."

"Mummy is Daddy's third wife," said Michael, "but we're the only children."

"Are you sure about that?" I asked.

"Daddy," said Kate.

"I had my hair done and wore a sexy new dress and – "

"Mummy!"

" – and he didn't even say I looked nice."

"Then what happened?"

"They drank champagne."

"Daddy's first wife became famous and – "

"We know that already."

" – and she did that yucky ink drawing he has. Period."

"It's worth a lot of money now," said Michael.

"You would think of that," said Saul.

"It sure doesn't sound very romantic," said Kate, "his puking like that on your first date."

"The truth is I was terrified of making a bad impression on your mother."

"Didn't you?"

"She'll have to answer that one."

"His approach was original. I'll give your father that much."

"So you talked and walked," said Kate, "*and then what?*" she asked, big-eyed, the boys now equally attentive.

"Not everything is your business," said Miriam, and there was that dimple in her cheek again.

"Aw, come on. We're old enough now."

"I can remember," said Kate, "all of us being in the car in Toronto that time – "

"The Toyota."

"It happened to be the Volvo station wagon."

"Will you please both stop interrupting me. And we passed a certain apartment building – "

"Where Mummy used to live."

" – and Daddy gave you one of those looks and your cheeks turned red as tomatoes, and you leaned over and kissed him."

"We're entitled to some secrets," I said.

"When Mummy was living in that building Daddy was still married to that fat woman," said Kate, puffing out her cheeks, sticking out her belly, and struggling across the room.

"That's enough. And she wasn't fat then."

"I'm dieting, for Christ's sake."

"Mummy says neither were you."

"We don't want you to have a heart attack, Daddy."

"It's not the smoked meat, it's the cigars I'm worried about."

"And is it true that Mummy had to pay your bill at the Park Plaza the next morning?"

"I forgot my credit cards in Montreal and they didn't know me there in those days. Christ, isn't anything sacred?"

"Boy, are you ever lucky she married you."

"That's not a very nice thing to say," said Kate.

"Period or comma? You didn't say."

"He's a good dad."

"I went to the Park Plaza to meet him for breakfast," said Miriam, "and there was a commotion at the hotel desk, everybody watching, and of course it was your father. He hadn't brought his personal cheque book or any identification with him, and naturally that was the desk clerk's fault. The manager came out, and was gesturing for the security man, when I intervened, offering my credit card. But the clerk was outraged. 'We will accept your credit card, Miss Greenberg,' he said, 'but first Mr. Panofsky must apologize for calling me names too filthy to repeat.' Your father said, 'All I did was to call him a typical Toronto prick, but then I've always been given to understatement.' 'Barney,' I said, 'I want you to apologize to this gentleman right now.' Your father, as he is wont to do, bit his lip and scratched his head. 'I will apologize for her sake, but I don't really mean it.' The clerk snorted. 'I will accept Miss Greenberg's credit card in order not to embarrass her further.' Your father was about to lunge when I shoved him back from the counter. 'That's most understanding of you,' I said to the clerk, and of course we had to go elsewhere for breakfast, your father growling throughout. Now, if you don't mind, I must get dressed or I'll be late."

"Where are you going?"

"Blair Hopper is lecturing on 'The World of Henry James' at McGill and he was thoughtful enough to send us two tickets."

"Don't tell me you're going, Daddy?"

"He most certainly is not. Michael, would you like to come with me?"

"Daddy said he'd take me to the hockey game."

"I'll go," said Saul.

"Oh, great," said Kate. "I'm staying home alone."

"You're being abandoned," I said, "because nobody likes you. Miriam, I'll meet you and Blair for a nightcap at the Maritime Bar afterwards."

"Would you now?"

"I'm sure they can come up with some herbal tea there. Or at least mineral water."

"Barney, you don't care for him. He knows that. But I'll meet you at the Maritime Bar."

"Still better."

SEVEN

BLESSED (or, rather, cursed) with hindsight, I now realize that Blair was after Miriam from the first day he caught sight of her at our cottage. I can hardly reproach any man for that. Instead, I blame myself for underestimating him. Give the bastard credit. Over the years, he kept turning up, insinuating himself into our family, undermining it, like dry rot nibbling at the beams of a house built to last. When the kids were still young and a handful, and we were once in Toronto for a couple of days en route to visit friends in Georgian Bay, Blair arrived at our hotel with a discreet bunch of freesias for Miriam and a bottle of Macallan for me. He offered to take the kids to the Science Centre, so that Miriam and I could enjoy an afternoon off. Mike, Saul, and Kate returned to the hotel laden with toys. Educational toys, of course. Not the warmongering water pistols and cap guns, enabling me to play cowboys and Indians and other racist games with them. "Bang bang. That's what you get for scalping nice Jewish widows and orphans, and not doing your homework."

When Michael won the mathematics prize on his graduation from Selwyn House, there was a letter of congratulation from "Uncle" Blair and an inscribed copy of a book of essays on Canadiana that he had edited. I read it with rising anger, because the truth is it wasn't that bad.

On another trip to Toronto, this time without the children, Miriam asked, "I suppose you're busy for lunch?"

"With the Amigos Three, alas."

"Blair has offered to take me to lunch and to a vernissage at the Isaacs Gallery."

I told her about the afternoon I had run into Duddy Kravitz at a gallery on 57th Street in New York. Duddy, who was then furnishing his Westmount manse, pointed out three pictures that interested him, and sat down with the epicene, hyperventilating owner. "How much if I take all three off your hands?" he asked.

"That would come to thirty-five thousand dollars."

Duddy winked at me, unstrapped his Rolex wristwatch, set it down on the tooled leather desktop, and said, "I'm prepared to write you a cheque for twenty-five thousand, but this offer is only good for three minutes."

"Surely, you jest."

"Two minutes and forty-five seconds."

After a longish pause, the owner said, "I could come down to thirty thousand dollars."

Duddy closed the deal for twenty-five thousand dollars with less than a minute to spare, and invited me back to his suite in the Algonquin to celebrate. "Riva's getting her hair done at Vidal Sassoon's. We're going to Sardi's and then to see *Oliver!* House seats. If you ask me, Oswald was a patsy. That Jack Ruby is connected, you know."

We consumed eight Scotch miniatures out of his mini-bar, and then Duddy fetched a full teapot he had hidden under the bathroom sink, lined up the miniatures on a table, refilled and capped them, and set them back in place. "How about that?" he said.

Whenever an academic conference brought Blair to Montreal, suspiciously often I realized too late, he would phone in advance to invite us both out to dinner. Once, I remember taking the call, covering the receiver with my hand, and passing it to Miriam. "It's your boyfriend."

As usual, I pleaded a previous commitment, and urged Miriam to go. "Why hasn't he ever married?"

"Because he's hopelessly in love with me. Aren't you worried?"

"Blair? Don't be ridiculous."

Once all the children were at school, Miriam's former producer, Kip Horgan, urged her to ease herself back into work, if only as a free-lancer to begin with. "You're sorely missed," he said.

Out to lunch together at Les Halles, Miriam waited until I was into my Remy Martin XO and Montecristo before she said, "What would you say if I went back to work?"

"But we don't need the money. We're loaded."

"Maybe I need the stimulation."

"You're at the CBC all day, what would I do for dinner when I get home?"

"Oh, you're such a bastard, Barney," she said, leaping up from the table.

"I was only joking."

"No you weren't."

"Where are you going? I haven't finished my drink yet."

"Well your wifey has finished, and I'm going for a walk. Even maids are allowed an afternoon off."

"Hold it. Sit down for a minute. You know, we've never been to Venice. I'll go straight from here to Global Travel. You go home and pack. We'll get Solange to stay with the kids and we'll leave tonight."

"Oh, terrific. Saul is leading his debating team against Lower Canada College tomorrow night and I promised to take Kate to see *Lawrence of Arabia* on Saturday afternoon."

"Bellinis in Harry's Bar. Carpaccio. Fegato alla veneziana. Tiramisu. The Piazza San Marco. The Ponte Rialto. We'll stay at the Gritti Palace and hire a launch to take us to Cipriani's for lunch on Torcello."

"I'm surprised you haven't offered me a mink coat."

"Everything I do is wrong."

"Not everything, but enough. And now, with your permission, I'm going for a walk. I might even take in a movie. So don't forget to drop off the cleaning at Miss Oliver's, it's on the back seat of the car. Here's the shopping list for Steinberg's and the receipt for the hassock I left to be recovered at Lawson's at the corner of Claremont. If you don't mind circling the block three times, you're bound to find a parking spot. You won't have time to take Saul for a new pair of shoes at Mr. Tony's, but you could stop at Pascal's to get me eight picture hooks, and I want you to return and get a refund for that toaster while you're there, it's no good. I'll leave dinner to you. I adore surprises. Toodleloo, my darling." And she was gone.

We ate Chinese take-out that night. Luke-warm. Gluey. "Isn't Daddy clever?" said Miriam.

The children, sensing bad vibes, ate with their heads lowered. But after they went to bed, Miriam and I shared a bottle of champagne, and made love, and laughed about our luncheon quarrel. "I know you," she said. "I'll bet you never returned the toaster, but threw it in the nearest wastebin and only pretended you got a refund."

"I swear on the heads of our children that I returned the toaster, as instructed by my housekeeper."

The following evening, a Thursday, I came down with the grippe, couldn't go to the hockey game, and had to watch it on TV, bundled up on the sofa. Guy Lafleur, intercepting an errant Boston pass behind his own blue line, swept over centre ice, his hair flying, as a roaring rocked the Forum. "Guy! Guy! Guy!" Lafleur weaved round two defencemen, deked the goalie, and was just about to go to his backhand . . . when Miriam started in on me again. "I do not need your permission to free-lance."

"How could he miss an open net like that?"

"I wasn't born to pick up your socks and wet towels, and drive kids to the dentist, and do the household chores, and to pretend you're out when you don't want to take a phonecall."

"The period will be over in three minutes."

As Milbury tripped Shutt behind the net, Miriam stepped immediately in front of the TV set. "Attention must be paid," she said.

"You're right. You don't need my permission."

"And I apologize for that crack about the mink coat. You didn't deserve that."

Damn damn damn. I had gone out and bought her one that very morning. On St.-Paul Street. "How much for that *shmata*?" I asked.

"Forty-five hundred. But we can forget the tax, if you pay me in cash."

I'd taken off my wristwatch and set it down on his counter. "I'm prepared to pay three thousand dollars," I said, "but this offer is only good for three minutes."

We stood there, staring at each other, and when the three minutes were over, he'd said, "Don't forget your watch."

"I'll take it, I'll take it."

Fortunately, the coat was still hidden in my office cupboard. I could return it. "You never should have made that crack about a mink coat," I said to Miriam. "I was deeply insulted at the time. I'd never do a thing like that."

"I said I was sorry."

So Miriam resumed work for CBC Radio, doing the occasional interview with authors who had hit the road to peddle their books. I did nothing to encourage her but, of course, tree-hugger, refuser of non-biodegradable plastic bags Herr Professor Blair Hopper né Hauptman did. "Who were you talking to for so long on the phone?" I asked one evening.

"Oh, Blair heard my interview with Margaret Laurence and called to say how impressed he was. What did you think?"

"I was planning to listen to the tape tonight."

"Blair says if I did a set of ten with Canadian writers, he is sure he could find a publisher for it in Toronto."

"There aren't ten, and anything can be published in Toronto. Sorry. I never said that. Hey, do McIver. Remind him about the time he read at George Whitman's bookshop in Paris. Ask him where he steals his ideas. No. They have to be his own. They're so prosaic. What's wrong?"

"Nothing."

"I'm going to listen to the tape right after dinner."

"I'd rather you didn't."

It was Miriam who insisted that Michael continue his studies at LSE.

"He'll come back from London a snob. What's wrong with McGill?"

"Mike needs to get away from us for a while. You're a bully and I'm too caring. A Jewish mama, in spite of myself."

"Mike said that? How dare he?"

"I said that. You cast too long a shadow. You take too much pleasure in demolishing him in argument."

"LSE?"

"Yes."

To come clean, I had barely made it out of high school, just managing to matriculate with a third-class pass, and envying class-mates who went on to McGill with ease. In those good old days, there was still a Jewish quota at McGill. Our bunch needed a seventy-five per cent mark to gain admittance, while goyboys qualified with sixty-five per cent, so even if I had converted on the road to McGill's Rodham Gates, I was a non-starter. So ashamed was I of my failure that I avoided student hangouts, like the Café André, and would cross the street if I saw one of my old classmates heading in my direction, anointed with that white sweater with the big red M sewn into it. After all, the most I could say for myself at the time was that I had graduated from busboy to waiter at The Normandy Roof. So I was inordinately proud that our children had excelled in their studies, winning prizes, and going on to one university or another. On the other hand, I doubt that Cardinal Newman, never mind Dr. Arnold, would have been impressed with the winds that blew in the latter-day groves of academe. Glancing through Kate's Wellington syllabus, I noted that she could take a course on Household Science, that is to say, how to boil an egg. Or vacuum. Saul, looking for a Mickey Mouse credit, had signed on for Creative Writing at McGill, taught by, you guessed it, Terry McIver. Superannuated *Gazette* reporters were teaching Journalism at Wellington, arranging their lecture hours so as not to conflict with their A.A. meetings.

Mike met Caroline at LSE, and, when we flew over to London on a visit, we were invited to dinner at her parents' home in The Boltons. Nigel Clarke was a well-known barrister, a Q.C., and his wife, Virginia, wrote the occasional gardening piece for the *Tatler*. Such was my apprehension (or insecurity, according to Miriam) that I pre-judged both of them as snobs and virulent anti-Semites, whose families – no doubt listed in *Debrett's* – had probably conspired with the Duke of Windsor to impose a Nazi regime on the U.K. in 1940. Clinching matters, I discovered that the Clarkes' country estate was not far from the village of Eaglesham, in Scotland. "I hope you realize," I said to Miriam, "that's where Rudolph Hess landed in 1941."

"Virginia phoned to say dress will be casual, but I bought you a tie on Jermyn Street all the same. Oh, for your information, that's spelt J,E,R,M,Y,N."

"I'm not wearing one."

"Yes, you are. She also wanted to know if there were any foods that disagreed with you. Isn't that nice?"

"No, it isn't. Because the sub-text is are we so Jewy that we don't eat pork?"

Nigel wasn't wearing a tie or a jacket, but a sports shirt and a cardigan with a missing elbow, and the imposing Virginia had on a loose sweater, what we used to call a sloppy joe, and slacks. Dressing down for colonialists, I thought. I must remember not to tear my meat apart with my fingers. Forearmed by a good deal of Scotch, consumed alone in a Soho pub, which was a violation of a solemn promise to Miriam, and riding my second glass of Marks & Spencers champers, I set out to shock at the dining-room table. Filling my father's office, I slid into telling tales of his days with Montreal's finest. The time they tied a felon to the hood of the car like a deer. Izzy's methods of persuasion. The courtesies he was shown in bordellos. To my chagrin, Virginia guffawed at my stories, and begged for more, and Nigel responded with steamy anecdotes about his divorce cases. So once again I got everything wrong, but instead of warming to the Clarkes, a nifty couple, I sulked at the failure of my strategy, Miriam covering for me as usual, until I loosened up.

"We are absolutely delighted with your brilliant son," said Nigel. "I do hope you don't mind his marrying out of the faith."

"That thought never occurred to me," I lied.

Then Nigel invited me to join him on a salmon fishing trip on the Spey. We could stay at the Tulcan Lodge. "I wouldn't know how to manage a fly rod," I said.

"You see," said a roused Miriam, "when Barney was a boy he fished in a brackish pond, with a twig cut from a tree in lieu of a proper rod, and a line made up of string saved from butchers' parcels."

A delighted Virginia pressed Miriam's hand. "You simply must come to the Chelsea Flower Show with me," she said.

On our return to Montreal, among the plethora of messages on our answering machine, there were three from Blair. Could we join him for lunch at the University Club next Wednesday? "You go," I said to Miriam.

Kate said, "How come you're so sanguine about Mom meeting Blair so often?"

"Kate, don't be foolish. This marriage is a rock."

EIGHT

HOLD it. This is not to suggest for a minute that Miriam was having an affair with Blair Hopper né Hauptman. She enjoyed his company, that's all. Possibly she was flattered by his attentions, but there was nothing in it. I'm the one who is responsible for the breakup of our marriage. I failed to respond to minatory signals sufficiently loud to alert a village idiot. And I sinned.

Wolves, I read somewhere, establish territorial rights to their domain, warning off trespassers, by pissing on its borders. I did something similar. I was amazed that a woman as intelligent and beautiful as Miriam would marry somebody like me. And so, fearful of losing her, I made her my prisoner, methodically alienating the friends she had made before we met. Whenever she had former CBC colleagues to dinner at our place I behaved abominably. My truculence was not entirely unjustified. Charged with virtue, those intellectual mice from the People's Network tended to condescend to me as a money-grubbing TV shlock-meister, even as they selflessly protected us from the cultural vandals to the south. Maybe this cut too close to the bone. In any event, I replied by ridiculing the Canadian content quotas for radio and TV, a licence for mediocrity (a profitable chunk of it supplied by me, as Miriam pointed out mischievously); and I accused them, as Auden put it,[1] of having hung their arses on a pension years ago. The worst case was Miriam's former producer Kip Horgan, a cultivated and irreverent man, a drinker, who was disconcertingly capable of puncturing my sharpest digs with a witticism of his own. Had he not enjoyed such a rapport with Miriam, we could have become chums. Instead, I loathed him. One night after he finally staggered out of our house, the last guest to quit a dinner party, Miriam turned on me: "Did you have to sit there yawning for the last hour?"

"Were you and Kip lovers?"

"Barney, you amaze me. It was before we had even met."

---

[1] Actually, Louis MacNeice in "Bagpipe Music."

"I don't want him coming here for dinner again."

"And, correct me if I'm wrong, but I do believe you were twice married before we got together."

"Yeah, but you're a keeper."

That did not earn me a dimple on her cheek. Miriam was not amused, but distracted. "Kip told me that Martha Hanson – she was no more than a script reader in my time, and not that good at it – is going to be appointed head of Radio Arts."

"So?"

"In future I will have to submit any ideas I have to her."

Another evening we flicked on the CBC-TV National News just as a new young woman correspondent was reporting from London. "I don't believe it," said a distressed Miriam, "it's Sally Ingrams. I gave her her first job."

"Miriam, don't tell me you'd like to be a television reporter."

"No. I don't think so. And I'm sure that Sally will be very good at it. It's just that it sometimes bothers me that everybody I used to know seems to be doing interesting things now."

"Don't you think giving birth to and bringing up three wonderful children is an interesting thing?"

"Usually I do, but there are days when I don't. It doesn't command much respect these days, does it?"

As long as our children were still living at home, in unending need of Miriam's support, our little tiffs were rare, usually culminating in hugs and laughter, and we continued to be passionate lovers. But in these days of rampant sexual self-advertisement, I remain unfashionably committed to reticence, so I will say no more than I did things in bed with Miriam that I never did with anybody else, and I believe it was the same for her. After the last of our brood quit the nest, we celebrated our new-found middle-aged freedom by treating ourselves to more frequent trips abroad, but Miriam was suddenly given to bouts of depression and dissatisfaction with the quality of her free-lance work, adjudging herself inadequate. Foolishly, I made light of her problems. Count on me to dismiss them in my oafish manner as an irritating but only passing menopausal phase.

Mike got married and Saul moved to New York. And one night before we made love in that parador overlooking Granada, I said, "I think you've forgotten your diaphragm."

"It's no longer necessary, but of course you're still capable of having children, aren't you?"

"Oh, Miriam, please."

"Do you envy Nate Gold?"

Nate, who had divorced his wife of thirty years to marry a woman twenty years his junior, could now be seen pushing a stroller with an eighteen-month-old babe in it down Greene Avenue.

"I think he looks foolish," I said.

"Don't knock it, darling. It has to be rejuvenating."

One afternoon after Kate got married in Toronto, I came home early from the office to find a McGill syllabus on the dining-room table. "What's this for?" I asked.

"I'm thinking of registering for some courses. Anything wrong with that?"

"Of course not," I said, but later that night, fearful of coming home to an empty house while she was sitting in a lecture hall, I stupidly launched into one of my anti-academic harangues. I insisted that Vladimir Nabokov was right when he told his students at Cornell that D.Phil. stood for "Department of Philistines," and went on to say the most gifted people I knew had never been to university.

"What about your children?"

"There are exceptions to every rule. Take Boogie, for instance. He was at Harvard."

"I doubt they've put a plaque in place to commemorate that."

We could never agree about Boogie and I didn't share Miriam's reverence for professors. In fact, just in case I haven't mentioned it before, the pride of my office wall is my framed high-school graduation certificate, lit from above. Miriam has reproached me for it. "Take it down, darling," she once pleaded. But it still hangs there.

The day after my ill-advised anti-academic rant, I found the McGill syllabus in our kitchen garbage pail. "Miriam," I said, "I feel terrible. Go back to McGill if that's what you want. Why not?"

"Never mind. It was just a passing whim."

One day we were a newly married couple, joy unconfined, and the next, it seemed, we had two grandchildren in London. Miriam could never bring herself to throw out the clothes Mike, Saul, and Kate had worn when they were kids. Neither would she let me get rid of our library of torn and crayoned Dr. Seuss books. But as she was assigned an increasing number of radio jobs she was less often depressed, more like her old self. Unfortunately, as the years passed, I dealt ineptly with her infrequent dark periods, arriving at Dink's earlier in the day and staying on later than usual. I would come home to one of Miriam's elaborately prepared dinners, a feast for two, and then boorishly fall into a drunken sleep on the living-room sofa, shaken gently awake by Miriam in time for bed. "Solange invited me to go with her to the Théâtre du nouveau monde tonight, but I said no. I didn't want you to be alone."

"I'm so sorry. Honestly, darling."

One afternoon I was seated on my usual stool at Dink's, gabbing away to a couple of young women Zack had brought in, when Betty gave me the eye. "Miriam just came in."

"Where?"

"She came in, turned around, and left."

"Didn't she see I was here?"

"Yes."

"*Tempus edax rerum,*" said Hughes-McNoughton.

"John, you're a horse's ass."

I hurried home to find Miriam in a state. "I got into a dress you favour and went to Dink's to surprise you, thinking it would give you pleasure if I had a drink with you there for once, and then the two of us could go out to dinner. Then I saw you chatting up those two women, young enough to be your daughters. I wasn't jealous. I was just sad."

"You don't understand. Zack brought them in. I was just being polite."

"I'm soon going to be sixty. Maybe you'd like me to get a face-lift."

"Miriam, for Christ's sake."

"Should I start dyeing my hair? What do I have to do to please my husband, the lounge lizard?"

"You're jumping to conclusions."

"Am I?"

And then, not for the first time, she lapsed into a denunciate of her father. The philanderer. The cheater. The murderer of her mother. After all these years, her father's promiscuity remained an obsession of Miriam's. The first betrayal she had known, perhaps. I learned to tolerate her outbursts. I didn't think it mattered. Certainly not to us. *Shmuck*.

I had to slip out of bed early the next morning to catch a flight to Toronto and when I got back that night Miriam wasn't there. She had left a note on the dining-room table:

> Darling,
>   I'm flying to London tonight to visit Mike and Caroline and the kids. I apologize for being hysterical last night, so please don't misunderstand. It's just that I can do with a break and so can you. If you come home early enough you are not to go to Mirabelle to fetch me. Please, darling. I won't be away for more than a week. I love you.
>
>   Miriam
>   P.S. You are not to go to Schwartz's to eat smoked meat and fries every night. It's bad for you. I've left some things in the fridge.

I opened the fridge to find a pot of spaghetti meat sauce, a pot of leek and potato soup, a roast chicken, a meat loaf, a bowl of potato salad and a cheese pie. Feeling sorry for myself, I ate in front of the TV set and went to bed early. Miriam phoned at seven a.m. "Are you okay?" I asked.

"I'm fine. I feel like a little girl playing hooky. I should do things like this more often."

"Well, I don't know about that. Are you sure you're okay?"

"Yes. Caroline is taking me to Daphne's for lunch, so I've got to get ready now. Will you be home this evening?"

"Of course. I had the spaghetti for breakfast and I think I'll have the roast chicken and the cheese pie for dinner."

"I'll phone you later. Kiss kiss. Goodbye for now."

I don't want to talk about what happened that night. It wasn't my fault. I was drunk. It meant nothing to me. Damn damn damn. The one evening I would give a year of my life to take back, I lingered at Dink's past the old farts' hour into the time when the raunchy singles begin to trickle in. Zack, who had once worked for, you know, that newspaper about money. Not the *Wall Street Journal*.

The Canadian one. The *Financial Report* or *Post*. Whichever.[2] Spaghetti is strained with a ... Hell, I got it right before. The Seven Dwarfs are called Doc, Sleepy, Sneezy, Dopey, Grouchy and the other two. Lillian Hellman did not write *The Man in the Brooks Brothers Suit*. Or *Shirt*. Fuck it.

Zack, who had once worked for a money newspaper, was telling me about his first encounter with Duddy Kravitz: "I was sent out to interview new young Montreal millionaires for a feature we were doing. One rich white-bread Wasp after another protested that they were certainly not millionaires, even on paper, and anyone who suggested as much was slandering them. They told me about their mortgages and bank loans and the problems they had coming up with school fees. The French-Canadian brokers I spoke to were no more forthcoming. Anglophone bankers discriminated against them. The big investors wouldn't trust their portfolios to anybody named Bissonette or Turgeon. They think we're stupid. It's a struggle, they said. They couldn't sleep because of the money they owed. Then I went to interview Kravitz, reconciled to even louder protests of penury. Instead, Kravitz beamed at me. 'Boy, am I ever a millionaire. Maybe three times over. You think I'm bragging? Let me show you some documents. Hey, did you bring a photographer?' I've had time for him ever since, no matter what other people say. Where are you going?"

"Home."

"Come on. One for the road."

"Okay. But just one."

That's when she sashayed into Dink's, the bimbo who ruined my life, snuggling onto the bar stool next to Zack who immediately began to chat her up. I can't even remember her name any more, but she was a bleached blonde, wearing a tight sweater and a miniskirt. Reeking of perfume, maybe thirty years old, if that. Obliging Zack to tilt backwards on his stool, her own head bobbing forward, she said, "Aren't you Barney Panofsky?"

I nodded.

"I had a part in a 'McIver' episode a couple of months ago. I played the investigating reporter from the Toronto *Globe*. Do you remember?"

---

[2] It was the *Financial Times*, defunct in Canada since March 18, 1995.

"Sure."

"They said it might be a continuing role, but I haven't heard from your people since."

That's when I should have left Dink's. Or when I should have had myself tied to the mast like Ulysses, not that she had anything on Circe or the Sirens, whichever it was.[3] But when Zack got up to pee, she slid onto the stool next to me, and the street boy in me was roused. Hotcha hotcha. Zack may be fifteen years younger than me, and better looking, but I'll show him I've still got the moves. *Not that I was interested. Or intended to take it any further.* I know I had a good deal more to drink, and so did she, but I still don't remember how come I got to her apartment, wherever it was, or how we ended up in bed. But I do recall I never meant for it to happen. I merely wanted to outshine Zack. Honestly.

It must have been three o'clock, possibly later, when I got home, filled with self-disgust, undressing, and staggering into the shower.

Miriam wakened me at eight. "Thank God you're there," she said.

"What do you mean?"

"I don't know what got into me, but I was up at five a.m. here, worried sick about you, I don't know why, and I rang and I rang and I rang and there was no answer."

"I was out late drinking with Zack."

"You don't sound right, darling. Are you sure you're okay?"

"Hung-over, that's all."

"You're not keeping anything from me? You haven't been in a fight at your age? There hasn't been an accident."

"*I'm all right.*"

"Something's wrong, Barney. I can tell."

"There is nothing wrong."

"I'm not sure I believe you."

"Come home, Miriam."

"Thursday."

"Come home tomorrow. Please, Miriam."

"I'm going to the theatre with Virginia tomorrow night. The

---

[3]It was to resist the Sirens, not Circe, that Ulysses was bound to the mast.

new Pinter. But I'm glad that you're missing me. I miss you too. I keep edging over to your side of the bed and you're not there."

That afternoon, having showered twice more, I started out for Dink's, as was my habit, and then stopped short. What if that bimbo was lying in wait for me there? What if she thought we were into something more than a drunken one-night stand? I made a U-turn and stopped at the Ritz for a drink instead. Shedding years, I sat once again on the terrace of the Colombe d'Or with Boogie and Hymie, the sun sinking behind those olive-green hills, seemingly setting them alight. A donkey-drawn wagon, led by a grizzly old geezer wearing a blue smock, passed clippity-clop below the terrace's stone retaining wall, and we caught the scent of its cargo of roses on the evening breeze. The roses were bound for the perfumerie in Grasse. A fat baker's boy puffed past our table, one of those huge wicker baskets of freshly-baked baguettes strapped to his back, and we could smell that too. Then one of those truly obnoxious Frenchmen, obviously past it, his belly sunken, pranced onto the terrace to claim the woman young enough to be his daughter who sat two tables to our left. *Madame Bovary, c'est moi*, that Frenchman who had the parrot once wrote[4], and I had become that odious Frenchman of unblessed memory. Feeling tears of self-pity coming on, I called for my bill and was about to go home when I stopped short again, troubled by second thoughts. I pulled Zack into a quiet corner. "You are never, never, never to joke with me, or anybody else, about that girl last night, or we are no longer friends. Do you understand?"

"Easy does it, Barney."

Then Betty said, "Somebody called Lorraine phoned for you." And handing me a piece of paper, she added, "She left her phone number."

"If she ever calls again, I'm not here. What do you know about her?"

"I think she's a model or an actress. She did that sexy bank commercial that used to be on TV. You know, the Canadiens take a penalty, Dick Irwin says we'll be right back after these messages, and there she is dancing all alone on a moonlit beach in Bermuda.

---

[4]Flaubert.

Wearing a sarong. Jiggle, jiggle. 'I got my vacation loan from the Bank of Montreal.' The guys at the bar used to howl."

I couldn't sleep Wednesday night. In the morning, I cut myself shaving and spilt my coffee. Then I bought Miriam a long string of pearls at Birk's and went to pick her up at Mirabelle. We no sooner got through the front door when she said, "Something's wrong."

"Nothing."

"Did anything happen to Saul while I was away?"

"He's fine."

"Kate?"

"Honestly."

"You're keeping something from me."

"I am not," I said, cracking open a bottle of Dom Pérignon to welcome her home. It didn't help.

"Is it the office? Have you had bad news?"

"There is absolutely nothing wrong, darling."

Like hell there wasn't. Miriam had been home for two days and we still hadn't made love, which baffled her, but I knew about that bar in the Hôtel de la Montagne, and what if I had contracted herpes, a dose, or, God help us, that thing that queers and druggies get? You know, that disease that sounds like a fund-raiser. AIDS, that's it.

I beat Miriam to the phone whenever it rang and lingered at home in the morning long enough to collect the mail, just in case. Returning from Dink's in time for dinner, my stomach churning, I was ready with a lie in case that bitch had phoned in my absence.

Years ago, luxuriating in my undeserved happiness with Miriam and the kids, I feared for the anger of the gods. I was convinced something dreadful lay in wait for me. An avenging monster who would rise out of the bathroom drain like an invention of Stephen King's. Now I knew. The monster was me. I was the destroyer of my loving refuge from "the world of telegrams and anger."

In those days I was still obliged to simulate enthusiasm for the dreck that enriched me, suffering mediocre, functionally illiterate actors, hack writers, no-talent directors, and TV executives at lunches in New York or L.A. It was degrading. A sewer. But until I cheated, I was blessed with a sanctuary. Miriam. Our children. Our home. Where I was never required to be deceitful. But it was with apprehension that I now turned my key in the front-door lock, dreading discovery. So I took preventive measures at the office, calling in Gabe Orlansky and Serge Lacroix for a meeting. "Remember that girl who played the investigative reporter from the *Globe* in a recent McIver episode? I think her name was Lorraine Peabody, but I could be wrong."

"Yeah. So?"

"I want her written into a couple more episodes."

"She can't act."

"You can't write and you can't direct. Do as I say."

Chantal lingered behind. "What is it?" I asked.

"Whoever would have thought – "

"*Thought what?*"

"Nothing."

"That's better."

"I was mistaken about you. You're no different than the others here. You don't deserve a woman of Miriam's quality. A dirty old man is what you are."

"Get out."

My heart hammering, I arranged to meet Lorraine for lunch at one of those quaintsy, tourist-trap restaurants in Old Montreal, where nobody knew me. "Look here," I said, "what happened the other night was an aberration. You are not to write to me, phone, or ever attempt to contact me again."

"Hey, it was no big deal. Relax. We shared a fuck, that's all."

"I assume our casting people have been in touch with you."

"Yes, but if you think that's why I – "

"Of course not. However, there is something you must do for me in return."

"I thought I wasn't supposed to contact – "

"As soon as we leave here, I'm driving you to Dr. Mortimer Herscovitch's office where you are going to have a blood test."

"You're kidding me, tiger."

"You do as I say and there will be more work for you. If not, not."

Guilt ridden, I swung wildly between remorse and aggression. When bolstered by too much to drink, I concluded that I hadn't behaved that badly and it was Miriam who was at fault. How dare she suspect I would be without blemish. Impervious to temptation. Guys weren't like that. Guys tended to stray on occasion and I was a guy too. I deserved a medal, not obloquy, for having cheated only once in thirty-one years. Besides, it meant nothing to me. I still don't remember how I got from Dink's to her apartment. I was giving her a lift home, that's all. I didn't want to be invited in for a nightcap. I was helplessly drunk and didn't ask that bitch to come on to me in the first place. Young women have no business tempting respectable old family men by dressing like hookers. I was taken advantage of and now I was not going to wear a hair-shirt or go in for self-flagellation. Considering the behaviour of the other guys at Dink's, I was the very apogee of correctitude. Miriam was lucky to have a husband like me. Tender. Loving. A wonderful provider. In that mood, I would stumble home from Dink's and start quarrels over picayune matters. "Must we eat chicken again tonight?"

"You won't eat fish, and red meat is bad for you."

"So's white wine. It killed James Joyce."

"Then open a bottle of red, if you prefer."

"There's no need to snap at me."

"But you're the one who's . . ."

"Yeah, sure. It's always me."

Saul phoned me at the office. "I want to know why Mummy was crying this afternoon."

"It was nothing, Saul. Honestly."

"That's not what she seems to think."

I was losing it. My wife. My children.

"Barney, I want to know why you're turning up here drunk every night."

"Am I now obliged to account for how many drinks I've had before dinner?"

"You're not going to like this, but I'm afraid that at your age you can no longer handle it like you used to. You come home in such an unspeakable mood that to tell you the truth I'd rather eat alone," she said.

Miriam turned away from me in bed that night and wept quietly. I wanted to die. The next morning I seriously considered charging across Sherbrooke Street against a red light. I would be hit by a car and rushed to the Montreal General in an ambulance. Miriam would sit by my side in intensive care, holding my hand, forgiving me everything. But I chickened out. I waited for the light to turn green.

Correction. These meandering memoirs do have a point after all. Over the wasting years I have levered free of many a tight spot leaning on a fulcrum of lies large, small, or medium-sized. Never tell the truth. Caught out, lie like a trooper. The first time I told the truth led to my being charged with murder. The second time cost me my happiness. What happened is that Miriam, as achingly beautiful as I had ever known her, came into my study on a Saturday afternoon, carrying a tray with a pot of coffee and two cups and saucers. She set the tray on my desk and sat down on the leather armchair opposite, and said, "I want to know what happened while I was in London."

"Nothing happened."

"Tell me. Maybe I can help."

"Honestly, Miriam, I – "

"The way you cough in bed these nights. Those cigars. Are you hiding something from me and the children that Morty Herscovitch told you?"

"I haven't got lung cancer yet, if that's what you mean." And that's when I broke down and told her what had happened. "I'm so sorry. I'm absolutely miserable. It meant nothing to me."

"I see."

"Is that all you have to say?"

"It never would have happened if you weren't available," she said, and then she went to pack a suitcase.

"Where are you going?"

"I don't know."

"Please, Miriam. We have a life."

"Had. And I'm grateful for it. But before you can corrupt it any further and I end up hating you – "

"We can work this out. Please, my darling."

But there was no point, because Miriam was twelve-years-old again. Looking me in the eye, it was her father she saw. Humping factory girls. Trolling downtown bars.

"Why do you put up with him?" Miriam had asked.

"What should I do?" her mother had answered.

Miriam would not be so helpless.

"I need some time alone," she said to me.

"I'll do anything you want. I'll sell the business and we'll retire to a villa in Provence or Tuscany."

"Then what will you do all day, a man with your energy? Build model airplanes? Play bridge?"

She reminded me of the last time I had promised to ease up with a hobby. I had hired a contractor to build a state-of-the-art workshop on our country property, and equipped it with a complete set of Black & Decker tools. I made one lopsided bookcase, cutting my hand with a power saw, requiring fourteen stitches, and used the workshop for storage ever since.

"We'll travel. I'll read. We'll manage, Miriam."

"Barney, you only pretend to hate your production company. The truth is you love the deal-making and the money and the power you enjoy over the people who work for you."

"I could go to my bank and help them with an employees' buy-out. Miriam, you can't leave me over a stupid one-night stand."

"Barney, I'm weary of pleasing everybody. You. The children. Your friends. You've been making all the decisions for me ever since we married. I'd like to make some decisions of my own, good or bad, before I'm too old."

Once Miriam had moved into a bachelor apartment in Toronto, and resumed full-time work for CBC Radio, she sent Saul round to pack and collect her things.

"Whoever would have thought it would come to this," I said, offering my son a drink.

"You miserable old bastard, I'm glad she left you. You never deserved a woman of such quality. The way you treated her. How you took her for granted. Shit shit shit. Now you have to show me which of all these books and records are hers."

"Take whatever you want. Pack the lot. Now that I've raised a family of ungrateful children, and my wife has abandoned me, I'm not going to need a big house like this any more. I think I'll sell out and move into an apartment downtown."

"We had a family. A real family. And you fucked it up and I'll never forgive you for that."

"I'm still your father, you know."

"There's nothing I can do about that."

Kate pleaded with Miriam, unavailingly, to forgive me my embarrassing lapse, and Mike refused to take sides. I flew to Toronto every weekend and took Miriam out to dinner, and made her laugh, and began to suspect that she was enjoying this second courtship as much as I was. "We're having such a good time together. Why don't you fly home with me?"

"And ruin everything?"

So I risked another tactic. I told Miriam that if she wanted a divorce, she would have to make the arrangements, I would have nothing to do with it, but she could have whatever she wanted. I would sign anything her lawyers presented me with. Meanwhile, I added, we still had a joint bank account, and she must continue to use it as she saw fit. Instead, humiliating me, she allowed that she had drawn ten thousand dollars on the account, which she considered a loan, but she had also written to the bank, returning her cheque books and volunteering that her signature was no longer valid for our account.

"What are you going to live on, for Christ's sake?"

"My salary."

"You're no longer a young woman, you know."

"But you have already made that abundantly clear, haven't you, darling?"

Mike phoned: "I want you to know we've invited Mummy to come over and stay with us for a while, but that invitation holds good for you too."

Kate said: "She starts on a story about a trip you made together to Venice and Madrid, and then she bursts into tears. Hang in there, Daddy. Keep plugging away."

Friends tried to cheer me up. Women Miriam's age, they assured me, often did squirrelly things before they settled down. Be patient, she would soon come home. The Nussbaums were foolish enough to invite me to dinners, providing a sparkly widow or divorcee whom I insulted gratuitously. "My wife never found it necessary to dye her hair, and she is still beautiful. Mind you, I suppose the loss of beauty is not something that ever troubled you."

O'Hearne reported at Dink's: "Your Second Mrs. Panofsky took the news well. She hopes the divorce costs you a fortune. And that it brings on a stroke or a heart attack."

"God bless her. Oh, incidentally, I'm thinking of committing another murder."

Blair was the candidate. I had phoned Miriam to say I would be arriving in Toronto late Friday night. "I can't see you this Saturday,

Barney," she said. "I promised to go to North Carolina with Blair for the weekend. He's presenting a paper at Duke."

Shit. Shit. Shit. I had Chantal phone Duke's Department of Canadian Studies, pretending to be Blair's secretary, saying he had mislaid the paper with his hotel reservations. Where was he staying? The Washington Duke Hotel. Next I insisted Chantal phone the Washington Duke to ask for a confirmation of Professor Hopper's reservations. "We have a single room booked for Dr. Hopper and another for Mrs. Panofsky," said the clerk.

"Feel better?" asked Chantal.

I invited Solange out to dinner. "What can she see in that prick?" I asked.

"I'll bet he doesn't correct or contradict her at dinner parties. Possibly he is considerate rather than ill-tempered. Maybe he makes her feel cherished."

"But I love Miriam. I need her."

"What if she doesn't need you any more? It happens, you know."

Six months passed before she moved in with Blair Hopper né Hauptman, and I thought I would go out of my mind. Imagining them in bed together, that bastard daring to fondle her breasts. One drunken night in our empty Westmount house, I swept crockery off the kitchen shelves, tore pictures off the walls, overturned tables, smashed chairs against the floor until the legs broke off, and took out our TV with one swing of a floor lamp. I knew how much of Miriam's love and thoughtfulness had gone into the acquisition of even the tiniest item in our home, and I hoped the racket I was making, destroying what she had put together, could be heard even in that sinbin she was sharing with Blair in Toronto. The next morning with rue my heart was laden. I collected some of her favourite pieces, hoping they had not been splintered beyond repair, and hired a furniture restorer to mend them. "Do you mind if I inquire as to what transpired here?" he asked.

"Break-in. Vandals."

I moved into this downtown apartment, but couldn't bring myself to sell the house at once, just in case. I could not abide the idea of strangers in what had once been our bedroom. Or some mod con yuppie bitch installing a microwave oven in the kitchen where Miriam had baked croissants to perfection, or cooked *osso bucco* even as she helped Saul with his homework, and kept an eye on Kate banging pots together in her playpen. I certainly wasn't going to tolerate a dentist, or a stockbroker, tramping on the living-room carpet on which we had made love more than once. Nobody was going to taint our bookshelves with the collected works of Tom Clancy or Sidney Sheldon. I didn't want some oaf playing Nirvana at 10,000 decibels in the room where Miriam had retired to the chaise longue at three a.m. to nurse Kate, while she listened to Glenn Gould, the sound turned down low so as not to waken me. I had no idea what to do with a basement closet full of skates, and hockey sticks, and cross-country skis and boots. Or the white wicker bassinet that had seen Miriam through three pregnancies. Or Mike's abandoned attempt at making his own electric guitar.

Striding up and down in my apartment in the early morning hours, drinking alone, pulling on my umpteenth Montecristo of the day, I shut my eyes and summoned up Miriam as she appeared at my wedding to The Second Mrs. Panofsky. The most enchanting woman I had ever seen. Long hair black as a raven's wing. Striking blue eyes to die for. Wearing a blue chiffon cocktail dress, and moving about with the most astonishing grace. Oh that dimple in her cheek. Those bare shoulders.

– I've got two tickets for tomorrow's flight to Paris in my jacket pocket. Come with me.

– You can't be serious.

– Come live with me and be my love. Please, Miriam.

– If I don't leave now I could miss my train.

Miriam has been gone for three years now, but I still sleep on my side of the bed and grope for her when I waken. Miriam, Miriam, my heart's desire.

NINE

OKAY, here goes. The trial. Me and the great Franz K., both falsely accused.

Were I a real writer, I would have shuffled the deck of my memoirs so that this would be a real nail-biter. Worthy of Eric

you-know, he wrote *The Something of Dimitrios*. Eric like I was
going for a walk. Eric Stroller? No. Eric like that publication Sam
Johnson used to write for. *Idler*. Eric Idler?[1] No. Never mind.
Forget it. I've got a better example. More recent. Worthy of John
Le Carré. But you already know I was adjudged innocent by the
jury, if only for lack of a corpse, but not by the gossips of this city,
most of whom still believe I got away with murder.

O'Hearne grinned as Lemieux put the cuffs on me, and I was
taken to the police station in St. Jérôme, where I was fingerprinted,
and sat still for a mug shot. If I ended up entrusted to the hangman,
I resolved to feign cowardice – just like James Cagney of blessed
memory – as a favour to my priest, Pat O'Brien, so that the Dead
End Kids would no longer regard me as a hero (or role-model, as
they say now), but instead would join the local Rotary Club. I was
locked into a cell not up to the Ritz standards, but an improvement
on the dungeon that the Count of Monte Cristo had to endure. I
was also blessed with a turnkey eager to supplement his meagre
salary. Well now, it's easy to joke about it today, but at the time I
was terrified, given to crying jags and shivering fits. Charged with
murder, I was denied bail. "It won't go any further than a preliminary hearing," said Hughes-McNoughton. "I'm going to plead a
total lack of evidence."

Later I learned that the Crown, their case weak, was not gung
ho to prosecute, even though O'Hearne had assured them it was
only a matter of time before he dug up the body. But a rampaging
Second Mrs. Panofsky had hired a fire-eater of a criminal lawyer, a
man with political influence, who insisted I be charged; and naturally that *yenta* waived spousal privilege. Nothing would stop that
chatterbox from enjoying her day in court. The hell with her. What
worried me was Miriam, who flew in from Toronto and was allowed
to visit me on my second day in the slammer. "Whatever happens,"
I said, "I want you to know that I didn't murder Boogie."

"I believe you," she said.

"I'll be out of here in a week," I said, hoping that saying it
aloud would render it true. "Meanwhile, I'm making some useful
connections. If I want my house or business burned down, I've got a

---

[1]Eric Ambler, author of *The Mask of Dimitrios* (1939); U.S.A., *A Coffin for
Dimitrios*.

guy here who will do it on reasonable terms. Something else. I'm not the only innocent man here. We've all been falsely accused. Even the guy who took out his wife with an axe because the eggs were supposed to be sunny-side up, not turned over. Actually what happened is she suffered a dizzy spell, tumbled down the steps to the cellar, and landed head first on the upturned axe. He got blood on his shirt when he tried to help her. Please don't cry. They won't keep me here long. Honestly."

I had to wait eight days for my preliminary inquiry before a magistrate, who denied Hughes-McNoughton's plea and ruled there was "sufficient evidence to justify a trial, namely evidence on which a reasonable jury, properly instructed, might convict." The clincher, according to Hughes-McNoughton, were my initial lies to O'Hearne about the gun, which made me suspect. "Now Barney, old pal," he said, "I don't want any surprises in the courtroom. Is O'Hearne going to find a body?"

"Where?"

"How in the hell would I know?"

"I didn't kill him."

Five long weeks would pass before my case was scheduled to be heard at the autumn assizes in St. Jérôme. Miriam flew in every weekend, putting up at a local motel, and brought me books, magazines, Montecristos, and smoked meat sandwiches from Schwartz's.

"Miriam, if by some fluke, I am sentenced to rot in prison, I don't expect you to wait for me. You're free."

"Barney, would you please wipe your eyes. Nobility doesn't suit you."

"But I mean it."

"No, you don't, my darling."

My good companions in the hoosegow included the idiot who held up the local grocery, making off with eighty-five dollars and change, and ten cartons of cigarettes, and was nabbed trying to unload his booty in a bar the same afternoon. There were a couple of car thieves, a guy who dealt in stolen TV and hi-fi sets, a small-time drug dealer, a flasher, and so on.

One glance at the trial judge and I sensed that I was for the long drop into nowhere. I saw my feet dangling and prayed that my bowels wouldn't betray me during my last moments on earth. Mr. Justice Euclid Lazure, a slender, severe-looking man with dyed black hair, fierce bushy eyebrows, a hooked nose, and a slit of a mouth, had an interesting history. Like most thoughtful *québécois de vieille souche* who had come of age in the Second World War, he had flirted with fascism as a sensitive young Outremont fop. He had cut his intellectual teeth on the then racist daily, *Le Devoir*, as well as the Abbé Lionel-Adolphe Groulx's rabidly anti-Semitic *L'Action Nationale*. He had been a member of the *Ligue pour la défense du Canada*, a pride of French-Canadian patriots who pledged to fight like mad dogs were Canada attacked, but declined to risk their arses in what they adjudged to be yet another British imperialist war. He had been among that merry throng that had marched down the Main in 1942, smashing plate-glass windows in Jewish shops and chanting, "Kill them! Kill them!" But he had since publicly regretted his youthful indiscretions. He told a journalist, "We had no idea of what was going on in 1942. We had not yet learned about the extermination camps." But, as Hughes-McNoughton pointed out, there was an up side to that bastard's sitting in judgment on me. Euclid's missus had run off with a concert pianist. He enjoyed a well-earned reputation as a misogynist. In an earlier case, before sentencing a woman who had buried a kitchen knife in her husband's heart, he said: "Women have climbed higher in the scale of virtue, higher than men, and I have always believed that. But people say, and I believe it, that when they fall, women reach a level of baseness that the most vile men could not reach."

So I could hardly wait for my garrulous, shockingly unfaithful wife to testify.

"Poor Mr. Moscovitch," she said, "was trembling and I only got into bed with him to keep him warm, because I have empathy for anybody in distress, regardless of race, colour, creed or sexual proclivity. I am a tolerant person. People have commented on that quality in me. But, m'Lord, we do have to draw the line somewhere. No offence to anybody in this courtroom for I have the greatest respect for French-Canadians. I adored our maid. But, speaking frankly, I think your people should give up the tradition of having all of a bride's teeth extracted before her wedding. If you ask me, there are better gifts you could give a groom.

"Now only the dirty-minded could read anything sexual into my getting into bed with Mr. Moscovitch, although speaking as an attractive woman in her prime I do have my needs, and my husband hadn't enjoyed his conjugal rights in months. Why, he even failed to consummate our union on our wedding night, the date of which he wanted to have changed because it conflicted with the Stanley Cup playoffs. Never mind the deposit my father had put down at the Temple, or that the invitations had gone out and more than one Gursky was coming. We're friends of the family. Long-standing. There was no expense spared at our wedding. For my princess, my father used to say, only the best will do, which was why he bitterly opposed my marriage to Mr. Panofsky. He comes from another *monde* my father said, and he was right, boy was he ever right, but I thought I could uplift Barney, you know, like a feminine Professor Higgins from *Pygmalion*, that play by the great Bernard Shaw. Maybe you saw the movie version with Leslie Howard, which must have earned him that part in *Gone With the Wind*. I absolutely adored the musical version, *My Fair Lady*, with Rex Harrison and Julie Andrews, and I'm not surprised it was such a big hit. I can remember when I left the theatre with my mother, the tunes still playing in my head, I said – "

The judge, suppressing a yawn, intervened: "You got into bed with Mr. Moscovitch . . ."

"To keep him warm. So help me God. I was wearing my pink satin nightgown with the lace fringe that I bought at Saks on my last trip to New York with my mother. We go shopping together the saleswomen take us for sisters. For a woman her age she has some figure . . ."

In 1960,[2] women were still considered too dim for jury duty in Quebec, so my fate was in the hands of twelve men, good and true citizens. Local yokels. Pig farmers, and a hardware clerk, a bank teller, a mortician, a carpenter, a florist, a snow-plough operator, and so on, all of whom obviously resented their wasted time in court. Educated, as they were, by backwoods priests, I figured they were waiting to see if I had a tail. I even considered turning up barefoot one day, if only to prove I did not have cloven hoofs. Opening for the Crown, Mario Begin, Q.C., said, "My learned confrère will no doubt remind you again and again that there is no body, but the truth is we do have sufficient facts at our disposal to

---

[2] It was not until 1928 that women were declared "persons" by the Supreme Court of Canada.

prove that a murder was committed. And far from there being no body, I prefer to put it to you that the corpse of the murdered man has not yet been found. Look at it this way. Between the accused's first phonecall to the police, which was awfully clever of him, and the second inquiry by Detective-Sergeant Sean O'Hearne, he had a long day in which to dispose of the murdered man. And, remember, we are dealing with a self-acknowledged liar. Mr. Panofsky has admitted that he lied twice to the Sûreté. I put it to you that he lied not twice but three times about that revolver. First of all he told Detective-Sergeant O'Hearne that he had no idea how the revolver got to be lying on his very own bedside table. And then confronted with the fact that there was an empty chamber in the revolver, he lied again, saying that the revolver had been left behind by his father, who never knew how to load a gun properly. I find that amazing, considering that his father had been an experienced police officer. But the third lie is what concerns us here. Yes, the accused finally admitted he had fired the revolver, but only in jest, over the victim's head. But as you will learn from Detective-Sergeant O'Hearne, the accused did break down in the end and confess to murder. He said, quote, I shot him through the heart, unquote. These were his own words. I shot him through the heart.

"Now this is not easy for me. Like you, gentlemen of the jury, I am not without compassion. We are talking about a husband who came home to find his wife and best friend in bed together. Surely he couldn't have been pleased. But, without making light of the accused's distress on finding his unhappy wife in bed with another man, it was no licence for murder. Thou shalt not kill is one of the commandments in the covenant that his people made with the Lord, and, as we all know, when it comes to the Chosen, a deal's a deal. I will not detain you here with a windy and fanciful opening statement, because I can rely on the evidence to hand to prove that the accused is guilty of murder. There is the revolver, and the missing bullet, and the victim who we are told was last seen diving into the lake. Had he drowned, his body was bound to float to the surface within weeks, if not days. But maybe he's still alive, and just possibly I'm the last descendant of the Czar of Russia, whose family was most cruelly murdered on the orders of the Communist Leon Trotsky né Bronstein. Or possibly Mr. Moscovitch – without money – his passport left behind – climbed out of the lake on the opposite shore and, clad only in his bathing suit, hitchhiked back to the United States. If you can believe that, I've got a property in a Florida swamp that I'd like to sell you.

"Gentlemen of the jury, you must not let your feelings for a wronged husband impose on your good natures. Murder is murder is murder. And, once you have heard the evidence, I expect you to find the accused guilty as charged."

Then it was John Hughes-McNoughton's turn to shine.

"I honestly don't know what I'm doing here. I'm amazed. In all my years at the bar, I've never had a case like this. Open and shut, if you ask me. I'm expected to defend my client, to the best of my humble abilities, against a charge of first-degree murder, but there is no body. What next? Will I be asked to defend an honest banker against a swindling charge, when there is no money missing? Or a respectable citizen accused of burning down his warehouse, when there has been no fire? I have such respect for the law, our distinguished judge, my learned confrères, and you, gentlemen of the jury, that I must apologize in advance for this case ever having come so far, an insult to your intelligence. But here we are, *faute de mieux*, so I must get on with it. As you have already heard, Barney Panofsky, a loving husband and provider, turned up expectedly at his cottage in the Laurentians one morning and found his wife and his best friend in bed together. Imagine the scene, those of you who are also loving husbands. He arrives, bearing treats, and discovers himself betrayed. By his wife. By his best friend. My learned confrère will ask you to believe that Mrs. Panofsky was not committing adultery. Oh, no. She was not wanton. Consumed by illicit lust. Wearing an alluring nightgown, she snuggled into bed with Mr. Moscovitch because he was trembling, and she wished to warm him. I hope you are touched. But, to come clean, I'm not. Were there no more blankets available? Or a hot-water bottle? And how come when the accused surprised the two of them in bed, how come the wife to whom he was devoted *was no longer wearing her revealing pink satin nightgown*? Was Mrs. Panofsky, unlike the trembling Mr. Moscovitch, insensitive to cold? Or was she obliged to shed her protective nightgown in order to facilitate penetration? I leave that up to you to decide. I also trust you to decide why a married woman, entering another man's bedroom, in the absence of her husband, did not stop to put on her readily available dressing-gown. I also must

ask if her embracing Mr. Moscovitch was so innocent, why did she
flee the cottage in such haste? Why didn't she stay on to explain?
Was it because she was consumed by shame? Justifiably, if you ask
me. You will hear medical evidence of a residue of male sperm
found on Mr. Moscovitch's sheets, but don't let that worry you. He
probably masturbated during the night."

Savouring the jury's laughter, an emboldened Hughes-
McNoughton went on to say, "But, given that the accused was
understandably shocked by what he chanced on in that bedroom . . .
his adored wife, his cherished friend . . . it was still no licence for
murder, and I put it to you there was no murder. Or there would
also be a body. Mr. Moscovitch and the accused quarrelled, that's
true, and both of them had a good deal to drink. Too much to drink.
Mr. Moscovitch elected to go for a swim, a bad idea in his condition,
and Mr. Panofsky, unaccustomed to the intake of so much liquor,
passed out on the sofa. When he wakened, he could not find Mr.
Moscovitch anywhere inside the house or on the dock. He feared he
had drowned. Mark you, he did not flee the scene, like Mrs. Panofsky. Instead, he immediately summoned the police. Hurry, he
said. Now does that sound like the action of a guilty man? No.
Certainly not. But, as you have already heard, a shot was fired
from the service revolver that belonged to Mr. Panofsky's father,
Detective-Inspector Israel Panofsky. A good deal has been made of
the fact that the accused initially lied about the weapon found on the
premises. Given that the officers of the Sûreté are our protectors,
this is regrettable. But it is also understandable for, at the time,
Barney Panofsky was both grieving and fearful. So he twice tried on
fumbling, evasive responses about the provenance of the revolver.
But he finally *volunteered* the truth when he could have remained
silent and asked to speak to his lawyer. Remember, this son of a
detective-inspector, raised to revere the law, was not coerced into
telling the truth. Happily the citizens of this province," he proclaimed, pausing to nod at O'Hearne, "do not live in a Third World
country where suspects are beaten up by the police as a matter of
course. No sir. We are fortunate in our Sûreté and have every
reason to take pride in the decorum of its officers.

"So Mr. Panofsky told Detective-Sergeant O'Hearne the truth.
He had fired a shot over the head of Mr. Moscovitch in jest. Surely
had it been otherwise, our astute officers would have found

blood . . . in the cottage, on the grounds. *Somewhere*. They searched inside and outside, they brought in dogs, but could find no blood, or evidence of a struggle anywhere, and these are men who know how to go about their business. They came up empty because Barney Panofsky was telling the truth. So where, you may well ask, is the missing Mr. Moscovitch? He is surviving somewhere, *not for the first time*, under an assumed name. Really, as the Crown has already argued, then how come he left all his clothes behind? Well, *did he*? Does Detective-Sergeant O'Hearne know exactly how many clothes Mr. Moscovitch brought with him? Can he testify, under oath, that Mr. Moscovitch did not in fact make off with a shirt, a pair of trousers, and shoes and socks? Ah, but he left a bank book behind, and there have been no withdrawals from his account since. But how do we know there are not other accounts in other banks? Other countries, even. Mr. Moscovitch was no ordinary man. He was sick, a drug addict, and a reckless gambler. Did he flee, and assume another identity, to evade drug dealers, bookmakers, or casino proprietors to whom he owed great sums of money? You will hear from witnesses, including a celebrated Canadian novelist and an internationally famous American painter, who knew both Mr. Moscovitch and Mr. Panofsky in Paris, that Mr. Moscovitch has disappeared before, for months at a time. And I will introduce into the evidence a short story by Mr. Moscovitch, but I am obliged to apologize in advance for the obscene, and occasionally blasphemous, language, which may offend you. The story is titled 'Margolis' and is about a man who walks out on his wife and child, and assumes a new identity elsewhere. Mr. Moscovitch, you will be surprised to learn – as Barney Panofsky was astonished to discover – does in fact have a wife and young child, living in Denver, and they hold him in such high regard that they are not here today. You will learn from witnesses, and I will introduce cheque stubs to prove, that time and again Mr. Panofsky bailed out his friend when his gambling debts became insupportable – the very same friend he would find in bed with his wife.

"I will not suffer the grieving Mr. Panofsky to testify in this courtroom. Falsely accused, he has already endured enough. Two betrayals. His wife. His best friend. But I am counting on your good sense to acquit him. In conclusion, and at the risk of being adjudged indiscreet, I must confess that there is nothing like a lawyer's life.

Why, this case is so nonsensical, so lacking in substance, that I feel guilty accepting my fee. And from here I go on to defend a man accused of stealing the Crown Jewels from the Tower of London. But there is a problem. There are no jewels missing. You have a similar problem to deal with here. A respectable man charged with murder. Problem. There is no body. Thank you very much."

O'Hearne testified that when he had come to the cottage he had discovered that I had fresh calluses on the palms of my hands, which I claimed to have acquired digging an asparagus trench. Far from being happily married, it seemed, on questioning me further, that I kept a mistress in Toronto, a Jewish woman. "You fucking keep her name out of this," I had said. I had lied three times to him about the hidden (*sic*) revolver before I said, "I got him right through the heart, and then I buried him out there in the woods, where those pricks are searching right now." I had been a hostile witness, given to obscenities, taking the name of Our Lord Jesus Christ in vain more than once. Finally I became violent and had to be restrained. Obviously contemptuous of the gentile officers of the Sûreté du Québec, I had called him, said O'Hearne – apologizing for the crudity of my language before quoting me – a functionally illiterate prick.

I had to admire that bastard. The accused, O'Hearne went on to say, whose library included many books on the Index, some by Freemasons, others by known Communists, many by his co-religionists, had said, "I'll bet the last book you read was your Dick and Jane reader and you're still probably trying to work out the plot. Where did you learn how to question a suspect? Watching 'Dragnet'? Reading *True Detective*? No, I would have known. Your lips would still be chapped." Obliged to give me the benefit of the doubt, in spite of his detective's instincts, O'Hearne had made inquiries in New York. They revealed that the murdered – or missing man, he said, smirking – had never returned to his apartment. His bank account was untouched to this day.

Hughes-McNoughton tried his best to defuse the dumb and damning statement I had made about shooting Boogie through the heart, pointing out that I was a sarcastic guy, with a weakness for irony, and that my so-called confession was actually torn from the rock of my outrage. But, as he glanced at the jury and then at me, I could sense Hughes-McNoughton took me for a gone goose.

Increasingly desperate, he fell back on a melodramatic ploy that would have been unworthy of even Perry Mason. "What if I told you," he said, addressing the jury, "that I was now going to perform a little miracle? What if I now counted to five, and then Bernard Moscovitch walked right through those doors into the courtroom. One, two, three, four . . . FIVE!"

The jury sprang awake, all eyes on the doors, and I also wheeled about, just about spraining my neck, my heart thudding.

"You see," said Hughes-McNoughton, "you all turned to look, because you all have more than reasonable doubt that there ever was a murder committed."

The stunt backfired. The jury was clearly resentful of being suckered, the victims of a cheap trick. Mario Begin, Q.C., could not restrain his glee. Compounding my distress, I caught a glimpse of Miriam, in the rear of the courtroom, seemingly about to faint.

Hughes-McNoughton paraded witnesses to my good character, unavailingly. Zack, less than sober, an obvious roué, cracked too many jokes. It would have helped if Serge Lacroix had not recently dyed his hair blond and worn a diamond earring. Leo Bishinsky should not have flown in from New York with an adoring bimbo half his age, who stood up and waved to him as he sat down in the witness box. But if I was going to be hanged, it was the lovable Irv Nussbaum who was to blame. My pal Irv insisted on being sworn in on the Old Testament, wearing a yarmulke. He said I was a pillar of the community, a fund-raiser of fund-raisers, who had done more than his share for the Israeli Bond Drive. He would be proud to call me his son.

Sliding in sweat, I felt I was now destined to join a long line of Jewish martyrs. Captain Dreyfus, languishing on Devil's Island for years before he was not adjudged innocent, yet accepted a pardon. Menahem Mendel Beilis, victim of a blood libel in Kiev in 1911. Accused by the Black Hundred of the ritual murder of a twelve-year-old Christian boy, he endured two years in prison before he was acquitted. Leo Max Frank, son of a wealthy Jewish merchant, charged with the murder of a fourteen-year-old girl, tried and convicted, and lynched by a mob in Georgia in 1915. I passed the time making mental notes for my address to the court before I was to be sentenced. "I did not poison your wells," it began, "and neither did I murder your babes in quest of blood for my Passover matzohs. If you prick Panofsky, does he not bleed? . . ."

And then, eureka, that unredeemed rapscallion, maître John Hughes-McNoughton did produce a miracle, calling his surprising last character witness to the stand. It was the good Bishop Sylvain Gaston Savard, then still a total stranger to me. The wee, twinkly, black-robed bishop pitter-pattered into the courtroom, beaming beneficently at the startled jury, three of whom immediately crossed themselves. In his ringed, manicured hands that noble churchman carried the leatherbound hagiography he had written in praise of his aunt, Sister Octavia, that anti-Semitic bitch. As I looked on amazed, but reduced to silence by a swift kick from Hughes-McNoughton, the bishop announced how I – notwithstanding I had been born a Jew, like Our Saviour, come to think of it – had agreed to pay for an English translation of his little book. In his grating, squeaky voice, he went on to say that, furthermore, I had volunteered to manage a campaign to finance the building of a statue of Sister Octavia that would stand at a crossroads in St.-Eustache, and I was a fund-raiser of fund-raisers, as somebody had noted earlier. His testimony done, the bishop acknowledged me with a nod like a blessing, arranged his skirts, and sat down.

The rest was a charade, and a crestfallen Mario Begin, Q.C., knew it. But all the same he went through the motions, producing witnesses of his own who testified to my violent nature, recounting insults, bar-room brawls, and other unseemly behaviour on my part.

Forget it.

I'm sure most of you have seen *The Godfather, Part II*, by Martin what's-his-name. You know, like the name of that guy, the opera singer, who played the lead in *South Pacific*. Martin Pinza? No. Wait. I've got it. Well, nearly. Marty with a second name closer to Don Quixote's squire. Marty Panza? Marty Puzo?[3] Anyway during the investigation of the mafia in *The Godfather, Part II*, one of that band of criminals, a protected witness, had agreed to serve as a canary. But Al Pacino flies that man's father in from Sicily, and just as the treacherous mafioso is about to start singing, the old man enters

---

[3] My father has confused two Italian-American filmmakers, the novelist and screenwriter, Mario Puzo, and the director Martin Scorsese. Puzo wrote the Godfather films and Scorsese directed *Raging Bull*, among other films.

the courtroom, sits down, and glares at him. The would-be canary is struck mute. And now, even as a flustered Mr. Justice Euclid Lazure was summing up, my darling of a bishop smiled sweetly at the jury, his hands folded on his lap.

The jury deliberated for a respectable two hours before pronouncing me innocent in time for them to hurry home and catch an exhibition hockey game, the Canadiens vs. the Washington Caps, on Radio-Canada. I leaped up to hug Hughes-McNoughton and then rock Miriam in my arms.

One final thought. In the years leading up to my trial, whenever I was caught in bumper-to-bumper traffic on the highway leading to my cottage, creeping along behind a battered, rust-eaten pickup truck with a sticker on its rear bumper that read JESUS SAVES, I used to think don't count on it, buster. Now I am no longer so sure.

TEN

BAD news. Check out page one of these meandering memoirs and you will see that Terry was the spur. The splinter caught under my fingernail. I started out on this story of my wasted life as a riposte of sorts to the scurrilous remarks McIver had made in his autobiography about Boogie, my three wives, and the scandal I will carry to my grave. Okay, okay. It's a bummer of a first book. But not as embarrassing as the great Gustave Flaubert's initial efforts. In *Rage and Impotence* he told the story of a man buried alive who devours his own arm. In *Quidquid Volueris*, his hero is the son of a black slave girl and an orang-utan. Mind you, he wasn't sixty-seven when he sat down to scribble those yarns, but a mere fifteen-year-old. ·

Anyway my point is that after having written a kazillion words, this door-stopper of a manuscript has suddenly been deprived of its *raison d'être*. That inconsiderate bastard has died on me. Heart attack. He was en route to a reading-cum-book-signing at McGill when he went into a spin on Sherbrooke Street and collapsed on the sidewalk, clutching his chest. Had he been rushed to the hospital he might have been saved, but passers-by took him for a lush, and simply walked around him. *Bonjour la visite*.

McIver never married. "I already serve the most exacting of mistresses," he once told a *Gazette* reporter, "literature." But in his declining years he did enjoy the favours of rich women: culture-vultures. I'm told he maintained scrapbooks of his reviews, each page protected by cellophane. The last years of Montreal's very own G.O.M.[1] were rich in rewards. His study was filled with wall-to-wall honorary degrees. The Harbourfront Festival of Authors, in Toronto, paid tribute. He served on the board of the Canada Council and was a governor of McGill University. There were rumours that he was in line for an appointment to the senate, where he would have been able to exchange ideas with the esteemed tenant of our penthouse apartment, Harvey Schwartz. The former Gursky *consigliere* is also in the news these days. He is founder and principal financier of the Pan-Canadian Society. "I am determined to dedicate the rest of my life to saving this country, which has been so good to me," said that inside trader, currency speculator, property-flipper, hostile takeover bidder-cum-asset-stripper, tax evader, millions hidden in the Schwartz Family Foundation.

I'm in two minds about funerals. At my age, staring down into one of those six-foot-deep pits gives me the chills, but there is some satisfaction to be squeezed out of witnessing the burial of somebody else. Anybody else, save for Miriam or any of our children. But, to my astonishment, I wept hot tears at McIver's funeral. We had once been young and footloose together in Paris, roistering provincials, and, looking back, I regret that we had never become friends.

Digression, but a pertinent one. I recently flew down to New York to see Saul, and to catch Gregory Hines and that young prodigy, Savion Glover, in *Jelly's Last Jam*. I think Glover is the most gifted tap-dancer I have ever seen, and I was back to watch him again the following night. The next afternoon I met Leo Bishinsky for drinks at the Algonquin. "I'm sixty-eight fucking years old now," he said. "I don't get it. It had to happen while I wasn't looking. I'm sixty-eight years old, married and divorced four times, and worth forty-eight million dollars, even after my handlers have

---

[1] Grand Old Man.

stolen all they can. I've been on the cover of *Vanity Fair. People* have done me I don't know how many times. I'm quoted in Liz Smith's columns. I used to do Johnny Carson and now it's Leno or Letterman. I've had a retrospective at MOMA. I'm famous. My father would have been amazed to learn that paint brushes can pay better than mix-and-match ladies' wear. My mother would be proud. But that Aussie shit-face Robert Hughes does me in *Time*, it's a carve-up. The guys I used to shmooze with at Le Coupole, or is it La, who cares, or the Select or the Mabillon, all hate me now. I go to one of their vernissages and they either cut me dead or say, wow, we've got a star here, you slumming, Leo? Goddamn it, we used to sit together in those cafés, cracking up, waiting for Walter Chrysler, Jr. to come over and look at our stuff, and maybe buy something. We were friends for life I thought. Going through the fire together. The hell with them. These days I'm invited to A-list dinners on Park Avenue or in the Hamptons. Hey, show some respect, you're looking at a guy who's had a nosh at the White House. I'm invited to these dinners and my esteemed host is either an arbitrage guru or a former junk-bond shark with a gabby trophy wife, and there could be one of my *chatchkas* hanging on the wall, it cost the prick maybe two million, and I want to carry it away with me, because sitting with any of them for more than five minutes drives me crazy. I'm sitting there, I'm so ashamed, and I ask myself did I do all this for you? When I was eating one meal a day, was it their approval I was striving for? I've got six different kids from four wives and I can't stand any of them, or the thought that they're going to be so rich when I croak. One of them is a producer of hip-hop records. From Mozart to rap, or hip-hop, is some trip. Who am I to talk? From Goya to me is also a stretch. They did a biopsy on my prostate yesterday and I'm waiting for the bad news. Meanwhile everybody envies me my bimbos, but I get into bed with one of them and I'm terrified of being limp and laughed at. Shit, Barney, we used to have so much fun. I don't understand where it went and how come it was so quick."

McIver, to give him his due, persevered against long odds. He rode a small, unnecessary talent to recognition in his own country, which is more than I ever did, or dared. I should not have been so cruel to him. Following McIver's burial, I repaired to Dink's and read the *Gazette*'s obit, which was headed: TERRY MCIVER DUG DEEP

INTO HIS OWN PSYCHE FOR INSPIRATION. Oh, dear. But, all the same, that night I wrote a letter of tribute that was published in the *Gazette* three days later.

I'm not giving up on this scribbling, just because McIver has let me down. Instead I'm rededicating these all but finished confessions anew. They are now for my loved ones: Miriam, Mike, Saul, and Kate. Solange and Chantal. But not Caroline.

On my last visit to Mike and Caroline in London, I can remember being served a vegetarian dinner one evening: artichoke, followed by ratatouille, assorted cheeses and organically grown fruit. When Caroline came round with the decaffeinated coffee, I pulled out my cigar case, lit a Montecristo, and offered one to Mike. "Sorry it isn't a Cohiba this time," I said, testing.

As Mike lit up, Caroline slid out of her chair, ever so discreetly, to open a window.

"But I'm sure you enjoyed that box of cigars, didn't you?"

"Damn right I did."

Provoked, I went on to say, "Let's get into the cognac now, you and me, and tell sad tales about when we were still a family, carnivores born and bred, and your kid brother, that naughty boy, was dealing in pot at Selwyn House."

"Mike can't tolerate cognac," said Caroline.

"Oh, just a little one, an ounce," said Mike, who tended to measure out drinks precisely with a little chrome cup, "if only to keep Dad company."

"And then you'll be up at four in the morning, your heart hammering, and I won't get any sleep either."

The next morning, long after Mike had left the house at exactly 8:06, as was his habit, for the twenty-four-minute drive to his office, I sneaked downstairs, hung-over, treading tippytoe, determined to grab a taxi that would take me to Bloom's for some salt beef and latkes, when Caroline waylaid me. She had missed out on her yoga class to prepare a beneficial brunch for the old reprobate: freshly-squeezed carrot juice, steamed broccoli, and tossed green salad. "It's rich in iron," she said.

Trapped but defiant I spiked my carrot juice with a couple of fingers of vodka. This earned me one of Caroline's patented reproachful looks. "Isn't it a bit early, Barney?" she asked, the "even for you" left unstated, but dangling in the hostile air between us.

"It's fucking eleven o'clock," I said.

I'm not a total boor. I never say "fucking" to proper young women. But I liked to make her wince and maybe register that for all her *pur sang* heritage and aristo connections and la-de-da education she had married into a coven of jumped-up Jews. The non-U descendants of the *fusgeyers*, hooligans who hiked out of their *shtetls*, singing:

> *Geyt yidelkeh, in der vayter velt;*
> *in kanada, vet ir ferdinen gelt.*

> Go, little Jew, in the wider world;
> in Canada, you will earn a living.

It was perverse on my part. Churlish. I know, I know. Especially when you consider that Caroline is such an intelligent woman, attractive, a faithful wife so far as I can make out, and a good mother. She adores Mike. But what irked me was that like some women who knew my story, she would rather not be left alone with her father-in-law, in case what they whispered about me was true. So that morning I taunted her with it. "Caroline, my dear, now that we know each other so well, why don't you come right out with it and ask me if I did it?"

She rose abruptly from the table, collecting dishes, putting the kitchen counter between us, and beginning to sponge imaginary stains. "All right, then. Did you?"

"No."

"There we are, then."

"But I would say that, wouldn't I?"

Later, I heard Mike and Caroline quarrelling.

"Is he so pathetically naïve," she asked, "that he thinks he can shock me by saying 'fuck'?"

"Couldn't we discuss this tomorrow?"

"Tomorrow. Next week. He's a tyrant." Then she told him about our little contretemps in the kitchen. "He brought it up. I didn't. He said it wasn't true, but then he added, with that teasing smile of his, 'But I would say that, wouldn't I?'"

"Only he knows for sure."

"That's no answer."

"It was before I was born. I simply don't know."

"Or you don't want to know. Which?"

"Leave it alone, Caroline. It hardly matters any more."

"I have no idea how your mother put up with him for all those years."

"He wasn't always so bitter. Or afraid of dying. Now let's get some sleep."

"You didn't have to smoke that cigar last night. You could have told him you'd given up smoking."

"But I wanted to please him for once. He's such a lonely old man now."

"You're afraid of him."

"Caroline, you never should have given away those Cohibas without asking me."

"Why not?"

"Because they were a gift from my father."

"But it was you I was thinking of. You had so much trouble giving it up. I didn't want you to be tempted."

"All the same . . ."

Shit shit shit. Mike, I apologize. I'm sorry. I've misjudged you yet again. But I thought it better not to say anything. Typical of me, that.

I WANT ALL my loved ones to know the truth. I need them to understand that when Hughes-McNoughton pulled that dumb trick, counting to five, and suggesting Boogie might now stride through those courtroom doors, I also turned to look. I thought wouldn't it be just like my perverse old buddy to appear in time to save my skin? I did not murder Boogie and bury him in the woods. I'm an innocent man. Of course this late in my own endgame, and given that Boogie was some five years older than I am, he could now be dead of natural causes. Not that The Second Mrs. Panofsky would ever believe that.

Whoops. I forgot to mention something. My mountain-sized second wife turned up at McIver's funeral, if only to glare at me, and she later responded to my maudlin letter in the *Gazette* with a one-worder delivered by courier: HYPOCRITE!!! She had struggled up the hill to McIver's graveside, supported on two canes, her breath coming in whistles, draped in a tent of a kaftan. Her head was bound in a turban, and sneaking peeks at her, I could not make out a single wisp of protruding hair. So I concluded that the poor thing was on chemotherapy and that she too might precede me into one of those six-foot-deep pits. This would save me something like $13,750 a month. Following my trial, our divorce was sanctioned by a private member's bill in the senate, Resolution 67, March 15, 1961. She was awarded alimony of $2,000 monthly, big money at the time, to be adjusted for inflation, and the house in Hampstead. Even so, I never wished cancer on that demented harridan.

Unable to sleep, still troubled by my attendance at McIver's graveside, I thought it might be useful to renew my animus against him by dipping into his autobiography again. Flipping it open anywhere. As it turned out, the book opened on his charming account of my wedding to The Second Mrs. Panofsky:

Montreal. April 29, 1959. Since my return to Montreal, ensconced in my basement apartment on Tupper Street, I've managed to avoid running into P——, although I have heard news of his exploits. Predictably, he'd gone seriously into trade on his return to Montreal, peddling everything from scrap metal to Egyptian artifacts, rumoured to have been stolen. Today my luck ran out. We all but collided in the rain on Sherbrooke Street,[2] and P——, devious as ever, feigning pleasure at our fortuitous encounter, insisted that we repair to the Ritz for a drink. It had to be the Ritz,[3] à coup sûr, if only to taunt me with his new affluence. He bragged that he was now a TV producer, contemplating film production, but I knew the truth was he was actually a vendor of odious TV commercials and industrial films. Then, as is his wont, he reached for his switch-blade. "I'm sorry your first novel didn't get better reviews," he said. "I certainly enjoyed it."

And how was I managing, he wanted to know, bleeding empathy, asking direct questions comme d'habitude.

---

[2] Or Stanley Street, see earlier.
[3] The Tour Eiffel, according to my father.

I told him I was hard at work on a new novel, surviving on a grant from the newly formed Canada Council, and teaching creative writing one night a week at Wellington College.

He said he was developing a television series about a private eye, and had the effrontery to ask if I would be interested in trying my hand at some script work, which made me laugh.

Realizing that he had gone too far, P— then insisted that I come to his wedding, if only for old-time's sake. Boogie would be there, he said, as if that were an added incentive. My first instinct was to respond with an emphatic no, but honouring my writerly bounden, the unending quest for grist for the mill, I acquiesced. After all, I had never witnessed Jewish nuptials before, so I elected to suffer it in the name of ontology. As might be expected, there was no lack of comestibles or usquebaugh. But given that even in Paris P— would seek out restaurants in the Jewish quartier that served gefilte fish, and chicken soup with matzoh balls, globules of fat floating on the surface, I was surprised that the culinary fare was not of ethnic origin, but, instead, nondescript. As I anticipated, there was hardly a Burbank with a Baedeker to be seen, but many a Bleistein with a Cigar.

Snatches of *conversazioni* from my notebook:

1. "Oh, you're a writer. How interesting. Should I know your name?"

2. "What do you think of Sholem Aleichem? Mind you, I expect you don't understand Yiddish. Such an expressive language." ·

3. "You ought to read my daughter's letters from camp. Laugh, you could die."

4. "Have you ever appeared on the best-seller list?"

5. "The story of my life. That would make some book, but I haven't got the time to sit down to it."

I caught sight of the bride at the dessert table, where melon balls and berries spilled out of the maw of a sculptured ice dragon.[4] She heaped her plate impossibly high and then balanced a chocolate éclair on top of the fruit. I was immediately put in mind of how "Rachel née Rabinovitch tears at the grapes with murderous paws."

Small wonder the groom seemed so melancholy, imbibing endlessly, and in constant pursuit of an attractive young woman, who was doing her best to avoid him. In later years, however, she would become his third wife, rather, I'm told, than abort his child.[5] But that evening, not yet entrapped, she said she was an unqualified admirer of my first novel. "Had I known you were going to be here," she said, "I would have brought along my copy for you to inscribe."

We took to the dance floor, where P—— (his betrothed in his arms, licking chocolatey fingers clean) contrived to bump against me twice, his elbows to the fore. Ironically, this only thrust me closer to my partner, and, interpreting her body language, it appeared she found this far from displeasing.

ELEVEN

THE hard-fought referendum of October 30, 1995, did not disgrace *la belle province*'s time-honoured election traditions. I watched the proceedings on TV with the rest of the gang at Dink's. It was a squeaker all right: NO to independence, 50.57: YES, 49.43. But within days we learned that it wasn't quite so close. The scrutineers, all of them appointed by our separatist government, had rejected something like 80,000 ballots, just about all of them from strongly federalist ridings. The ballots were adjudged unacceptable because the X was too dark, or too faint or crooked, or exceeded the perimeters of the square.

---

[4]Or was it a hunter's horn? See earlier.
[5]I was born six months after my parents' marriage.

When I was in seventh grade Mrs. Ogilvy once turned her dynamite bum to our class and wrote on the blackboard:

CANADA IS——
a) a dictatorship
b) a post-colonial democracy of limited culture
c) a theocracy.

None of the above answers apply. The truth is Canada is a cloud-cuckooland, an insufferably rich country governed by idiots, its self-made problems offering comic relief to the ills of the real world out there, where famine and racial strife and vandals in office is the unhappy rule. Buoyed by this thought, I hurried home, and had just poured myself a nightcap when the phone began to ring. It was Serge Lacroix. He had to see me urgently.[1]

A few months earlier, after sitting through a "McIver of the RCMP" episode that Serge had directed, I had turned to Chantal and said, "I don't believe this. We've got to dump him. Would you fire him this afternoon, please?"

"Do it yourself."

But coward that I am, I couldn't, not after all those years he had been with me. So I procrastinated, even as his work deteriorated further. But now that he had insisted on a twelve o'clock meeting in my office, surely to plead for more money, making things easier for me, I decided to act, with Chantal as my witness. "Sit down, Serge. What can I do for you?"

"I'll come right to the point. Your friend Dr. Herscovitch established that I was HIV Positive after my little adventure in Parc Lafontaine. And now I have been diagnosed as suffering from full-blown AIDS."

"Oh, shit, Serge, I'm so sorry."

"I'm still capable, but I would understand if you wanted to be released from our contract."

"As a matter of fact," said Chantal, "Barney asked me to rewrite

---

[1] I fear that by this juncture my father's memory was unreliable, even somewhat scrambled, and that pages of this manuscript were put together in a haphazard fashion. The referendum was on October 30, 1995, but what follows, happened months later.

your contract only yesterday. He wants you to be cut in for a percentage of the syndication gravy."

"Retroactively?" I heard myself ask, glaring at Chantal and wishing that I had bit my tongue instead.

"Yes. As you like," she said.

"I need some advice, Barney."

So the three of us went to lunch at Le Mas des Oliviers.

"What about Peter?" I asked.

"He seems to be one of the lucky ones. I think he's immune. Barney, there's an insurance broker in New York who buys life policies from guys like me. I make him beneficiary and he advances me seventy-five per cent of the capital due on my death. What do you think?"

"You don't need to traffic with such bloodsuckers. Tell me how much you want and I'll lend it to you. Isn't that what you were just about to suggest, Chantal?"

"Yes."

After Serge left, Chantal lingered behind, and we continued to drink.

"You know something, Barney? You're not such a bad guy."

"Oh yes I am. You don't know the half of it. My sins are legion. So I've got to put some points on the board while there's still time."

"Have it your way."

"Christ, I'll soon know more dead people than live ones. Why don't you marry Saul?"

"For sure, when it comes to knowing what's best for me, it's a toss-up. You or my mother."

"I don't like to see you quarrelling with Solange."

"Why don't you marry her, Barney?"

"Because Miriam will come home one of these days. I'm willing to bet on it. Hey, for a guy named after a character in a comic strip I haven't done too badly, wouldn't you say?"

"Barney, there's something I've always wanted to ask you."

"Don't."

"Did you really murder that guy all those years ago?"

"I think not, but some days I'm not so sure. No, I didn't. I couldn't have."

TWELVE

BAD days my memory functions no better than an out-of-focus kaleidoscope, but other days my recall is painfully perfect. Today I seem to be pumping on all cylinders, so I'd better get down on paper what I've been avoiding until now before I expunge it again. I didn't lie about those last two days[1] with Boogie, but neither did I tell everything. The truth is the Boogieman who came to me to kick his habit was no longer the friend I revered. Over the wasting years all those drugs he ingested, not to mention time and fevers, had scrambled his head, burning away his individual beauty.[2] He was, for instance, no longer generous about other writers, except for McIver – "He showed some promise" – but that was proffered only to needle me. Something else. On one of my forays into his favoured New York watering holes, following his disappearance, I discovered that he had latterly come to be regarded as a man who promised better than he paid.

When we pulled up in front of my house in Hampstead, so that he could shoot up one more time, he said, "You must be rich now."

"Boogie, don't make me laugh. I'm heavily in debt. I never should have gone into TV production. If not for the commercials and crapola industrial documentaries I'm obliged to do, I'd be dead in the water."

Boogie was amused by our split-level home and The Second Mrs. Panofsky's flair with its furnishing. The enormous mirror shot through with gold flake. The collection of porcelain cats perched on the mantelpiece. The sterling silver tea set and cut crystal whisky decanter on the sideboard. "There's something missing," he said.

"What?"

"Cellophane covers for the lamp shades."

Surprising myself, I rose to the defence of The Second Mrs. Panofsky. "I happen to like what she's done here," I lied.

Boogie sauntered over to a bookcase, plucked out my copy of

---

[1] Three days.
[2] A paraphrase of lines from W.H. Auden's "Lullaby."

Clara's *The Virago's Verse Book* and, with his expert eye, immediately found two lines that didn't scan, and read them aloud with unseemly pleasure. "A woman from bloody *Life* magazine came to interview me. 'What was Clara like in those days when she was in her creative mode?' she asked. Crazy, I said. A compulsive shoplifter. Everybody's screw. 'What is your favourite or most germane Clara Charnofsky anecdote?' Oh, go away. *Fiche le camp. Va te faire cuire un oeuf.* 'When did you decide to make communications your field of endeavour?' Well, I'll be damned. 'Do you resent not being worldrenowned like Clara?' Go away. 'With all due respect, I think you suffer from low self-esteem.' Shit. I still can't understand why you married Clara."

"How come you never married?"

"Didn't I?"

"You did?"

"Take off your tie and knot it round my arm."

It took three bloody probes before he was finally able to drive the syringe into the vein, and then he dozed on the ride out to the lake, moaning, muttering incomprehensible complaints against what I imagined to be intolerable dreams. He slid into sleep again at our dining-room table and I put him to bed. I drove to Montreal the next morning, had far too much to drink, and when I returned to the cottage earlier than expected a day later I found the Boogieman in bed with The Second Mrs. Panofsky.

"It's your fault," said a giggly Boogie. "You were supposed to phone before you left town."

My hysterical wife, seated at the wheel of her Buick, hollered, "Some friend. What are you going to do about him?"

"Oh, I'm going to kill him is what I'm going to do, and then maybe I'll come after you and your mother."

"Fuck you," she shrieked and, hitting the accelerator, she raced down the driveway, her rear tires spitting pebbles. Boogie and I got into the Macallan.

"I ought to knock your teeth out," I said, but my manner was playful.

"Only after I've had a swim. Oh, she asked a lot of questions about Clara. You know, on reflection, I think I was no more than a convenient *deus ex machina*. She wanted to get even with you for that woman you're keeping in Toronto."

"One minute," I said. I hurried into my bedroom and returned with my father's old service revolver, which I set down on the table between us. "Scared?" I asked.

"Couldn't that wait until I've done some snorkelling?"

"You could do me a service, Boogie."

"Like what?"

"I want you to agree to be a co-respondent in my divorce. All you have to do is testify that I came home to my beloved wife and found you in bed with her."

"Why, you planned this, you bastard."

"No, I didn't. Honestly."

"You set me up."

"I didn't. But possibly it's time you came through for me once."

"What's that supposed to mean?"

"I can't remember how many times I bailed you out with cheques over the years."

"Oh."

"Yeah. Oh."

"Payment in advance, was it?"

"Shit."

"What if I took money from you because that's all you've got to give?"

That crackled in the air between us for a bit before I answered in a voice not my own, "I had to borrow on your behalf, Boogie."

"This is getting to be very interesting."

"*In vino veritas.*"

"Don't tell me they taught you Latin in that high school of yours."

"Boy, was that ever a cheap shot."

"No. You're the el cheapo here. You're the old friend who has been keeping accounts, not me."

"Have it your way. But now that we're into it, do you mind telling me whatever happened to that novel of yours the world was waiting for?"

"Are you inquiring as a friend or an investor?"

"Both."

"I'm still working on it."

"Boogie, you're a fraud."

"I've let you down."

"You were once a writer, and a damn good one, but now you're just another druggie with pretensions."

"I've failed in my duty to you. I was supposed to amaze the world so that one day you could brag, 'If not for my help . . . ' "

"You're pathetic."

"Oh, no. I'll tell you what's pathetic. Pathetic is a man so empty that he needs somebody else's achievements to justify his own life."

I was still struggling to recover from that hit when he smiled and said, "And now if you don't mind, I'm going for a swim."

"I want to know why you can no longer pick up anybody else's novel without sneering at it."

"Because what's being published and praised today is second-rate. And I've still got standards, unlike – "

"Here, you want to read a real writer," I said, and I threw my copy of *Henderson the Rain King* at him.

"Leo Bishinsky used to say how can you tolerate that know-nothing kid from Montreal?"

"And you no doubt pointed out that we were friends."

"I took you in hand and educated you, for Christ's sake. I put the right books in your hands. And look what you've become. A TV hustler. Married to a rich man's vulgar daughter."

"Not so vulgar that you didn't bang her last night."

"Yeah, but she's not the only wife of yours I had in bed. Clara, I said, what do you see in him? A breadwinner, she said. But I'll give her this much. She made a great career move dying so early."

"Boogie, maybe I ought to punch you out after all. That was fucking nasty."

"But true," he said.

I couldn't handle any more. I was too frightened. So, natural coward that I am, I retreated into humour. I scooped up the gun and aimed it at him. "Will you testify?" I demanded.

"I'll think it over on my swim," he said, rising shakily to fetch my snorkelling equipment and flippers.

"You're too drunk to swim, you damn fool."

"You come too."

Instead, I fired that shot well over his head. But I only raised my gun hand at the last minute. So if I wasn't guilty of murder in fact, I was by intent.

THIRTEEN

"WHAT'S wrong?" asked Chantal.
"I can't remember where I parked my car, and don't look at me like that. It could happen to anybody."

"Let's go," she said.

It wasn't on Mountain Street. Pardon me, rue de la Montagne. Or on Bishop.

"Somebody has stolen it," I said. "Probably one of your mother's separatist buddies."

We tried de Maisonneuve, formerly Dorchester Boulevard.[1]

"What's that?" she asked, pointing.

"If you blab to Solange, you're fired."

Saturday afternoon I was just drifting off to sleep when Solange phoned. "What time are you picking me up tonight?" she asked.

"Am I? What for?"

"The game."

"Ah, I think maybe I'll give it a skip tonight."

"*The hockey game?*"

"You know something? I've had enough of hockey. Besides, I'm very tired."

"It could be the last time we'll ever see Gretzky play."

"Big deal."

"I don't believe this."

"You want the tickets? Take Chantal."

Ten days later, according to Chantal, I dictated the same letter to her for the third time in a week. Leaving the office, I'm told I automatically reached into my pocket and pulled out a key, but didn't know what it was for.

"What are you staring at?" asked Chantal.

"Nothing."

"Open your hand."

"No."

---

[1] Actually, it was called Burnside until 1966,

"Barney."

I opened it.

"Now tell me what that is?"

"I know damn well what it is. Why are you asking?"

"Tell me."

"I think I'd better sit down."

Next thing I knew, strolling home from Dink's late one afternoon, I opened the door to my apartment, and found Solange and Morty Herscovitch lying in wait. Shit. Shit. Shit. "I know times are tough, Morty, but don't tell me you bastards make house-calls now."

"Solange thinks you may be suffering from fatigue."

"Who isn't at our age?"

"Or maybe it's merely a brain tumour. We're going to have to do a CATscan and an MRI."

"Like fuck we are. And I'm not chewing any of your tranquillizers or anti-depressants either. I remember when doctors were doctors and weren't working on commission from drug companies."

"Why would I prescribe anti-depressants?"

"I'm now going to pour myself a drink. You can both join me before you leave."

"Are you depressed?"

"Chantal took away my car keys and won't give them back."

"I want you at my office at nine o'clock tomorrow morning."

"Forget it."

"We'll be there," said Solange.

Morty was not alone. There was another guy there. A fat guy, introduced as Dr. Jeffrey Singleton, M.D.

"You a shrink?" I asked.

"Yes."

"Let me tell you something, then. I don't hold with shamans, witch doctors, or psychiatrists. Shakespeare, Tolstoy, or even Dickens, understood more about the human condition than ever occurred to any of you. You overrated bunch of charlatans deal with the grammar of human problems, and the writers I've mentioned with the essence. I don't care for the glib manner in which you stereotype people. Or how easily you can be paid to be a professional trial witness. One for the defence, the other for the prosecution. Two so-called experts at odds. Both pocketing big cheques. You play mind games with people, doing them more harm than good. And from what I've read recently, like my friend Morty here, you've given up the couch for chemicals. Swallow these twice a day for paranoia. Munch this before meals for schizophrenia. Well now, I take single malts and Montecristos for everything, and I recommend that you do the same. That will be two hundred dollars, please."

"I'd like you to do a little test."

"I pissed before I got here."

"It won't take long. Think of it as a game."

"Don't you dare patronize me."

"Barney, that's enough."

"Will this take long?"

"No."

"All right, then. Let's go."

"What is the day of the week?"

"I knew this would be ridiculous. Shit. Shit. Shit. It's the day before Tuesday."

"Which is?"

"You first."

But he wouldn't bite.

"Let me see. Saturday, Sunday . . . *it's Monday.*"

"And the date today?"

"Look, you're barking up the wrong tree. I could never remember my car licence number, or my social security number, and if I'm writing a cheque I always have to ask somebody the date."

"What month is it?"

"April. Gotcha, didn't I?"

"The season?"

"Boy, I'm going to be first in the class. If it's April, it has to be summer."

Tears began to slide down Solange's cheeks. "What's wrong with you?" I asked.

"Nothing."

"What's the year?"

"In the calendar of my people or in the Christian area? I mean era."

"The Christian Era."

"1996."

"Where are we?"

"This is child's play. We're in Morty Herscovitch's office."

"What floor are we on?"

"My father was the detective in the family, not me. We got into an elevator. Solange pressed a button, and here we are. Next?"

"What city are we in?"

"Montreal."

"And the province?"

"This is getting to be fun. We are in the blessed province that is squeezed between Alberta and the other one, on the continent of North America, the World, the Universe, as I used to write on the brown paper cover of my grade four whatcha-ma-callit book."

"And the country we're in?"

"Canada for the time being. Solange is an *indépendantiste*. Sorry, slip of the tongue. She's for here. For Quebec going-it-alone. So we've got to be careful what we say."

"I want you to repeat the following words for me. Lem—"

"She's a separatist, for Christ's sake. Mornings are not my best time."

"Lemon, key, balloon."

"Lemon, key, balloon."

"Now I want you to begin with the number one hundred and count backwards by seven."

"Look, I've been very patient until now, but this is just too silly. I'm not going to do it. I could. But I'm not," I said, lighting up a Montecristo. "Hey, I bit off the right end. Do I get any points for that?"

"Would you be good enough to spell the word 'world' backwards for me?"

"Did you read Dick Tracy when you were a kid?"

"Yes."

"Remember, when he went undercover, he called himself Reppoc. That's cop spelled backwards."

"How about 'world' backwards?"

"D, r, l, and the rest of it. Okay?"

"Do you remember the three words I asked you to repeat before?"

"May I ask you a question?"

"Yes."

"Wouldn't you be nervous doing a test like this?"

"Yes."

"Orange was one of them. The words. I'll give you the other two if you can name the Seven Dwarfs."

"What is this I'm holding?"

"It's a fucken not ink-point-pen, for sakes Christ, and you know what you strain spaghetti with? A colander. Ha."

"What's this on my wrist?"

"It's what you use to tell the time with. A clock."

"Excuse me," said Solange, fleeing into the waiting room.

"Now I'd like you to take this paper in your right hand, fold it in half, and put it on the floor."

"No. I've had enough. Now you tell me something. How did I do in your childish little test?"

"Your mother would be proud."

"So you're not going to put me in a strait-jacket?"

"No. But I want you to see a neurologist. There are some tests that should be run."

"Brain tests?"

"We've got to eliminate certain possibilities. You could be suffering from no more than fatigue. Or benign forgetfulness, not uncommon in a man your age."

"Or a brain tumour?"

"Let's please not jump to unpleasant conclusions. Do you live alone, Mr. Panofsky?"

"Yes. Why?"

"Just asking."

Early the next afternoon I bluffed my way into the McGill library and looked it up in a reference book:

When Alzheimer (1907) described the disease which now bears his name, he considered it an atypical form of dementia ... Family histories illustrating either dominant or recessive inheritance have been reported ... Alzheimer's disease is indistinguishable histiopathologically from senile dementia, and Sjogren *et al.* (1952) found a higher than expected incidence of senile dementia in Alzheimer families ...

Oh, my God. Kate. Saul. Michael. What have I done, Miriam?

Pathology
The brain shows extreme atrophy. Coronal sectioning confirms the uniform gyral atrophy, widening sulci, reduction in white matter and ventricular dilatation . . .

Yeah yeah yeah.

Clinical features
The first sign is mild memory loss. A housewife mislays her sewing, burns the toast, and forgets one or two items while shopping. A professional man or woman forgets appointments or disconcertingly hesitates in the middle of a lecture, unable to find the appropriate word. No more serious failure may be observed for a year or longer because of the slow progress of the disease . . .

"Morty, it's me. Sorry to call you at home. Have you got a minute?"

"Yeah, sure. Just let me turn down the TV."

"It's Alzheimer's, isn't it?"

"We're not sure."

"Morty, we've known each other for a hundred years. Don't fuck with me."

"Okay. It's a possibility. The thing is your mother died of – "

"Never mind my mother. She had hardly any marbles to begin with. What about my children?"

"The odds are long. Honestly."

"But shorter than for those with no family history. Shit. Shit. Shit. Saul reads about any disease in the *Times* and he's sure he's got it."

"We've scheduled the CATscan and MRI for tomorrow morning. I'm going to come and pick you up at eight."

"I've got to arrange my affairs, Morty. How long have I got?"

"If it's Alzheimer's, and that's still a big if, the memory lapses will come and go, but I'd say you've got a year before . . ."

"I'm totally gaga?"

"Let's not assume anything before we know for sure. Hey, I'm not doing anything tonight. Would you like me to come over?"

"No. But thanks anyway."

FOURTEEN

I'VE already mentioned "Margolis," but there is an even more chilling story of Boogie's that I read while I was in prison. "Seligman," written in Paris in the early fifties, wasn't published in the *New American Review* until months after Boogie's disappearance. Like all his stories it went through endless drafts before it was distilled to less than 3,000 words. It's a story about a bunch of affluent New York lawyers, Harold Seligman among them, who have taken to relieving the tedium of their lives by playing practical jokes on each other, constantly upping the ante. But there is a rule to the game. In order for a jest to pass muster it has to pinpoint and attack a flaw in the dupe's character – in Seligman's case, say his uxorious relationship with his libidinous wife. One morning, Boris Frankel, the criminal lawyer who is a member of the group, entices Seligman, just for a gag, to join a police station line-up in a case of alleged burglary and attempted rape. To the astonishment of the bunch, watching behind a one-way mirror, the victim, a still traumatized woman, identifies Seligman as the true culprit. The lawyers instantly fear that for once a jape has gone too far, but Seligman is sanguine. He has a sure-fire alibi. The night in question he and his wife had dined with Boris in their apartment. But Boris, consulting his desk diary, denies that was the case, and Seligman's wife confirms there had been no dinner party at their apartment that night. And then Boris and Seligman's wife repair to a motel to tear off each other's clothes and resume their heated affair.

Rereading that story this morning, and recalling the Boogie-man's taste for cruel pranks, I could no longer believe, as I once did, that he had been sufficiently angry following our quarrel to betray me out of spite. And yet – and yet – turning to McIver's Paris journal, I consulted the entry for September 22, 1951:

> ... In passing, I once said to Boogie, "I see you've got yourself a new friend."
>
> "Everybody is entitled to his own Man Friday, don't you think?"

No. Boogie never said that, I decided, setting out for one of my aimless morning strolls. It's a malign invention, typical of the lying McIver. There had been such warmth between Boogie and me. I was not his flunkey. Comrades is what we were, brothers kicking against the pricks. I couldn't be wrong about that. I wasn't going to allow that Boogie, even given his drugged-out state on the lake, that once soaring talent addled beyond repair, would take off forever just to get back at me. More likely we were to blame for his self-destruction, having anointed him, when we were young and foolish, as the only one of our bunch destined for greatness. And those publishers who had courted him in New York, pledging lavish advances against a novel only he knew he couldn't deliver, could only have added to his burden. I had solved the problem at last. Boogie, in flight from unbearable expectations, had gone to ground somewhere, assuming a new identity, just like Margolis. "Rest, rest, perturbed spirit." I forgive you.

I must have walked for an hour, maybe more, so self-absorbed that I had wandered into unfamiliar territory. I had no idea where I was until I recognized that I was standing outside the Provincial Bus Terminal. And, oh my God, that's where I caught that unnerving glimpse of the lady of my sometime wet dreams, Mrs. Ogilvy of the pubic hairs that used to glisten with pearly drops for me. Eighty years old now, I reckoned. Knobby hands clutching the rails of her walker to which she had defiantly fixed a Union Jack. Humped now. Shrivelled. Eyes bulging. Gathered with others, chanting:

One, two, three, four,
what are we for?
Wheelchair access,
Wheelchair access.

There must have been thirty-five of them there, maybe more, all of them wheelchair-bound. A Hieronymus Bosch sprung to life. Or a scene out of a Fellini film. Amputees and double-amputees. Survivors of strokes or polio, with wasted legs thin as rake handles. Victims of Parkinson's and multiple sclerosis, heads jerking, spittle trickling down their chins. Fleeing the scene, I hailed a taxi.

"Where to, mister?"

" . . . um, drive . . ."

"Yeah, sure. That's what I do. But where to?"

" . . . ahead . . ."

"Do you want a hospital?"

"*No.*"

"What, then?"

" . . . downtown . . ."

"Right."

" . . . it's the street next to, you know, I want . . ."

"Gotcha."

" . . . it comes right after where the hotel is . . ."

"Which hotel?"

"That's right."

"I'm taking you to a hospital."

"*No.*"

" . . . you know where the bookshop is on the corner?"

"If you feel like you're going to be sick, for Christ's sake, not here, let me know, and I'll pull up to the curb."

"I'm not going to be sick."

"There's always a silver lining, eh?"

" . . . it's where they serve drinks I want . . ."

"A bar?"

"Of course a bar. I'm not stupid, you know."

"This has to be my lucky day," he said, pulling over. "You got a wallet on you, maybe with a card with your home address, I'll take you there."

"I know where I live."

"Tell me, then. I won't squeal."

" . . . it would be close enough to where I'm going if you drop me on that street with a saint in its name."

"Oh, that's a big help in fucking Montreal."

" . . . Catherine. On the corner, please."

"*Which corner?*"

Shit shit shit. " . . . on the corner right after the religious street . . ."

"Religious street?"

"Not rabbi, or mullah. Catholic."

"Cardinal?"

"Bishop."

"Hey, this is fun. You want the corner of St. Catherine and Crescent. Right?"

"Right. I'm going to Dink's."

Hughes-McNoughton was lying in wait for me there. "Are you okay, Barney?"

"I know my own name, if you don't mind."

"Of course you do. Bring him a coffee, Betty."

"Scotch."

"Sure. But a coffee first."

I waited until my hand had stopped trembling before I drank the coffee. Hughes-McNoughton lit my Montecristo for me. "Feel better now?"

"I want you to do the paperwork so that I can give power of attorney to my children."

"You don't need a lawyer for that. A notary will do the trick. But what's the hurry?"

"Never mind."

"Let me tell you a story, if only to validate my role as *advocatus diaboli*. When I was a young and inexperienced lawyer, still trusting in human nature, I had a client, a nice old Jew in the *shmata* trade, who decided to sign over his flourishing business to his two sons in order to avoid estate duties. I did the dirty deed. We drank champagne together – the old boy, his two sons, me. When the old boy turned up at his office in the factory the next morning, his two sons told him he wasn't to come in any more. He was through there. So be careful as you go, Barney."

"Very amusing, but my children aren't like that."

I couldn't handle more than one Scotch in my state. Strolling back to my apartment, still feeling somewhat unwell, wary of when my next memory failure would strike, I thought, so much unfinished business. Miriam, Miriam, my heart's desire. My children, my children. Mike has no idea how much I love him. I fear Kate's marriage won't last. And what will become of Saul?

When Saul was no more than eight or nine years old, I might send him upstairs to my bedroom to fetch a sweater or a script I needed. A half-hour could go by and still he would not have returned, and I knew he had passed a bookcase, pulled out a book, and was now lying on his stomach somewhere, reading. When he was absorbed in *A History of the Kings of England*, Saul brought conversation at our dinner table to a full stop one night, complaining, "If Daddy was the King then after he died Mike would inherit the throne and get to rule the empire, and I would just be the duke of something or other."

Only ten years old at the time and my second-born son already grasped that he had been delivered into an unjust world.

Oh my oh my, if I were an angel of the Lord, I would mark the doors of each of my children's homes with an X, so that plague and misfortune would pass over them. Alas, I lack the qualifications. So when there was still world and time enough I fretted. I nagged. I corrected. I got everything wrong.

Damn damn damn.

Following the death of his wife, Sam Johnson wrote to the Reverend Mr. Thomas Wharton, "I have ever since seemed to myself broken off from mankind; a kind of solitary wanderer in the wilds of life, without any direction, or fixed point of view: a gloomy gazer on the world to which I have little relation."

But my wife wasn't dead, merely absent. Temporarily absent. And I had to talk to her. I had to talk to her right now. She's in that city in Ontario, I thought. Not Ottawa. The city with the Prince Arthur dining room, remember? Yes. I'm not totally wacko yet. I can even remember how to strain spaghetti. It's with that thingumajig I keep in a kitchen drawer. There are Seven Dwarfs, who cares what they're called? Lillian Kraft didn't write *The Man in the Brooks Brothers Shirt*. Or *Suit*. Whichever. It was Mary McCarthy. I picked up the phone, started to dial – stopped – and began to curse. I couldn't remember Miriam's number.

AFTERWORD

by Michael Panofsky

AT 10:28 a.m., on September 24, 1996, a surveyor and two lumberjacks, employed by Drummondville Pulp & Paper, stumbled on scattered human remains in a clearing near the crest of Mont Groulx: a skull, a severed spinal cord, a pelvis, a femur, cracked ribs and broken tibias. The Provincial Police were summoned, and the bones were collected and delivered to a pathologist at the Notre-Dame Hospital in Montreal. Dr. Roger Giroux declared that these were the remains of a Caucasian male, thirty something years old, who had died of unknown causes thirty to forty years ago. He speculated that the cracked ribs, severed spine, and broken tibias could be attributed to the fact that the unknown male had been severely beaten with a blunt instrument, or had fallen from a considerable height. But a more likely possibility, he ventured, alluding to the teeth marks, was that coyotes, or other animals, had cracked the bones, trying to get at the marrow. The story, reported in the *Gazette*, caught the attention of a retired Sûreté du Québec detective, Sean O'Hearne. On his insistence, an old file was opened, and a New York dentist was flown in to examine the skull. Shortly thereafter, it was confirmed that these were the remains of Bernard Moscovitch, who had disappeared in the vicinity on June 7th, 1960. A triumphant O'Hearne was interviewed by the *Gazette* and *La Presse*, and appeared on several local TV shows, as did my father's second wife, always with a framed photograph of Mr. Moscovitch on her lap. "He pledged undying love to me," she said. Accounts of my father's trial in St. Jérôme were resurrected under the rubric, DID JUSTICE TRIUMPH? or THE AVENGING BONES. My father's defence lawyer, John Hughes-McNoughton, entrapped at Dink's (a bar, on Crescent Street, in Montreal), dismissed one reporter, saying, "*Credo quia impossibile*," and another, who confronted him with the renewed charges, saying no more than, "*Argumentum ex silentio*," before waving him away. An enterprising *'Allo Police* photographer managed to slip into the King David's Nursing Home to snap a picture of my father being spoon-fed roast brisket by Solange. I flew in from London, Kate from Toronto, and Saul was driven in from New York by a young woman called Linda. We met at the cottage in the Laurentians, where we had once been such a happy family, to cope with the revelation that Barney had lied and was a murderer after all. Kate, naturally, disputed the irrefutable evidence.

"Boogie was drunk, and he could have wandered up there, had a bad fall, broken both his legs, and died of starvation. How dare you both be so quick to blame Daddy when he can't even answer to his name any more?"

"Kate, you're not the only one who is upset here. Be reasonable, please."

"Sure, reasonable. Daddy was a homicidal maniac. Obvious, eh? He shot Boogie, dragged him to that mountaintop, and broke his legs with a shovel."

"I'm not saying that's how it – "

"There wasn't any evidence of even a shallow grave having been dug. Do you think Daddy would have just left him there for the animals to pick over?"

"What if there wasn't time?"

"In all these years."

"The remains were found not far from where Daddy used to have that lean-to he once told us about. They found broken glass nearby. From a bottle of Scotch."

"So what?"

"Kate, we know how you feel, but – "

"They were both drunk. He could have killed him accidentally. I'll give you that much."

"He never stinted on any of us, and we owe him the benefit of the doubt. So you believe what you want, but if I live to be a hundred, I'll still know he was innocent. Furthermore, I happen to know that he never gave up the idea that Boogie was alive somewhere, and would turn up one day."

"Well, he has now, hasn't he?"

We had gathered at the cottage to come to a decision about Barney's incomplete manuscript, which we had all read; and also to salvage whatever mementos that appealed to us, and to close the cottage which we had already put up for sale. The omens weren't encouraging. The real-estate agent said, "The day after the referendum, I had calls from forty-two people out here wanting to sell their properties, and I have yet to see an offer for any one of them."

This wasn't our first family conclave, or our second, since we had learned that Barney was suffering from Alzheimer's Disease. At the time, Saul had reminded us that our grandmother had also been stricken, so we were all at risk.

For starters, said Saul, we shouldn't use underarm deodorants that have a zinc base, or cook in aluminum pots, which are also suspect. A subscriber to both the *Lancet* and the *New England Journal of Medicine*, he went on to point out that nicotine had recently been adjudged a brain stimulant, and that smokers were less likely to be afflicted.

"Only because they die of lung cancer first," said Kate, "so you can put that cigar out right now."

"Period?"

"Period," said Kate, falling into Saul's arms, sobbing brokenly.

The Alzheimer's diagnosis had been confirmed four months earlier, at a meeting in the offices of Totally Unnecessary Productions, on April 18, 1996, with Dr. Mortimer Herscovitch, and two specialists in attendance, as well as Solange and Chantal Renault, and of course Kate, Saul, and me. Saul went on to Toronto by train to tell Miriam. Reduced to weeping by the news, she phoned Barney as soon as she could trust her voice, and asked if she could come to see him.

"I don't think I could handle it."

"Please, Barney."

"No."

But he started to shave again every morning, cut back on his alcohol and cigar intake, and jumped whenever the phone or the doorbell rang. Solange phoned Miriam. "Come as soon as you can," she said.

"But he said no."

"He won't even go out for a short walk in case you should turn up and find him out."

Miriam arrived the next morning, and the two of them went to lunch at the Ritz, where the maitre d' didn't help matters, saying, "Why, I haven't seen you two together here for years. Just like old times, isn't it?"

Later Miriam told Saul: "I could see that the menu baffled him, and he asked me to order for both of us. But, to begin with, he was light-hearted. Even playful. I'm looking forward to games of hide-and-go-seek, and spin-the-bottle, with the other loonybins in whatever hospital I end up in. Maybe they'll have tricycles for us. Bubble gum. Triple scoop ice creams. Stop it, I said. He ordered champagne, but what he actually said to the waiter was bring us a bottle of, you know, with the bubbles, what we used to have here, and the waiter laughed, thinking he was trying to be witty, and I was so insulted for him. When my husband, I wanted to say, intends to be witty, he is witty.

"Wouldn't it have been grand, Barney said, if I had agreed to fly to Paris with him on his wedding night. We recalled the good times, our salad days, and he promised not to be sick as he had been at our first lunch together. Although come to think of it, he said, it would make for a certain symmetry, wouldn't it? But this needn't be our last lunch together, I said. We can be friends now. No, we can't, he said. It has to be everything or nothing. I had to get up twice to go to the ladies' room for fear of breaking down at the table. I watched him pop I don't know how many different-coloured pills, but he drank his champagne. He reached for my hand under the table, and told me I was still the most beautiful woman he had ever seen, and that he had once dared to hope that we would die simultaneously, in our nineties, like Philemon and Baucis, and that a beneficent Zeus would turn us into two trees, whose branches would fondle each other in winter, our leaves intermingling in the spring.

"Then, I don't know, maybe he shouldn't have had the champagne. He began to mispronounce words. He had trouble dealing with his cutlery. Selecting a spoon when it was a fork he needed. Picking up a knife by the blade rather than the handle. An embarrassing change came over him, possibly prompted by frustration. His face darkened. Lowering his voice, he motioned me closer, and said Solange was forging cheques. She was swindling him. He was fearful she might force him to sign a will she had fabricated. She was a nymphomaniac who once yanked his apartment doorman into the elevator with her and raised her dress to show him she wasn't wearing panties. The bill came and I could see that he was unable to add it up. Just sign it, I said, which made him laugh. Okay, he said, but I doubt if they'll recognize my new signature. Hey, I still remember some things, he said. I once brought her here with her mother, and that old bitch said, 'My husband always tips twelve-and-a-half per cent.'

"Then his manner altered yet again. He was tender. Loving. Barney at his most adorable. And I realized that he had forgotten that I had ever left him, and obviously assumed we would now go home together, and maybe take in a movie tonight. Or read in bed, our legs tangled together. Or catch a late flight to New York, the way he used to pull surprises out of a hat. Oh, in those days he was so much fun, so unpredictable, so loving, and I thought what if I didn't return to Toronto, and did go home with him? That's when I went to the phone and called Solange and asked her to come at once. I got back to the table and he wasn't there. Oh my God, where is he, I asked the waiter. Men's room, he said. I waited outside the men's room, and when he came out, shuffling, his smile goofy, I saw that his fly was still unzipped and his trousers were wet."

While he was still enjoying some relatively good days, our father called in John Hughes-McNoughton and insisted on signing papers that granted power of attorney to his children. Totally Unnecessary Productions Ltd. was sold to The Amigos Three, in Toronto, for five million dollars in cash and another five million's worth of shares in Amigos Three. According to his will, the proceeds from the sale, as well as all his other holdings, including a considerable stock portfolio, were to be split three ways: fifty per cent to his children, and twenty-five per cent each to Miriam and Solange. First, however, the estate would be responsible for a number of bequests:

Twenty-five thousand dollars for Benoit O'Neil, who had been caretaker of the cottage in the Laurentians for years.

Five hundred thousand dollars for Chantal Renault.

His two tickets in the reds in the new Molson Centre were to be maintained for five years, and left to Solange Renault.

The estate was obliged to settle John Hughes-McNoughton's monthly bar bill at Dink's for as long as he lived.

One hundred thousand dollars was to go to a Mrs. Flora Charnofsky in New York.

There was also a surprise, considering how often our father joked about *schvartzers*. A two-hundred-thousand-dollar trust fund was to be set up to establish a scholarship at McGill University for a black student who excelled in the arts; the aforesaid scholarship in memory of Ismail Ben Yussef, a.k.a. Cedric Richardson, who had died of cancer on November 18, 1995.

Five thousand dollars was to be set aside for a wake at Dink's, to which all his friends were to be invited. No rabbi was to speak at his funeral. He was to be buried, as he had already arranged, in the Protestant cemetery at the foot of Mont Groulx, but there should be a Star of David on his stone, and the adjoining plot had been reserved for Miriam.

Saul undertook to consult our mother. Before hanging up, all she could manage was, "Yes. That's how it should be."

FOLLOWING THE settling of his affairs, my father's decline was precipitous. From an increasingly frequent inability to find the right word for the most commonplace objects, or to remember the names of those near and dear to him, he might waken unaware of where or who he was. Summoned again to Montreal, Kate, Saul, and I had another meeting with Mr. Herscovitch and the specialists. A pregnant Kate offered to have Barney move in with her, but the doctors cautioned that unfamiliar surroundings would only compound Barney's difficulties. So, to begin with, Solange moved into the apartment on Sherbrooke Street with Barney. If he addressed her as Miriam, and denounced her as an ungrateful whore who had ruined his life, she continued to feed him and to wipe his chin with a napkin. When he dictated a letter to her, the words incoherent or mispronounced, jumbled phrases repeated, she promised to mail it at once. If he turned up at breakfast with his left arm in his right shirtsleeve, or his trousers back to front, she didn't comment. Then he began to rant against his reflection in the mirror, taking the image to be somebody else's, addressing it as Boogie, Kate, or Clara. Once, mistaking his own mirrored image for that of Terry McIver, he butted his head against it, and required twenty-two stitches in his scalp. So Kate, Saul, and I came to Montreal again.

Over Solange's objections, on August 15, 1996, we had our father committed to the King David Nursing Home. Although he is now beyond recognizing anybody, his children included, we have not abandoned him. Kate comes once a week from Toronto. As luck would have it, she was playing Chinese checkers with Barney on an afternoon when Miriam appeared, Miriam, who had only recently recovered from a minor stroke. She and Kate had a fearful row and would be estranged for months. They weren't even on speaking terms when Saul brought them together for a lunch in Toronto. "We're still a family," he said. "So behave yourselves. Both of you." His gruff manner, so reminiscent of Barney's, won them over. Saul visits the hospital frequently. Once, sending Barney's building blocks flying, he hollered, "How could you let this happen to you, you bastard," and broke down and wept. His visits are dreaded by the nurses in attendance. If he detects an egg stain on Barney's dressing-gown, or bed sheets that don't appear freshly laundered, he threatens mayhem. "Shit. Shit. Shit." One afternoon, arriving to find the TV set turned to Oprah Winfrey, he yanked it off its perch, and smashed it on the floor. Nurses came running. "This is my father's room," he shouted, "and he doesn't watch such crap."

My younger brother is the one who has inherited something of our mother's beauty as well as our father's hot temper. Between Barney and Saul it was always a gladiatorial contest, strength pitted against strength, neither one ever yielding an inch. Barney, who had secretly adored the teenage left-wing firebrand, and never tired of telling the story of The 18th of November Fifteen, later came to abhor his shift to the unforgiving right. All the same, he remained the favourite son, if only because he was the writer our father always longed to be. On the opening page of my father's memoir he ventured that, violating a solemn pledge, he was scribbling a first book at an advanced age. This, like a good deal of what he went on to write, was not quite true. Going through Barney's papers, I discovered several attempts, over the years, to write short stories. I also found the first act of a play and fifty pages of a novel. He was, as he claimed, a voracious reader, an admirer of stylists above all, from Edward Gibbon to A.J. Liebling. Flipping through his Noter's Write Book, I saw that he had transcribed many a sentence of Gibbon's. Take these two, for instance. Gibbon on the Emperor Gordianus:

His manners were less pure, but his character was equally amiable with that of his father. Twenty-two acknowledged concubines, and a library of sixty-two thousand volumes, attested the variety of his inclinations; and from the productions which he left behind him, it appears that both the one and the other were designed for use rather than ostentation.[1]

And from A.J. Liebling, on the boxing trainer Charlie Goldman, a.k.a. The Professor:

"I never married," the Professor says. "I always live à la carte."[2]

"Like Zack," he wrote underneath.

I am the beneficiary of Barney's gift for money-making. Alas, it is an attribute he always deplored in himself, which is why, I suppose, I was the least favourite of his children, the one who bore the brunt of his sarcasm. His rush to judgment. In spite of what he has written, Caroline and I have sat through *Don Giovanni* more than once. As my footnotes amply testify, I have also read the *Iliad*, Swift, Dr. Johnson, and others. But if I happen to believe that this exclusionary Eurocentric pantheon has to be revised, and enlarged, and if I also find merit in Mapplethorpe, Helen Chadwick, and Damien Hirst, surely this is my prerogative. I cannot deny my resentments. Even so, I try to fly over to see Barney once every six weeks. Possibly, I suffer least from his altered state, because the truth is we never did communicate.

Barney does not lack for other, more regular visitors. Solange is there just about every day to bathe and help him crayon colouring books. Old drinking companions from Dink's often pass through: a disreputable lawyer called John Hughes-McNoughton, an alcoholic journalist named Zack, and others. Only after I was sent a severe letter from a hospital administrator did I learn that a certain Ms.

---

[1]Gibbon, Edward. *The Decline and Fall of the Roman Empire.* Vol. 1, p. 191. Methuen & Co., London, 1909.

[2]Liebling, A.J. *A Neutral Corner, Boxing Essays,* p. 41. Farrar, Straus and Giroux, New York, 1996.

Morgan came by once a week to masturbate him. A sprightly old man, Irv Nussbaum, pops in often with a bag of bagels or long strings of *karnatzel* from Schwartz's delicatessen. "Your father," he once said to me, "was one of your real wild Jews. A *bonditt*. A *mazik*. A devil. I could have sworn he was out of Odessa."

On Barney's most recent birthday, he surprised us by responding to his name with an impish grin. We brought balloons, funny hats, noise-makers, and a chocolate cake. Miriam and Solange, conspiring together, had what seemed like an inspired idea. They hired a tap-dancer to perform for him. A gleeful Barney clapped hands and sang bits of a song for us:

> Mairzy-doats,
> anddozy-doats,
> andlittlelambseativy,
> akid'lleativytoo,
> wouldn'tyou.

But Barney stumbled and fell, and wet himself when he tried to emulate Mr. Chuckle's steps, and Miriam, Solange, and Kate fled into the hall and fell into each other's arms.

I remember another moment of recognition, as it were. A letter came for my father from California. It was incomprehensible to me, but not to my father who read it and wept copiously. It read:

HANG IN OLD FRIEND

Mother explained that the letter was from Hymie Mintzbaum, who had suffered a bad stroke some years earlier. In London, back in 1961, she said, Hymie had taken her to lunch and said that she simply had to marry Barney. "Only you can save that bastard," he had said.

To DIGRESS briefly, as Barney was so fond of saying, all my recent

trips to Montreal have been depressing. This, not only because of
our father's condition, but also in recognition of what has become
of the city I grew up in. When I got out the phone book, hoping to
get in touch with old friends who had been to McGill with me, I
discovered that all but two or three had moved to Toronto, Vancouver, or New York, rather than endure the burgeoning tribalism.
Of course, looked at from abroad, what was happening in Quebec
seemed risible. There are actually grown men out here, officers of
the *Commission de protection de la langue française*, who go out with
tape measures every day to ensure that the English language lettering on outdoor commercial signs is half the size, and in no
brighter colour, than the French. In 1995, after a particularly
zealous language inspector (or tongue-trooper, as they are known in
the local argot) discovered boxes of unilingually labelled matzohs
on display in a kosher grocery, the offending product was ordered to
be withdrawn from the shelves. Such was the protest, however, that,
in 1996, the Jewish community was offered special dispensation:
unilingually labelled boxes of matzohs were declared legal for sixty
days of the year. Old Irv Nussbaum was delighted by the ruling:
"Listen here," he said, "marijuana, cocaine and heroin are banned
here all year round, but, come Pesach, Jewish druggies are now a
special case. Sixty days of the year we can munch matzohs without
drawing the blinds or locking the doors. Please don't think I'm
meddling, but I know your father always hoped that your children
would have a proper Jewish education. You want to treat them to a
trip to Israel, I'd be glad to help with the arrangements."

My father's manuscript created problems for us. Kate was for
publication, Saul argued for both revisions and cuts, and I vacillated, distressed by his gratuitously cruel remarks about Caroline.
But the truth is there was nothing to be done. Barney had already
come to an arrangement with a publisher in Toronto, and a codicil
in his will absolutely forbade any changes or cuts being made. It
also stated, surprisingly, that I was to be responsible for seeing the
manuscript through to publication. After protracted negotiations
with the publisher, it was agreed that I could add footnotes, correcting the most egregious factual errors, a chore that obliged me to
do a good deal of reading. I was also granted two other privileges. I
was allowed to rewrite the incoherent, faltering chapters, dealing
with Barney's discovery that he was suffering from Alzheimer's,

after consultations with Solange and Drs. Mortimer Herscovitch and Jeffrey Singleton. I was also authorized to add this Afterword, subject to the approval of Saul and Kate. But they were not pleased. We quarrelled.

"I'm clearly the writer here," said a sullen Saul, "and I should be the one to handle the manuscript."

"Saul, I'm not looking forward to this job. If he picked me, I have to accept that it was his ultimate putdown. Because, just as he wrote, in that patronizing manner of his, I'm so punctilious. I could be counted on to correct his most glaring memory lapses."

"I happen to know," said Kate, "that many of his so-called errors, quotes attributed to the wrong author here and there, were actually traps baited just for you. He once told me I know how to make sure that Mike finally gets to read Gibbon, and lots of other writers. My system is fool-proof."

"As it happens, in spite of what he thought, I had already read most of those people. But we have a problem."

"Boogie?"

"Here we go again."

"Kate, please. Don't start. He was my father, too. But when he wrote again and again that he was still expecting Boogie to turn up one day, he was obviously lying."

"Daddy did not murder Boogie."

"Kate, we're just going to have to come to terms with the fact that Daddy wasn't all he pretended to be."

"Saul, you're not saying anything."

"Shit. Shit. Shit. How could he do such a thing?"

"The answer is he didn't."

I put the question to John Hughes-McNoughton. "As a rule," he said, "a lawyer doesn't ask his client. The answer could be unhelpful. But Barney volunteered more than once that the story he told O'Hearne was the unvarnished truth."

"Did you believe him?"

"A jury of twelve honourable men adjudged him innocent."

"But now there is new and damning evidence. We have a right to know the truth."

"The truth is he was your father."

OUR FATHER, before he was reduced to a near vegetable state, cast a large shadow. Kate's husband, for instance, had always felt diminished in his presence, and did not enjoy his visits to Toronto. Barney's pathetic condition, and Kate's slow, reluctant acceptance of what he had done, not that she would ever acknowledge it, drew them closer together. But something within her broke and was badly in need of mending. Happily, however, giving birth to a baby boy did a good deal to restore her sunny disposition. She has named her son Barney.

In the months that followed the discovery of Bernard Moscovitch's bones on the top of Mont Groulx, my younger brother's politics took a surprising U-turn. He has reverted to the left-wing politics of his adolescence, his polemics now appearing in the *Nation, Dissent,* and other venues he once considered abominations. Saul strongly objects to my theory that his conversion came about only after he no longer felt obliged to contend with our father. Miriam, who now walks with a cane, has asked to be spared mention in this Afterword, beyond my saying that she and Blair have retired to a cottage near Chester, Nova Scotia.

Before his brain began to shrink, Barney Panofsky clung to two cherished beliefs. Life was absurd, and nobody ever truly understood anybody else. Not a comforting philosophy, and one I certainly don't subscribe to.

THESE LINES are being written on the porch of our cottage in the Laurentians on what will surely be my last visit here. Any minute now the real-estate agent will arrive with the Fourniers, and I will hand over the keys. Here, where we were once such a blessed family, it is gratifying to be able to conclude on a note that has nothing to do with incriminating bones. I phoned Caroline to tell her what had happened. I was sitting on the porch, I said, remembering old times, when suddenly a big fat water-bomber came roaring in. It lowered on to the lake, and without even stopping, scooped up who knows how many tons of water, flew off, and dumped the water on the mountain.

I wished I had brought my camcorder with me. It was an incredible, truly Canadian sight, and the children would have adored it. Certainly they'll never see anything like that in London.

Benoit O'Neil explained that it was a practice run by forest fire fighters in training. Years ago, he said, they used to fly over more often. Maybe once or twice in a summer, testing new airplanes. But I had never seen such a thing before.

"Oh," he said, "for sure, I'm talking about before you were born."

Then the real-estate agent arrived with the Fourniers. After an exchange of niceties, I excused myself, driving off. I had covered a good ten miles before I hit the brakes and pulled over on the shoulder. Oh my God, I thought, breaking into a sweat, I had better call Saul. I owe Kate an apology. But, oh God, it's too late for Barney. He's beyond understanding now. Damn damn damn.

Acknowledgements

Lines from "In Memory of W. B. Yeats" by W. H. Auden from *Collected Poems* by W. H. Auden, edited by Edward Mendelson. Copyright © 1940 and renewed 1968 by W. H. Auden. Reprinted by permission of Random House, Inc., and Faber and Faber Limited.

Extract from *In the Fifties* by Peter Vansittart. Copyright © 1995 by Peter Vansittart. Reprinted by permission of Sheil Land Associates Limited, and John Murray (Publishers) Limited.

'Mairzy Doats' by Al Hoffman, Milton Drake and Jerry Livingston. Copyright © 1943 (Renewed) by Al Hoffman Songs Inc., Drake Activities and Hallmark Music Co. International Copyright secured. All rights reserved. Reprinted by permission.

Lines from "The Truly Great" by Stephen Spender from *Collected Poems 1928–1985* by Stephen Spender. Copyright © 1934 and renewed 1962 by Stephen Spender. Reprinted by permission of Random House, Inc. and Faber and Faber Limited.

First four lines from "Howl" from *Collected Poems 1947–1980* by Allen Ginsberg (Viking, 1985). Copyright © 1955, 1985 by Allen Ginsberg. Reprinted by permission of HarperCollins Publishers Inc. and Penguin Books Limited.

www.vintage-books.co.uk